Significance

A Significance Series Novel

SHELLY CRANE

Editing services provided by Jennifer Nunez

Printed in paperback October 2011 and available in Kindle and E-book format as of June 2011 through Amazon, Create Space and Barnes & Noble.

Printed in the United States

10 9 8 7 6 5 4 3 2 1

More information can be found at the author's website
http://shellycrane.blogspot.com/

ISBN : 1463695403
ISBN 13 : 9781463695408

Significance
A Significance Novel
SHELLY CRANE

To imprint:
To change an image, memory, opinion or idea in a vivid and lasting way.

For Axel,

You have always loved me through my baggage and craziness and you still do. You are everything important to me and I'm the luckiest for finding someone to be myself with.

I love you, infinity.

One

I waited for this day, for this one thing to complete me. To wrap up seventeen and three quarter years of my life and set a pretty bow on it in the form of a graduation cap. I waited for this one sheet of paper to tell me that I had done something right.

I sat in my assigned seat, along with my classmates, in alphabetical order in front of the gym. The ones up front were in order by achievements, their faces lit with the relief of scholarships and graduation parties with gifts and family and friends...and getting out of this town.

I was numb. I had waited for this moment, but now, I didn't feel good inside. I didn't feel complete, didn't feel achieved. I felt like I'd slid by and barely made it, which was exactly what I'd done. I despised school. I was in the early release program for students who work after school, so we got out at 1:00 instead of 3:00 like everyone else. I was barely here and when I was I didn't want to be.

I know I sound bitter. Believe me, I know. But I was seventeen, graduating a year early, and on the fast track to being valedictorian or whatever else, but things happened to me that I just couldn't handle. And so, there I was, sullen, slightly unhappy and skidding by.

The 'things' I speak of, well, number one was that my mom left. She was an upstanding, stay at home mom, PTA loving, frugal grocery shopping, coupon clipping guru of the community. And she just left us, just like that. She decided out of nowhere that my dad had been holding her back all these years. She didn't love him and she needed time to start a new life, without me there to pester her. So she did.

She moved to California along with every cent in my dad's checking account and the one supposed to be for my college fund. I wanted to laugh at the Cali cliché, but I guess it didn't suit her for long. She moved somewhere else, but I refused to speak to her anymore when she called. All she ever talked about was how sorry she was, that she just couldn't do it anymore, that she was happy now, that I didn't know what it was like to live with my dad. Yeah right. I'd counter that I was the only one *still* living with him and she'd hang up.

I was sure her newest boyfriend, who was ten years younger than her, could console her.

So here we are, present day, graduation day. I was waiting patiently for the m's to roll around so I could grab my diploma and hear the one person that'll be in the stands clap for me, my dad.

I glanced up in front of me to see Kyle looking back. He smiled. "You look like you're in your own little world back there. You ok?"

"Yeah, I'm just ready to be done with this."

He turned more fully in his chair, putting his arms on the back of it. "Come on. It's graduation day. Shouldn't you be happy?" he reasoned. I just shrugged. "You wanna do something tonight? My parents are throwing this lousy party for me, but I'm looking for an excuse to leave early."

"I don't want to be your excuse, Kyle."

He paled, his brow bunched together. "Ah, Mags, I didn't mean it like that." He sighed. "My party is from five to seven. I'll have plenty of time to do something with you, I just didn't want it to seem so much like a date, you know," he explained and looked at me bashfully. "In case you said no, again."

"Oh." I felt an inch and a half tall. "Kyle, I…" I was this close to telling him no, once more but I thought about it. I had always told him no. I hadn't been on a date in a year, ever since my life fell under my mom's pointy heels. He was always sweet to me and he was probably leaving soon anyway for college. What could it hurt? "Ok. Yeah, we can do something."

"Really?" he said shocked.

"Yeah. What time do you want to go?"

"Is your dad throwing you a party or something?"

"No." Ha. Yeah right.

"Oh. Uh, how about I text you? I'm sure it's fine, but I've gotta ask my dad for the car. Mine's in the shop."

"Ok, let me give you my number," I said and started to pull up my gown to reach my pocket.

"I have it." I looked at him curiously and he grinned. "I asked Rebecca for it a couple weeks ago. I was going to call you, but I never, uh, got up the nerve."

He looked a little embarrassed and I couldn't help but giggle a little at his obvious hand-in-the-cookie-jar expression. He was nice looking. No movie star stud, just a normal, light brown hair, brown eyed nice guy. We'd hung out a lot over the years in our group of friends, but never alone.

"Well, maybe you should have."

"Would you have talked to me?"

I didn't want to lie and I didn't want to give him false hope, so I just smiled and shrugged, hoping to pull off a little flirt. It must have worked; he grinned wider. "Ok, I'll text you tonight."

"Great," my mouth said, but my head was already dreading it.

Then I saw the people ahead of him start to stand one by one as their names were called.

"Kyle Jacobson." He looked back and grinned at me once more as he made his way on stage. There were still about eight people before me. I watched him make his way to the stage and saw his parents and a large group of others stand and applaud loudly for him, a couple whooping and hooting. He grabbed his diploma and then made a show of muscles. Everyone laughed as he bounded down the stairs. He was a crack up. Everyone liked him and voted him class clown in superlatives. He was popular, but never really dated anyone. He was always nice to me though. I used to hang out with that crowd, before everything happened.

After my mom left, my dad was lost. He went a little 'nuts'. He quit going to work and got fired from a job he'd had for over fifteen years at the school board and now works at the wood mill for a quarter of what he made before. So, I had to get into the work release program and get a job because we had no extra money for anything other than food that I needed or wanted.

When I told my mom all this, when I explained how I had to get a job to help and how Dad was so destroyed by what she'd done, she said it was good for us to experience a little bit of heartache and hard work for a change. That was it. That was the last straw.

That was the day I decided to never speak to her again.

"Maggie Masters."

I heard my name and looked up. Everyone was looking and I realized that my name had been called more than once. I blushed and giggled nervously as I made my way up to the stage. I chuckled under my breath as I half expected the announcer to call out Mags or Magster or Maggsie. No one called me by my real name, hardly ever.

I took my diploma and turned to look for Dad. He was sitting there. Just *sitting there*, not taking pictures, not clapping, not smiling, just watching stoically.

I frowned and made my way down to the end of the platform and was lifted into warm arms. *Familiar* warm arms.

"Congratulations," he whispered into my hair.

"Chad, don't."

"Mags, come on." He put me down, but didn't let me go as he looked at me pleadingly. "We graduated. Let's celebrate! Can't you let go of the past, just for today?"

I looked up to his black hair. The dark, short locks that any girl would love to run her fingers through. His tan skin and brown eyes with his lean Friday night football arms that always held me like I mattered. Oh, how I missed him, but he was the one who left me.

"You certainly know how to let go of things," I countered.

"Maggie." He sighed exasperatingly, like I was being unreasonable and it made me fume even more. "Look. That was almost a year ago. And you know I wouldn't have broken up with you if you'd told me what was going on with your mom and all."

"Oh. That makes me feel so much better," I said and let the sarcasm drip.

"You know what I mean. We'd had that talk, a lot. I'm leaving, we both knew it when we started seeing each other. I thought we agreed it'd be easier if we calmed down a little and just were friends the last year of school. I didn't date anyone else, you know that. It wasn't because I didn't want you."

It was true. He hadn't been on one date this whole school year that I'd known about. He and his friends even made a pact to go to prom together as a group. There were a lot of angry girls over this pact as it appeared it caught on and almost the whole football team went stag.

"I know that. But you haven't talked to me all year," I said softly.

"Maggie. You wouldn't return my phone calls. You avoided me at lunch and then started working after school. What else could I do?"

He was right. The only time I talked to him was to yell at him one month after he broke up with me and my mom left. Coincidentally, it was three days after she left that he decided to make the decision for the both of us; the decision that we'd talked about but not come to a conclusion to.

I told him he sucked for deciding that right then was the time to dump me. He said he was sorry, he was there for me. He tried to take it back, even tried to kiss me and hold me but I would have none of it.

I missed him. He was such a nice guy but his timing was just terrible and I was angry at him for it. I was angry that he still wanted to leave me here and go through with his plans. Everyone left me. I tried to summon a semblance of calm.

"You're right," I admitted. "I just needed you and I wanted you to want to be there, but not for you to come back because I begged you to."

"You didn't beg me, silly girl," he crooned and pulled me closer for another hug. He spoke into my hair. "I'm so sorry, Mags. I thought I was making things easier for you, for both of us by just trying to be friends instead. I knew how hard it was going to be to leave you. Look at me." He waited for me to look up, which I did with a sigh. "The last thing I wanted to do was hurt you. I've missed you."

"Chad, you're still leaving. Don't, ok? I'm sorry for how I acted, but it doesn't change anything does it? You're still leaving, University of Florida football."

"I know. I just hate that this year was wasted like this. I'm sorry."

"I'm sorry, too." I pulled from his embrace and boy, was it painful. "I've gotta go."

"Please write me. Or call me, text, something. I miss you. I never intended for us to just never speak to each other again. I want to know how you're doing."

"I will. I promise. Congrats on the UF scholarship. I always knew you'd get it."

"Thanks, Mags. I still love you, you know," he whispered and kissed my cheek, so close to my lips and I fought for composure.

Then he was gone.

I turned to look at him once more and he was walking backwards, watching me, his black grad gown flapping at his sides and his diploma in hand. He waved sadly and then took off towards his truck. If possible, I felt worse than I already had.

Two

"It still boggles my mind how you can eat those things," my dad said, as he'd said a hundred times before, but this time he sneered it instead of joking with me. "I mean, it's pure sugar. Sugar and starch and bad for you carbs."

"Are you saying I need to lose some weight, Dad?"

We sat at the kitchen dinette. I say dinette because it barely fits two people. This was where we'd been ever since that ride home from graduation. It was an utterly silent ride except for one 'congratulations' muttered from Dad, nothing more. I had been sitting there for almost an hour now, checking my phone and waiting for Kyle to text me. I never thought I'd ever be waiting for Kyle, but I would have done anything to get out of that house tonight.

I did, however, have a text from Bish.

Congrats, kid. I'm really sorry I couldn't come, but the boss is on me and interns can't really negotiate, you know. But I love you and can't wait to see you. I'll come home soon for a visit, I promise.

"No." Dad cut through my moment of happiness with more grumbling. "I'm not saying that, stop being dramatic. I'm saying they're not good for you."

"Dad, I've eaten honey buns almost every day since birth, along with thousands of other Americans. I'm sure they're not lethal."

"Stop the sarcasm, Maggie. I'm just saying you could watch it to make sure your weight doesn't get out of control one day. Your mother always said-"

"Ok, stop right there, please, Dad. I have no interest in what that woman thinks of me. She left, so she definitely doesn't get a say so anymore. She doesn't care."

She was always on me about my weight. Of course, back then I just thought it was motherly protection, you know. Now, who knew what was going on in her head.

I'm kinda short, I guess; five-three. My mom has always said I should watch it and maybe start doing more activities, such as joining the cheerleading squad again. I quit my sophomore year. I was already on the track team, but apparently, our running shorts weren't cute enough for her.

I have always liked my body, always. I wasn't fat. I wasn't one of those girls that griped and complained and had conniptions every time I had to put on a bathing suit. And I'd never had any complaints from anyone else either. Especially not Chad, who constantly told me how he loved that I ate real food and looked normal and didn't ask him if I looked fat every time I changed my clothes. No one except *her* ever had a problem with it or ever said anything to me about it. I refused to get a complex because of one high strung woman. And now Dad had to start this crap?

"She does care. We just didn't do what we needed for her. We took advantage. She wouldn't have left if we had been more..."

"More what, Dad? More perfect?"

"You know what I mean."

"No. You don't love people for what they can give you. You don't love them because of what they do for you or how good you make them look. Love is blind, love does not boast, love is not vain. Remember, Dad?"

"I know what the bible says, Maggie, but since when do you care what God has to say about anything?" Ouch. True, we hadn't been to church not one Sunday since my mom left. "Your mom loved us, we just didn't show her enough love to keep her here. We failed her."

I stood up, not caring that Kyle hadn't texted me yet. I looked at the sad, mean, black haired, pale and thin man in front of me with his wrinkled navy blue shirt and his hair greased back, uncared for.

"Dad, I love you, but I'm not taking the blame for something she did. I'm going out with a friend. I won't stay out too late."

"Chad?"

"No, not Chad. Chad's too busy trying to leave this town."

"Well, good for him and you knew it was coming. You could learn a few things from that boy. He was a little out of your league anyway, I think. Probably why it didn't work out. You've gotta be more realistic, Maggie. You expect too much from people," he muttered.

"Ok, Dad. Bye."

I left without another word from him or me. I grabbed my green cargo jacket from the hall coat rack and stuck my phone in my pocket. I looked at myself in the hall mirror. I remembered this mirror. It was bulky and huge, made from antique silver. Dad had to wrestle to get it in the car after mom found it at an old, out of the way antique shop. I looked in it and I saw my light brown hair with a little wave at the ends passed my shoulders. I saw my green eyes. I saw the freckles smattering my nose and cheeks on tan skin. I wasn't gorgeous, but I still didn't understand why I wasn't good enough for anyone.

I searched through my backpack for the ten dollar bill I knew was there and stuffing it in my pocket with my phone, I headed out the door.

It was cold and humid. The air was thick with fog and moisture, making a glow around the street lights as I made my way down Broad Street. One street over was Main. I lived right smack in the middle of town my whole life. I didn't have a car because I didn't need one. I could walk anywhere I needed to go and the diner I worked in was only five blocks down and over.

But I wasn't headed to the diner. I had no idea where I was going, but I just needed to get away. Dad had completely changed. We used to get along; play games, go to movies, cook together, rake leaves together. We were a typical uptown normal street family from Tennessee. But, when my mom left, my dad may as well have left too. He would never have said anything about my weight before, especially since there's nothing wrong with it, and never ever would have just sat there while his only daughter graduated. He also wouldn't have let me get a job just so I had money to buy things I needed because he was too buried in his grief to go to work anymore. He was not the same man and I missed him.

I also have an older brother, Bish, who was adopted, but he'd been out of the house for a long time now. My parents decided when I was eight to adopt a kid from the state. They got a boy, a sixteen year old kid who'd been pulled from a foster home. He'd apparently been in lots of them and was pretty happy to actually be adopted being so old.

I liked him right off and he liked me. He let me follow him around and pester him. He played games with me and took me shopping. I helped introduce him into the youth group at church because he'd never been to church before. But he left to go to art school on a scholarship and moved to New York to be an intern for some jerk at a law firm. I rarely saw him anymore. We text, but he was so busy and I couldn't seem to find anything to talk about but how much life sucked here without him.

I made my way to the stop light and waited for it to turn red so I could cross. There was only one other person there, a guy with his back to me. He was wearing his earbuds and bobbing his head a little to whatever beat he was listening to with his hands in his pockets. He looked back, smiled slightly and nodded before facing forward again. I checked my phone again and saw that I still had no text. I wondered why I was so worried about it. I wasn't even thrilled about going with Kyle in the first place, but now I couldn't seem to stop thinking about it.

I thought maybe I'd get a coffee while I waited. If Kyle didn't text me, at least I could sit there. Maybe read a little from the Kindle app on my phone before heading home. I put my phone back in my pocket and looked up just in time. The light turned red, but the guy was already walking without looking to the side first and was crossing. I saw the red truck turning, the driver's head turned left, but he was turning right.

It all happened so fast I didn't even get a chance to think. I just reacted. I ran forward, grabbed the back of the guy's jacket and pulled him backwards with all my strength just as the truck sped by in front of us. We tumbled back and he landed hard on top of me, his backpack banging against my face. My breath slammed into my chest painfully.

I heard a screech and looked to see the truck slam to a stop just a ways ahead of us. He yelled some obscenities out his window; something about stupid kids, but more colorful, and then sped away.

The guy immediately rolled off me, yanking the buds from his ears and looking at me with awe and concern.

"Are you ok?"

"Uh...yeah, I think so," I groaned.

"I can't believe I just did that. You- you saved my life."

"It's fine. It's a good thing I was here, I guess."

He scooted a little closer and winced as he brushed my hair back from my face. "You cut your head," he said breathlessly and looked a little dazed.

"I did?" I felt it with my fingers and squinted as it stung. My fingers had a little blood on them, but nothing alarming. "I guess I did. It's all right, really, just a bump."

I tried to stand, but he held me down with a hand on my shoulder.

"Whoa. Wait, ok? Let me call an ambulance. If something happened to you after you saved me..."

"Really, that's not necessary. I'm fine."

He frowned and paused, screwing up his lips like he was debating it. I looked at him in the soft glow of the streetlights. He was tall, that I'd seen from before, and broad, but his hair was brown and shaggy, curling around his ears and forehead, and his eyes were light, blue maybe or hazel. His lips were fascinating as he sucked them in and out of his mouth in contemplation. He was wearing a gray hoodie that said 'VOLS' in big orange letters on the front. Great.

That was one of my biggest problems with Chad. He'd been so set to go to Florida to be a Gator when the University of Tennessee was right here. Right down the road. His dad went to UF, I get it, he wanted to follow his dad's footsteps but it just felt like he wouldn't compromise. I don't know.

The guy's eyes drifted to mine and we just sat there, eyes locked on one another's. Then the corner of his mouth rose slightly. And it was unnerving.

"Please, let me take you to the hospital at least." He brushed my hair back again and leaned closer to inspect. I heard my swift intake of breath at his closeness and he did, too. He looked down into my eyes again and watched me closely. "It doesn't look too bad, but...let me call someone for you. I'd feel better," he said softly.

"There's no one to call," I muttered, but wished I could take it back when I saw his face. "Really, I'm fine."

"I'm so glad you were here. I can't believe I did that. And I'm sorry you got hurt. I must have hit you with my book-bag when we went down. That's a pretty good grip you got there," he said and smiled and I had one of those moments where you stare and can't look away.

He smiled wider when I didn't say anything and chuckled right as I came back to myself.

"Uh, thanks. Are *you* all right?" I asked and he nodded.

"So. There's no one to call? Your parents? A boyfriend?"

"My dad won't come and my boyfriend and I- Well, we aren't together anymore. I wouldn't feel right about calling him now."

"You don't think he'd come?"

"Oh, he would. That's why I don't want to."

He seemed confused and amused at the same time. "Ok. I'm gonna assume there's a story there and you're not just suffering from a head injury."

I realized then that we were still sitting on the sidewalk next to each other, in the middle of town.

"No, I'm fine. Look, I'm sorry. I'm fine, I promise. I didn't mean to hold you up," I stammered and stuck my hair behind my ear.

"Are you kidding? You saved my life. The least I can do is make sure you get where you're going. Here." He grabbed my arm gently and helped me stand, keeping it there to make sure I was steady. "You good? No stars, no spots, no blurs?"

"I'm good."

"Where you headed?"

"I have no idea. Nowhere. I'm just waiting for someone to call and needed to get out of the house."

"Did you go to graduation?"

"Yeah, I graduated."

"Really? You look too young to be graduating."

"Seventeen. My birthday's in a few weeks. I, uh, skipped a grade so I graduated early."

"Aha. So, I was saved by a genius. This just keeps getting better," he said grinning.

"I'm not a genius," I laughed. "I just used to like school. I loved tests." I saw his expression. "I know, I know. I'm a freak. But I liked it, for whatever reason."

"Not anymore?"

"Long story. Bad year."

He nodded and seemed to know to leave that one alone.

"You're not a freak, by the way." He leaned close and stage whispered to me. "I love to do geometry speed drills. Love it."

I raised my eyebrows and dropped my jaw in mock shock.

"No way. That's crazy."

"I know."

"Maybe you're the freak."

"Hey!" We both laughed and then smiled at each other. "So, where can I take you?"

"Really, I'm fine. Where were you headed?"

"Oh, my uncle's house a couple streets over. My cousin graduated, too. My mom and dad are here with me, partying it up with the family. You know."

"Yeah," I said bleakly as I most certainly did not know. "Who's your cousin?"

"Kyle Jacobson."

My jaw dropped for real this time. "Kyle is your cousin?"

"Yeah, you know him? Oh, of course you do."

"Yeah, I've been friends with Kyle since...forever. He's actually the one I'm waiting on. I thought his party was from five to seven?"

"It is. I snuck out for a walk. I can't handle so many Jacobsons in one room." He put his hands back in his pockets and rolled his shoulders, looking a little uncomfortable. "So, you're Kyle's big date, huh? He kept talking about you earlier."

"It's not a date. Well...I guess it is. We're just friends. He's sweet."

"Well, I'll tell you, he definitely thinks this is a date and wants to be way more than friends, trust me."

I bit my lip and he smiled sadly at me. "Really? I wasn't trying to get his hopes up, I just wanted to do something and he's asked me out a few times already. I just didn't want to say no again. You know?"

He nodded and rubbed the back of his neck. His hair fell across his forehead and I wanted to fix it for him. In fact, my fingers twitched with wanting to, but I clenched my fist and mentally shook myself. I was not one of those girls who got all swoony over a cute guy. I wasn't about to start being one.

"Well, I can walk you there since that's where I'm headed anyway. Kyle will be happy to see you."

He looked as disappointed as I felt at that prospect. I'd never been attracted to anyone but Chad before. And I was definitely attracted to mister blue eyes.

"Ok, but we're just friends. I've never even been to his house before. You don't think he'll mind my just showing up when he said he'd text me, do you?"

"Positive that he won't."

"Ok."

We started walking in that direction. I knew where Kyle lived but it was nice to have someone to walk with in the dark. "So, what year are you?" I asked to fill the silence.

"Heading into Sophomore. I'm studying to be an architect."

"Really? That's neat. I guess that's why you like geometry."

He smiled and nodded. "What about you? Are you headed to school anywhere?"

"Uh." I sighed. "To be honest, as lame as it sounds, I haven't even thought about it. I kind of blew it this year with my grades and haven't even applied to any colleges yet. I have no idea what I'm going to do. My dad, he…he kind of needs me right now. I work at the diner in town. I guess I'll work there until I figure it all out."

"Hey, taking care of family is just as important if not more than taking care of yourself. You're doing a good thing, staying with your dad while he needs you."

It was the first positive thing I'd heard someone say about anything I was doing all year.

"Thanks. Wow, I can't believe how much I needed to hear someone say that," I admitted and smiled bashfully.

He smiled back. Then he pulled me to a stop by a hand on my arm and pushed my hair back once more to inspect my head. I looked up to his face, refusing to look away no matter how much my cheeks wanted to flush. I refused to be swoony. He looked back down at me, his hand still in my hair, and I felt butterflies attack in my gut. He cocked his head to the side a little and seemed to inspect my reaction. I licked my lips nervously. His eyes flashed and he immediately looked away and dropped his hand.

"It looks better. I think you'll be fine. Hey, Kyle, look who I found."

I turned to see Kyle standing behind us. An irritated gaze latched onto his cousin. "I can see that. Do you two know each other?"

"Nope, but your friend here saved my life." He looked back down at me and smiled. He looked back up to Kyle's incredulous look. "Seriously, I almost got hit by a truck. She pulled me out of the way. I would be standing here dead, if not for her."

Kyle looked at me with a new admiration. "Really? You did that?"

"Uh, yeah, it was nothing." I waved off their flattery.

"Mags, I can't believe you." Kyle came and grabbed me in a hug that lifted my feet from the ground and I could tell he was just doing it because of what he saw between his cousin and me. His cousin could, too, from the way he rolled his eyes and crossed his arms over his chest. "Come inside. Wait until I tell Aunt Rachel what you did."

"No, please don't take me in there. I'm not really in the mood for a crowd."

"Ok," he said reluctantly. "I was just about to text you anyway. Sorry, the party ran a little late. We were waiting on a certain someone," he looked pointedly over his shoulder, "to come back so we could eat, but now I see he was preoccupied."

"Well, late's better than dead, right?" I spouted and then winced.

Kyle raised an eyebrow at me, but his cousin burst out laughing from behind him. "She's got you there, cuz." He slapped him on the back. "And I'm glad to see you're so worried about me."

"Whatever. Are you ready?" Kyle asked me and I wasn't.

I so wasn't ready to leave the stranger I'd saved, but saw no way to invite him to go with us when I could see there was clearly tension between them. I looked at him and he was looking at me. I could tell he didn't want me to go either and it made the butterflies worse.

"Uh, yeah, sure," I muttered.

"Ok. I've already got the keys. Let's get going."

"Hold on." I walked up to his cousin a few feet away. I looked up into his face, at least half a foot higher than mine, probably more. "I'm really glad I was there."

"Me, too. Thank you. If you ever need anything; a new pair of rollerblades, a popsicle, a kidney, it's yours."

I laughed and tucked my hair behind my ear as he chuckled, too, and shuffled his feet. "Ok. I'm Maggie by the way."

I stuck my hand out toward him and smiled.

"Maggie," he repeated and I bit my lip at the sound of my name on his lips. "Caleb." He took my hand and I felt an instant jolt go through my body that made me gasp.

Not like a girly wow-he's-touching-me jolt. I mean an actual jolt. Like it felt as if fire was racing through my veins and I was standing in water with a blow dryer. My breaths ceased to exist and my blood felt cold in my hot skin. My eyes fluttered automatically at the pleasure pain of it. I saw images, flashes of things. Me on a porch with tan arms going around me from behind and a brown haired head sitting atop mine then leaning down, kissing my neck. Then that image vanished and a new one appeared.

Me running, someone chasing me, but I wasn't scared, I was laughing. I looked back and a brown haired boy was hot on my tail, grabbing me and throwing me over his shoulder as I squealed in delight. Behind them was a house with a for-sale sign, but 'SOLD' was stamped over it, a moving truck parked beside it.

Then, a man and woman took a walk through a lot of white sand. The man pricked a finger on a cactus as he swung his arms. I kissed his finger and then pulled him back to the house, through big bay doors into a bedroom. He pushed me to the bed and followed me, kissing me senseless as we rolled around in the white sheets.

Then I saw me, right now, holding the hand of a tan, dark haired boy. The look of pleasure and confused delight on my face was also on his. His eyes opened and he smiled at me like he understood everything, like *I* was everything.

I was jolted back to the present when my eyes saw what was actually in front of me and not a strange vision of happy times. I was still looking at Caleb's face. He was still looking at me, but just like in the vision, he was smiling, ecstatically.

"It's you," he whispered in wonder. "You're the one."

"What's going on?" I heard Kyle behind me, but I couldn't look away from the blue eyes looking at me with such want.

Caleb came closer to me, releasing my hand and framing my face with his hands and I felt a flood of calm and warmth.

"Breathe, Maggie." I hadn't realized I was holding my breath. I took a deep breath and felt the air rush in and out frantically as I blinked. My head cleared a little. He smiled. "Everything's going to be ok. All right? Just don't be upset. You don't have to be scared."

"What are you doing?" Kyle asked and pushed Caleb's hands away. The second he did that, I felt cold and oddly desperate and heard myself gasp. "Dude, not cool. Look, I understand that she saved you and you feel - whatever - but I told you about this girl. You can't just-"

"She's the one, Kyle," Caleb interrupted, never taking his eyes from mine. It felt like an eternity had passed since he'd first taken my hand and I was still tingling in my veins from whatever had taken place. "It's her."

"What?" Kyle said loudly, almost angrily. "She can't be. I mean you just...met." He sighed harshly and ran his hands through his hair. "You gotta be frigging kidding me."

"What's going on?" I asked softly and finally pulled my eyes from Caleb to look between the two. Kyle looked pissed and angry. Caleb looked in awe and blissed out. He stepped closer to me, but didn't touch me this time.

"Maggie, we have a lot to talk about."

"Not tonight, Caleb," Kyle said, coming to stand between us. "She has no idea what you're talking about. You're going to scare her."

"I'm not going to scare her. She knows me, inside. She knows me, just like I do her, Kyle. It's exactly like they always described it. I can feel her heart beating."

Kyle cursed and shook his head. "This is bull. I can't believe you did this. You knew how I felt and you still did this."

"You know that's not how it works. We don't get to choose. I'm sorry, Kyle, I am."

"Well, fat lot of good that does me."

"Ok," I stopped them both. "Please tell me what's going on." I felt a little light headed and blinked to clear my vision.

Caleb came around Kyle to grab my upper arms gently.

"Maggie, everything's fine. Just wait. It's new, it'll calm down some. Just breathe."

I felt something strange. It felt like an invader, a welcomed invader. Like something was pushing its way into my thoughts or my body somehow. I felt *him*. I gasped and looked up at him. He smiled, realizing what I felt.

"I can feel…your heart beating. I can feel your…happiness," I admitted and had no idea how I knew these things, I just did.

I brought one of my hands to my heart to feel it under my fingers. I could feel each beat of his heart as if it was my own. I felt his concern over me, he was worried that I was going to run when he told me everything, he felt an intense sense of longing and protection for me, but more than anything, I felt his utter joy at what was happening between us, whatever that was.

"See," he continued to explain to his cousin, but his eyes stayed on me, as did his hands. "She can feel me already." He laughed a breathy chuckle and his next words were barely whispered. "Wow, I can't believe this."

"You're too young," Kyle countered. "And she's only seventeen. You're both too young."

"Tell that to my imprint."

"You know what? No." Kyle once again came and got in between us and as soon as Caleb's hands released me, his heartbeat went with him. I was beginning to be irked with Kyle but wasn't sure why. "We have a date. And we're going on it."

"You want to take my significant on a date?" Caleb asked and cocked a brow at his cousin.

I couldn't speak. I just stood there and let them fight.

"Yes, exactly. If she is your significant, she still will be when we get back, won't she?"

"We have to talk about this, Kyle. We have to tell the family."

"I know. But I've been waiting for this all year and I think you can spare her one night, since you'll apparently be spending the rest of your life with her," he said snidely.

"Kyle, don't be like this."

I finally found my voice. "Ok, ok, ok. I have no idea what's going on. I feel strange. I feel...really strange. Why are you both talking like I'm not standing right here?"

"Maggie, I'm sorry." Kyle turned to look at me. "I never wanted you to get mixed up in all this. I never would have thought that *this* could happen."

"What? What could happen?" I said a little hysterically. "What are you talking about?"

"There's some stuff we need to discuss, but first, let's just go, ok? We can get away from here and I'll explain when you have a clear head."

"But…what are you...I mean…I don't understand."

Kyle grabbed my arms to steady me as I swayed. "Caleb. Tell her. Tell her it'll be all right."

I looked up and there he was as Kyle handed me over to him. He was the most beautiful thing I'd ever seen. How had I not noticed this before? He looked the same to me; same cute, sweet guy, but so different now. It was like a new light had been shone on him to illuminate all the perfections I'd been blind to before. My blood was singing in my veins at having him touch me. I wanted to touch him, too, hug him, pull him to me to see what his scruffy chin felt like on my jaw, anything.

He smiled and leaned close to whisper to me, "There will be plenty of time for that." I gasped and blushed furiously as I realized he'd heard my thoughts. "It's ok. Don't worry." His warm hands closed over my shoulders and his fingers brushed my neck sending another sense of warm calm through me, which I'd started to think wasn't a coincidence. "It won't always be like this. You'll learn to control it, where I'll only hear the thoughts you want me to hear. But for now, go ahead and go with Kyle. He's right. You need to clear your head and I have to talk to my father and the family anyway, and it'd probably be better for you if you weren't there the first time. They're a little zealous." He bent to look closely into my eyes. "Don't be scared. You feel that I'd never hurt you, don't you?"

I did, loud and clear. I nodded and said, "Why? Why do I feel that?"

"Because you are my significant, my soul mate, and I'm yours. We imprinted with each other. I guess because you saved me...I'm not sure. It usually doesn't happen when we're this young. And it hasn't been happening at all with the families."

"Imprinted?" I replied breathlessly.

"Imprinting is when we sort of…stamp a seal on each other. You're imbedded in me and I in you. And it's very rare to imprint with a human."

I gasped again and he smiled sadly. "Human? If I'm human, what are you?"

"I'm human just not completely. We're Virtuoso, or Charmed. We call ourselves Aces. We have abilities once we reach a certain age after we imprint."

"What kind of abilities?" I asked dazedly.

"Lots. Look, Maggie, I'm going to tell you everything, I promise. But first, I have to inform my father. He's the champion of our clan, the leader. He has to know what happened and then we'll talk, ok?"

"So, we imprinted," I mused and thought about what that could mean. "Like werewolves or a vampire novel or something?" I asked and they both chuckled.

"Kind of. You read vampire novels?"

"Sometimes."

"Me, too." He smiled and then sighed. "Ok, Kyle, you know you have to be careful with her." He looked at his cousin sternly. "Don't bombard her with information, just wait, she's very fragile. And don't start your crap. It's harder on humans-"

"I know all this. I grew up a Jacobson, too, you know."

"Yes, I know. Sorry."

"Whatever. Come on, Mags."

I tried, but my legs wouldn't go. "I can't. I mean, I don't want to," I realized.

"That's just the mojo working. Fight it, Maggie."

"Hey," Caleb said harshly. "That's what I'm talking about, right there. If you're going to take it out on her the whole time because you're angry about this, then I won't let you take her."

Kyle nodded and sighed. "Ok. You're right, I'm sorry. Help her so we can go."

"Help me? What does that mean?" I asked.

"It's so new," Caleb explained. "It's hard on us. Our imprints don't want to be apart, but I can help you by telling you that I want you to go. Our bodies are in tune with each other. I have to take care of some things here so I want you to go with Kyle and know you're safe, ok? I can feel you," he palmed his chest, "in here, if you need me. You don't have to worry about anything." I needed him to touch me. It was like my veins were screaming for it. And he did. He cupped my face with his big tan hands and we both sighed at the contact. I heard Kyle muttering behind me, but couldn't think to care right then. "I'll come to you tomorrow. Ok? Everything will be fine and I'll explain it all to you. Are you going to be all right?"

"Yes," I said and I felt it. Whatever he was telling me, it was like it went straight to my brain, bypassing everything else. He said it was fine, so it was. "Yes, I'm fine. I'm not sure why I'm fine, but I am."

He smiled beautifully. "Good girl." He glanced over my shoulder. "I told you she'd be all right with this. You shouldn't underestimate her."

"Ok. Ready?" Kyle asked, still clearly exasperated, but willing to cooperate.

"You'll come tomorrow?" I grabbed Caleb's shirt front and felt strange for doing so, but I had to. "To see me?"

His thumbs caressed my cheeks, sending embarrassing shivers down my arms. "I'll come *get* you tomorrow," he corrected. "You are very special, Maggie. My family will be anxious to meet you."

I nodded. "Ok."

"Just remember, there is nothing to worry about."

"Ok."

He kissed my forehead and I closed my eyes at the pleasurable burn, feeling him. Letting his pride at how well I was taking everything wash over me in waves of warmth. "I'll see you soon, Maggie."

I nodded and bit my lip as Kyle grabbed my hand and towed me to his dad's silver Audi. My body felt like it was being split. I didn't want to go. I so didn't want to go. But Caleb said I would be fine.

Kyle buckled me in and we started to back up down the driveway. The whole time, my significant's eyes were locked on mine.

Three

"Significant? What does that even mean?" I asked Kyle after about five minutes of silence. He'd been driving around not really going anywhere since we left his house, his thumb beating an angry rhythm on the steering wheel. "And why am I ok with all this? I mean, you just told me you're not human? I think I would normally freak out about that."

"You're one of us now," he said quietly.

"What? You mean I'm an Ace or whatever?"

"Yes. Look." He looked at me quickly. "I'd explain it all to you, but Caleb was right. You can't handle it right now. Your body is going through enough just being away from him."

"I don't understand."

"You're his mate, his one, his partner, his companion, his soul mate, the person he'll be with forever. Take your pick." He waved his hand in the air.

"But I just met Caleb. I don't even-"

I was about to say I didn't even feel anything for him, but that was a lie. In fact, just saying his name was bringing on a little round of hysteria all on its own. My heart clenched, my palms were sweaty and tingly. I had the strange need to grab the door handle and make a break for it.

And I knew that was crazy, but I couldn't stop thinking it.

"Why do I feel like this? Why do I-" I stopped and tried to breathe through it.

Caleb told me everything would be ok. I knew it would, but I had no idea how or why.

Kyle grabbed my hand.

"Why do you want him? That's what you were going to say? It's because you're meant for each other. It's like...both your souls saw each other and decided they wanted the other. It's something that's always happened in the clans. We've always imprinted to find a wife or husband. Usually it happens when you're older, like about twenty two or three. I've never heard of it occurring this young, and it rarely happens with a human, but sometimes it does."

"So what does that mean? I have to marry him now?"

I thought about getting married at seventeen and what everyone would think of me, that I was loony or worse - pregnant.

"No, silly." He laughed. "You just...belong to each other, now." He chuckled again sadly and squeezed my hand. "Just when I finally got you to go out with me, too."

"I'm sorry."

"You don't have anything to be sorry about. You can't control it." He let loose a growl of a noise. "Ok, let's stop talking about this. You don't need the stress and it's sure depressing me. What do you want to do?"

"I don't know. I'm pretty hungry."

"Ok. Pablo's it is."

We pulled into the restaurant parking lot and he got out, running to my side to open my door for me. He grabbed my elbow to help me and I thought, he's sweet but going overboard, but then I started to wobble. I felt lightheaded and he grabbed my other arm to steady me.

"What's wrong with me?" I croaked.

"It's like withdrawals. You just have to bear through them. They'll get better."

"Withdrawals from what?"

"Caleb," he said and curled his lip like it was disgusting. "Come on. You're with me, you're fine. We're gonna have fun but we gotta stop talking about him, all right?"

"All right."

His hand slid down, his fingers locked on mine and I had a strange sense that I was doing something wrong.

"Stay close, ok?" He opened the door to the restaurant and we went in, wafted by a strong sent of delicious pasta and garlic.

Pablo's was the best half Italian half Mexican place in town.

"Hey, look, there's Rebecca and the guys."

I pulled him to a stop.

"Please no. I don't want to see anyone tonight," I begged.

"Because of what happened? You'll be-"

"No, not because of what happened. I had a fight with my dad and I don't feel like being in a crowd, ok? Please?"

"Ok. Let's go sit back here." He towed me to the back and we sat in a dark booth. Our waitress came over immediately. It was a junior from my Lit class. "Hey, Callie, I'll take a root beer. What do you want, Mags?"

"Sweet tea."

She eyed us both with a little smile. "Congratulations on graduating, both of you. I can't wait."

"Thanks," Kyle muttered and she went to fetch our drinks. "You ok?"

"Yes."

"What'd you and your Pops fight about?" he asked as he fingered his silverware.

"He's a jerk."

"Aha," he replied, like that explained everything.

"My mom left last summer right before school started. Did you know that?"

"Yeah, Chad said something about it."

"He did?" I said with surprise.

"Yeah, he was pretty strung out there for a while after you guys broke up. Of course, I only really saw him at football practice and lunch."

"Yeah."

"So why did you break up with him, anyway?" he asked and I looked up to see that he was serious.

I started to tell him the truth but Callie came back with our drinks. "What'll you guys have?"

"I'll have the...parmesan eggplant," he answered.

"Cheese ravioli."

"Ok. I'll get that right in for you. No appetizers?"

"No thanks," I answered and as soon as she was gone I turned my glare on him. "Chad broke up with me. He didn't want to date anyone his last year because he knew he was leaving."

"What? Then why was he so upset about it? I just assumed it was you...I mean, that's why I kept asking you out, because I thought you broke it off with him which meant you didn't want to be with him anymore."

"We had talked about it. He thought it'd be easier that way, but I didn't want to. He did it anyway."

"Ah, man. What an idiot. I actually felt sorry for him moping around."

"Well, I mean, he had a point, but I guess I just thought it'd be better to spend our last year together than apart, even if it would be hard for him to go, you know?"

"Yeah."

"Ok, enough about Chad. Where are you going to school?"

"Good old University of Tennessee."

"So, is that where all your family goes?"

"Pretty much. We try to stay together as much as possible."

"So, where's, uh..." Just thinking his name made me feel shaky all over again. "Where's Caleb from?"

"From here, well two towns over. His family lives there along with the rest of our clan. We're the black sheep who decided to live somewhere else."

"Why?"

"This is where my mom's parents were from. She and my dad are the last members of our clan to be imprinted. Something is wrong and it's stopped happening. There are a lot of single people in our clan right now."

"So, nobody in your family has gotten married since your parents?"

"Well." He took a long sip of his drink and leaned back. His feet touched mine under the table. I scooted them back. "My uncle got married but it was a big scandal. He wasn't imprinted, he just married someone from a clan that he fell in love with. Big no-no."

"Because he could imprint with someone while already being married to someone else," I said, understanding.

"Yep. I mean, he was thirty one when he got married, no one ever imprints that late, but still. Why chance it? You can't control it. Think about what his wife would feel if he imprinted with another woman. He wouldn't be able to control the way he felt."

"So you can love someone even if you aren't imprinted with them?"

"Yeah," he said softly and looked down quickly so I tried to act like I didn't notice.

"So, what happens after you imprint? Caleb said something about abilities."

"Nuhuh. That's his territory. He has to explain it to you."

"Another no-no?" I asked, sensing there was probably gonna be a lot of rules.

"Nope, I'm just not gonna be the one to break it to you."

"Ok, so." A silly question popped in my head but I hoped it'd lighten the mood. "What about Werewolves? Real?"

He laughed. "No. Not even close."

"Wizards?"

"Hardly."

"Angels?"

"Bible."

"Aliens?"

"Science Fiction."

"Vampires?"

"Young adult science fiction," he said, laughing loudly.

An older couple beside us gave us a *not happy* look at his outburst and we laughed harder before I started quizzing him again. "So, none of the myths are real?"

"None that you would think of. Food's here."

"That was fast."

"They always are. Good ol' Pablo."

"Here you go," Callie said and she set our food down. "Ravioli and eggplant. You need anything else?"

"Nope. I think we're good. Thanks, Callie."

"Ok." She lingered and looked a little uncomfortable, twirling her pen in her fingers before turning to me. "So, um, you and Chad broke up, right?"

"Yeah," I answered and hoped this wasn't going where I thought it was.

"Would you mind if I called him? I mean, we're both going to Florida. I'll be there next year. I just figured, since you dumped him you wouldn't mind if I asked him out."

"Jeez, Callie, blunt much?" Kyle said and looked at her like she had two heads.

"What? She's the one who dumped him. He's moped around all year waiting for her. He needs to have some fun for a change."

"She didn't dump-" he started to defend me, but I stopped him.

"No, Kyle. It's ok. Yes, Callie, call him to your little heart's desire."

"Are you funning me?" Her hand went to her hip. "Cause I don't always catch the sarcasm."

I wanted to sigh, and I had to mentally push out the blonde joke rattling around in my head. "Look. Call him. If he wants to go out with you, fine. Thanks for the ravioli. We don't need anything else right now."

"Ok," she said warily. "I'll check on you in a bit."

She walked away and Kyle looked at me sympathetically. "She's such a ditz. Some people have no couth."

"No, really it's fine." I had an epiphany; a revelation that made my cheeks spread in a smile. "I don't care. For the first time in a year...I don't care about Chad."

"It's the bond." He shook his head. "You won't care about anyone but Caleb now," he said almost grudgingly.

"So, there's no way to break it or stop feeling it...or whatever?"

"No. Why, do you want to?"

"No," I answered too quickly and he grimaced.

"Yeah, didn't think so."

"So," I sang, sensing a need to change the subject. "What are you gonna do at Tennessee?"

"Architecture."

I remembered Caleb telling me that's what he was doing. "Is that a family business?"

"Mmhmm," he mumbled around a bite.

I pursed my lips and waited, but he didn't say anything further. So we ate. He asked me about school, why I'd dropped out of everything. Why I hardly came to school anymore and stopped eating lunch with them. This whole time, he thought it had been because of my dumping Chad.

I told him everything. I don't know why, I just did. I told him things I didn't even tell Rebecca and she was the closest thing to a best friend I ever had but I even felt withdrawn from her lately. I told him how my mom left, taking everything of value with her: all our plates and dishes, the money, our savings, my college fund, my parent's bed. My dad had slept on the couch in the den for ten months. I told him how she used to call me and try to explain how much she had hated her life and everything in it. I told him how my dad was bitter now and spiteful, his life just spiraling down and he was slowly taking me with him. I told him how I had to get a job to help out because my dad lost his.

He listened quietly as he ate. He waited to see if I was done, watching me closely.

"I'm sorry, Mags. Everyone just assumed you'd ditched Chad and just didn't want to hang out with us anymore. No one knew- I mean, we knew your mom left but the rest...you should have said something."

"I didn't know what to say. How do you tell someone that your boyfriend dumped you three days after their mom left and their dad sits in his room and doesn't even speak to you? No one wanted me around anymore," I said softly and stared at the ravioli I no longer wanted.

"I wanted you," he admitted just as softly. I looked up and caught his hazel brown gaze. "I've always wanted you. But it was always you and Chad. And now, it'll be you and Caleb. And not only that, but I'll have to see you together, every day, because you'll be family."

"Kyle." I pushed my plate away and began to toy with my hoop earring. "I'm sorry. I don't know what to say."

"No." He sighed roughly and grunted. "I'm sorry. I shouldn't have said that. I still want to be your friend, Mags. Now I get to be your cousin, too." He forced a grin. "The Jacobsons are a weird bunch, I'm warning you now, but they are fiercely protective. You don't have to worry about anything anymore. Your mom and dad are idiots for leaving you, but you have a new family now."

I didn't know whether to smile or run at his comment so I just bit my lip and chuckled under my breath.

"So, you ready to get out of here? Wanna see a movie?"

"Sure. We can't go back to your house can we?"

"No. Not tonight. There's gonna be a lot of crap going down tonight at my house with the whole family there. Believe me, you don't want to be there anyway."

I could beg to differ. Caleb was there and whatever this imprinting thing was, it wasn't a joke. I could still feel his heart beating if I thought real hard about it.

"Ok. What do you want to see?" I asked as he flagged down Callie for the check.

"Anything you want, even a chick flick if it'll cheer you up."

I wrinkled my nose. "I'm not really into chick flicks. I'm more of a Sci-Fi girl."

"Ah, you're gonna fit right in." He grinned and took my hand to pull me up. "And I know just the movie."

I let him pull me to the car, again feeling that ping of wrongness for holding his hand, but not before Rebecca and the rest of them saw us. Her eyes bulged and I saw her glance at our hands. Then I saw Chad, sitting in the very back of the group. I should've known. That was why Callie was asking about him.

He was there.

His face was a textbook description of hurt and confusion and anger. He looked like he wanted to stand, but thought better of it. He leaned back in his seat, crossing his arms and glared at Kyle. Boy were they all wrong about what was going on, but I was sure it still looked bad. It might have been better if he saw me with Caleb instead. They didn't know Caleb, but he knew Kyle. This was like betrayal to Chad.

I quickly turned and left the restaurant before any of them could move towards us.

"Kyle, you shouldn't have done that. Those are your friends. Now Chad's going to be all weird around you."

"I'm leaving and so is he. It's not like I'm going to talk to him anymore. We only hung out in our group and at football. I wasn't really his friend. Besides, from what you just told me back there, he's a complete idiot anyway."

"Still." Then a thought hit me and I pulled him to a stop. "Did you do that on purpose? Did you see him back there?"

"No. But I might have done it on purpose if I had. He's not worth your time. He cared more about football than you. He proved that when he ended it when you guys could have tried to work out some long distance relationship or something. That's the dumbest thing I've ever heard."

"I know," I started as he towed me again, "but that doesn't mean I want to hurt him on purpose."

"You're too sweet, you know that? You can't let people just do away with you. You are too good for him, even your parents, if they can't see how great you are."

He opened my door and put me in, reaching over to do my seatbelt. "Uh, Kyle, I can do it."

"Oh. Right." He smiled bashfully before going to his side. "So, are you a popcorn or candy girl?"

"Popcorn," I answered.

"Ah," he groaned and shook his head. "You're killing me here."

"What do you mean?"

"Nothing, just...you're pretty awesome." He gave me a sidelong look at the red light, staring with a little smile and I blushed involuntarily, looking away. "Huh," he said smiling wider, looking entirely too pleased with himself. "Maybe Caleb's got some competition after all."

"Kyle-"

"Ok, I know. I know," he said, his hands raised in surrender before taking the wheel and turning into our spot in front of the theater.

It was literally two blocks from Pablo's.

I opened my own door this time, feeling a little more like my old self. I was even starting to wonder why I was taking everything so well. I mean, I just found out there are people out there with powers or abilities or something. Not human. I had bound myself, unintentionally, to one of these people I just met and couldn't get him out of my mind. Shouldn't I be freaked?

"Two for Battlestar National, please," Kyle said to the attendant then smiled at me. "You're going to love this. Have you seen Lord of the Rings?"

"Of course," I scoffed.

"Well, this is nothing like that."

I laughed and he laughed, too. The attendant rolled her eyes as she passed him the tickets. He took them and we made our way in the doors and to the concessions stand. I took off my jacket, stood behind him and waited.

My mind drifted to Caleb. I scolded myself. I'd never been so smitten in my life. I mean, this was borderline boy crazy. I didn't even remember being like this with Chad. I felt a little foggy thinking of Caleb. I had an urge to leave, right then. Head out the door and straight to Kyle's where I knew Caleb would be. A lump grew in my throat the more I thought about it. My hands twitched at my sides and I took a deep, steadying breath.

Kyle looked back at me and frowned. "Don't think about him, I told you."

"What's happening to me?"

"It's just new. It'll fade," he grimaced, "some."

"You both keep saying that. What does that mean?"

"Just stop, ok? Don't think about him and you'll be fine," he said, irritated.

He turned to place our order and handed me a drink while he squirted butter on our huge bucket of already pretty yellow popcorn.

We started towards our theater and I heard someone call Kyle's name from behind us. I groaned as I turned, thinking it was guys from school but it wasn't. I'd never seen those guys before. There were six of them and they were all black haired and tall. Kyle groaned beside me, so I didn't feel much better.

"Jacobson," the guy said lilting and sardonically. "What brings you out? Oh, I see," he said like he hadn't seen me already. I raised an eyebrow at him as his eyes perused me openly. "My, my, I *do* see. Hello."

"All right, Marcus, enough," Kyle barked and I balked at his tone.

"What? I only said hello. So, Kyle, you breaking your clans rules now? I always knew you were a rebel at heart. What movie are you seeing?"

"Not interested in adding to our group, but thanks."

Kyle tried to turn us but Marcus grabbed my arm. I had another jolt and for just a second I worried that I was imprinting with someone else. But I realized, that was the last thing I was doing. My veins screamed in protest and my skin burned hot on my arm. My body was warning him; my blood, whatever, however it worked. This guy's intentions were not to keep me safe and the imprint reacted.

He released my arm with a curse like I shocked him. He and his group eyed me with wide, scared eyes and something else; anger.

"She's your significant! Impossible!"

"Not mine. She belongs to Caleb. Now back off."

"She's human. She's what...fifteen?"

"Seventeen," I butted in, annoyed.

"Impossible," he repeated, but this time he growled it and I stepped back, Kyle pulling me behind him.

"Don't freak out. You'll call Caleb and all hell will break loose. Breathe," he told me quietly and waited for me to take a deep breath, then turned back to Marcus. "Back off. You know now that Caleb's imprinted, it'll only be a matter of time until he gets his ascension. You're not stupid enough to mess with his girl, are you?"

"Marcus, let's go," one of the guys said behind him. "Enough already."

"For now, human," Marcus spat and eyed me evilly before they moved on.

One guy hissed at me. Hissed! I shook my head. "What was that?"

"Bad news. Crap, why tonight? They are a rival clan. They haven't been imprinting for a while either. This will definitely stir up the pot now that they know about you."

"Why is everyone so hard pressed to date? I don't get it. So you don't find your soul mate. There are tons of single people out there. It's not like you can't live that way."

"No. You don't get it. Wait." He looked around and pushed our theater door open, taking us to the very back to sit down. "See, if we don't imprint with anyone, we don't ascend. If we don't ascend we don't get our abilities. It's not just about being single. This is our whole life, our heritage, being an Ace, protecting our family, having the power to do that. But without finding our mate, we can't do that and it's crippling our clans, making us vulnerable."

The full weight of what he'd been trying to tell me hit me like a ton of bricks. That's what Caleb meant when he said I was special. This was a big deal. No one had imprinted in years. Caleb was the first one of his kind in a long time and they were gonna make a fuss about this, good or bad, and I was stuck in it with no way out, but wasn't sure I wanted out.

The screen blinked with an advertisement for concessions then went straight into a movie preview. I settled back in my seat and tried not to think about Caleb. Whenever I did, I felt a zing in my chest, an ache, but a pleasure as well. It was all very confusing and frustrating. While I sat and pretended to watch the movie, my mind was somewhere else. On a blue eyed, brown haired boy. And though it made me feel anxious, his heart beat coming to me in waves and pulses the harder I thought, and I fought to stay in my seat, I did it anyway. I thought about that boy.

A boy that apparently now belonged to me.

Four

I woke the next morning and felt terrible, like I had the flu or something. I rolled over in my bed and clutched my queasy stomach, feeling a pounding in my head and chest. The pound coincided with my heartbeat.

I sat up and saw stars. That had never happened before. At first I was alarmed. Maybe it was something worse than the flu. I stood and went to the mirror. I looked haggard.

Kyle had brought me home right after the movie last night. It wasn't that late when I got home, but Dad was nowhere to be seen, as usual. I went straight to bed, feeling more exhausted than I had in a long time.

And now, I could see my face was dark with fatigue. My eyes were dull and shaded. What in the world? I lifted my arm to push my hair back to check the little gash on my forehead and froze. There was a black handprint burned into my skin, black and grayish like it was charred, right by my elbow on my right arm. What the-

Then I remembered. My arm burned hot when that Marcus guy grabbed me yesterday. And now, I had a strange black grip burned into my skin. What was going on here?

I heard the phone ring, but didn't answer it. It was probably Chad, looking for answers, though he had no right to any claim over me anymore. So I went to take a shower instead.

That was one of the best showers I'd ever had. I still felt bad, but better. The hot water did wonders for my skin color. My face seemed back to normal and my eyes were brighter. But, I still needed some serious makeup. Then I remembered. Caleb. He said he was coming to get me today.

I scrambled to my room and pulled some clothes out. I actually thought about what I was putting on. I had jitters. I was freaking out. I slipped on my blue chiffon peasant blouse over my black cami and some jeans with some silver hoop earrings then I went to fix my hair and slick on some make-up.

All the while, I felt a bubble of anxiety and nerves. What had happened last night? I couldn't believe I saved some guy's life. I couldn't believe I was bound to him in some twisted soul mate thing. I couldn't believe Kyle had a crush on me. I couldn't believe I was so crazy about some guy I barely knew. I couldn't believe they weren't human.

I started to have a mini-panic attack, swallowing down the lump in my throat. Then it began to escalate to full blown.

What if Caleb didn't come today? Why did I need him to so badly? What was going to happen to me? Would I just marry some freak guy and live in their cultish community forever? Could I run away before he got here? Did I really want to? No, I didn't and if he asked me to marry him right now I'm not sure I could say no. What was going to happen to me now?

My breathing was crazy out of control and I grabbed the sink to hold myself up. I felt all wrong and my muscles twisted in my body as I kept Caleb in my thoughts. I was just about to really worry, maybe call somebody, though I didn't know who, when I felt arms around me, turning me and pulling me to them.

"I'm sorry." He pulled me to his chest, wrapping his arms around me and whispering in my ear as his hand ran up and down my arm. "I got here as fast as I could."

Caleb.

I sighed in relief as I felt a release of all the tension, the queasiness, the aching muscles, the painful breaths, everything, as I settled my arms around his waist. I felt brand new, like he was a drug and I'd just gotten a hit.

I pulled back to look at him slightly and was wowed. He was even better looking in the daylight. I blinked up at him and he looked back down at me. I could see into his mind as if it was made of glass. He had felt me begin to panic he was already half way here. He ran. He knew I'd be upset when reality crashed down on me this morning. He was feeling withdrawals for me, too, and pestered Kyle for over an hour before he got out of bed to give him my address, though once the panic attack hit he didn't need it. He could find me anywhere. He also loved my freckles and thought I looked gorgeous in blue.

I smiled and bit into my bottom lip at his thoughts.

"Hi," was my masterful greeting.

"Hi," he said smiling widely, his arms still around my back. "Are you all right now?" He reached up and brushed my hair back from my forehead. "How's the head?"

"It's fine. It doesn't hurt anymore."

"Did you sleep all right?"

"Yeah, I slept great, actually." We both seemed to realize the awkwardness of it all and stepped back to give a little space. "And I was fine, I mean I felt a little weird, like I had the flu," he nodded to confirm, "but it wasn't until I started to think about things…um, you, that I freaked."

"I know. It happens, especially the first few days after an imprinting."

"Why?"

He shrugged. "Doesn't matter. I'm here now, and I have no intentions of going very far."

"Good," was all I could say.

He seemed to like my answer. "Did you have fun with Kyle last night? I didn't have a chance to talk to him much. I waited up for him last night but he went straight to bed. I'm sure he would have told me if something had happened."

"Yeah, we had an ok time, mostly."

"Why mostly?" he said, suddenly concerned. "What-" He saw my arm and his eyes went wide. I'd forgotten the angry, black, burned hand print. His face twisted in anger. "What happened? I can't believe Kyle didn't tell me about this. Who did this to you?"

"Some guy called Marcus." I rubbed it like it could come off.

He pushed my fingers away gently to run his thumb across it, almost reverently. "Marcus touched you?" he said softly and I knew not to mistake the softness for anything but fighting for control.

"He grabbed me when we tried to walk away. But as soon as he knew that I- you- we..."

"That we imprinted," he supplied.

"Yes. He left. I didn't see this until this morning."

"It's what happens to warn them that you don't belong to them."

"I know, I felt it, but why didn't it do that when Kyle touched me?"

"Kyle touched you?" he said with a slight edge.

"He held my hand a couple times," I explained truthfully. "Mostly to make me keep up with him, but it never did that with him."

"It only happens if the person's actions aren't of pure intention. Your body can sense it when someone means you harm."

"So, that Marcus guy wanted to hurt me?" I said breathlessly at the prospect.

"Don't worry about that just yet." His big hand came up to my cheek, making me want to shudder. "One thing at a time. I'll explain it all to you, but right now, I need to get you over to Kyle's. My family is all there, waiting for us."

"Eh," I cringed. "I don't like crowds."

"You'll like this crowd. They were so happy last night when I told them what happened. They can't wait to meet you."

"Caleb," I said and he sighed, closing his eyes like he was in ecstasy at the sound of his name from my mouth. "I have no idea what's going on. I mean, what does all this mean? Why am I meeting your family after only knowing you for one day?"

"Well," he looked slightly unsure, "I, uh...you're my significant. I mean, I would never force you to do anything, but this means something to us; to my family. You are so important and the sooner you learn all about what's going on, the sooner you can make the decision if you want anything to do with it or not."

"I thought I didn't have a choice."

"Kyle and his big mouth," he muttered. "There are so many things you don't know. So many things that I need to tell you and explain. But if after you hear everything today you want nothing to do with any of it, or with me, I won't stop you from leaving if that's what you're asking."

"Ok. I'm ready to go." I nodded. "I need to tell my dad where I'm going."

"All right. Should I go wait outside since I burst into your house without knocking," he said with a cocky grin. "I'm sure your pops would love that."

"It's fine," I said, laughing slightly. "He won't know whether anyone's been up here or not."

"Are you sure?"

"Yeah, come on."

"I guess it's only fair if you're meeting my family that I meet yours, too, right?"

"I don't think the word 'family' constitutes as one person."

"Sure it does." He stopped in the hall at a family picture of us four in front of the Christmas tree from two years ago. Bish had his arm around me and I was poking his stomach, making him laugh. "Is that your brother?" I nodded. "Wow. You really look like your mom."

"Yeah, everyone has always said that."

"What happened to her?"

"She left," I said, shrugging before heading downstairs.

"I'm sorry. That sucks."

"Yeah," I agreed and then called to Dad before we went into the den. Just in case he was in his underwear. "Dad?"

I heard him grunt and felt a grip on my hand tighten. I didn't realize we were holding hands. Caleb smiled at me and I tried to think of how in the world to explain him to my father.

"What, Maggie?"

"Uh, Dad, I'll be leaving for a while. I'm not sure how long I'll be gone. I just wanted to let you know."

"Fine, as long as you don't miss work."

"I'm off today."

"Fine."

"Dad. This is my...friend, Caleb."

I glanced up at him and he was fighting a smile, the twinkling of amusement in his eyes giving him away. My dad barely glanced at him, looking right back at the television and scratching behind his ear.

"Uhuh."

"Dad," I said more pointedly.

He looked up again. I really regretted not letting Caleb wait outside. Dad was sitting on our couch in the den, his boxers and a white t-shirt, with white socks up to his mid calves, watching the Today Show of all things.

"Oh, yeah. Hi, Calvin, nice to meet you," he muttered and returned to his show.

"Caleb, Dad."

"It's fine, Maggie," Caleb assured me with a squeeze of my fingers. "Nice to meet you, too, sir. I won't keep her out too long."

"Mmhmm. Fine."

As we made our way out into the hall, I remembered when my father always used to joke about how when I finally started dating he'd be all mister-shotgun-on-the-porch about it. He sure gave Chad a hard time, though most of it was in jest. It's like an alien took over his body or something. He's not even my dad anymore. And the only reason the house is clean right now, is because I cleaned it before leaving for graduation yesterday. I couldn't remember a time I'd been more embarrassed.

Caleb was apparently tapped into my thoughts again.

"Hey." He bumped my shoulder as we walked. "Don't sweat it. Your dad is apparently going through something. He'll come around one day. You don't ever have to be embarrassed with me, ever, about anything."

"Caleb, I barely know you. Why do I feel so...fine with everything? This is all so strange."

"I know and I'm not going to rush you to understand everything. But other people don't get to decide who you are to me, not even your parents. Just know, you can't ever say or do anything to make me not want you anymore."

I sighed, wanting to sag in relief, because that's exactly what I always wanted someone to tell me, that they wanted me for me, no matter what. "Thank you, Caleb."

"You're welcome," he said sincerely. "Do you need to grab anything before we leave for Kyle's?"

"Uh, my phone. It's in my jacket pocket upstairs. Be right back."

I ran up to get it and ran back down. He was waiting at the bottom of the stairs for me with a smile. He didn't take my hand this time, just opened the door for me and we walked slowly, side by side, but not touching all six blocks to Kyle's house.

I was thinking and listening. Listening and absorbing his feelings as he worked through what we were about to do. He was scared. Scared that I was not going to be able to accept what his family would tell me. Scared that I was gonna hate him, blame him and want nothing to do with him for taking my choices for a different life with someone else.

This confused me, because yesterday, he seemed so sure that I would take everything fine. Accept it and want it. Now he wasn't so certain. I wondered what I had said or done since then to make him change his mind about me.

We reached Kyle's front yard and I stopped, taking a deep breath. Caleb saw me and came back to stand in front of me.

"I'm a freak, aren't I?" I asked.

"What? Why would you say that?"

"You said this doesn't happen to humans."

"I said it's rare."

"What if they don't like me?" I spouted quickly and shot my gaze to the grass, my insecurity raring its ugly head.

"What's not to like?" he said sweetly.

"What if they think your imprint made a mistake? What if they think I'm too naïve and young? What if they think that you're definitely going to have your work cut out for you with me? I'm scared of walking through that door and hearing what they might say. I'm nobody, mediocre, I'm not special, I'm not rich, I'm boring, I'm shy and I'm only seventeen."

"Maggie-"

"And I'm terrified that the more you get to know me, you'll realize it, too."

He put a tentative arm around my lower back and pulled my face up with a finger under my chin making me automatically lean towards him and his warmth. He smiled and it was gorgeous.

"Imprints don't make mistakes, Maggie. All an imprint is, is our souls seeing what's perfectly right for it in someone else. In here," he palmed his chest "I saw something in you that I couldn't live without. I chose you, inside of me, and you chose me. It's not one sided, it only works when both people choose the other. You are perfect for me in every way. I don't want to scare you with it all. I mean, you're so young and you don't know me. Yet. But...we will always be drawn together. We'll always crave each other. We'll always be in tune with each other, physically and mentally. There is nothing that can change or break that. And even if there was, I wouldn't want to. Not for the world." His hand moved to my cheek and he caressed it with his thumb. "I've seen you. You can't fake or glimmer what's inside your mind. And you are sweet and caring and absolutely lovable in that head of yours. I promise that my family will love you. In fact, I'm sure they already do. You're one of us now and they can sense how I feel about you."

"How you feel about me," I repeated and nodded.

"Yes. They all know how it is. How we feel...about each other isn't uncommon. It's normal for you to feel so pulled and drawn to me even though you don't know me, just like I am to you, but worse. It gets better and with all our connections and abilities we'll grow to know each other very quickly."

I couldn't deny that and I definitely felt something for him. Especially right now with his arm around me, tentative, fighting with himself because he wants to touch me more but also wants to make sure I'm ok with it too. His concern for me was extremely endearing.

"This is all so strange," I said breathlessly.

"Just wait," he leaned in to whisper in my ear. "It'll only get stranger." He chuckled and the vibrations gave me goose bumps. "Come on." He pulled back to look at me. "If you're ready, let's go on in so everyone will stop staring out the window."

I didn't dare turn to look, but I shifted my eyes that way and sure enough, there were more faces than I could count, all packed in and peeking out of the curtains. I felt my cheeks blaze red as I groaned and he chuckled again.

"Don't worry about them. I promise. Look at me." I did, but slowly. "They will love you. Don't let them overwhelm you, all right? Everything will be fine. Ready?"

"No." I did turn then. I looked at them. They were all smiling, watching us. A little girl waved frantically to me. I waved back and she jumped up and down and even though I couldn't hear her, I could tell she was squealing. I took a deep breath and smiled. "Let's go, but be prepared to answer about a million questions."

"I'm counting on it."

We made our way to the door and before he could even reach the handle, the door was snatched open and I was enveloped in a hug by a large woman with gray and brown hair who smelled like Freesia. She swayed me side to side and all I could do was let her.

I heard Caleb behind me, along with a lot of other chatter. "Gran, come on. She's freaked out enough as it is."

"Oh, hush, Caleb. Let me have my fun." She pulled back to look at me. "My, my, you are a pretty little thing, aren't you?"

"Am I?" I asked lamely and everyone giggled and cackled.

"Well 'course you are! Look at those freckles. And these cheek bones," she mused and ran a cool finger down one to accentuate.

"Thanks," I said, doubly lame.

"Gran, please." Caleb pulled my arm to make her release me and she did. I couldn't help but latch onto his arm and try to keep my eyes up to look around the room with confidence instead of looking like a trapped rabbit. I didn't want them to feel like they were bothering me. I could do this, but…there were at least twenty people in there. "All right, can you all give her some breathing room, please? Jeez, guys."

"Why don't you bring her in the living room, Caleb," a pretty petite woman with brown hair that matched Caleb's said. She was very well dressed in gray slacks and a white button blouse. She walked right up to me and smiled. "Hello, Maggie. I'm Caleb's mother, Rachel, and you must call me that. None of that Mrs. Jacobson stuff."

"Ok, nice to meet you."

"No, sweetie, it's nice to meet you." She squinted and leaned closer. "What happened to your head?"

"I did that, Mom. Remember? I fell on her after she pulled me back," Caleb explained and looked at me sideways, a little guiltily.

"Oh, yes, how stupid of me to have forgotten." She hugged me tightly and I heard her voice straining to get her words out. "You saved my boy. It's hard to think that if you hadn't been *there,* my boy wouldn't be *here*."

"It was nothing, really. Just good timing," I insisted into her shoulder.

"You don't honestly believe that anymore do you? After what happened I would think you'd be a big believer in destiny."

"Mom. Jeez," Caleb breathed out in protest.

"Go ahead," she waved us toward the living room, "I'll bring you something to drink. Tea?"

"Sure. Thanks," I answered and heard her high heels clicking on the tile as she scampered away through the throng of onlookers.

Caleb took my hand, smiled at me shyly and nodded for me to follow him into the living room, as instructed, as everyone stared, but had warm smiles and parted the way for us. I felt like a specimen in a Petri dish, but a welcome one. Caleb hadn't been exaggerating. They were all thrilled I was there and it was plainly written all over their faces.

He brought me to a plush, brown couch in the middle of the room. The room was bright and yellow with pictures everywhere of brown haired people. I sat down and he sat close beside me but not touching. It was so quiet, like everyone was waiting for something to happen. I decided I'd show Caleb I wasn't some shy silly girl. I could handle his family.

"I've always loved this house. From the outside anyway," I said, loud enough for most to hear and some chuckled.

"Well, I'm glad you like it," a deep voice answered back. A tall, dark haired man stepped forward and took the club chair in front of us. I saw him glance at the black handprint on my arm, frown, and then look back to my face. "This was my wife's parent's house."

"You must be Mr. Jacobson," I stated and jolted a little when everyone laughed.

"Sweetheart, we're all Mr. Jacobson."

I blushed and looked up at Caleb from under my lashes. He was smiling and shaking his head...and he was glowing with happiness. It took my breath away. I continued to look at him. He had a little dimple in one cheek that I hadn't noticed before and it made me ache to look at it and not touch it.

He was wearing jeans and a yellow polo shirt today. It was a nice fit, hugging him, and I bit my lip as my eyes met his and my heart jumped. He actually blushed, as he felt what I felt, which was pretty hilarious.

He rubbed his chin and smiled crookedly at me which made me smile. I turned back to see everyone else grinning at us, which made me blush again. I ducked my head and let my hair curtain my face.

"Here you go." Rachel handed me and Caleb a glass of sweet tea and sat on the loveseat near us. "Now, Maggie," she leaned forward on her knees with her elbows, "tell us about yourself."

"Mom, that's not why I brought her here," Caleb rescued me. "First, she needs to hear the history of our kind. She needs to understand what's going on. Where's Dad?"

"He'll be here shortly. He had an errand to run, but while we wait, I don't see why it would hurt to ask Maggie some questions."

"Mom, why don't we let her talk to grandma instead?" He turned to me. "Grandma is the only other living member of our clan who was human."

I gasped inwardly and looked up searching for her. I forgot he had mentioned that there were others. I felt desperate to talk to her. To find out if what my body was telling me was real.

I saw her moving forward and she sat in the only empty chair left in front of us. She pulled a silver, oval locket out of her dress, on a long chain around her neck, opened it and thrust it forward for me to see. She, too, glanced at my arm, the handprint, before settling her gaze on me.

I took the locket gently and saw the black and white picture of a man, a handsome man who looked shockingly like Caleb. I glanced between the two several times. Caleb's grandma chuckled.

"Yes. Caleb does look an awful lot like my Raymond did. He's Caleb's grandfather and you can call me Gran, everyone does."

I nodded and she went on, pulling the locket from my grasp and looking at it longingly before replacing it.

"So, I met Raymond at a buffet." She cackled. "I was with my parents, eating on a Saturday night out at our first buffet in town. We never ate out and it was such a treat. We both reached for a roll at the same time. Our fingers touched and that was it," she said and smiled sadly.

"So, it's the touch that triggers this...whatever it is?"

"Imprinting. Yes, touch is what triggers it. Now granted, I felt some attraction to Raymond before that, as I'm sure you did, but after that it was impossible to stay away. I was human too, so it made it doubly worse. Humans aren't prepared for the changes that occur. We aren't knowledgeable and understanding of what's going on. We have a most difficult time. His parents of course knew but my human parents did not. We were both twenty two. I was in college and so was he, in another city. My parents thought I was smitten and silly and made us leave right then, forbidding us to ever see each other. We were separated for a week before he was able to find me, get to me and sneak past my parents to make it back to me."

I remembered this morning. The strange flu like feelings and aches I had and how Caleb took them all away with one touch this morning. I looked up curiously and she nodded.

"Yeah, think about what you went through this morning but everyday, all day, non stop for a week." I hugged myself while she shook her head. "My parents thought I was crazy, that I'd have some kind of breakdown and were thinking about having me put into an institution."

"Wow."

"So, you see why we are all so concerned for you two, especially you, dear. You are human. You have human parents who will not understand your need to be with Caleb, among other things. Plus you are so very young and not yet legal, the youngest I've ever heard of being imprinted in all the clans. I am worried about causing problems between you and your family."

"Well," I started. "I graduated already."

"Yes. Kyle told us. Skipped a grade?"

"Yes, ma'am, but even if I hadn't, my parents won't cause any problems, so you don't have to worry about that."

"What do you mean, child?" she said with a scowl.

I felt so uncomfortable. I did not want to hash out my sad sob story in front of these twenty or so people, all with their waiting eyes. They wanted the dirt and life story of the strange girl who had been thrust into their lives. I did not want their sympathy. I licked my lips nervously.

Then I felt a hand on mine and it all went away, like wind blowing fog to clear the air. I only felt calm and warm when I looked up into those blue eyes. He was rescuing me again, with a little encouraging smile to boot. So I told her what she wanted to know.

"My mom left last summer. It's just been me and my dad and he's depressed and a little...bitter. I barely see him. I don't have any other family except one adopted brother who lives in New York. No grandparents. No uncles or aunts. No cousins. Just us."

I waited for the onslaught of 'ahhs' and 'you poor things' but they didn't come. His grandmother just nodded. "That's hard. But if nothing else it'll make this a lot easier on you. Do you have a plan for college or anything yet?"

"Um, no. Not yet," I said and picked at the fabric of my jeans.

"Well, we'll talk about that later." She glanced meaningfully at Rachel and Mr. Jacobson, the one I'd talked to, and then back to me.

"What do you mean it'll make it easier on me?"

"Well, honey, to be blunt, you can't live without Caleb."

Five

"Gran!" Caleb's hand released mine as his hands flew in the air. "This is not the way I wanted to explain things," Caleb said and I could feel how exasperated he was.

"It's gotta be done. It'll be worse on her if we don't get it all out in the open. We all know it. She's human. The deed is done. Nothing can be changed now. We can pretend all we want to that there's another choice, but the girl will have to be with you."

"I have to be with him," I repeated before Caleb could say anything else. "You mean with him physically around, like all the time, or I'll get sick like I did this morning?"

"Yes. It's worse in the beginning, but it fades some. You will always need each other. After you ascend, things will be even more different than now, in a good way. I know it's scary right now-"

I cut her off. I wasn't scared. I was feeling an eclectic rainbow of emotions, but scared wasn't one of them.

"I get all that. Don't worry, I'm not scared. I'm not upset. I'm just not sure how to make it all work. This is..." I rubbed my temples and closed my eyes for just a few seconds. "Crazy. I mean, yesterday I was a nobody seventeen year old who graduated high school and had normal problems like everybody else."

"Look." She leaned forward and patted my hand. "I know this is a lot to take in but you wanted the facts. I'm not a baker, so I'm not about to sugar coat it for you. The thing is, there's a reason this happened. You are the first imprint in twenty years in our clan. That's a big deal. The fact that you're human and incredibly young has to mean something."

"This isn't just because I saved him, is it? Some miss-fired imprint false alarm or something?"

Everyone laughed again. Even Caleb beside me. I could feel him shake, and though I was slightly teasing, I was also dead serious.

"Caleb was right. You are fabulous." I looked at him and he winked as she went on. "No, honey, no false alarms with imprints."

"Ok. So, I'm not sure what it is I'm supposed to do. Or be. I mean, what happens to you after you imprint? Kyle said something about ascending and getting abilities. And if you don't imprint you don't ascend and you don't get any abilities. That's why this is such a big deal, right? Because no one is getting any of these...gifts?"

"Exactly," Mr. Jacobson said.

Then I felt something. That little push I felt yesterday when Caleb was in my head. But this time, my mind didn't welcome it. It didn't hurt, but it was annoying and fuzzy. I felt my brow furrow and something zapped in somehow. There were images moving in rapid form and fashion, images of kicks and punches and techniques. My eyelids fluttered and I heard my breath come in and out quickly. Then it all of a sudden just stopped.

Everyone was staring at me expectantly. Caleb had one arm around me and the other holding my hand. I looked up to his face. He looked a little peeved actually, but waited for me to catch my breath.

"You could've warned her," Caleb growled to someone and then looked back at me. Finally he spoke softly, though I knew they all could hear. "What did you see?"

"I saw...um, karate?"

"Very good, Maggie." Mr. Jacobson scooted to the edge of his chair and smiled at me. "I was *teaching* you basic karate actually."

"I'm sorry?" I squeaked.

"That's my gift or ability or power, whatever you want to call it. I can learn at an exponential rate. Then, I can help my family by teaching them anything I've learned that they need to know to protect them or help them do a task by sending those images to their mind. I learn just as quickly as you just did and I then teach you that quickly as well. You, for example, just learned basic beginner's karate in less than ten seconds. I figured if I was going to teach you something, it may as well be something useful to you," he said and smirked.

"You mean, I know karate? Like...real karate?" I made a wide motion with my hands to accentuate. "I don't feel like I do. I don't remember anything."

"That's because you haven't used it yet. Right now it's just an…imprint burned in your mind of my memory of how to do it. The first time you need it, it'll fire your brain receptors and teach you along the way, but you'll remember instantly how to do whatever your instincts think you need to at the time."

"Ok." I took a deep breath, taking it in. Trying not to frown or show discomfort at what he was telling me. "So, is that what everyone does? Is that everyone's ability?"

"No. Everyone is different."

"When will Caleb get his ability? And what will it be?"

"It usually doesn't take long after the imprint. But as far as a what, we have no idea. He'll show us when he's fully ascended. And so will you."

I looked up at him gaping. "Me? You mean I'm going to have some ability, too?"

"Absolutely."

I thought of something and fiddled with the hem of my shirt. "This is what you meant by 'easier for me', that my parents aren't involved, because not only do I have to stay in physical contact with Caleb or I go crazy, but because my family would be suspicious of my abilities pretty soon."

"Yes."

I was shocked to say the least. I pulled my hand free from Caleb, not meaning to upset him, but I just needed myself for a minute. I needed to feel whatever it was that he was shielding and taking from me with his touch.

Then it all rolled over me. Now, I was scared to death. I didn't want to be a freak in their clan that everyone wanted to observe because I was so special. I didn't want to be different or strange to my own world either. I didn't know what I wanted.

My breathing began to be loud and erratic, my hands were shaking. I closed my eyes and steepled my hands in front of my face. I heard someone tell Caleb to help me, he said he was helping. He was letting me work through it. I was grateful that he seemed to know exactly what I needed, but it didn't calm me down any.

I felt the tingling push of his mind in mine, checking to make sure I was all right. I knew he was listening to me, but I couldn't stop the string of thoughts that followed.

Does this mean I'll never have any privacy in my head? Caleb told me I'd learn to control it. Do I love him? Is that what this is? Would I have wanted him if we hadn't imprinted? Yes, I knew I had, but would it have evolved into more? What would have happened if I hadn't been at that light? What's going to happen to me now?

Are we dating now? Do we just jump right into kissing and whatever else dating people do, because we know we're soul mates? I had no idea how to proceed with him. I felt embarrassed and naïve all of a sudden. It was all too much, too fast. I heard a commotion in front of me, but I couldn't break free from my panic.

Kyle.

"What are you doing? Don't just sit there. Help her!"

"She pulled away from *me*. She needs to work through all this, Kyle. If she doesn't do it now, she'll do it tonight or tomorrow when I'm not with her and it'll be a lot worse for her. She knows what she needs. I would never hurt her. "

"Bull. You just want to act like you know her so well, now. You don't know her. Just because you can get in her head and read her feelings doesn't mean you know her."

"I am in her mind and I'm going to do what's best for her. Always. Go away, Kyle, if you can't handle it. She's my responsibility."

"She was my friend before she was your responsibility!"

I heard shuffling and finally a booming voice, Kyle's father, saying Kyle's name and pushing Kyle's voice further away.

I felt my hysteria dwindling. Finally dying down as I felt the push and pull of Caleb in my thoughts and mind and a steady pulse ran through my body. It was loud and a little bit fast, but steady. I realized what it was. Caleb's heartbeat.

There was no denying it. As much as I was confused about all this, I was intrigued. As much as I was wary of how to proceed, I was excited at the prospect of being important to someone. As much as I was scared of what was to come, I was dependant and leaning on someone who had all the answers. His heartbeat pulsed in my veins. How could I deny that?

I felt him rub my arm soothingly and my mind instantly cleared at his touch. I opened my eyes and we were alone. Just us. His family gone.

He was watching me cautiously, waiting for my reaction. He squinted and looked guilty. His fingers came up to brush a tear away, barely brushing my skin. I hadn't even realized I was crying. His guilt flooded me. He was worried that he let it go too far and he'd hurt me, that I was ready to bolt. He was worried that I didn't want any part of this, any part of him.

I felt an ache to soothe him. My hand moved, almost on its own accord, to touch his cheek. "You didn't hurt me."

He looked surprised. "You did it. You can read me?"

"Yeah. I could last night, too."

"Wow, Maggie," he breathed as I dropped my hand back to my lap. "It usually takes a while to adjust, to have any control, especially humans."

"I think we've established I'm not a normal human," I joked.

"No, you're not." He smiled, but then sobered. "Maggie, I'm not expecting anything here. I mean, I know it's awkward. It's even awkward for Aces when they imprint with each other, to just wake up one day and have all these feelings for someone you didn't have before. We'll take it slow. You can set the pace, ok? I'm not gonna rush you into anything. I just want to...spend time with you and get to know you. Everything else will just fall into place when it's the right time, all right?"

I could have cried with relief. "That sounds perfect."

"Are you ok?" He scooted closer so our legs were touching. "I know it's a lot to take in. It must sound pretty crazy."

"I'm...fine. I mean, I should be freaking out. This *is* crazy. I guess I would be if you weren't here. But you are here. So it doesn't matter I guess," I said softly.

He smiled slowly and I gave in to the innate urge I'd had since I'd opened my eyes. I needed to touch him. I worried my bottom lip with my teeth, then timidly reached my arms around his neck to hug him. His arms went around my back and he sighed into my hair. One of his hands moved to hold the back of my head. His neck, where my face was pressed, smelled heavenly. The warmth I felt from his normal touch warmed even more. I felt so put together, so content. He was like a balm to every sore.

"Ahem," an annoyed voice said, interrupting.

Kyle.

We pulled back reluctantly, but Caleb was still holding my wrists. "What, Kyle?" he asked, looking at me.

"Just checking on Mags."

"I'm fine," I said, still not able to look away from Caleb yet either.

"Of course you are. You let everyone run all over you and lover boy here is no exception," he said sarcastically.

"Kyle, that's enough of that, son," the lowest baritone voice I'd ever heard spoke from behind Kyle. We all looked up to see a man who I could only assume was Caleb's father. He was tall and broad with brown hair. I could see Caleb in him. "Give them some slack, why don't ya, Kyle? Sorry, Caleb. I got held up." He walked around Kyle to sit in front of us. "Hello, Maggie. I'm Peter, Caleb's father." He smiled. "How are you doing this morning?"

"I'm all right for the most part. How are you?"

He laughed, deep and wonderful. "Splendid. Thank you for asking, my dear."

"Dad is the champion of our clan," Caleb explained, "like I was telling you last night. He's the main man around here."

"All right, now." His dad laughed. "Don't go filling her head or bloating up my ego. I'm basically a glorified superintendent. So," he slapped his hands on his knees, "you're my son's significant. I never thought I'd see this day. I can't tell you how happy I am to meet you, young lady."

"All right, Peter." Grandma came back in and resumed her seat from before. "Why don't we give the girl a break? She's had a big day already. It's almost lunch time anyway. Maggie, I was wondering if you might want to stay. You can help me whip up something for dessert if you like."

"Sure. That'd be great."

She extended her hand to help me up and I took it. Once standing she took my arm in her other hand and laid her fingers precisely lining up to lay over the black handprint on my arm. She looked into my eyes and I saw her gray eyes swirl a bright green. I gasped a little and she smiled at me.

I began to see the scene in my head of when Marcus had grabbed me, but it was all backwards. It played like a movie in reverse. It was freaky. Then the vision stopped just that quickly. When she removed her hand, the handprint was gone. My jaw dropped.

"How did you do that?"

"It's my ability, dear. I can heal things of the supernatural. But broken arms and cuts from slicing tomatoes, now those have to be healed by your significant."

I jerked to look at Caleb. "You can heal me?"

"We can heal each other, after we ascend. It's one of the things all significants can do for each other."

I blinked. "Are there a lot of things that we can do like that?"

"Yes. Lots," Gran answered. "You complete each other, two halves to one circle. You are no better matched physically, mentally, temperamentally, spiritually and by abilities than with your significant." She pulled up Caleb, too, by his arm and spoke to us both quietly as she held our hands. "Now, listen. I know what you're feeling right now. And I know how quickly things can get out of hand if you aren't careful. You're human. It's gonna make your feelings and reactions to him much more potent and stronger than it would for someone else." She looked at Caleb. "And you're gonna have a hard time, too, because you're gonna feel what she feels. You'll have to keep yourselves controlled. Aces get pregnant the human way, ya know."

I wondered if Caleb was blushing as furiously as I was. I looked over and saw that he was. This was by far the strangest and most uncomfortable conversation I'd ever had with a grandma. But at least he said something.

"Gran, I'm only gonna ask this once. Please don't have sex talks with me, ok? Especially with Maggie in the room. Do you think we could do that?"

"Oh, now, don't be embarrassed. It's natural-"

"Dad! Little help here," he called out.

"All right, Gran," Peter laughed. "Why don't you take Maggie to the kitchen and I'll talk to Caleb. But first." He came and stood in front of me. He smiled and reached around me to hug me to him. "Thank you so much for saving my son, Maggie. Even if you weren't his significant, I would still owe you everything." He pulled back and released me.

"It was nothing, really," I insisted.

"Nothing, smothing. Come on, pretty girl. I need help with the banana pudding," Grandma chimed.

"Aces eat banana pudding?" I asked as she looped her arm through mine, but I felt stupid for my question.

"Yep. Aces *love* banana pudding. Well, my Aces do anyway."

She towed me with her. I glanced behind me at Caleb and he mouthed a 'sorry'. I smiled, shrugged and made my way to help a bunch of Aces make dinner.

Six

Gladly, Gran did not continue her plight for safe sex with me. In fact, she didn't speak about our imprinting at all. She just asked me questions about things; school, my dad, my brother, growing up.

The other ladies in the kitchen listened intently when I answered. The little girl I'd seen in the window had apparently been held back from the meeting we had earlier and was now bouncing around me as I sliced bananas. She was about seven years old I'd guess, and was very cute in her green dress and ponytail.

Everyone decided to eat outside, so I helped set the tables and bring out dishes of hot concoctions. I texted Bish really quickly while I had a few seconds.

Hey. Thanks for the congrats. I miss you. I can't wait to see you. The sooner the better. Dad's pretty bad, but we're making it. How's things in NY?

As expected, the fastest typer in NY, who always had his phone attached to his hip, answered within thirty seconds.

Man, I miss you, too, kid. I'm sorry about Dad. I'll try to send a little bit more money in a couple weeks, but things are crazy expensive here. Other than that, things are...ok. I'll start looking at when I can get a few days off soon. Love ya.

I typed back.

Don't worry about us. We're fine. Love you, too.

When I made my final trip into the kitchen to help I saw the men had moved outside and were already parked in their chairs. Most of the women were seated as well. I saw the empty seat next to Caleb, put my dish down and started to make my way over to him.

I felt like everyone was watching me. I'd felt like that all day and was glad I hadn't just grabbed a hoodie and jeans like I would have any other Saturday.

The little girl who was following me around grabbed my hand before I could reach him. She smiled up at me angelically and swung our arms as we walked.

"I'm Maria."

"Hi, Maria. I'm Maggie."

"I know that, silly. Everyone knows who you are."

"Oh. Well." I was sure I grimaced, so I thought of something to say. "Where are you sitting?"

"Well, I usually sit next to Uncle Caleb, but since you're here, momma said I have to give up my seat."

"Oh. You can sit by him. Really, I don't want to take your seat."

"It's ok. Hi, Uncle Caleb!" She ran to him as he got up and hugged him tightly. "I brought Maggie to you."

"I can see that," he patted her back and smiled at me, "thank you."

"So," she said more loudly and I was leery of the mischievous grin on her chubby cheeks. "Do you love my Uncle Caleb, Maggie? He's really nice and he plays sports," she said as if trying to convince me.

Everyone looked and I swore my heart stopped. I laughed nervously and tucked my hair behind my ear, but Caleb rescued me again.

"Maria, don't you want Maggie to come back?"

"Yes."

"Then let's try not to embarrass her, ok?"

"But she's gonna marry you, isn't she?" she spouted with sudden alarm. "I heard Momma say that you were! You can't get married unless you love each other. 'Cause then all the babies will be born with no love in them-"

"Maria," her mother whispered loudly. She covered a laugh in her fist. "Come sit down. I think you've scared Maggie enough for one day."

I felt my cheeks blazing and bit my bottom lip. I wondered if I'd be permanently colored from all the blushing in one day. I looked up at Caleb and he was sighing and shaking his head as everyone chuckled around us.

"I'm so sorry. They're all crazy. Don't judge me by them, please," he joked as he pulled my chair out for me.

The birds were jabbering as we sat under the shade of a huge oak in the backyard. I looked around at his family as they all passed the dishes around, laughing, talking, and bickering. It all looked so perfect. I missed it, though I'd never had this before. I missed it something fierce.

"Are you kidding? Your family is so great. I'd give anything to have a big family like this. I mean, you all drove over here to see Kyle graduate, right?" I asked and he nodded.

I smiled remembering Kyle's cheering and clapping section, and his obvious enjoyment of it as his name was called. I'd never know what that felt like.

Caleb leaned in to whisper in my ear. "Yes, you will. They are your family now, too."

I looked over and his face was so close our noses almost bumped. My heart galloped and I turned back to focus on my garlic bread. I decided I needed to talk to him. Understand him. Know him. I knew he went to Tennessee and was studying to be an architect, other than that, I had no clue. "So, you live with your family?"

"Yeah. When I'm not at school I stay with my parents about thirty five miles from here. When I'm at school, I have a little apartment there."

"And, Maria's mom is your sister?"

"Yep. Jen."

"What does she do?"

"She works with us."

"Us?"

He looked at me and warred with whether to tell me or not. "We all work together. Our great, great grandfather started *Jacobson Buildings and Things Architecture*. It grew and now it's a pretty big company."

"So, you all go to school to be architects and go work for the family firm?"

"Pretty much."

"What if you didn't want to be an architect?"

"You could be an accountant, lawyer or secretary. Anything you wanted as long as you work for the company. There's a lot that goes into a big business like that."

"Ok, so what if you didn't want to work for them?"

"Uh, I'm not sure. That's all we've ever done. That way we can stay together and work together. We all have knowledge of how to take care of the family in case something happened to one of us. Everyone's taken care of. It's a security thing."

I nodded. "So, when do you go back to school?"

"August first."

"That's eight weeks," I sighed.

"Yep." He looked at me and rubbed his chin. "I talked to my uncle and he's agreed, in fact he insisted, I stay here with them until I go back to school. That way I'll be closer to you."

"And when you do go back to school?" I asked softly.

He leaned close. "One thing at a time, Maggie."

"Yeah. Ok, so now what?"

"Well, it's Saturday. I was going to ask if you wanted to do something with me tonight."

"Yes," I said a little too quickly and rolled my eyes at myself.

He laughed softly and scooted his hand close to mine on the table, a few of his fingers grazing over my knuckles. "Great. We can go see your dad if you need to ask him first."

"Nah," I mumbled, relishing the way my mind cleared of anything negative every time he touched me. "He won't care."

"You're sure?"

"I'm sure. You saw him, he's almost catatonic."

"He's been like that since your mom left?" I nodded as I picked at my pasta. "And what about the diner? Are you still going to work there over the summer?"

"Well, I have to if I want money. My dad sure won't give me any for anything."

"So, you only work there for extra cash?"

"Basically. School stuff, clothes. What is it?" I asked at his relieved expression.

"Nothing. That'll just be one less thing to worry about later," he said cryptically.

"What do you mean?"

He smiled and bumped my shoulder with his. "Nothing. Try the pudding. My grandma won county prize three years in a row for it."

I allowed his subject change, but put it away for future reference.

"So where are we going tonight?" I asked as I tasted a bite of pudding and found that yes, it was delicious.

"Mugly's."

"Mugly's?" I said, thinking I'd heard him wrong.

"Yep. A little place in my town, if you don't mind the drive. They have awesome homemade corn nuggets and barbeque."

"Mmm. I love barbeque," I crooned.

He laughed around his spoon of pudding at my enthusiasm. "Well, I'll file that little tidbit away for later use. What else do you love? I'm making a list here."

It was my turn to laugh. "Um, popcorn, cherries, coffee, anything pasta. My all time favorite, honey buns. I eat at least one every day."

He smiled, leaning on his elbow watching me as if he was thoroughly enjoying himself. "What else?"

"Concerts." He made a noise to indicate he did, too. "Sci-Fi movies, the beach, the color blue, convertibles."

"Really? Convertibles, huh? Well, then you're in luck."

"Why? Do you drive a convertible?"

"I do indeed."

It hadn't slipped my mind the cute, flirty banter that was flowing easily between us, that every time he smiled at me there were sparks in my veins. That I suddenly realized he was way out of my league and there is no way this guy would have given me the time of day had we not been imprinted.

But I remembered yesterday, when he walked me to Kyle's, he did seem somewhat interested then. In fact, he seemed outright disappointed when Kyle was ready to go. Hmm.

Then I remembered he could read my feelings and peeked at him. He was still watching and shaking his head in amusement. I wrinkled my nose and he laughed.

"You said there was a way to turn that off, right?"

"Yep," he answered, "it takes practice and concentration."

"I'll work on it."

"Hey," I heard from behind me. I turned to see Kyle. "You done?"

"Uh." I looked down at my plate. I'd barely touched any of it. I'd spent most the time talking to Caleb. "Sure, I guess. What's up?"

"How you holding up?"

"Good. Your family is really nice."

"I told you they would be. You didn't have anything to worry about. So, since you're feeling all right, what are you doing tonight?"

I glanced at Caleb. He was watching Kyle with annoyance. "Caleb and I are going to dinner."

He laughed humorlessly. "Are you? Well at least he's gonna *try* to date you."

"What is that supposed to mean?" Caleb asked.

"It means this is some fluke. Some joke. She's nothing like you. She already got rid of one jock in her life and now you think you can just take her out on a date, like everything was normal, and it's all just gonna be hunky-dory from now on?"

"Kyle, I don't know what's wrong with you." As Caleb spoke, I looked around and saw that everyone was watching them with concern. "I'm sorry. I already said that."

"Oh, yeah, you're real sorry. Strutting around here, *in my house*, like you're just king of everything," Kyle spat and I was shocked by the venom in his voice.

"Kyle, that's not fair at all. I didn't choose-"

"But you were still the chosen one, weren't you!" he sneered.

"I can't change that she's my significant, no matter what you feel about her. This right here is a prime example of why they have the no-dating rule."

"You hated that stupid rule just as much as me!" he yelled and pointed angrily.

"I know, but I didn't break it," Caleb countered quietly. "If you'd spent less time trying to get her to go out with you, you wouldn't feel this way about someone who doesn't belong to you."

Kyle paled and then turned beet red. "That has nothing to do with it, though if I had touched her first instead of you, things would be a little different, now wouldn't they? But she's my friend."

"I disagree," Caleb said steadily.

Kyle's hand shook with his drink in his grasp at his side. I wondered what was going on. I mean, I knew Kyle had a little crush on me, but Caleb knew an awful lot about it. Then Kyle's dad came forward and put his hand on Kyle's shoulder.

"Son," he said softly, "I know this situation isn't ideal, but Caleb's right on this. What are you doing? Don't stir trouble where there doesn't have to be any."

"I'm not, but, Dad, you should have heard the things he used to say. He hated this whole thing. He wanted out."

"Kyle!" Caleb yelled and stood up.

"He thought the whole significant thing was a joke. He said it was fake or something. He wanted to leave and go to school in Arizona."

"Kyle, shut up, man! That was before it happened to *me*, ok! It's different now. And it'll be different when it happens to you, too."

"But it's not going to happen to me, is it? You're the special one and I'll be stuck alone forever. The one girl I thought I'd risk it for." He stuck one finger in to the air to drive home his point. "The *one girl* and you stole her right out from under me! Literally!"

This was more uncomfortable than sex talks with Granny. I just wanted to crawl under the table. And the following silence after his statement was deafening. They were in front of me, but I could slip behind Caleb to the house and get a refill or something. So I did. But Maria caught me. "Where are you going, Maggie?"

I turned to look at them over my shoulder, completely embarrassed and uncomfortable. I started to walk again, shifting my gaze to the ground.

"Maggie. I'm sorry," Kyle blurted loudly while Kyle's dad said, at the same time, "Let her go, Kyle," while Caleb said, "Maggie."

"Um. I think I'll just go home, but thanks for lunch. I really enjoyed it. I want to change before tonight." I looked at Caleb. "I mean, if you still want to go."

"Of course I do." He sighed and came to stand in front of me. "I'm sorry about this," he mostly whispered.

"It's ok." I needed to flee the eyes. "Can we talk, later?"

"Do you want me to walk you?"

"No, I'm fine. Really."

"Can you even leave?" Kyle said condescendingly. "I mean it's only day two. Last night you were on the edge the whole time. Go ahead. Try to just walk out of here without his help."

I already felt and knew that what he was saying was true. The minute I told Caleb no to walking me home, my body clenched with the knowledge that I'd leave him here.

"Shut up, Kyle! You claim to be her friend, so stop it already. You think you're helping right now?" Caleb took my arm gently and pulled me with him to the back gate. I looked back and saw Kyle and his father in a heated discussion.

Gran, Rachel and Jen were looking at me with nothing but sympathy. They'd been through this. They knew what it was like. And I was already hurting.

"I'm so sorry, Maggie. I don't know what's gotten into him."

"It's ok."

"No, it's not." He spoke gently and my head started to hurt, the pounding behind my eyes suddenly almost unbearable. My eyes closed and pinched. He sighed and framed my face with his hands. I instantly felt better and opened my eyes to look up at him. "It's so much worse when you're upset."

"I'll live. I just didn't want to be in the middle of all...that, ya know?"

"Yeah. Me neither," he said dryly. "Are you ok, now?"

"Yeah. So, Arizona? Is that true?" I asked, still looking up at him.

"Yes." His thumbs moved across my cheeks, causing my eyelids to flutter with pleasure. "And I never would have said a word to him if I'd known he'd tell everyone. This'll stir up crap, for sure."

"So," I said thoughtfully, "we've got Arizona and some sport you love to play, that I have yet to learn what it is. What else?"

"What?"

"I'm making a list."

He laughed softly. "I'll give you the full list tonight, which I can't wait for, by the way."

I nodded. "Ok. I guess I'll see you in a couple hours."

"I'll pick you up at five thirty."

"In your convertible," I teased.

"Absolutely," he said, grinning.

"Ok."

I wanted to move. I wanted to. He knew what I needed. "I want you to go home and wait for me. It'll be better this way, now you can see your dad for a little bit before we leave. Everything will be fine," he crooned soothingly. "And I'll see you very soon."

"Ok."

I started to pull away, but he pulled me closer and kissed my forehead. I looked up and smiled at him before pressing through the big wooden gate, not looking back at his multitude of family watching our every move.

Seven

I walked home slowly. I felt the pull to go back to Kyle's house. It didn't seem quite as bad since I understood what was happening this time.

Kyle only lived six blocks away. I paused at the red light and remembered the last time I was here on the other side; watching a dark haired boy bob his head to his music. I'd thought he was so normal, so human, but boy how wrong had I been?

The light turned red and I looked before making my way across. As soon as I turned the corner I saw her flames of red curls blowing in the breeze. Her scowl was firmly in place as I made my way down my walkway.

Rebecca.

"So, you've completely just cut me out. Is that it?"

"What? No. Look, I know seeing me with Kyle last night looked bad, but we aren't dating. Far from it. I didn't leave you out of the loop. I promise."

"It certainly looked like there was a loop and that I was out of it."

"Nope. No loop. Nada. Kyle is just a friend. He was...helping me with something last night, that's all."

"You know it's been a week and a half since I've even talked to you. You haven't returned any of my text or voicemails, even at the diner."

"Beck, I'm sorry, all right? I've been having a hard time lately. I just didn't want to drag you down with me."

She stood up off the steps and came to stand in front of me. "Mags, you know better than that. I'm a glutton for drama and baggage. You know this," she joked but stepped forward a little and looked at me seriously. "You could have talked to me."

"I just didn't want to talk about it. I don't want to think about it."

"Look. Your mom is a skeez for leaving, but your dad has no right to treat you like this just because he's angry or depressed or whatever. He needs to chill and take a Prozac. He's still your dad. He still has responsibilities."

"*I* know, but he apparently doesn't, or doesn't care."

"So you thought Kyle - class clown Kyle - could help you with your problems and not me?"

She looked so hurt and bothered, I felt terrible. I had ignored her and purposely avoided her and there really was no good reason for it.

"I'm sorry. Really." I grabbed her purple nail polished hand and squeezed. "You're right. I've been avoiding you. I've been avoiding everyone and everything. I completely screwed myself this year and I didn't know what to do. I just didn't want you to see me like that. I was almost as bad as my dad."

"That's impossible. Your dad's practically catatonic," she scoffed.

"That's what I said." I grinned at her. "I love you, Becky Wecky."

"Ahh, you haven't called me that since second grade." She smiled widely and it felt so good to see. I missed her. "I love you, too, Maggie Waggie."

She grabbed me in a hug and squeezed me. Then she grabbed my hand and started to tow me down to the sidewalk.

"Come on. You're spending the night at my house."

I stopped her. "I can't. I have a...date."

She screwed up her lips. "Kyle, again."

"No. Kyle's cousin, Caleb."

"Wow." She grinned deviously. "You're really making the rounds, aren't you?"

"Shut up!" I yelled playfully. "I'm not dating Kyle."

"So, Caleb is Kyle's cousin. Where did you meet him?"

"At the main street red light. He stepped into traffic and I pulled him back."

"What! For reals?" she shrieked.

"Yeah."

I realized with painful acceptance that that was about all I could tell her. Everything else was complicated and crazy and unbelievable. I was going to have to keep secrets from her. Mmmmm. That sucked.

"Wow. So you saved him and now you're going on a date? When did this happen?"

"Last night."

"Ahh. He's smitten because you saved him and asked you out to thank you. How cute."

I felt a sudden bristle at her nonchalant words. "It's a little more than that."

"What do you mean?"

I sighed and relented. There was no point. "Nothing."

"So, how old is he?"

"Nineteen. He's a sophomore at U of T."

"Really? Football?"

"Not sure. But he's studying to be an architect."

"Oooh. A money maker. Sweet." She sighed dreamily. "I bet he drives a Lexus."

"I don't know, but it's a convertible."

"Definite Lexus. Is he hot?"

"He's perfect," I answered quickly, my mouth answered without my permission. I blushed and she laughed.

"Aha! Wow. You really like him, huh? So, what time is Caleb coming to pick you up?"

My heart clenched each time she said his name. I tried to focus on her face and remain calm. My fingers were starting to twitch.

"Five thirty."

"What?" she exclaimed loudly and grabbed my arm. "That's only two hours. We gotta get you ready!"

"What? Why? What's wrong with what I have on?"

"Nothing, but this is a college guy, babe." She pulled me as she walked backwards. "They expect a certain kind of girl. And no offense, but your age isn't exactly going for you right now. Unless he's a pedophile. Do you think-"

"Beck! Eew! Stop!"

"Anyway, he's been at college for a year already, seeing all those mature girls with their expensive cars and flat ironed fake blonde hair. It's a lot to compete with."

"I'm not going to worry about that."

I wanted to contradict her. Tell her I was his soul mate. That he would like me even if I wore a sack. I knew this must be true because I could picture Caleb in one and I still wanted him. I giggled to myself at the picture, but then I remembered what he wore today. His yellow shirt and how much I liked looking at it on him. I suddenly wanted to look my best. Not just ok, not just presentable. I wanted him to look at me and think that I looked…amazing.

That brought me back to this morning in my bathroom when he thought I looked gorgeous in blue, how he loved my freckles. And how even after all that, I still felt young and inadequate.

I wanted him to want me because he wanted me. Not because he was imprinted with me and couldn't help himself. So I smiled at Beck and told her to have her way with me.

"Really!" she squealed and she shut my bedroom door. "You never let me play doll with you!"

"I know. Now's your chance. Don't go overboard," I warned.

"Ok. What are we going for here? Where's he taking you?"

"A barbeque joint in his home town."

"Boo. That gives me nothing to work with." She pressed a finger to her lips as she thought. "What do you want?"

"I just want him to look at me and think there's no one else he'd rather be with."

She smiled. "So, sex vixen?"

I gasped, "Rebecca!"

"Kidding! Kidding. I have the perfect thing in mind. Don't worry about a thing, Mags. We'll have him drooling, in a very tame and respectable way, of course."

I rolled my eyes, but smiled at how much I missed her. I took a deep breath and let her work.

An hour and forty seven minutes later I stood in front of the oval floor mirror in my room. My very 'me' room that I completely redid when my mom left. She had it all coordinated with different squares of color. I always hated it. So when she left I took everything down and now it's just a room. The walls are white, the bed is white and green with a dark brown poster frame. Not a very girly room, but I loved it because it was all me.

So, I stood looking at what Beck had done. I didn't look like a different person. I didn't look vamped up with a crazy outfit or makeup. I wasn't glamazonned in a preppy, peppy outfit that wasn't me. I was just me.

She'd made me shower while she looked through my closet and decided nothing would do. So, she took a dark green knee length dress out that had thin brown stripes down the length of it. She cut the sleeves off to make it a tank dress and pulled a wide brown ribbon off of a pillow on my bed to push my hair back with like a headband. She was always so crafty, always coming up with crazy things to do. It's like her brain never turned off.

She pulled her long gold chain necklace off, with an open heart at the end that hung half way to my navel and put it around my neck.

"Perfect. Now shoes. Aha."

She handed me my strappy gold flat sandals and I pulled them on before she dragged me back to the bathroom. My hair has a natural curl at the ends, always has, but she wanted them to curl *her* way. So she curled and did my makeup and then painted my nails a barely there pale pink. She ended the ensemble with small gold studs in my ears and smiled at my reflection with approval.

And that's where we are. And I'd never been this nervous in my life. What if he thought I was overdoing it, trying too hard? I pushed that thought away. That had to be some side effect of the withdrawals from him because I'd never acted like this before. I wrung my hands and smoothed my dress over and over.

"Why are you so nervous? You're going to sweat through your dress if you don't calm down."

"I'm ok."

"What's wrong with you? I don't remember you being this way before. Even with Chad. It's just a date," she reasoned.

Yeah right.

I shook my head to clear it and thanked her for helping me right as the doorbell sounded. It took all my strength to stay put and not bound down the stairs for him. The ache in my stomach and back had returned already, but not as bad as before and I wondered if he was feeling it, too.

"Wow. College boy is four minutes early. He must be trying to impress," she joked. "Sorry. I meant to be out of here before he came."

"It's ok." I thought real hard before my next statement and decided it was ok. "I want you to meet him."

"Really? It's not weird I'm meeting some guy you barely know on your first date?"

"No." I chuckled as I pushed my bangs over to cover the wound on my forehead. "I'm sure he'll be fine with it."

I rushed to answer the door, at a ladylike pace, but Dad beat me to it. Caleb was trying to make small talk with the man known as my father, standing in the same outfit as yesterday just another color, thankfully, but still his boxers nonetheless.

Caleb was wearing something different than earlier; a button up blue and green shirt and brown boots with his jeans. He looked up at me coming down the stairs to greet them and his face lit up and he couldn't stop himself anymore than I could. It was like a dam broke.

He reached for me just as I raced to the bottom step and embraced me. I wrapped my arms around his neck, lifting my feet from the floor. I breathed him in and everything else fell away. He was just as happy to see me as I was him, as strange as it all was. And once again, the second he touched me the ache of being away and silly girl worry over what he'd think melted away.

I somehow found my sanity and pulled back. He smiled shyly and put some space between us. He looked me over, making my cheeks beg for permission to scarlet, but I forbid them to, standing my ground.

"You look gorgeous, in case you didn't know."

"Thanks. You, too."

"Wow," I heard Beck mutter behind me.

I turned and beckoned her down the stairs. "This is my best friend, Rebecca. Beck, this is Caleb."

"Hi," he said easily and reached for her hand.

For a split second I imagined the whole imprinting process again, but with her and Caleb instead. She already seemed half in love from her glazy stare.

"Hey, there." She grabbed his hand and removed it quickly. "Do you have any single brothers?" He laughed.

"Beck!" I chastised.

"I'm just saying," she rationalized. "All right, have fun. I'm out. Text me if you need me." She leaned to whisper in my ear. "Do you remember the text code for a 911 emergency date exit?"

She pulled back to look at me seriously. "Uh, 911?"

"Good girl." She smiled at me and then at Caleb. "Have fun you two!" She waved over her shoulder.

I turned back to Caleb who stood amused and patiently waiting. I completely forgot my father standing there by the door. I looked at him and saw how he was looking at me, as if he was actually seeing me. Like he was looking at me for the first time in ten months, which was true. I didn't know if that was a good thing or bad.

"Where are you taking her?"

"To a place called, Mugly's. It's a barbeque place my family loves to go to," Caleb answered.

"Hmm. Well, I expect her back before midnight." He turned to me and scowled. "I know you think because you graduated you're all grown up, but you still live with me, so my rules."

"Dad, I didn't say anything. Midnight is fine. It's only five thirty. We're just going to dinner," I said at a complete loss for his outburst and his sudden concern for my whereabouts.

"Well, good." He seemed off put, like he expected a fight. "You have your cell?"

"Yes." I grabbed it off the hall table and put it in my bag. "All set."

"Ok. Call me if you need *anything*." All I could do was stare at him like he was speaking Chinese. So he sighed harshly. "What?"

"No offense, Dad, but since when do you care if I have my cell or not? Since when do you care what time I come home?" I asked softly.

"Since you started bringing a boy home that's too old for you."

"He's only two years older than me, Dad. And I'll be eighteen soon."

I glanced back at Caleb and he smiled, letting me know he'd wait.

"Well," Dad mumbled. That seemed to bluster his resolve. "Still, with Chad it was safe. I knew he was leaving for college. I knew there would be no chance of you getting all silly over him because he'd keep you at arms length. Everyone always knew he was leaving; everyone but you. But this boy, he is not safe." He looked over at Caleb. “She is still a minor and I’m not thrilled about you taking her out.”

“I understand, sir. I promise you I’m not up to any trouble,” Caleb answered respectfully.

“Dad, if I’m old enough to work almost full time and go to school in clothes that I paid for all by myself, I think I'm old enough to go on a date and know to be careful and come home at a reasonable hour.”

His face went pale and he nodded sadly. “I guess you’re right. We’ll talk later.”

He walked off into the kitchen and I saw the light turn out as he made his way through the house. I was astounded. What just happened?

I looked at Caleb and felt the need to explain. I’d told him earlier that my dad was docile and uncaring, but now he was all about my every move.

“I understand,” Caleb said. “I feel how confused you are. It’s fine. Maybe he’s just waking up. I told you it probably wouldn’t last forever.”

“Yeah, but why now? Why when I’m going to need…” I stopped myself from saying anything else.

“I know. I need you, too.” He came and hugged me to him, making sure to touch his palm to my arm so as to get skin contact, to take my troubles away. “Don’t worry. We’ll figure it out. In the meantime, are ready to go?”

“Yes,” I said, pushing away the weirdness. “I’m sorry about Beck. She’s a little quirky.”

“It’s fine. My best friend is pretty *quirky,* too. Vic. He’s pretty much insane.”

I followed him out to his car...only it wasn’t a car. It was a motorcycle; a sleek, black Yamaha.

“I thought you said...” Convertible. Oh. I got it. “Ha ha.”

He grinned and laughed. “Hey, I didn’t lie. This is as convertible as you can get.”

“I guess I have to agree with that,” I said laughing.

“First things first.” He grabbed my bag and put it in the compartment under the seat. “This won’t do.” He motioned to my dress and lifted his seat again to pull out a jacket. He placed it around me and pulled the zipper up.

“It’s pretty warm out,” I said mildly, wondering why he thought I needed a jacket in May.

“Not on the back of a bike it’s not.”

“If you say so.”

“Here,” he came and put a small black helmet on my head, buckling it under my chin, “now you can keep that pretty head all nice and in one piece.”

“And where’s yours?”

"Right here." He pulled one off the handlebars and put it on. He climbed on and looked back at me expectantly. He flipped a switch on his bike and I could hear him in my ear in the helmet. "One leg at a time."

I sighed and climbed on behind him. I settled myself as close to him as I could get. Our legs lined up, touching all the way down. I blew a breath to steady myself and tried to play off my shakiness as anxiety about the ride instead of being so close to him. "I have never ridden a motorcycle before."

"I assumed as much, so I promise to take it easy on you…this time."

I heard him laugh as he cranked up the beast. I got queasy as I could feel its every rumble. I dreaded this ride now, for more than one reason and wondered if there was some way to back out of it. I thought I was trembling, but couldn't tell.

His hand came back to pat my bare knee, easing and soothing me.

"It'll be fine. I promise you'll love it."

"I'm ok." I lifted my feet to rest on the foot props. "I'm ready."

"Arms around me," he ordered, "and hold on tight."

I did as he said and leaned against his back as my arms hugged his midsection. I smiled at how comfortable it was. I felt him swirl his hand once on my knee before grasping the handlebars and slowly pulling away from my house. Then my street. Then my town.

Eight

The helmet did an okay job of shielding my hair from most of the wind. He blocked a lot of it himself. He'd been right about the jacket. My legs were freezing.

We drove for about thirty minutes that way. We talked through the mics the entire time. He told me some about his family member's abilities. Like his Aunt Kelly and Uncle Max, Kyle's parents, she could decipher any language or code; anything that is meant to hinder and confuse, she could figure it out. She could do any crossword puzzle and learn any computer password and then turn around and speak Chinese even though she never learned it. And his uncle could learn anything and teach anything, which I learned earlier today, at a crazy fast rate.

Then he told me his dad's ability was that he could detect the earth elements. It was one way they had enough money to pay for college for everyone and get the real estate they wanted. He could find precious metals and gems. They go on expeditions once a year for it.

Wow.

And his mom, Rachel, could move and bend metal. The family jokingly called her Magneto, but she could only move small objects. The biggest thing she ever moved was a Volkswagen and that was pushing it.

And his grandfather, the one he looked so much like, he could look at someone and see their intentions. Good or bad, he could see if you were planning something malicious or helpful, if you were lying to hurt someone. He couldn't see the actual act, but could decipher and sift through it.

There were many more people in his family that I had not met yet. Some didn't make it to Kyle's for the meet and greet. I tried to imagine what having such a huge close family would be like.

He also told me that the families are clans. Each family is separate from the other and most are civil, but some are rivals who vie for land and 'territories' or areas. They don't like to be close to each other and they don't ever mix if you are a rival clan. There has never even been an imprint between rival clans before, ever.

Once you imprinted with someone, generally they would then be part of the clan of whoever the male is, since they share the same last name. For instance, he said his mother was from the Mitchell's clan and when her and his father imprinted, she became part of the Jacobson family and clan. She does see her original family some but scarcely. For the most part, you gained a new family.

I was fascinated by it all. I was a sponge and soaked up everything he told me, but soon we pulled into the parking lot and he stopped the bike under a tree on the edge of the lot. He kicked the stand and let me get off first. I was wobbly, my legs tingling and unsteady.

He grabbed my arms to steady me before removing his helmet and laughed softly as he removed mine. I could only imagine the nest my hair was, but he smoothed it back for me with his fingers, running them through and giving me shivers.

"You did good for your first time. I was worried you'd squeal and shake the whole way."

"You say that to all the girls who ride on your bike?" I teased, but the thought of another girl on his bike made me tense with something...

Jealousy?

He smiled as his hands coasted down my arms and then to his sides. "Never had a girl on my bike before." He motioned his head for me to follow him.

"Why?" I asked as we moved slowly through the parked cars to the door.

"Well, our family has this rule. When they realized that we weren't going to imprint, some of them wanted to try to find a wife or husband without being imprinted first, when they got older than the rest of them did when they found their significant. The clan decided it was best for no one to date at all since they didn't know what was going on. They didn't want anyone to marry someone and then imprint on someone else. Therefore, there has never been a girl on my bike."

"You've never dated anyone, at all?"

"Nope." He waved to the hostess as she made her way to us. "Hey, Mrs. Amy."

She was about forty I'd say, pretty with a high ponytail, and I could tell right away she would be quirky and loud.

"Hey there, Caleb. What have we here?" she asked as she looked me over.

"This is Maggie. Maggie, this is Mrs. Amy. The owner."

"And the cook, waitress, dishwasher and hostess. He always forgets that," she said sweetly and laughed. "Well come on you two. I'll give you a table in the back," she said conspiratorially and winked at Caleb.

We followed her and passed a packed dining hall full of laughing people and waitresses wearing cowboy boots to the back. She sat us at a corner table and left with our drink order.

It was a small booth that only fit three people, if tightly, so we sat beside each other instead of across from one another. I wondered if that had been Mrs. Amy's plan.

I turned to him a little so I could see his face. I fiddled with my silverware and put my napkin in my lap so my hands would have something to do.

"So, if you're not supposed to date, why was Kyle taking me out that night?"

"Only I knew about it. His parents didn't. He told them he was going to a grad party. That's why he wanted to text you about leaving."

"Aha. So you brought me to his house thinking he'd get caught, huh?" I smiled and bumped his shoulder.

"Maybe. He *was* breaking the rules." He smiled crookedly. "Plus, I was pretty disappointed when I found out that you were the one Kyle had been talking about."

I bit my lip to stop the smile and looked toward our new waitress as she placed our drinks on the table. I told Caleb since we hadn't looked at the menus at all to order something for me, whatever was his favorite, and so he did. Then I started to quiz him again.

"So, what sport do you play at Tennessee? Maria said you played something."

"Swim team, 400 Meter, freestyle."

Oh, boy. That thought brought a whole new line of thinking. Shorts, arms, legs, water... "Mmm. Are you any good?" I leaned my chin on my hands and watched him as he scratched his chin.

"Uh, yeah, I'm ok," he played off modestly, "I guess. We made it to conference this year. Do you play any sports?"

"I ran track."

"You any good?" he taunted and smirked.

"I guess so."

"What did you run?"

"200 meter."

"My sister ran, too, but she wasn't very good. Don't tell her I said that." We chuckled. "So, did you place?"

"State, two years."

"Nice. So, uh-"

"Caleb, hi there." I looked up at a sweet voice and saw a face just as sweet. It was a girl, looking at Caleb like he was everything she ever wanted. She was blonde, of course, tall and slender with a blue halter dress and very pretty. "Sorry, I don't mean to interrupt," she said sweetly and lifted one bare, tan shoulder.

"Hey, Ashley. How's your summer?" he said not looking at her and twirling his straw in his glass.

"Well, it just started, silly," she giggled and fiddled with her necklace, "but it's good so far. My parents are making me do a summer internship at a law firm in Chattanooga."

"Sounds fun."

"No way. It'll be torture. The last six weeks of my break will be spent working like a dog with no pay and no credits for it."

"Yeah, but you get the experience." He turned to me before she could say anything else. "Ashley, this is Maggie. Maggie, this is Ashley. She's in my Economics class."

"And your Geometry class. But you're always so focused that you barely notice anything in there." She turned to me and fixed a not very pleasant smile on her face. "Nice to meet you, Maggie. Is that short for Margaret?"

"Nope, just Maggie."

She perched her petite behind on the edge of the seat next to Caleb and I felt an instant irritation. I could only assume this sweet faced girl would be trouble. And then trouble started to spew from her lips in the form of sugar coated degradation.

"So, are you Caleb's cousin from out of town?"

"Uh, no."

"Hmm. Are you his sister? I always assumed from the many times Caleb and I have talked that you were older."

"No, I'm..."

Boy, oh, boy. I had no idea what the crap to say. What was I? Would Caleb be upset if I said I was his girlfriend? *Was* I his girlfriend? Could I blurt out soul mate? I could tell this girl was interested in him and waiting anxiously for my reply, but I just couldn't fit an explanation into my mouth.

Once again, Caleb came to my rescue. "Maggie and I are on a date, Ashley."

"Oh?" she asked, her voice shrill and vexed. "And how did you meet? You don't go to school with us, I know."

"She graduated with my cousin, Kyle, the other night."

"Oh." She looked genuinely crushed and hurt, and then pissed. "I thought you said you didn't date."

"I didn't date," he answered and seemed to look for an explanation that wouldn't hurt her feelings.

"So, what? You just didn't want to date *me*? Is that it? I'm not good enough for you? You could have just said that instead of making up some stupid 'I don't date' story," she sneered.

"Look, I didn't date, that wasn't a lie, but Maggie is..." he looked at me, "different." He looked back to her. "I'm sorry if I hurt your feelings, but I wasn't trying to. Besides, aren't you leaving for Vassar in a couple semesters anyway?"

"That's not the point." She glared at me. "Can you even enroll in college yet? You look like you just got out of preschool."

"Ok, that's enough." His hand came around the front of me as if to shield me. "I'm sorry if you think I led you on - which I didn't - but you will not sit here and talk to her like that."

She got up huffing and stomped her sandaled foot before walking away swiftly. He turned to me quickly. "I am so sorry about her."

"It's ok."

"I'm sorry about this, too." He pulled his hand back. "I got this feeling like I needed to protect you or something. I don't know, weird. I really am sorry about her."

"It's pretty obvious she has a crush on you."

"Yeah." He rubbed his face. "She's pretty persistent. She's asked me out since the beginning of freshman year, but..." he shrugged.

"The rule," I supplied. He nodded. "So, would you have dated her if the rule wasn't there?" I asked and felt a ping of guilt for acting like a jealous girlfriend when I had no idea what I was to him.

"Uh, no." He smiled. "She's definitely not my type. I prefer girls with morals and substance over new cars and attitude."

I nodded and looked down at my hands, but wasn't so sure. I had to find out what I was to him. What were we doing? I know I only met him yesterday, but this was far from some crush. We were soul mates.

He didn't seem too bothered by the whole no-dating thing, but maybe he regretted it or wished some other girl - an older different girl - had imprinted with him. Someone that lived in his city so it would be easier for him. He already had to move to Kyle's to stay the summer because of me, changing his plans and barging in on family. All because he'd imprinted with me, the only reason.

If he'd never touched me, I wouldn't be here right now with him. She could have talked to him like they apparently did normally and she wouldn't be all upset. And he could've talked to her and not felt the need to come to poor little me's rescue.

He was only with me because of the imprint. I knew it. His body reacted to me and needed me, but other than that, I was nothing to him. He would never have picked me over Ashley if he had a choice. A real choice.

I felt a warm, calming finger under my chin as my face was pulled up and I tried not to look at him, but his gaze pulled mine to it. He looked serious and his blue eyes were blazing.

"That is absolutely not true," he insisted, reading my feelings, before laying his forehead against mine.

I felt the push and tingle of our skin, his heartbeat steady beside mine, and then I was seeing him, a vision of him. He was standing at a stoplight, listening to Cage The Elephant on his mp3 player and thinking about Kyle coming up to join him at Tennessee the next semester. He looked back and did a double take as a beautiful young girl made her way to the crosswalk.

I couldn't believe that was what I looked like to him. I didn't look like some silly high school girl. I looked pretty and confident, distant and a little sad.

The girl looked around and even in the dim light he could see her freckles. He liked them. She checked her phone and stopped behind him to wait. He wanted to turn and get a better look, but didn't want to seem like he was checking her out so he peeked back and smiled and nodded when she caught him instantly. He turned back and wished he could talk to her, but there was no point. It would just make it worse.

He waited impatiently for the light to turn so he could leave and get the girl out of his mind. He had no idea why he was so struck by her anyway. The light turned and he peeked back once more and started to cross but she wasn't looking, she was checking her phone again. He didn't look both ways before crossing because he was looking back, to get one last peek before never seeing her again. Me.

When he turned back it was too late, then he felt a jerk on his back and tumbled backwards on top of something. When he rolled off and realized it was the girl he was at a loss for words. Then he realized what had happened. The sad, anxious, beautiful girl had saved his life.

He didn't know what to say or do. He asked if she was ok and when he finally heard her voice saying that she was, he thought it was the sweetest sound ever to hit his ears.

He could see a cut on her brow and reached his hand to push back her hair. It was soft and curly. He could smell her shampoo and it was doing marvelous things to his senses. Add that to the sweet green eyes looking up at him and that was it.

He started to question right then if he was imprinting with her, but no visions came, no jolts or tingles or fire as was described by his family. Just butterflies and a racing pulse.

And he was disappointed.

He'd never found anyone he really *wanted* before. There was no one he ever thought about breaking the no dating rule with, no one that made his heartbeat race and trip, until now. And he was so very disappointed that he couldn't have her, especially after she saved his life.

He asked if she needed an ambulance or ride, but she refused. She seemed dazed by him when he got close which made him smile. He flirted with her a little. He wanted her to like him, no matter how pointless it was.

He convinced her to let him walk her, but then he found more disappointment when she told him that she was headed to see Kyle. So this was the girl Kyle was breaking the rule for. He'd talked about this girl for two years. No wonder, he thought. She's pretty awesome and funny and sweet and thoughtful. And those green eyes...

She asked him questions and they laughed and talked all the way to Kyle's. Caleb couldn't hide his disappointment anymore and used her injury to touch her hair once more. Then Kyle had shown up and gave him the look of death over the girl's shoulder while Caleb's hand was in her hair.

Kyle asked if the girl was ready to go; she wasn't, he could tell by her hesitation and it thrilled him even if just to piss off Kyle for being a jerk.

Then she came to him. She said her name was Maggie and she smiled. All breath left his body. He managed to mutter his name, took her hand and was shocked by a bolt of lightning in his veins. His hand felt on fire where he touched her and his lungs burned for breath that wouldn't come. Visions swam in front of his eyes.

I couldn't tell what the visions were and I got a sense that I wasn't supposed to see them. Those particular visions were just for Caleb, just like mine were meant for me. So all I saw were swirls of light and haze as I watched Caleb's face change from happy to elated as he witnessed each vision.

Then he was jolted back to himself and looked at her odd expression of confusion along with longing. He knew exactly what had happened. He could feel her heartbeat banging against his just as loudly as his own and his body knew exactly what to do to comfort and protect her.

He knew it. He had just imprinted with the girl he wanted more than any other, the girl who had saved his life, the girl he thought he'd never have. She was his.

I was brought back to the present when Caleb pulled his head back a little, but kept his face close.

"Now, you see. Don't doubt how I feel about you. This has nothing to do with an imprint and everything to do with you."

I was breathless and in awe of what Caleb had shown me, his memories. They were clear and vivid and had seemed all too real. It was strange to watch the same event through different eyes.

What was stranger still was that Caleb had wanted me before the imprinting. Before. I couldn't stop the smile that spread my cheeks.

I knew I needed to say something.

"You almost got hit by a truck because you were checking me out?" I joked and he laughed loudly.

"Yeah. It's a good thing you saved me. It would have been all your fault if I didn't make it," he said through a grin.

I laughed, nodding and then stopped. I looked at him, really looked at him. He wanted me. Me. Not imprinted me, not high school me, not track shorts me. Just me. I decided that was all the proof I needed. I leaned into him and rested my head on his shoulder. "I'm really glad I was at that stoplight, Caleb."

He sighed happily and placed his arm around me, his hand brushing my arm making us both shiver. I noticed a tattoo of a half circle or moon on the inside of his wrist.

"Me, too, Maggie. Me just a little bit more than you, I think."

I giggled silently and felt him shake with a chuckle. "So, was that one of your abilities or can we always do that?"

"We haven't ascended yet. All significants can do that with each other, among other things."

"Healing," I chimed.

"Yep. Healing. What we just did is called memory transfer. I know. Sounds romantic, right?" I laughed again. "But it's useful sometimes to figure things out, to get another point of view of something. We can also find each other. And if you are ever in trouble or extremely anxious or distressed, your body calls to me and I can find you anywhere and you, me. I can also feel your pain or if you're uncomfortable."

"Mmm. That's..."

"Freaky?"

"No. I was going to say neat, but I was looking for a less dorky word."

He laughed just as our food came and Mrs. Amy gave him a knowing smile as she topped off our sweet tea. I tried all his favorite foods. Corn nuggets, beef brisket on garlic bread and baked sweet potato with cinnamon butter. Then for dessert we had blueberry cobbler with vanilla bean ice cream.

I was stuffed and felt happier than I had in a very long time.

We finished up and made our way up to the cash register to pay. Then back out to his motorcycle. He started to put his helmet on, but stopped and looked at me.

"I'm not ready to take you home yet."

"I'm not ready to go home yet."

Nine

"Well," he grinned, "there's a pond in back. People fish and swim in it during the day, but it should be quiet tonight. There's a walkway and benches. Do you want to go sit with me for a while?"

"Yeah, I do."

"Good. Here." He reached under his seat, got the leather jacket and once again reached around me to wrap it around my shoulders. "It's getting a little cold."

"Thanks."

He held his hand out to me and smiled crookedly. I slipped my hand into his and felt the familiar calm wash over me. He started to pull me with him, but I stayed my ground and looked up at him. "Caleb."

"Yeah?"

"I thought you were pretty great, too, before all this. I was disappointed when I thought I'd never see you again. I just wanted you to know that it's not just the imprint to me either."

He came closer and took my face in his hands. For a second I thought he'd kiss me. But he just looked at me for a long time, smiling, so I just stared up at him. Finally he spoke. "Thank you, Maggie."

He kissed my forehead. It burned a good heat where his lips touched me and my eyelids fluttered. Then he took my hand again, and led the way to the path and benches. There were a lot of them lined up on the boardwalk under Dogwood trees and the moon was casting a hazy glow on the water.

"Wow," I said as I sat and looked up. "You can see every star out here."

"The darker it is with less city lights, the more stars you can see."

"Wow," I repeated as I leaned back to get a better view. "Thanks for dinner. I really like this place."

"It's my favorite. Mrs. Amy is an old family friend. We've been coming here since as long as I can remember."

"And does she know about your family?"

"No. We don't ever tell anyone."

His pocket buzzed and he pulled out his phone.

"So, I can't tell Rebecca?" I knew the answer but felt the need to ask anyway.

"I'm afraid not. Sorry," he said as he typed something into his phone and then slipped it back in his pocket. "Sorry. My friend, Vic, texts me like a jealous girlfriend."

I laughed. "No. It's ok. And I kind of figured that I couldn't tell anyone, but it didn't hurt to ask."

He stretched his legs out beside me, not touching me, and crossed his ankles, laying his head back against the seat as if he was settling in for a long haul talk. I smiled to myself. "So, how long have you known each other? You and Beck," he asked.

"Birth."

"That right?"

"Yep."

"And what about your brother? Where is he?"

I told him about my parent's adoption of Bish, how he moved to New York and I never see him anymore but we text all the time. That he left for school before mom left so he missed all the drama.

"So," I asked, "what about Jen? I don't remember seeing her husband there this morning. Where did she meet him?"

"Uh." He sat up slowly, setting his elbows on his knees and looking uncomfortable. "Well, remember we told you that no one has imprinted in a long time."

"Yeah, I remember."

He waited, watched me and I thought hard because it seemed he wanted me to figure something out. Then it clicked. His sister couldn't be but a few years older than Caleb. So, she couldn't have imprinted with anyone if no one has in twenty years. Yet she had a daughter. Hmm.

"Yeah, I remember you said that. So, if she didn't imprint and didn't get married what happened, if you don't mind my asking? Is Maria adopted?"

"No, she's not adopted." He turned to look at me and smiled sadly. "That sweet little girl is the product of a crazy end of the summer party and the date rape drug."

I gasped and covered my mouth with a hand.

"It's ok," he assured me.

"Caleb. Oh, my gosh, I'm so sorry for her."

"Don't be." He scooted closer and placed his hand on my elbow to draw off some of the anxiety that had my heart racing. "She was angry, extremely angry, for a while. She was a different person and dropped out of school, which was understandable. You see, there is usually more than one of us from the family at Tennessee together, we watch out for each other. It just worked out that her first year she was alone. Remember I told you there is still a lot of family that you haven't met. Well, we've never had any problems, except that one year, that one time. This is why we stay together. This is why they want us to go to school and work together and live near each other. Because things happen and it's just easier if we're all there to help each other or prevent stuff from even happening. I know it happens to humans too, but we have so much to hide. And things like that could expose everyone."

"Yeah. So, she had the baby anyway."

He scoffed and chuckled. "Of course she did. The police told her they couldn't find out who did it and she should just have an abortion and even set her up an appointment at the clinic before telling her. Well, you don't tell Jen what to do. She dropped out of school, came home and sulked and was a zombie for nine months. Then Maria was born and that was all it took, one look. Maria was born with a full head of dark curly hair." He smiled remembering and I picked up bits and pieces from his mind but mostly just listened. "She was herself again after that. She said as morbid and twisted as it seemed, she was happy, because she wouldn't have imprinted and never gotten a chance to have a baby otherwise. That she considered it a gift and wasn't angry anymore."

"Wow."

I couldn't imagine that. But Maria is pretty adorable. And I'm sure his close knit family made a huge fuss over her and cared really well for them both. It made me smile.

"Yep. So, don't feel sorry for her. She doesn't regret it. In fact she went back to school two years later and finished her two year degree and then started work at the firm with everyone else. She loves it."

"Your parents didn't try to make her have an abortion?"

"No, they wouldn't anyway, but I think they understood her point of view; that she'd never get the chance for a baby otherwise and if that's what she wanted, they'd support her for it."

"Wow."

"That's like your favorite word, huh?" he teased and chuckled.

"Oh, yeah." I bet I sounded so young and stupid. "I just can't believe that she-"

"I was just joking." He put his arm around my shoulder and squeezed me to him. "It's cute. I like it, a lot actually."

"Cute?" I said, playfully incredulous.

"Yep. Cute."

"I'm not sure if that's a compliment or not," I said and leaned away in mock distress.

He grinned and followed me as I inched away laughing. He inched closer. "Oh, it's a compliment." I came to the edge of the seat and stopped. But he didn't. He smooshed right up next to me and smiled deviously down at me. "Where you gonna go now, cutie?"

"Um. Away." I bolted from him and took off down the boardwalk.

I heard him chuckle and then footsteps pounding behind me on the wood planks. The moon was bright and there was plenty of light to see him. He chased me and was fast but so was I. I was on the track team for crying out loud.

"Hey! Jeez, you're fast."

"I'm sorry you can't keep up," I yelled as I ran backwards. "I figured a big bad swimmer could handle a little jog."

"Ooooh," he feigned anger. "You are so going to get it now!"

"You have to catch me first, slow poke!"

"Ok! Ok. I give!" he called out and bent down to rest his hands on his knees.

I came back to him slowly and stood next to him.

"Hmm. I'm not sure I can be seen with you anymore. I'm thoroughly disappoint- Ah!" He grabbed me around my stomach from behind and lifted me, swinging me around. "You tricked me!"

He pressed his face to my ear. "And you totally fell for it, too."

This savored strongly of the vision I had had of us when we imprinted. His breath on my ear, so close to my neck... I felt goose bumps glide down my skin rapidly and instantly blushed because I knew he could feel them too.

"Yeah, I guess I did," I said, but it was all wrong and breathless.

He set my feet to the ground, but didn't let me go, his hands moved to my upper arms. We stood looking out at the lake for a minute. I could feel every breath he took behind me. I pressed into his mind, focusing on him, to see what he was thinking. He was wondering the same about me. I could feel his pulse in my veins and it was faster than normal. I took some comfort that he was just as affected by my presence as I was by his.

"I think I'm more affected if you ask me," he said suddenly.

"You are getting really good at that," I said dryly.

He laughed softly. "You get better at it the more time we spend together. You'll only block me when you're trying to. Soon, you'll be able to pick up exact thoughts, too, not just my feelings."

"Are you nervous about your ascension? Getting your abilities?"

"Nah. I've waited for this all my life. Are you nervous?"

"Terrified," I breathed truthfully.

He turned me in his arms to look at my face, his arms held me firmly to him. "Don't be. It's not that painful."

"Not *that* painful?"

"Yeah. And the chills, fever and convulsions only last a couple days."

"What?" I said and even though he was touching me, I felt a spike of terror.

"Yeah, but don't worry. The little green spots that appear all over are mostly under your clothes."

I gaped at him and he smiled widely and cockily. "Caleb!" I pushed at his chest playfully. "I believed you."

"I know, I'm sorry." He hugged me to him so I couldn't see his face as he spoke into my hair. "You really think I'd be so happy about something that would hurt you and I couldn't fix it?"

"I don't know what to think."

"I don't want you to be scared about it. It's a good thing and it doesn't hurt at all. And it won't happen if I'm not around." He pulled back to look at me. His hands moved down, slid really, to rest on my lower back and I thought my pulse couldn't possibly race more than it was already. "We'll be together and I'll know exactly what's happening so don't be scared. My parents said it feels kind of like the imprinting. You feel hot and cold, your heart races. Our abilities will complement the other's so we'll be even more in tune and drawn to each other after that."

"I don't see how that's possible," I muttered and then realized I'd said it out loud. I pressed my lips together and he smiled. "So, you'll be with me when it happens and it won't hurt?"

"I'll be with you and it won't hurt," he assured and his hands flexed on my back.

"Ok. So what do you think your ability will be?"

"No clue. But none of us have the same ability. So it will be something that no one else in the family has."

"Can it be something like making honey buns appear out of thin air, because I could get used to that."

He laughed and pulled me closer, pressing his forehead to mine. "I don't think so, cutie."

"Dang," I whispered.

We sat for a few minutes just like that, eyes closed. I breathed him in and enjoyed the feeling of clarity and calm from his touch. "Are you ready to go home yet?"

"No, but I guess I better. It's getting late."

"Here," his hands went inside my jacket and he pushed my arm through the sleeve, "better zip this up. It's dark so it'll be even colder on the bike."

I let him pull both my arms through and zip my jacket up before he took my hand and we made our way back to the parking lot.

"I picked a good day to wear a dress, huh."

"It may not be practical, but you look very pretty."

"Thanks. So, um." I had wanted to ask him this question since I first found out about all this, but couldn't get up the nerve. "Do you…" I sighed.

"What is it?"

"Do you, uh, feel withdrawals like I do?"

"Of course, yeah. Significants always feel withdrawals for each other, especially in the beginning."

"But are they like mine? I mean, this morning I thought I was having a heart attack or something."

"Well," we made it to the bike and he leaned against it, "no, from what Gran says, humans feel it a lot more than we do. This morning I felt sick and sore, just like you said, like I had the flu. It sucked, but I knew what was going on and got to you as soon as I could but I wasn't in pain. I'm really sorry about that. I'll be there sooner tomorrow."

"It's ok. I think it'll be better tomorrow now that I understand what's going on."

"So, that's what you wanted to ask me?" he asked and looked unconvinced.

"Not all of it. I…" I so didn't want to say the words.

Then a thought hit me. He could read my thoughts earlier, my actual thought. I decided to try it again. I thought about how I feel when he touches me. How I feel calm and collected and have no worries. I wondered if he felt that way with me. If my touch calms him and makes him feel better like his does me. Like a balm to soothe and comfort.

I pushed my thoughts to him and watched his face to see if he heard me. He looked at me expectantly and then his mouth opened. He looked shocked and surprised. He smiled and laughed.

"You did that all by yourself. I wasn't even trying to read you!" I smiled, too, enjoying his happiness as he moved to stand in front of me. "Wow. You are amazing, you know that? You're constantly surprising me. But even with that, I feel like I've known you my whole life." I stood listening and looking at him in complete agreement of what he was saying and complete awe at how we seemed to always be feeling the same thing. Then he pushed my hair behind my ear as he stepped a little closer. "And to answer your question, yes. Every time I touch you, it's like a switch is flipped. I do touch you a lot when I feel your anxiety, but I do it for me too. It's like everything that was wrong is right and it'll all be fine if I can just touch you. It takes everything away that I don't want to feel. I could touch you all day long." And as to demonstrate, he let his fingertips coast down my cheek. "I can't believe I only met you yesterday."

"Me either," I breathed and then sighed. "And you won't see me tomorrow if we don't get me home before midnight."

"Right. Yeah, let's get going," he said hurriedly, not liking the outcome of that.

He put on our helmets and climbed on, then I hopped on behind him.

"Hang on, gorgeous. I'm not taking it easy on you this time," he said. My heart flipped and I heard him laugh through the helmet.

Whether it was because he could hear my thought or he could feel my excitement through my heartbeat, I didn't know, but I didn't care.

"Ok."

"You trust me?" he asked as he cranked it up and I gripped him tight around his stomach. I could feel his muscles were hard and bunched through his shirt.

"I trust you."

We rode in almost silence the way home, except for the occasional squeal from me. I let him ride as fast and as crazy as he wanted to. I was scared sometimes, especially on the curves where we leaned the bike into them, but I was having just as much fun too. I'd laugh and I'd hear him laughing too, through the helmet mics. He'd reach up and grip my hand or sometimes he'd reach back and rub my knee to soothe me and I felt instantly calm yet excited at his touch at the same time.

We pulled up in front of my house with twenty three minutes to spare. I got off and handed him his helmet and jacket. He took his helmet off too and we stood by the bike for a minute as I thanked him again for dinner and he thanked me for going.

I wondered again if he was going to try to kiss me.

"All right, I better let you go. I'll be here first thing in the morning."

"Ok. I'll see you then."

I started to go, but he stopped me by grabbing my hand.

"Maggie, I just need one more thing." He pulled me close and I knew this was it, he was going to kiss me, but he didn't. He pressed his forehead to mine and his arms went around me. "I just needed to touch you one more time," he confessed softly. He kissed my cheek and ran his hand down my arm. "You're really soft," he said too quietly, more to himself.

"Thanks," I muttered breathlessly and lamely.

"Bye, Maggie."

"Bye," I said, but couldn't take a step to go. "Caleb."

He glanced at me. "I'm sorry," he said sincerely. "It'll get easier, I promise. Maggie, I want you to go inside and get some sleep. Don't worry about anything. I'll see you in the morning, I promise. And I can't wait."

Then somehow I turned and made it to the steps, albeit wobbling and stumbling in my stupor. It was actually painful to watch him mount the bike and drive away. My gut twisted and pulled as I closed the door and leaned my back against it. My feet tingled and begged to take off running after him. I closed my eyes and took a deep breath, smiling and remembered his words to me about seeing me in the morning.

I pushed off the door and stepped into the foyer and saw my dad, sitting at the kitchen table. "Did you have a good time?"

I was flabbergasted. What was up with him? "Uh, yeah. Sure, Dad."

"Not too good I hope."

"Dad. Eew," I said as I poured myself a glass of water.

"I'm still your father, Maggie. You may not like it, but you are not an adult yet. I want you to be careful with that boy. And I don't remember you getting permission to ride on a motorcycle."

"I didn't think I needed permission. He had a helmet and jacket for me. He's very responsible."

"I'm sure, but that's not the point."

"What is the point, Dad?"

"That you're seventeen and still live under my roof. You can't just do whatever you want to do."

"I'm not. I told you I was going out and you said it was fine."

He grunted and ran both his hands through his hair. "That's not what I'm talking about."

"What *are* you talking about?" I asked exasperated.

"Look, I-" He choked on his words.

Like really choked up. His head bowed and he sniffed. I saw his shoulders shake. His hand came up to swipe his face and I couldn't take it anymore. I walked swiftly to him and knelt down in front of him.

"Aw, Dad. What is it?"

"Maggie, I am so sorry."

"What for, Dad?"

He looked at me closely. "I did everything I could for your mother. She was everything to me. And then you came along and you were everything too; my girls. Then your mom left for no reason, out of the blue, and took everything with her. She was spiteful and hateful. She didn't care what happened to you or me and I couldn't handle it. I loved her with everything I had and she gave me no reason, no *real* reason, for leaving. Just that I held her back. I don't know what I did to her and I know that I've been a horrible person, let alone father, to you lately. I was bitter and nasty. I know you've been angry with me - for good reason. You just look so much like her and are so independent, I just assumed you didn't need me or didn't want me like she didn't." He took my face in his hands, the first time he'd touched me at all in almost a year and I saw another tear roll down his chin. "But I love you so much. It took me seeing you walking out that door with someone who could actually take you away for me to remember that. I'm so sorry, Maggie."

He hugged me to him tightly, crushed me to him really. My body was rebelling. It wanted to remind me of all the things he had said to me. All the things he needed to have done or said and didn't. He let his grief over my mom ruin his life and I let my grief for him ruin mine.

I felt utterly at his mercy. My heart ached with wanting. I wanted him to be telling the truth so badly that it hurt. I needed him. As much as I took care of myself, I still needed my dad.

"Maggie, please forgive me. I know you're about to turn eighteen and you'll probably be leaving home soon. I can't live with knowing how I've hurt you without trying to fix it."

He sniffed again and pulled back to look at me.

"Dad, I understand. I do. I know it sucked for us both when mom left, but you more than me. She was my mom, but your wife. It's different, I know that, but I've missed you."

"I've missed you, too. I'm so sorry." He hugged me to him. "I love you, baby girl."

"I love you, too, Daddy."

"I have an idea. Why don't we go to the boathouse? I'm sure that old place is still available. We can just spend some time away, you and me?"

Before I could balk at his idea - for he knew nothing of my predicament with Caleb - the doorbell rang.

I went to answer it and peeked out the peephole.

Caleb. And he looked nervous.

I opened the door. He sighed with relief and pulled me to him. "Oh, thank God. Your heart was going nuts and I could feel you were upset. I thought something was wrong." He pulled back to look at me and wiped a tear from my cheek. I didn't even realize I'd been crying. "You *are* upset. What's wrong? What happened?"

"My dad and I were just...patching things up, I guess."

I heard my dad coming and pulled from Caleb's grasp, painful as it was. "Maggie, it's midnight. Who in the world could it...be?" Dad stopped in the doorway and stared with a mixture of curiosity and annoyance. "Caleb. It's kinda late, son."

"Yes, sir. I uh...just needed to check on something."

"What's that?"

"Dad," I interrupted. "Caleb forgot to tell me what time he was coming tomorrow. He wanted to make sure it wasn't too early."

"Well, Caleb. I think," he put his arm around me, "Maggie and I decided to head up to the lake for a couple weeks. So, she might not see you for a while."

Just saying the words let alone thinking about it sent my body in a panic. I gasped and let out a little cry of distress, to my embarrassment, but I had no control.

Dad looked at me sideways as Caleb stepped a little closer.

"Sir, please don't do that. I, um, have a few things that I asked Maggie to help me with before I go back to school. It's kind of important."

It wasn't completely a lie.

Caleb's hand snaked out slowly and low to touch the ends of my fingers with his, and him and I both sighed. I looked up to his face, he was just as upset as I was about the prospect of not seeing me. So much for no trouble with my dad.

"Yeah, Dad," I insisted. Dad glared at Caleb's fingers as he caressed mine. "Please. I'd love to go with you but I already promised Caleb I'd be here."

"All right," he said stiffly, "but I don't want you spending every day, all day with each other. It's not good for you, especially if he's leaving for school in a few weeks and leaving you here."

Another jolt of pain ran through me. "Dad, please don't say that," I almost moaned.

"Sorry but it's true. The sooner you break it off, the better in my opinion." I bit the inside of my cheek to keep from screaming at him. "All right. Say goodnight to Caleb."

Oh, crap. I couldn't move. Caleb had to release me or whatever it is that he does to let me leave him and my dad was standing right here. Oh, crap!

"Maggie," Caleb said immediately, I assumed he realized what I just had and I locked my eyes to his. "Go up and rest. We have a busy day tomorrow. I'm sorry I bothered you, but I'll see you in the morning, ok?"

I nodded. "Ok."

He waited to see if that was enough to help me go and when he saw me turn he blew a grateful breath and smiled. He waved to my dad and said a goodnight as my dad shut the door.

"That's a strange boy, Maggie. Are you sure he's who you want to waste your summer on?"

"Dad," I said, exasperated.

"Ok, ok. I'm going to go to bed. I have a lot to think about and an early start at the mill tomorrow. Goodnight, baby girl."

"Goodnight, Dad. And I really appreciate you telling me all that before. I've been really worried about you."

"I know and I'm sorry. But things are gonna be back to normal around here. You'll see. I love you, Maggie."

"Love you, too, Dad."

I smiled and made my way up the stairs to my bed. I had texts from Bish and Beck both and answered them eagerly. Once I had gone back and forth with them both for about half an hour I lay down and thought about Dad's new awakening. The 'event' was just something of the past.

In my opinion, even though things were looking up, or down depending on how you looked at it, morning couldn't get here fast enough.

Ten

I woke with the same aches and pains as the day before. But this time I understood them. Unfortunately for me, it didn't make them better. My head pounded, my back and stomach groaned and pulsed with painful jolts. My legs wobbled when I tried to climb out of bed.

I glanced at my alarm clock; 6:45, pretty early. Caleb said he'd be here earlier than yesterday so all I had to do was wait it out. I went to the mirror on my dresser and saw the same ashen and sickly skin as before as I looked past the stars in my vision. I decided I should change out of my pajamas for when Caleb would be here. But wasn't fast enough.

I heard the doorbell and my legs were wobbly no longer. They propelled me forward and down the stairs as quick as I could make it. I yanked open the door...only to find Kyle. My heart sank painfully at seeing it wasn't Caleb and I collapsed against the doorframe and slid to the floor as the ache in my bones engulfed me.

Kyle came and yanked me up into his arms and held me tight. Then he whispered into my ear.

"Maggie, I'm so sorry. I got here as soon as I could."

"Where's Caleb?"

"Who's Caleb?"

I pushed him away and stared at him incredulously.

"That's not funny, Kyle."

"Here." He reached for me again. "Maggie, I know you're withdrawing. I am too. Come here, you need me."

"What?"

"Maggie, it's just the withdrawals. Touch my hand and everything will be ok."

"Kyle, I am not your significant. What are you doing here? Where's Caleb?"

He looked hurt and shocked. He started muttering to himself.

"Dad never told me about this. I thought you'd need me, right away. I didn't think you'd fight me and hallucinate."

"I'm not hallucinating!" I yelled. "Where's Caleb?"

"Mags," he said more pronounced. "Who is Caleb?"

I started to falter. Had I just imagined it all? Kyle looked serious. He looked startled. He looked hurt and his eyes beseeched me to take his hand. I didn't know what was going on but I held my hand out and let him grasp it. His fingers were cold and rough, not like Caleb's and his touch didn't calm me or sooth me. In fact, it made my skin crawl.

"Maggie, what are you doing? You're blocking me somehow. Let me help you."

"I'm not doing anything. Kyle, come on. Where's Caleb? I need him, he's the one. This isn't right," I yanked from him and pleaded.

Even I heard the hysteria in my voice and I turned away from his betrayed expression.

Kyle pressed his mouth to my ear. "Caleb can't come out and play right now," the voice said but it was no longer Kyle's voice. It was deeper, more menacing and definitely not nice. "Neither can Kyle. Sorry."

I turned, looking around but saw no one. "Who are you?"

"You don't remember? I'm hurt, Maggie, really," the voice sang with sarcasm.

He appeared in front of me from the shadows off the porch and smiled as he saw recognition flash in my face.

"Marcus," I gasped. I backed into the wall. "You scared me. What are you doing here?"

"Oh, I scared you? Well, you're scaring me. You see, you're special. Not like in a get-a-big-head special, but special enough for us to be pissed about it. It's not fair that the Jacobson clan gets to start getting their ascensions back when we've been just as patient as they have. They will have the upper hand now, you see? We've had many a discussion about you in my clan. There is a reason for you, there has to be. There's something special about you and we can't let it come to pass."

"What? You can't let *what* come to pass?" I asked but was afraid of the answer.

"Your ascension. If we take you away from Caleb, you won't ascend and neither will he."

I gasped with pain at the thought.

"You can't do that! I'll die."

He laughed maniacally.

"You won't die, silly human!" He laughed again. "You'll be in agony, but you won't die. Well, not at first anyway. That's a sacrifice we're willing to make."

"No, please," I whispered my plea.

There was nothing else to do. He pointed outside. I saw a black car waiting on the curb for us. "Get in."

"No! No! Please!"

"Too late for that. If only you hadn't saved him. This is your fault, I want to make sure that you see that. He will be in just as much pain as you, you know. He'll writhe in wanting and agony just as you will, with no cure. Now, how's your conscience?"

"What did Caleb ever do to you to make you hate him so much?" I ground out.

"He was born," he growled and then we were standing beside the car and I had no idea how we got there.

He grabbed me around my arm and threw me into the darkness of the open car door.

I screamed and scrambled to get a footing but there was none. I fell farther and farther into a dark place of nothing. I felt nothing, I heard, smelled, nor saw anything. Except the burning black handprint on my arm and when I finally hit the bottom, a loud boom.

I was jolted awake in my bed like I'd been dropped. I was sweating and crying. I reached up to my cheeks and felt the wetness and then the aches in my body pounded into me. It was almost too much. Even though I knew what was happening, I wanted to freak out and cry more from the pain.

I heard the doorbell in the back of my mind, heard voices. I lay on my bed and tried to catch my breath, but it felt like I was suffocating as the stars danced in my vision.

Then I felt a hand on my forehead and wanted to sigh until I realized it wasn't the hand I needed. It wasn't Caleb. I opened my eyes to see Dad looking at me with clear worry, the stars bouncing in my vision behind him.

"Honey, Caleb's downstairs, but I'm gonna go tell him you're sick. You're burning up."

"No, Dad! I need him!" I yelled and kicked off the covers.

"Maggie," he scoffed and held me down. "Look, I know you like this boy, but he can wait a day to see you if you're sick."

"No. Please. Caleb," I breathed painfully.

"I'm right here." He actually pushed my father aside to get to me. Pushed!

His hands were on either side of my face and I almost cried with relief. Everything felt normal and right and I could breathe again. Except for when I opened my eyes and saw how pissed my father was.

"Excuse me, son, but I think you need to leave, right now," he boomed.

"Dad, wait. Listen-"

"You be quiet. No boy is coming into my home and pushing me around while he jumps into my daughter's bed in the morning like it was completely normal. What have you done, Maggie?"

"Nothing-"

"Sir," Caleb butted in as he set me and him up on the bed beside each other. He kept his arm around me for contact and I felt his protection seeping out. Even though this was my dad we were dealing with he was pretty red faced. "I'm really sorry. I just heard Maggie so upset and I panicked. I shouldn't have pushed you."

"You're dam- darn right you shouldn't have! I don't know who you think you are, but-"

"Dad, he said he was sorry," I begged and he looked at me finally.

Then he cocked his head and pressed the backs of his fingers to my forehead and then down my cheek. "What happened to your fever? You looked like death warmed over when I came in here."

"I feel fine," I said and shrugged, trying to seem nonchalant.

"Hmmm." He looked between us. "You can go with Caleb today, but he is not to come over so early in the morning like this anymore. Understand?"

"Dad-" I started to argue, but Caleb squeezed me and interrupted me.

"That's fine, sir. Thank you for understanding. I am sorry."

"Fine. Whatever. You be careful with her on that deathtrap of yours." He turned to go, but then pointed his finger at him. "And if I ever catch her on it without a helmet, so help me-"

"No, sir. Never. I promise you that."

"Fine," he said and huffed out of the room.

I turned to Caleb and reached my fingers around his neck just to have the contact and then started to protest about his non-protest.

"How can you say you won't come over in the mornings?"

"I will, he just won't know it," he whispered and smiled conspiratorially.

"Oh."

He pulled me close to him, hugging me to him and inhaled deeply from my neck, his nose grazing my skin.

"Wow, you smell good," he muttered and nestled closer. My heart rioted in my chest. My hand was still on his neck and I felt my fingers pulse with need to bury them in his hair. "And you look very cute in pajamas."

"Oh, yeah." I pulled back bashfully and crossed my arms over my chest. "I forgot."

"It's ok." He laughed. "You do look cute. But, something's not right. What happened this morning? That wasn't a normal withdrawal. You were terrified."

"I had a dream. It was so real." I rubbed my arm absently, remembering Marcus and his hateful grasp.

Caleb turned his head slightly. He looked concerned and then wary. He pushed my short sleeve up. I gasped as I saw a burned black handprint on my arm. But it was a dream right? He growled beside me. "I'm gonna kill him."

"But I was dreaming. How is this possible?"

"We need to go see my father. I wish you could show me what happened," he muttered.

"But I can can't I? Just like you did me?"

He shook his head.

"You can try but everything is harder for humans."

I turned to him, laying my knee on his leg. I pulled his face close and I saw a flash glimpse of a kiss. I realized it was him imagining me kissing him. I held my gasp in check and pushed that aside. It was good to know he at least wanted to since he hadn't done it yet. I was curious as to why. But now that I could see that in his mind, I wanted to smile but it wasn't the time. I pressed my forehead to his, just like he had done to me in the restaurant, immediately feeling his heartbeat unsteady and slightly faster, and remembered the dream.

It was just as real. Unlike any memory I've ever had and I guessed that it was just as real for Caleb as me when we memory transplant. I heard his fast intake of breath and knew he was seeing it too now, so I let it all flow between us.

His breaths sped up as he saw me in pain, getting out of bed. Then when I yanked the door open to find Kyle instead, he grunted in annoyance. And when Kyle told me he was my significant and Caleb didn't exist I had to grip Caleb's head harder to hold him in place.

Then we got to the Marcus part, he growled and huffed all the way through it. When I landed forcefully in my bed at the end of the dream, I pulled back and looked at him expectantly. But he surprised me by not talking about the dream right away.

"Maggie, I'm so proud of you for being able to do that. Everyone told me to warn you, to make sure that you understood how hard it was going to be and what a struggle it was for humans but you have blown all those theories out of the water. You are so amazing."

I blossomed under his praise. I tried to hide my smile but failed. He smiled too and cupped my cheek, bringing his face to mine, our noses touching, our lips so, so close.

But no kiss.

We sat like that, sharing air and listening to each other's thoughts as we allowed them to be open and tangible for the other about the dream, about each other, about everything. I could *feel* what he felt in his thoughts, like they were my own. It was amazing and breathtaking.

Too soon, he pulled back and sighed forcefully. "Can't put it off any longer. Let's go see my father."

"Ok," I said anxiously and practically jumped from the bed.

I wanted to know what had happened as much if not more than he did. I almost forgot Caleb was still here as I began to pull my shirt over my head. When the hem got to the edge of my bra I stopped, realizing what I was doing. I peeked at him and he was staring at me with a sort of gaze I'd never seen directed my way before, which is sad since I had a boyfriend for three years.

You see, I'm a virgin. Yes, Chad and I dated for three years and yes I loved him, in some way, but now all that has been questioned. I never longed to see him without a shirt, I never sat in bed at night thinking about kissing him, I never got butterflies or goose bumps, ever in my recollection of being with Chad. Our being together was like an arrangement or agreement from day one of high school and it was just implied from then on. We kissed some, we wrestled, we played just like any other couple, went on dates, snuggled watching movies. But it was more for comfort I think.

He felt more like a really good friend and someone who I was comfortable being with more than someone I was in love with. He was someone who'd known me forever. I didn't have to let him see anything in me he didn't already know. He was safe.

Just like my father had said, he was right. There was no way I would have ever gone too far with Chad because he was always one foot out the door and I was too complacent with being stuck on first base. And neither of us had any intentions of changing that, before he decided to end it.

How had I not seen this?

I loved Chad but I wasn't in love with him. I missed him because I could talk to him about anything because he'd hug me and tell me it'd all be all right whether it really was or not. I had wanted him because he was my home base, my safe zone, my constant. And now, I could never go back to something like that. Not after having passion for someone, after seeing what it's like to want and feel something in your bones, after blushing at the way someone looks at you, like I was blushing under Caleb's hot gaze, right then.

I pulled my shirt down swiftly but his eyes stayed fixed on my stomach, then jerked to mine.

"Sorry," he said gruffly and shook himself.

I wanted to giggle at him but I was still too shaken myself. I'd never had someone so fixated on me before. It was fascinating and exhilarating and terrifying, in that order.

"It's ok. Sorry. I almost forgot you were here."

"I'll wait downstairs while you get dressed. And try to avoid your dad and his wrath," he joked before rubbing his chin as he left, shutting the door.

I sat on my bed in a daze. Caleb had been in my room. I wonder what he thought of it.

I felt like I was crammed so tight. So much had happened in the past couple days, more then than ever, to change my life. I took a breath and went to my closet to pick something out, preferably something with sleeves to help cover the handprint. I was glad Dad hadn't seen it. He would never have believed me that Caleb hadn't put it there.

I dragged on a pair of jeans and a coral tank with a white cropped cardigan. Then I slipped on my flops and went to the bathroom to do the rest.

When I creaked down the stairs a few minutes later, I heard Caleb and Dad talking in the kitchen. So I stopped on the stairs and listened.

"Yes, sir. I understand all that but I'm not some frat guy trying to take advantage of your daughter. Yes, I'm in college and I live in another city but we'll make it work."

"How long have you even known my daughter?"

A hesitation. "A few days."

"So how can you possibly feel-"

"She saved my life."

"What?"

"She didn't tell you? I would have been hit by a truck but she pulled me out of the way."

I heard Dad grunt and pause. "So, that's what this is? You feel indebted to her?"

"No, sir. I feel very grateful to her for what she did but that's how we met, that's not why I want to be with her."

"Then why, son?"

"Forgive me if I'm being too bold, sir, but don't you know your own daughter? Don't you know how amazing she is? It can't be that hard to see why I'd be interested."

"I know she's cute-"

"I'm not talking about her looks."

"Look, she's only ever been involved with one guy and it was for...what, three years at least. But it wasn't serious. She's inexperienced about everything. She's too young to be so intense about you, and I see it. She's gonna get all crazy about you and then you'll be gone and who knows what silly notion she'll get then. Follow you to college or whatever but I won't have it. I don't care that she graduated, that doesn't mean-"

I'd had enough of this conversation so I bounded down and interrupted them.

"Hey. Ready?"

"Yeah. Good talking to you sir but I promise you have nothing to worry about with me."

"I hope so, Caleb."

"Bye, Dad," I shouted as I pulled Caleb from the kitchen.

"Helmet!" he yelled back as we shut the door.

"I'm sorry about him. He's a psycho or something."

Caleb laughed as he buckled our helmets and I noticed he was wearing a Hawksley Workman t-shirt. I loved them.

"He's just worried about you. It's better than him not worrying about you, right?"

"Debatable. Where are we going?"

"To my house. My dad had to work today so we'll catch him at the home office."

I was thrilled to be going to Caleb's house. He put the jacket on me again and I climbed on behind him as he cranked the bike. I grabbed on tight and held on as he pulled away from my house. I saw Dad peeking out the kitchen curtain and wondered why Caleb was going so slow. Then, when we hit the end of the street, I realized why. My dad had been watching.

"All right, all clear," he said. "Hang on."

He revved it up and sped away as soon as the light turned green. I squealed but this time it was excitement, not fright. He laughed as I squeezed him around the middle.

"I'm glad you like it. I was worried you'd hate it and I'd be forced to drive something else when I'm with you," he said through the headset in the helmet.

"No, I love it. What do you do when it rains?"

"Well, I have a truck, too. I just prefer to drive this."

"Oh." I wondered how he could afford two automobiles when he was only nineteen. "So, I heard you and my dad talking in the kitchen."

"Mmhmm. About Chad?" he said. "Yeah, Kyle actually told me some about him too," he said in a flat tone.

"He did?"

"Yeah. I asked him about you, he said you and this guy had gone out for a long time and that it was pretty intense."

"It wasn't really. I mean, I thought it was at the time but...he was just the only guy I'd ever known, ever been out with, you know?"

"So, what happened?"

"Kyle didn't tell you?"

"He did, but Kyle's a little begrudging on the details."

"Well, Chad has wanted to go to Florida to play football since... forever."

"The Gators," he said incredulously.

"I know, right? Anyway his dad went there and it's what he's always wanted. So I always knew he was leaving as soon as he graduated. He decided the beginning of senior year to end it then, that it would be easier that way on both of us."

"Ok," he said dragging out the letters. "So he dumped you senior year after three years of dating because he didn't want to hurt you?"

"Yep. And he did it just days after my mom left so...but he didn't know that she left, it just really sucked for me."

"Hmm. That's some logic he's got there."

"Yeah."

"So, if he hadn't done that you'd still be with him."

It wasn't lost on me that he didn't phrase it as a question. So, I answered truthfully.

"Yeah, more than likely. He was the only thing I knew. We've known each other since we were babies. He was my friend."

He nodded. "I'd hate to think what would have happened if we'd imprinted while you were still dating him."

"We wouldn't have imprinted," I mused. "I would have been with him instead of waiting for Kyle. Which means, you wouldn't be here. I wouldn't have pulled you back."

He nodded again and then spoke slowly.

"Well, don't take this the wrong way and I know it sucked for you this year but...I'm glad you aren't still with him. And I'm glad you were at that red light."

I squeezed his chest. "Me, too. It was worth it."

I felt a rush of hazy warmth from his mind at my words. He drove silently the rest of the way and safely but fast, I enjoyed it all the way.

We reached a long street and he began to slow. I saw the houses we were passing and wondered if he was turning down another street. Those houses were insane. They all had gates out front, like the people who lived there were important. I started getting a bit anxious. I mean Kyle's house was really nice, but it was nothing compared to these.

"Don't freak out." He chuckled reading my thoughts. "We share our house with family a lot of the time, plus Jen and Maria still live there. So we have to have a big place to have room for everyone, but we're not snobs. Promise."

"I know. It's just a little overwhelming compared to what I've seen before."

He pulled up to a big black double gate with a J in silver on each one and a half circle centered in the filigree work along the top of the gate and fence. Just like his tattoo on the inside of his wrist. He pressed a red button on the voice box.

"Yes? State your business here," a pompous British voice answered.

"It's me, Randolph. Cut the British crap."

"Oh. It's you, Caleb," a now normal American voice said. "I was trying it out. No good?"

"Nah," Caleb laughed. "I'd stick with the Aussie if I were you."

"Oh, well. Come on in, your father's in his study."

"Thanks."

"What was that?" I asked.

"Our butler slash security slash maintenance man, Randolph. He's a guy we keep around to handle all the house stuff since we're always in and out. Plus, he's a hoot."

"You have a butler?" I asked incredulously.

"*A* butler, as in one. And he's a jack of all trades. We don't have maids or chefs or groundskeepers, we do all that ourselves. We just need someone here all the time for safety reasons. Plus, he really needed a job at the time so my dad helped him," he explained. "And you're already on the list to come and go when you want, just in case you're ever in the neighborhood."

"I'll keep that in mind," I said with a smile.

Eleven

We parked in a huge garage and along side six other vehicles. Six. I saw his truck that he referred to earlier. It was a black Dodge Ram extended cab. The rest of the cars were expensive and had model names that were letters and numbers and I had no idea what they were, but they looked nice.

He got off first this time and lifted me from the bike. He set me down in front of him and took off my helmet.

"I'll have to keep a steady supply of rubber bands here if we keep this up," I mused as I tried to tame my hair.

He laughed softly. "Well, you can keep anything here you want. I told you, you're welcome anytime. In fact, I'm not trying to scare you, but we have a spare bedroom with your name on it."

"What?"

"We have a couple of extra rooms with beds. Nothing special but anytime you want to crash here you're welcome to. My parents insisted I tell you that."

"Oh, ok. Thanks."

"I mean it. I mean, we still have a lot of things to talk about, but one of them needs to be what you're going to do when I go back to school; when I come home and to my apartment. I can't live at Kyle's forever."

I nodded and unzipped the jacket, putting it under the seat. "Yeah, I know."

And I did, I just had no idea what to do about it.

"Ok. Let's go see Dad." He took my hand and we walked towards the door. "You really are taking everything well, you know. I knew you would, but I was still a little worried."

"Do you want me to run for the door screaming? Because I can do that if you want."

He laughed loudly, his dimple winking, and grabbed me around my stomach. "No, I don't want that."

"Just checking."

"You really are kinda perfect," he mused quietly.

Oh, I wanted him to kiss me. I wanted him to badly. I didn't know why he hadn't yet, but I knew he wanted to from that little flash from his mind. So why was he stalling?

His expression told me he read my mind, but as he opened his mouth to say something we heard a voice over the intercom.

"Caleb, is that Maggie? What are you doing here? Is something wrong?" Peter said frantically in his deep timber voice.

"Of course it's Maggie, Dad. Who else would I be about to kiss in the garage?" he called out.

I bit my lip to keep the smile from breaking, but kept my composure at his admission. About to kiss!

"Well, bring her in!"

"Ok, I am!" He looked at me and smiled. "I think he likes you."

"I like him, too. All of your family is great, especially Gran."

"She's everyone's favorite."

"So, what do you think your dad will know about...this." I rubbed my arm where the handprint sat under the fabric. "Have you heard of this before?"

"Not me. Maybe he has. I'll warn you though," he stopped me and looked at me pointedly, "I'm not thinking this is a good thing. But whatever it is, we'll get through it, ok?"

"Ok."

"I'm not going to let anything happen to you," he assured.

"I know."

"Good." He started towing me again, through the garage doors, and into the house. I was jumped by a big furry blonde creature and slammed into Caleb's side. "Bella! Down!" He righted me and looked apologetic. "Sorry. She's still only a puppy. Still learning aren't you, girl. Bad girl," he said, but crooned it sweetly like it was an endearment.

"A puppy? She's huge? What is she?"

"She's mostly Sheepdog. Only seven months old."

She did look like a Sheepdog, I could see it now. She was big, up past my knee with long blonde and white shaggy hair that hung over her eyes and legs.

"Well," I said and bent down to pet her. "She's pretty." Bella nuzzled my hand and then my neck, making me giggle while Caleb tried to pull her back. "And sweet. She's ok," I assured him.

I scratched behind her ears and she groaned a happy noise and flopped herself right on top of my lap almost. We laughed at her as she wagged her feet in the air and rubbed her head against my hand.

"She likes you. She usually doesn't like strangers." Then he groaned and squinted. "That really sounded like some lame pick-up line didn't it?"

"Kind of," I laughed. "How did you come up with Bella?"

"Don't laugh," he said sternly, took a deep breath and muttered something under his breath that I didn't catch.

"What?" I asked and leaned closer.

"Twilight! Ok! Twilight!" He laughed. "Maria, it's her fault. I told her she could name her and she's on this Twilight kick." He shook his head. "Jen drew the line at putting a cut out of Edward on her door."

I laughed and continued to pet Bella. "But she's only eight, right?"

"Yes, but she's really smart. She's read all the books."

"Well so have I, but I would never have read them when I was eight."

"It's not just that though. She reads everything. Murder mystery, fantasy, sci-fi. She's a freak, but I love her."

"Wow."

"Ok, Bella, that's enough belly rubbing," he crooned and patted her stomach. "I'm taking Maggie to see Dad."

We got up and she whined and tried to follow, but Caleb turned and put his hand up. "No, girl. Stay."

She did but she didn't look happy about it as her tail hung and she panted. He took my hand and pulled me down a bunch of winding halls and up some big white stairs.

"I can't stay here, Caleb. I'll get lost every time I go to the bathroom. It's like the Labyrinth in here."

He cracked up. "That's a good name for it. My dad designed the house to confuse anyone who doesn't live here. Burglars, you know. There's a trick to it. I'll show you later."

"Ok."

The next hall we turned had black walls and floors. There were pictures lined with white backdrops of all kinds of funky buildings all down the walls, floor to ceiling.

"These are my dad's designs," Caleb said proudly, pulling me to one that was particularly bizarre but in a good way.

"Wow, these are great. I had no idea you could do things like this with a building."

"Yeah. He's the best. And he loves it which makes it even better."

"Caleb?" Peter shouted down the hall. "Are you purposely keeping Maggie from me?"

Caleb rolled his eyes and pushed me forward with a hand on the small of my back. Peter was sitting at an insanely large cherry desk in a huge office with black walls as well. He smiled hugely when we entered.

"Here you go, Dad," Caleb said sarcastically and presented me like a gift. "I'll just wait over here."

Peter guffawed and came around to greet me. He was wearing black slacks and a blue Oxford button up with the sleeves rolled up.

"Oh, come now, Caleb." He hugged me tightly. "This is the only time I'll get this chance. Let me have my fun," he said just like Gran had yesterday.

"Ok, Dad," Caleb said smiling. "But can we remember that I saw her first?"

"Absolutely." He pulled back to look at me with amusement. "And how are you, my dear?"

"Great. And I love your house."

"I love it, too." He winked. "Did Caleb extend our invitation to you?"

"He did. Thank you, I really appreciate it."

"And?"

"And?" I said confused.

Caleb came over and stood beside me as Peter released me and leaned back on his desk.

"Dad, I haven't had a chance to talk to you yet. You see, Maggie's dad is going to be more of a...problem than we originally thought," he said and looked apologetically to me.

Peter sat up straight and crossed his arms, looking pensive. "That right?"

"Yes. We've already had a couple close calls. So, I told Maggie she can stay here when she wants to, but she won't be able to do anything more than that right now, Dad."

"Hmm." Peter rubbed his chin just like Caleb does. "Well, we'll have to figure something out."

"Yeah," I chimed in. "I don't know what's gotten into him but he's all of a sudden decided to start parenting again."

"Tell me." He waved to the couch in front of him for us to sit. "Tell me what happened with him. Why he's been so absent from your life until now."

I sat down with Caleb and thought how to process and word it all. With Dad having confessed and apologized and now was being so awkward and upset with Caleb, it was like a fresh wound. Caleb's hand came up to massage my neck, calming, soothing. I smiled at him gratefully.

"Well, he hasn't been absent. We've always been happy and together until last summer, before school started. My mom left. After that my dad has been like a zombie."

I told him the whole sad story up until present day. I watched his face as I told him and saw that he was concerned but didn't pity me.

"Hmm." He rubbed his chin again and then ran one hand through his hair. I saw the same tattoo Caleb had on the inside of his wrist except his father's half circle had Rachel's name around the curved side. "Well, he must see that what is between you two isn't going to just go away. That's why he's so frightened by this. I understand, I have a daughter myself. It's hard to watch them grow up. I think this is just what he needed to wake up."

"Yeah, but it couldn't have come at a worse time. He said Caleb can't come over in the mornings anymore."

Peter jolted up.

"Now that is a problem. Hmm. I'd hate for you two to have outs with each other when you've just gotten him back in your life."

"Me, too," I said truthfully.

"But you can't deny the need for Caleb-"

"I know, believe me. Dad almost kicked Caleb out this morning and I...completely freaked," I admitted quietly. "I don't know what we're gonna do but...we gotta figure it out somehow. If I just leave him like that, I don't know what he'll do. I'm all he's got."

Peter nodded and looked sincerely understanding. "We'll work it out somehow, Maggie. We'll figure it out. Don't worry."

"Ok, Dad. So, one more thing," Caleb inched into the topic at hand.

"Ok," he said warily.

Caleb pulled my sweater open and pulled the shoulder down to expose my upper arm. Peter growled his words out, just like Caleb had. "Again? How?"

"No, Dad, not again. This was a dream."

His dad paled and leaned against the desk further to keep from falling. I jumped up to him.

"Are you ok?" I asked.

"Dad, what is it?" Caleb asked at the same time.

"They have an echoling," Peter answered breathless and then banged his fist on the desk.

"What's that?" Caleb asked.

Peter looked at my arm and grasped it gently.

"This is an echo. A dream that is so real that it becomes real; tangible. They dream it and fashion it how they see fit and then send it, or echo it, to who the intended recipient is. They can imagine whatever they want and make it real. Make it happen to someone as if it were actually happening to them. They don't have to even be aware that you're asleep, you just receive the echo when you are sleeping. That's why you have the offense mark, because for all intents and purposes, it did happen."

I stared at him and waited for him to finish and to tell me that there was some way to stop it or make it go away. But he just sat there thinking.

"So, they can just climb into my dreams whenever they want and hurt me?"

Caleb came closer and laced our fingers.

"Yes," Peter said bluntly. "They can hurt you and drain you of your energy and essence. When you wake up you feel like you haven't slept at all when they are in your dreams. Unless..." He sighed. "The solution is a little ironic I guess in this case."

"What? Whatever it is, we'll do it," Caleb answered forcefully.

"Well, the only way to stop it is for Caleb to be with you. His touch calms you, it heals you and also keeps you from harm, from attack of another's ability. He anchors you, grounds you, so to speak. He's your shield." I guess Caleb and I continued to stare at him because he sighed and said more bluntly, "You have to sleep with Caleb. Just sleep," he insisted quickly, "but he has to be touching you while you sleep in order to keep Marcus or anyone else away. He's your barrier."

I blinked.

"I don't understand."

"Your imprint works so that you are always together, Maggie. You live best, work best, play best, love best and fight best when you're together. You'll even sleep best when you are. I know I do all those things best with Rachel."

"I have no idea how we'll pull that off with my dad the way he is lately."

"Me either. Let me think on it. In the meantime, just stay together as long as possible. Ok?"

I nodded and then had another thought. "I thought no one in their clan had ascended either? How can Marcus have abilities?"

"He doesn't. Someone's helping him. That's what worries me most."

I let Caleb pull me from the room. He called out over his shoulder. "Bye, Dad. Thanks."

"Caleb." He came to the hall to speak. "I know this is hard for you both. You're both young and you're trying not to hurt Maggie's father, but this is inevitable. You two can't be apart." He looked at me. "Maggie, I know this is strange for you, but I feel the need to stress the severity of the situation. It won't just make you ill if you're apart, Caleb will be ill, too. I'll work on trying to figure something out about your father, but if it doesn't pan out and he forbids you to see Caleb-"

"I understand. We have to be together, even at the cost of angering my father. I understand, I do."

He smiled sadly at me.

"I'm so sorry, Maggie. Usually, for us, these first few years after imprinting are very special and joyous times. I'm sorry that it doesn't seem to be that way for you now, but it'll get better."

"It's ok. Thank you."

"Will you stay? For a while? Rachel would love to have you both for dinner, I'm sure."

I looked at Caleb and shrugged.

"Yeah. We'll stay," he told him.

"Good. I've got to get back to work. See you in a few hours."

We made our way down the hall and into another wing, past a huge white foyer.

"The wing with Dad's office is for business. This wing is where the bedrooms are," he advised and we turned a corner, then he stopped at a wide door. "My room."

He opened the dark oak door and I was bombarded with his scent. The scent I smell when I inhale the skin at his neck, my favorite smell. I took a deep breath and walked in after him, he closed the door as I looked around.

It was a strange room for a college boy I thought. It was clean and his bed made. He had sheet music and guitars everywhere with a baby piano in the corner and a trumpet on the wall stand. There were no posters above his bed. Just a plain room with lots of shelves, filled with books and cd's.

"I like your room," I said truthfully.

"Yeah? I like it, too. Mom tried to guy it all up when I left for school, but..."

"Guy it all up?" I asked cocking a questioning brow at him.

"Yeah. When I came back my first break from college, she had decorated everything in swimming. Water waves bedspread, Michael Phelps posters, my old trophies and metals on my shelf. She even had a poster over my bed that said 'Swimmers Do It Right'." I laughed and then covered it with my hand. "Yeah, so I fixed it. I like things plain, not loud."

"Me, too."

He kicked his shoes off and walked to the piano. I took my flops off and sat on his bed while he played something I'd never heard before. It was sweet and slow.

"Did your uncle - the one who can learn and teach anything, whatever he's called - did he teach you to play all these instruments?"

"Nope. And he's called a Novice."

"A Novice? But doesn't that mean beginner?"

"Yes, smarty. Technically, he's a beginner until he learns it."

He looked back at me and smiled. I smiled back and then lay back on the bed and listened to him while I thought about what to do about my dad and everything that was going on.

I hadn't gotten very much sleep the night before. I went to bed after midnight and got up before seven. I hadn't realized how tired I was. I felt so at ease in his room, so comfortable in his bed, peaceful and safe with him there. And I fell right to sleep.

I felt cold. I was shivering and my teeth chattered. I found myself in Caleb's bed still but Caleb wasn't here with me. I felt that ping of anxiety rise up at that thought. I heard the door creak behind me. I rolled over slowly to see a silhouette of someone in the doorway. I squinted to see who it was.

"Caleb?"

"You wish," a deep voice answered me and I froze.

"Marcus," I whispered. "How did you-"

"Poor little Maggie. You're exhausted aren't you? Caleb keeping you up too late?"

"How?"

"How am I here? Well, you went to sleep. And your knight in shining armor is banging away at his piano, oblivious."

"What do you want?"

"I want you."

"Caleb. Caleb!" I shouted. "Caleb!"

"He can't hear you," he sang.

"Oh, yes he can."

I concentrated like I did before, so he could read my thoughts. I got it together and pushed it toward Caleb.

Caleb!

Marcus looked instantly peeved.

"I don't know how you can do that, but fine. He won't be right next to you all the time, little human."

I felt warm hands on my cheeks and woke with a gasp to see a concerned face over mine. I panted as my heart calmed at his touch.

"Maggie, are you ok?"

"It was him."

"I know. You sent me your thoughts. I saw him. Are you sure you're ok?"

"Yeah. I'm sorry I fell asleep. You were playing and I was so tired and..."

"It's ok. He didn't hurt you, did he?" he said and caressed his thumbs over my cheekbones.

"No, not yet." I was calm for the most part except Caleb was still over top of me. His legs straddled me and he rested on his elbows as his hands warmed my cheeks. Now I was getting breathless for another reason. "I'm fine," I breathed.

He frowned and sighed. "I can't protect you even when I'm in the same room with you," he sighed again harshly and tried to get up, but I grabbed his shirt to stop him.

"Don't. It was my fault. I fell asleep."

"No, it wasn't." He let his nose touch mine and I breathed deep. "You did nothing wrong. I'm sorry. I'm just not going to leave you again until we figure this out."

I nodded which made our noses bump. His eyes closed and I closed mine, too. I thought, this is it, he's finally going to kiss me...but he just stayed close, then his bedroom door opened.

"Caleb, your father said- Ah! Oh!" Rachel said startled and started to shut the door.

"Mom, wait," Caleb said scrambling off the bed to help me sit up. "It's not that. She had an echo attack."

"An echoling?" She pushed the door open all the way and it banged against the wall. "Oh, no," she breathed and covered her mouth with her hands.

"Dad's working on it."

"Well, he said you were here and you'd be here for dinner, but he didn't say anything about an echoling." She shook her head and grimaced. "Are you all right, Maggie?"

"Yeah. I'm fine," I insisted, but was no longer sure.

"Ok then, I'm going to go start some supper."

"I can help-"

"No, honey. Thank you, I appreciate it, but you need to just stay with Caleb, ok? Just stay together as long as you can."

She went out and shut the door behind her. I flopped back on the bed again and closed my eyes at the throbbing behind them. It was exhausting to worry so much. Caleb lay down beside me and I instinctively moved to my side to press against him. At first I was a little shocked at myself, but his arm came around to hold me to him just as instinctively.

It felt perfect, like it was right where I was meant to be.

"You're always so warm," I muttered sleepily and put one of my legs under his.

I heard him chuckle as he pulled a blanket over us from the end of his bed. Then he turned on his side facing me and wrapped his other arm around me.

"Just rest for a few, sleepy girl. I'm here this time. Nothing's going to happen to you."

"Thanks." I moved my hand to rest on his neck and felt my headache ease away. "Maybe just for a minute."

"Yeah."

He kissed my forehead and I felt his smile against my skin. I smiled, too, as I drifted off for a completely restful sleep.

I woke later, who knew how much later, to voices in the room. They were hushed but concerned and I peeked to see that Caleb was still asleep against me. Our arms were around each other and his face was right next to mine.

"I know all that, Peter, I'm just worried is all," I heard Rachel say. "She's so young, but it's not like we can stop them. They need each other. I just don't know how to control it."

"You know Caleb has a good head on his shoulders. He's responsible, he's reliable, and he's more careful, considerate and attentive of this girl than I've ever seen him with anyone."

"Well, of course he is, but he never cared about that dating rule anyway-"

"He's a nineteen year old college boy, Rachel. I guarantee you, he cared," he said dryly. "He just understood. He saw the merit in it. If anyone in our clan deserved to be the one to receive this gift, it's him. And I'm not just being biased because he's our son."

"I know. I know. I just remember being brand new with you." She laughed softly and it startled me how girly and young she sounded. "You couldn't keep your hands off of me."

"I remember," Peter said and I could hear the smile in his voice. "But they're different. They didn't know each other at all beforehand like we did. I've watched them together. Even though they feel the pull, they aren't giving into it. They both have incredible restraint. Don't worry about them."

"But when I came in earlier...and now."

"Sweetheart." I heard shuffling. I assumed he was embracing her. "He needs to comfort her. They have to touch, they have to be together and after this echoling situation, he'll have to sleep with her and be with her even more. I still haven't figured out a solution without her angering her father, we'll think of something. But, honey, they are soul mates. They are eventually going to be consumed with each other and there's nothing we can do."

"I don't want to stop it, I know how it is and how it needs to be. I just wish I could convince them not to go too far, too soon. They are so young."

"He loves her already," he said and I fought not to gasp. "I can see it. That's why he uses his restraint, Rachel. If he didn't, he would give in to his urges because they are uncomfortable for him, and it wouldn't take much persuasion for Maggie to give in, you know that. We didn't have to use restraint; we were older and ready for it. They are doing remarkably well for being so young and unprepared for the overload of emotions."

"You're right. You are. He's a good kid and so is she. I don't think I could've picked a better person for him. She's adorable and sweet. She's going to be so good for this clan. Just what it needs to perk up a bit."

"I can't wait to see what their abilities will be," Peter mused. "I have a feeling they'll be spectacular."

I felt the bed depress behind me and a hand on my leg.

"Sweetie." She shook my arm a little. "Maggie, if you don't get up and eat you'll be late getting home."

I roused slowly as she shook Caleb's leg as well. He pulled me closer and nuzzled my head when she tried to wake him. I heard them both chuckle. She shook him harder.

"Caleb, you have to take Maggie home."

His eyes instantly opened and he saw me, our faces almost touching. He smiled. "Hey. Did you sleep?" he asked.

"Yeah. Thanks."

"Come on, you two," Rachel beckoned. "Supper's been ready."

Her and Peter left and I slowly sat up and stretched. I felt so much better it was like night and day. He sat up beside me and ran a hand through his hair so I did the same.

"No dreams?" he asked as he stood.

"Nope. None."

"Well, I didn't want to take all your dreams, just the bad ones," he said softly and he lifted me by my hands to stand in front of him.

"I usually don't remember them anyway."

I couldn't believe how refreshed I felt. How my body seemed to sing with contentment. I came to see it was Caleb. We'd had physical contact for who knew how long now while we slept. Both of us calming and soothing the other. It was actually good for me to sleep with him.

Peter was right. It was pretty ironic that the thing I needed most was going to be the biggest fight with my father. I had no idea how to make it work, but I hoped we'd figure it out.

"I'm starving," I mused and smiled at him. "Come on." I grabbed his hand. "Point me towards the kitchen."

He laughed. "The dining room actually. Follow me."

I held his arm as we walked. I even put my head on his shoulder and could feel Caleb's happiness about it beaming through to me. He didn't want to push me, but wanted us to move forward in our relationship. He wanted us to be happy and at ease with each other, but he wanted things to go on my pace. He was happy that I was getting more comfortable with him.

I felt so strange yet utterly put together at the same time. It was the sleep, I knew, but I felt more bold and confident and comfortable with Caleb than I ever had.

Twelve

"This is so good, Rachel. Thank you," I said and then took another big bite of mashed potatoes.

The dining room was grand. The walls were a soft yellow with green floor tiles and a big oak table that could have easily sat ten. We all sat at one end together.

"Good, I'm glad you like it. It's one of Caleb's favorites."

"I can't believe how hungry I am," I mused.

"It's the echoling," Peter advised as he wiped his mouth with the white linen napkin and leaned back in his chair. "It drains you like I told you, but not only are you tired, but you're hungry. It also wouldn't hurt to drink some orange juice or take a vitamin when you get home."

"All that because a guy invaded my dream?"

"I'm afraid so. I'm sorry, Maggie, but unfortunately sometimes, we have to deal with these unpleasantries with our kind."

I nodded and sat back, stuffed. All I wanted to do right then was crawl back into bed with Caleb, but it was getting late and would be dark soon. I needed to get home if we were going to appease my father.

I looked at him and saw him watching me. When he saw he was caught, that dimple of his became more defined as his smile spread. He chuckled silently and I cracked a smile. But I didn't blush. Progress!

He leaned his elbows on the table. "Ready to go?"

"Yeah."

I thanked his parents again for dinner and everything else. Peter said he'd still be thinking about how to deal with the echoling and for me not to worry. He hugged me tight and then handed me off to Rachel who did the same.

"Be safe, dear."

I nodded and we walked to the bike slowly. As I was about to put my helmet on Caleb stopped me. “We can take my truck if you’d rather this time.”

“Um...if you want to.”

“You want to take the bike don’t you?” he said smiling.

“Yeah,” I admitted.

He laughed and helped me with my helmet. "You just keep getting better and better.”

I shook my head at him as I slipped on his jacket and then climbed on behind him.

“You want to drive?” he asked suddenly.

“Uh...maybe, but not tonight. I don’t want to add a timeline of pressure to my nerves if I’m going to be driving.”

“Ok,” he said amused, “next time.”

We pulled out of the garage, then the gate and headed down the driveway to my house.

“So, if your uncle didn’t teach you, how did you learn to play all those instruments?”

“Well, he wanted to teach me but I wanted to learn by myself. So I took piano lessons first, when I was six. Then my grandpa taught me to play guitar and the rest I just figured out on my own.”

“Your grandpa. The one who looks so much like you?”

“Yeah, Grandpa Ray. He died four years ago.”

“How?”

“Well...we aren’t sure. Old age, I guess. Significants heal each other so we usually live a really long time. We never have to go to doctors or anything like that, except for babies. We just heal whatever’s wrong without knowing it. But Grandpa Ray didn’t wake up one morning. I mean, he was eighty five years old, but we usually live longer than that. We can see it coming, but him...it was just out of nowhere.”

“I’m sorry,” I said and saw in his mind that significants usually die together or nearly. For Gran to live this many years after him was unprecedented. I could feel his anguish, remembering Gran crying and inconsolable for months. I would have put my hand on his to draw those feelings away from him, but couldn’t reach it on the handlebars so I improvised, needing to do something. I lifted the hem of his shirt and splayed my hand on his side. “I’m sorry,” I repeated.

“Thanks.” He pulled my hand in front of him, laced our fingers, his palm on the top of my hand. “It’s ok. We still don’t know what happened, but we just accepted it was his time. But now, with this echoling thing...I’m starting to wonder if maybe that had something to do with it. He was our Champion before my dad.”

“Wouldn’t Gran have been sleeping with him though?”

"Well, Gran said she'd been working on his birthday present. She was making him a jacket and had worked on it a couple nights in a row, waiting for him to fall asleep first, so she wasn't with him. That's why she was so upset. She thought he had a heart attack or something and she wasn't there to heal him. She blamed herself."

"Caleb. That's terrible."

"But she got better. And if Dad hasn't thought of the echoling thing as a reason, maybe it's not possible. Maybe I'm just trying to make something out of nothing."

He didn't believe that, but he wasn't sure if he wanted to open Gran's wounds or not.

"You'll do what's right. You guys are lucky to be so close to each other, your family."

"Yeah, we are. Most clans are this way."

"So, you said your mom was part of another clan until she met your dad. How do you meet other clans? Do you have an Ace's convention or something?"

He laughed and I was happy that the sadness of his grandparents was forgotten for now.

"Well...yeah, actually. Every year we get together in London. That's the central base for our kind. It's called reunification. Aces came over to America on the Mayflower, you know."

"Really?" I said intrigued.

"Nah." I bumped his back as he laughed. "But we did migrate here and all over the world over the years. We all make a trip for one week, every year, to London and get together to keep in touch and see the new couples, new babies. All the clans go, or use to, even rival ones."

"I bet you have a lot of imprints that week," I mused.

"Kind of. Imprints are a private thing and mostly, you won't imprint in front of anyone else, or at least not in front of someone you don't know well. Most of the imprints happen when they are saying goodbye, or when they meet up later for a visit or something. We've all known each other since birth so, it's not usually like it was with you and me, where we've never met before."

"I bet there's a line a mile long of Ace girls who hate me now," I joked.

"I doubt that." He laughed. "Kyle is the ladies' man, not me."

"I don't believe that. I think you just don't know the effect that you have on people."

He sighed in embarrassment. I saw glimpses in his mind of a big golden room and him being followed by girls of all ages throughout the days when he was in London. Then he pushed it away.

"Well, anyway. That's where my parents met, even though they both were from Tennessee. They got together after the reunification for a bi-family lunch and that's when it happened. Some of the clans that are close in geography will get together sometimes."

"So are there like...rituals they're going to try to perform on us at this thing?"

He laughed. "We're clans, Maggie, not covens."

"Ok," I conceded. "So is there like a million people there?"

"Nope. There's really not that many of us, only about three hundred around the world. There are three families here in Tennessee. There are two more families in the United States, in Chicago, and then two in London, one in Sydney, Australia, two in Paris, and one in Prague."

"Wow."

"Yeah. Some of the other families are a little eccentric, but for the most part, they're all pretty normal and want to seem as human as possible and with loads of cash of course." I laughed and he did too. "The next reunification is in six weeks, right before school starts back."

"Will I go to this with you?" I asked and felt timid about it, like I didn't belong or something.

"Of course you will, you're family. We'll work something out with your dad by then. From what I hear through my gossiping aunts, everyone in London is pretty anxious to meet you."

"Why? Because no one has imprinted in a long time?"

"Yes, that but also because you're human. There are only three humans imprinted out of three hundred people. You, Gran and a man named Philippe. He's a genius. He can name any capitol of any city in the world."

"What's his ability?"

"That *is* his ability. He can remember anything. He brings new meaning to the phrase *photographic memory*. Anything you say to him, he'll remember after only hearing it once. He's a walking dictionary."

"Hmm. That'd be useful."

"Yeah. I'd kill for that one for mid-terms."

"Ditto. So, I'm gonna be a freak show on display at this reunion thing, right?"

"Reunification. And no, you won't be a freak," he soothed and swirled his thumb over my knuckles. "They're just happy for us and hoping that the imprints are coming back. There are a lot of single people out there, but the other clans don't have the no-dating rule like us. A bunch of them have married since this whole thing started, without imprints. Now, I think they're afraid the imprints are coming back and they'll imprint on someone else. A lot of these people have kids and stuff."

"Hmmm, wow." I didn't know what else to say.

"Yeah. But don't worry about the reunification. Everybody's great. You'll see for yourself and I can't wait to go. I hope this is the start of something for our kind. They've been worried for too long."

The rest of the ride was cold but I could feel his warmth through his shirt. I leaned my helmeted head on his back and held on as I tried to relax and not get worked up again about everything. It didn't work a few times. Thoughts would creep in about how impossible it all seemed. I mean, I couldn't go to sleep. What was I supposed to do? And what about this reunification thing? I didn't like crowds and he was talking about a crowd of three hundred all staring at me like I was somehow the answer to all their problems.

But he would touch my hand, rubbing my knuckles with his, when these thoughts took over and I'd be instantly brought back down. Once he even brought his hand over his shoulder to caress my neck. I didn't remember Chad ever being like this.

Chad kissed me, yeah, but not hungry kisses. We never used tongues, they were more like pecks. He touched me, but it was just hand holding. He never caressed my face, never tried to go up my shirt or under my skirt, never tried to have sex with me. He never even kissed my neck, ever. And I realize I should be grateful for those things, for him not pushing me too far, but he should have wanted to do those things, right? I mean he didn't even try, he never talked about it, and I never saw passion in his eyes when he looked at me.

I hadn't realized what it was I was missing until Caleb.

So when we pulled up in front of my house to see Chad sitting on my front steps, I was more than a little blown away.

Caleb tensed when he saw him, then he pushed down the kick stand. I climbed off and let him help me take off my helmet but I kept the jacket.

"I have no idea what he's doing here," I whispered.

"I'm sure I have a pretty good idea," he muttered as he took his helmet off. "You want me to go?"

"No," I said quickly and then smiled at his smug smile.

"Well, at least there's that."

We walked up to the walkway. I grabbed Caleb's hand as he was giving me space. He didn't want to seem like he was claiming me or grandstanding that we were together now, though, in his thoughts, that's exactly what he wanted to do.

"Chad."

"Mags," he said and glared at Caleb.

I was shocked. Chad was never aggressive. He was nice to everyone and he never thought twice when someone else looked at me before. Why now?

"What's up?" I asked and he looked at me, his expression softening a little. "What are you doing here?" I asked, not unkindly.

"I wanted to come see you before I left to set up my apartment in Gainesville," he stated and glanced at Caleb nervously. Then he sighed. "I was hoping we could talk."

"Well," I said and didn't know what else to say.

"My dad is letting me go alone for two weeks to get settled in and then I'll come back to pack. I leave in a few days." He clucked his tongue. "Maybe we can go get something to eat?"

"I already ate at Caleb's house."

He scoffed. "So, first Kyle, now this guy? What are you doing, Maggie?" he asked sweetly, like it was an intervention or something.

"Chad, this is Caleb. Caleb, Chad."

"Hey," Caleb said smoothly, but Chad ignored him.

"Caleb is Kyle's cousin. I wasn't on a date with Kyle that night."

"It sure looked like one to me."

"Well, it wasn't. It's always been Caleb."

"Can we talk," he said exasperated and glanced at Caleb again. "Alone."

"I'd rather not."

"Maggie," Caleb said and pulled me a little bit away. "Maybe you should talk to him."

"What?" I scoffed. "Why?"

"Because you need to fix whatever it is that's wrong with you guys and this way, he'll go to school and not feel like he needs to apologize anymore. He feels guilty."

"He should," I insisted and felt my heart spike.

"I know," he insisted and framed my face with his hands. I sighed. "I'm not saying you should forgive him and run away into the sunset." He chuckled. "I'm saying it would be better for both of you if you have some - at the risk of sounding cheesy - closure."

"I guess," I conceded, "but I don't want you to go."

"I'll just go wait at Kyle's and let you guys talk for a while. Then I'll come back as soon as he leaves. Give me your cell."

I handed it over and he pulled his out, too. After a few seconds of pressing buttons he gave it back. "There, now I'm in yours and you're in mine. I can't believe I didn't have my soul mate's phone number," he said jokingly.

"Yeah, pretty crazy," I said and wanted to feel happy and secure like he did, but I just couldn't.

"Maggie," he said softly and I looked up at his face. "Are you scared to be with him?"

"No. He wouldn't hurt me."

"Then you're scared of Marcus? I'll be right back. You won't have to worry about falling asleep without me-"

"No, it's not that. I just don't want to do this with him right now. He's leaving and he doesn't want to leave with me mad at him, but if not for that, he wouldn't be apologizing to me right now."

"Hmm. I'm sure it's more than that," he insisted. "I'll be three minutes away. If it gets too bad just call for me and I'll come running."

I cocked a brow at him. "Why do you think he's here?"

He looked at me closely. "I think he saw you with Kyle and freaked. He's never seen you with anyone else and it made him jealous. I think he's coming to ask you to work it out with him, to give the long distance thing a shot or come to Florida with him for school."

"Nuhuh. He wouldn't ask that."

"We'll see," he mused.

"You're not worried?"

He shook his head. "Nah," he said, but looked at me crookedly. "Should I be?"

I smiled and shook my head. "Nuhuh. No way."

He smiled and pressed his face to mine. Once again, noses, foreheads and cheeks touching, lips so close, not even an inch between them. His hand came up to my cheek. I breathed him in and nuzzled his nose with mine.

"I want to. So bad," he whispered.

"Then why don't you?" I whispered back. I knew we were talking about the ever out-of-reach kiss.

"I told you I'd let you set the pace."

"You've been waiting on *me*?" I realized that was exactly what he'd been doing. He never did anything I didn't want to. He never pushed me to do more. Every time he'd pressed his face to mine, he had been waiting on me to close the distance.

"I never wanted it to be said that I pushed you into anything," he said and leaned back a little to look at me.

"I wouldn't think that," I insisted.

"I know, but you already gave up so many choices. I wanted you to have the choice as to when and if we kissed or not."

"If?"

"Yeah."

"So, if I never kiss you, you'll be perfectly fine with that?" I teased.

"Well," he grimaced, "not perfectly fine, but I'll live." He smiled. "I just want you to be happy, Maggie."

This was it, I was going to kiss him. I got closer, licked my lips. He saw and I enjoyed his reaction as he sucked in a breath. I smiled and really liked the idea that I could cause him to be so shaken. He leaned down and put his lips against my ear, making me shiver.

"It wasn't *my* pulse that just jumped from 70 to 120," he said smugly in response to my thought.

I smiled wider and laughed softly, tipping my head to him in agreement. Then I put my hands on his upper arms and pushed myself up on my tiptoes, feeling his nose against mine and... remembered Chad sitting on my steps. I turned and saw him eying us with clear disdain and disgust.

I pulled back with a sigh and heard Caleb do the same. "I'm sorry, Caleb. I forgot all about him."

"It's ok. I'll take that as a compliment."

I reached up and kissed his cheek, almost the corner of his mouth really, right on his dimple. "See you in a little bit?"

"Yeah," he said gruffly and nodded.

"I don't plan on hashing this out for very long, so come back soon, ok?"

"You got it."

I turned to go to Chad and heard Caleb behind me. "Uh, Maggie?"

"Yeah?"

He looked a little embarrassed and smiled bashfully. "A little help here."

"What- Oh, really?" He needed me to release him, to help him leave. "But why?"

"The tables have turned. I guess since you're the one walking away this time, it's my turn to see what it feels like."

"And so far?" I joked.

"It sucks."

I laughed and so did he. I walked up to him closely and peered up at his face. He looked amused. "Caleb, I want you to go home and pine for me until I'm done with this other guy." He groaned and grabbed me around my waist making me laugh. "Ok, ok. Go to Kyle's and wait a while until I'm done here. Then come back and I'll be waiting for you."

He laid his head against mine, his hands on my hips. "I can do that," he said softly.

"Bye."

"Bye, gorgeous." He left with a crooked smile, his dimple flashing at me. I waved and turned to see a very pissed Chad.

"Took you long enough. You act like you'll never see him again," he spat as I made my way to him.

"Jealous?" I got right to the point as I heard the bike crank and drive away.

"Yes!" he yelled. "You never acted like that over me."

"And neither did you."

"Look," he stepped closer, "I wanted to talk to you, seriously. Can we go inside?"

"I'd rather not. Dad's acting weird," I said though I was cold, I just wrapped Caleb's jacket tighter around me.

"Since when do you ride motorcycles?"

"Since Caleb drives one."

"Where did you meet this guy anyway?"

"This *guy* goes to Tennessee, but he was in town for Kyle's grad party."

"You just met him the other night?" he asked loudly coming to stand in front of me. "You don't even know him, Maggie!"

"Yes, Chad, I just met him. Why do you care? What do you want to talk about?"

"Us," he admitted softly. He closed his eyes and put his hand behind his neck, sighing. "You were always just Maggie. I'd been with you forever. I didn't want things to change but when I thought about going to college without you, I didn't hurt." I looked at him sharply. "I'm gonna be honest, Mags. I knew I'd miss you but I wouldn't ache for you. I thought we'd still be friends, still talk and eventually...I don't know. So I figured it would be easier on you if I broke it off. But you totally did the opposite of what I expected and I've spent all year suffering for it."

He grabbed my jacket clad upper arms gently in his hands. I tried to pull away but he held me firm. I sighed and gave in.

"Look," he continued, "I know I messed up but I didn't see how much until you weren't there anymore. I missed you so much. I didn't expect that. I've wanted to get back together all year but you kept blowing me off so I figured I'd just wait until I left for college and you'd eventually come around. I never thought in a million years you'd start dating someone else."

"Why is that so hard to believe?"

"It's not- well it shouldn't have been. That's what I'm trying to tell you. I took you for granted. Everyone here knew you were mine this whole time. I knew no one would go after you. Kyle sure shocked me though. But I just thought you'd wait for me. That one day we'd be back together, where we belong."

I wanted to scream. Was this not exactly what I wanted not five nights ago? Was this not what I'd hoped and wished for? Once again his timing was horrible.

"Chad, I'm sorry. But I don't want that anymore."

"Come on, Mags. He doesn't know you." His hands moved up a little. "He doesn't fill up your life of seventeen years like I do. It's always been us. Can he remember every time you've ever been sick? Can he count how many bones you've broken? I used to throw mud at you when our parents took us to the beach when we were four, can that guy say that?"

"No. But that guy didn't dump me for college football either." Chad leaned his head back to look at the sky in frustration but I kept going. "He didn't dump me to save me from myself. Chad, he does things you never did. You never touched me, I mean really touched me. You never looked at me the way he does. You wanted nothing more than a comfort zone girlfriend."

"I know that and I was an idiot for not seeing what I had. All I want is a second chance. I can touch you, I want to," he insisted and reached for my face but I backed away.

"You can't, Chad, not now. I'm sorry that things ended up like this for you but I'm happy. Don't you want that for me?"

"I think you're angry at me and letting this guy come in and tell you everything you want to hear."

I wish I could tell him how wrong he was but it looked like I'd have to settle for looking like the sulky ex-girlfriend hell bent on a rebound relationship.

"I'm sorry, Chad. I've gotta go, ok? I promised I'd keep in touch and I will. I hope everything works out great for you at Florida."

I started to walk around him. I should have seen it coming but I didn't. He grabbed my arm to halt me and swung me around. His hands gripped my arms and his mouth came down on mine gently, but with force.

My mind screamed at me to make him stop. That little thing I'd felt when Kyle held my hand, that feeling that I was doing something wrong, was a full force assault on my senses now. I tried to push him away but he held me tight. He pulled me closer and opened my mouth with his, brushing his tongue against my teeth, searching. He groaned when he found my tongue. I was so confused. Chad had never kissed me like this, with passion and whole bodies, and now he was trying to prove a point.

That he could and he wanted to.

But I didn't.

I pushed him with all my strength but he held me still. I focused my mind and tried to think of something. My mind cleared a little and seemed to lead the way as he continued to press and when his hand came up to tug in my hair I knew I had to end it. I pushed the thought through to stop. I thought it red hot and angry for him to stop. Then he released me with a gasp and grabbed his lip.

"Did you bite me?" he said in shock.

"No," I answered and rubbed my lips, as if to rub him off.

"It felt like you...shocked me."

I held in my smug satisfaction, knowing I'd caused whatever it was he felt. I had no idea how but didn't doubt that I'd done something.

"I don't know, Chad. Maybe it was the universe telling you that you shouldn't keep kissing a girl once she tries to push you away."

He paled.

"That's not what- I wasn't. I just wanted to make you see that I do want you."

"And you did. Maybe if you'd kissed me like that last year, we'd still be together," I said softly and made my way to the door. I turned once. "I really do hope everything works out for you, but I'm happy where I am." And then I closed the door.

"Maggie Masters." I startled at the harshness of my father's voice. "I did not raise you to behave this way."

I turned on the light in the foyer and but didn't see him. So I peeked in the kitchen. He was standing at the sink in front of the window. Aha. So he saw Chad's little love display. Great.

"That was Chad, Dad, not me."

"You let him."

"Did you see what happened? Because if you did, you must have seen him grab me."

How was I being blamed for this?

"Maggie, I'm not just talking about Chad. You can't lead these boys on like this."

"What are you talking about?"

"You leave with one guy this morning and not too long after another boy comes by, the Jacobson boy, Kyle, and then tonight, Chad sat on the steps for over an hour waiting on you. You can't do this, it's not right."

"Ok. First, Caleb is the one, ok. He's the only one I'm interested in. Kyle is a friend. And Chad dumped me. How was I supposed to know he was sitting here waiting for me like that?"

"Ok," he conceded and sat in one of the chairs at the table. "So Caleb. What can I expect with you two?"

"I don't know what you mean?" I asked as I jumped to sit on the counter.

"I mean are you going to get silly about him and try to follow him to college or something."

I sat and looked at him. There was no point in lying. He couldn't stop me from seeing Caleb; it was literally life or death.

"Maybe. I haven't decided yet."

"So...being boy crazy is what it's gonna take to get you to go to college?" he said dryly and his mouth turned up in amusement.

"What?" I asked, stunned by his question.

He actually seemed happy about the idea.

"You always had such big plans until last year, always had good grades, I assumed you'd go but after this year I wasn't sure if you still wanted to or not. You've barely made it to high school everyday, let alone thinking about college."

"I do want to," I admitted, "but no college is going to accept me, Dad. I blew it."

"Well, you won't know for sure until you try."

"So. You're saying you won't have a problem if I enroll at Tennessee with Caleb next semester?"

"Well, you won't be enrolling *with* him, you'll be enrolling in the college that he happens to attend, one year ahead of you. But yes, I'm saying, I wouldn't have a problem with that. In fact, I'd be thrilled for you to go to college. That is if Caleb doesn't mind you tagging along, of course."

"He won't mind," I said grinning.

"Well, still, I think I'll have a talk with him. I planned to anyway if you're going off to college alone together. He needs to know the boundaries-"

"I get it, Dad. You want to put him through the ringer about my virtue and respectability, sex and parties and staying at his place. I get it. I understand. Go ahead."

He scoffed and sat looking at me like I was blue or something. "Ok," he finally said.

"Ok," I agreed. I jumped off the counter and bent to kiss his cheek. "Goodnight. Love you, Daddy."

"Love you, too, baby girl."

Thirteen

After I brushed my teeth vigorously to get rid of anything Chad and took a shower, my bed was calling my name. I had no idea what Caleb had planned. He promised he'd come back, work it out somehow for sleeping tonight. I believed in him but no matter his powers of persuasion, there was no way my dad was letting him up here tonight.

So I texted him once I was out of the shower and I was so giddy to be texting him. I wrote-

Hey. Drama over. Ready when you are. - Maggie.

He wrote-

Good, I'm dying here ;)

I sat and started to read instead, because otherwise, I would just pace and if I sat on my bed I'd fall asleep in no time.

After careful consideration of my wardrobe, I curled up in my cami and cherry sleep pants in the club chair in the corner of my room. I didn't want him to think I was trying to be sexy, but I didn't want to look like a frump either. But I needed to be wearing something that he could easily reach my skin. I gnawed my bottom lip in anticipation of tonight. I mean it didn't mean anything really. I'd slept with him before, once. It's just sleep, I knew that, but for some reason, tonight it felt like so much more. Like this was a step for us towards something.

So I read my favorite book, Pride and Prejudice. I'd worn down the pages so much that the binding barely held anymore. I know it's the cliché favorite girl's book but I can't help it. It was a perfect story. Elizabeth is the typical girl with confidence yet insecurities and family drama and Mr. Darcy was a fine specimen of what a man should be like.

After I'd read for about twenty minutes I started to be curious. I didn't want to text him again and seem clingy or controlling but I was worried that he'd already tried to come and Dad had turned him away.

Then I heard the tink of something hitting my window. My heart leapt in giddiness. There's a guy tossing rocks at my window! It was a very classic movie moment for me. I eased it open and looked down to see Caleb smiling up at me.

It had to be the second floor, he thought to me.

I gasped at his words in my mind and laughed happily but quietly and shrugged. He began to climb up the drainpipe and then hooked his leg over the porch roof. He pulled himself up and walked over easily to the window.

"Can I come in?" he asked.

"Yes." I moved back so he had room. "So this was the big plan? To sneak in?" I jested.

"Yep. I couldn't think of anything else. Does your door lock?"

I went to it and turned the little bolt to lock it. I came back to him as he shucked his backpack.

"I brought snacks," he chimed and pulled out two packs of honey buns.

"Ah! Yay!" I took mine and unwrapped it enough to take a bite. "You totally get points for remembering."

"That's what I was going for," he laughed. He took a bite of his too and devoured it in two more bites. "Hey, pretty good."

"How have you not had a honey bun before?"

He shrugged. "Not sure. My favorite snacks are macadamia nut cookies. My mom always makes them for me and mails them to my apartment once a week."

"Aw, that's nice. I like cookies, too, but honey buns are just the right amount of sweet," I said and smiled, but that turned into a yawn.

"Sleepy again?" he asked and pulled me to sit on the bed beside him.

"Yeah. I can't believe it but I am."

"So, what happened with the guy?" His voice was a little hard. "Did I win the bet?"

"Yes," I sighed reluctantly. "I shouldn't feel guilty, he dumped *me*, but I do a little. He was pretty upset."

"He wanted to get back together, and you said no?"

"What else would I say?"

"I don't know; that you regret what happened."

"You mean you? I regret you?" He stayed silent, but that was answer enough. "No. Of course I don't. He hasn't given me half of what you have in just the few days I've known you and I told him that."

"He kissed you," he said so low I barely heard him.

"Yes," I answered truthfully and waited. Was he angry? Did his silence mean *he* regretted it? Was he disappointed because he thought I let him or wanted it? "I didn't let him if that's what you're thinking. In fact, I shocked him or... something when he wouldn't let go."

"Wouldn't let go?" he asked and I heard the edge to his tone.

"I handled it."

"Did he hurt you? Force you?" He moved to stand over me, tower over me. "Tell me the truth, Maggie."

"No, he didn't hurt me, just got a little carried away. I zapped him or whatever and told him I wanted you. And then I went inside."

His breathing was heavy and his face hard. "He better hope I don't see him walking around."

"It's ok." I stood, too, and placed my palm on his cheek. His breathing almost instantly calmed and he sighed, leaning into my hand. "Then Dad scolded me for it, like it was my fault. And then...he said he'd like it if I went to college next semester."

"He said that?"

"Yeah," I said softly and so hated to stomp on the hope in his voice. "But I can't go. I told you, I completely screwed up this year. The rest of the years won't matter. No one's going to let me in."

"Let us handle that. Will you? We have connections at Tennessee. If you're sure you want to go there, you're in."

"What kind of connections?"

"Well, Benjamin Franklin is the most famous."

"What was he your great, great, great uncle or something?"

"No," he laughed. "I meant hundreds, as in dollars. We furnished the library in the Jacobson family name. Plus all colleges give alumni special privileges."

My heart skipped at the idea, but plummeted in the next beat. "But I don't have any college money. My mom took it when she left and my dad let things go too badly to help me with loans."

"Don't worry about it. My dad wants to take care of it."

"What! Like pay my way to college?" I stared at him. "No way. I couldn't let him do that."

"Why not? He has the money, that's what it's there for; family." He brought his head to mine. "You're family now. Anything that's ours is yours."

"Caleb, it's too much."

"No it isn't. Just think about it, ok? I'm not guessing here. He already talked to me about it. Same way with the house. It's your house now, too."

I hadn't even kissed him yet and he was already trying to pay for my college.

"Not me, my father," he corrected, reading my thoughts. "He wants to, he lives for it. We all help each other. It's why everyone works so hard in our family."

I looked at him and saw he was completely serious and sincere.

"Ok, I'll think about it, but it's pretty crazy and I'm not really comfortable with the whole paying-my-way thing."

He nodded and continued to look down at me. "Did I tell you how cute you look in pajamas?"

"Yeah," I giggled. "I think you did. Nice subject change, by the way."

"It worked," he smirked and it defined his dimple.

I couldn't wait another second.

I bit my lip as I slid my hands up his chest to his neck to rest in his hair. It was curly and soft as I pushed my fingers through it. He closed his eyes and groaned a little when I scratched and ran them through the strands. It was exactly like I imagined it was.

"I've wanted to do that ever since you knocked me to the pavement," I said easily and smiled.

He looked like he was having trouble with his breaths. I remembered what he had said that day, about being more affected by my touch than I was to his.

He reached out and did the same to me, ran his fingers through my hair and down my neck. It felt better than anything ever before it. He leaned down to kiss my forehead. I pulled his face down, moving his lips from my forehead to my mouth. I paused for just a second and saw his eyes flash before I pulled him down and...and then we were *finally* kissing. His fingers tightened in my hair as I pressed my lips to his. When our mouths opened together, it was almost like imprinting all over again.

I felt a tingling burn start at my lips and move outwards down my neck, a cold in my veins and hot on my skin as my body zinged with a jolt of tremors and shocks and a heavy fog seemed to blanket the room, like morphine. I was calm, almost too calm, but also enraptured with him and his lips.

I got flashes and glimpses from Caleb and saw that he was feeling the same thing, but we didn't stop. I moved my fingers to the back of his neck and felt the gentle pressure of his tongue. I could barely take what was happening to me.

And then he gently pushed me back to lie on the bed, placing himself over me, never breaking the kiss.

While my pulse rioted in my body under his, my lips pushed harder. I pulled my knees up to be on either side of him as I was pressed into the mattress. I had a strange feeling like this is what Rachel and Gran had been trying to tell us about. That eventually it would be like a dam would break and we'd be unable to control ourselves with each other.

But I wasn't accustomed to letting something else control me. I knew we could be trusted with each other, that we could enjoy the other, but not get carried away.

I fought for control. I felt the fog lift slowly as I pulled away, our lips were barely apart and we shared breath as we panted and fought to get a grip.

"Ah," he breathed. "That's what I've been missing with you? You've got to be kidding me," he said hoarsely and then laughed a strained chuckle as he stroked my cheek with the back of his fingers.

I didn't know what to say. In my mind that may as well have been my first kiss because nothing before it even mattered. I smiled up at him. He eased off me slowly, pulling me to sit up even as he moved to sit in the chair.

"I, uh, think I better sit over here for a minute."

I felt confused. Did he really think he couldn't control himself? Why was he moving away? Did I go too fast? I thought he wanted me to? Was I not any good? It was almost funny to me that I'd never had any of these concerns with Chad.

He came back to kneel in front of me on the floor, between my knees. He put his hands on my hips and squeezed once. "Are you for real? Of course I wanted you to. And it was good. Too good. I just don't want things to get out of control."

"You don't think we can control ourselves?" I asked and gave him a questioning look.

"Well, my mom explained that it's really intense. And it was. I know you felt it."

"Yes, I did, but we stopped just fine. Look, no offense to your mad skills," he laughed and shook his head, "but I think I can handle it. I'm not afraid of you losing control with me and I'm not worried about me not being able to stop you either. You'd never hurt me. Your parents trusted us to be alone, didn't they?"

"Yeah, but my mom is worried about you. She thinks that I'll persuade you to do something you don't want to, even if neither of us meant to. That I'll let it control me."

I was so confused. "Will you explain it to me, please? You keep talking about this, but I don't understand. It's worse for you?"

"Yes, in a way. It's uncomfortable." His cheeks actually turned pink as he looked away. "The males are the protectors and leaders of the clan. The way I feel about you is more than just...affection, which I feel plenty of. I feel protective of you above everything else and concerned about your welfare. When I'm not with you, I spend the whole time trying to tell myself that you're ok, that you're safe, that you don't need me right that second. It's like a steady constant stream running through my mind."

I licked my lips nervously. "I'm sorry, I didn't know it was like that for you."

"No," he insisted and grabbed my face gently. "No, no. I want it that way. It helps me keep you safe. And it helps me keep you happy. I can't always read your mind unless I'm trying but I can feel what you feel, especially when you have a spike of adrenaline or emotion. And you know how you can feel my heartbeat sometimes?" I nodded. "I can always feel yours. Always, even when I'm not with you, beating right next to mine."

I thought about all the times he'd touched me and my heart raced. All the times I'd watched him and thought about him and it skipped and jumped. I'm sure my face was as red as a beet.

"This," he continued, "is why I didn't tell you all this yet. I didn't want you to feel weird around me or be embarrassed and I still don't. I wanted you to be yourself so you could get to know me."

I had a thought. "That's how you knew Chad kissed me?" I accused him, but it came out as barely a whisper, feeling the heat in my cheeks.

"Yeah," he said and flashed a second of irritation on his face before he settled for a slight scowl. "You see, your heartbeats sound different when you're excited and when you're distressed."

I flushed brighter, the heat almost unbearable. "I was not excited that he was kissing me," I said vehemently.

"I know that." His thumbs caressed my cheeks making me shiver. "But your body involuntarily reacts when someone kisses you. I figured it out and it took all my willpower to trust you and not come over here to pummel him." That made me laugh. He nuzzled his nose with mine. "What I was getting at, is that I feel everything you do, but because I feel my own feelings plus yours, it's just a lot harder for me. If I'm touching you and you like it... it all just adds together and makes me want to touch you even more," he said gruffly and wrapped his arms around my waist. "It feels sometimes like I couldn't stop touching you for anything." He brushed his lips against mine.

"I don't see why that's a bad thing," I murmured against his lips.

"It's not. I just want you to understand that if we get carried away, it won't be me that stops us. I don't know if I could."

"I'm not worried. I told you. I have no problem with making sure we don't go too far, ok? I trust you."

"I'm glad. I want you to trust me. I want you to feel completely safe with me. I would never hurt you, Maggie, and I'd never let anything happen to you."

"I know that," I insisted.

"You," he took my hand and held it to his chest where our hearts beat together, "are in me now. You're everything. All I want is for you to be happy and safe. I *need* you to be. Don't ever be afraid to tell me things. If I'm being too pushy, crowding or controlling you or getting on your nerves, just say the word."

"I don't think I could not like those things," I said sweetly.

"Maggie, I'm serious."

"So am I." I pulled him to me, wrapping my arms around his neck. "I want you to be happy, too. I want you to tell me the same things. Everything is going to be fine. We'll both be honest and it's not like we can't read each other's thoughts and feelings anyway. It's not like I could hide it if I was annoyed, right?"

He smiled sadly. "No, not really."

There was something he wasn't telling me. I could feel it hanging there. I reached out in my mind and pushed. His gaze shot to mine and he knew I was looking for something. He let down any resistance and closed his eyes. We were completely open to each other, connected.

I could see how he still felt my choices were being taken away. He thought I'd still be with Chad and would never have given him the time of day had things not happened like they did. He was so extremely worried and upset over this echoling thing, pissed even. He also wanted to kiss me again and it almost hurt to restrain himself and it hurt me to know that. To actually feel the way it pulled him to me and wanted him to just consume me with passion. I had no idea he was feeling this way around me.

But the most important thing I saw was that he loved me.

He had no intentions of telling me because he thought I'd freak and think it was way too soon. But what he didn't understand is that *I did*. I understood how crazy and unconventional this all was but we were bound together and I wasn't scared anymore. That could not be denied. And though I didn't know him that well, something in me did. It recognized him and chose him as he chose me because we were meant for each other.

And I loved him, too.

His eyes went wide at my thought. I didn't say it out loud, nor did he, but there it was and I didn't think I'd ever seen a bigger smile on his face.

He pulled my face close, his fingers bunched in my hair.

"Maggie," he sighed.

"You didn't take my choices away. And Chad and I were never meant to be together. You and I are," I insisted. "And I've set the pace now. You don't have to wait for me anymore," I whispered teasingly and smiled.

He wasted no time in pulling me the small space between us and letting me feel just how he felt about that. We kept the connection between our minds open directly as he kissed me sweetly. Usually I caught glimpses and flashes involuntarily but when we focused on keeping the wall down completely it was a tidal wave of emotions and thoughts.

I didn't lie back this time, knowing how intense everything was. But I did push myself to the edge of the bed and let him kiss me senseless as his arms enveloped me tight and warm, him still on his knees in between mine. And he was a perfect gentleman. Well... about as gentlemanly as one can be with their mouth devouring someone else's. His hands didn't try to wander to places they shouldn't, though in his mind he wanted to. His body so wanted to.

He was also embarrassed by that but I made sure he knew I wanted him to want me. That I wanted him. That was the point, wasn't it? The thing I never had with Chad, he didn't want me physically, sexually or long term relationship wise until he knew he couldn't have me. And to be honest, apparently neither did I. I wanted someone to want me in all ways and someone who I wanted the same in return. And I'd found him.

His hands on my hips flexed once, reminding me that it was late and it had been a pretty intense and emotional night already. So I pulled back easily. While we caught our breath I kissed him once more before shifting back to crawl towards my pillow and then threw the blanket back.

I nodded my head towards me for him to come.

He chuckled as he stood and shucked his shirt. I'm sure my eyes bulged, but I kept it together mostly. It was awfully nice under that shirt. He had a tattoo of a hollow green star on one shoulder and an armband of black swirl filigree on the other. I recognized it as the design on the gate of his house.

He turned the lamp off and I heard rustling of fabric so I assumed he was putting on sleep clothes. Then the bed ducked and he climbed in beside me.

I hesitated for only a second. Even Chad and I had never slept together, even only to sleep. I tentatively reached over and my hand brushed soft t-shirt and hard skin underneath. He didn't hesitate however. He pulled me right to his chest.

I saw a blue screen in the dark.

"Setting my cell alarm to vibrate so I'm out of here before your dad tries to come in," he explained.

"Good idea. Plus, I'm working tomorrow."

"How long is your shift?"

"Eleven to seven."

"Ouch. Ok, I guess I'll head over tomorrow night after your dad goes to bed. I have to go to my dad's tomorrow night and go over some things with him and some of my uncles, important family stuff, but I promise I'll come as soon as I'm done."

"This will be the longest we've been without each other," I mused, already feeling the sting of our imprints being apart.

"Yeah. You going to be ok? I can stop by your work maybe before I head to dad's?"

"Nah, I'll be ok. We need to try to make it work anyway, right? We can't spend every second together, especially when you go back to school. It'll probably be easier to wean ourselves," I said lamely and grimaced in the dark at my wording.

"But I so don't want to wean myself," he said as he nuzzled my ear making me giggle.

"Me either, but we need to. This'll be good practice."

"Yeah. Just remember, if it gets too bad just call me in your mind. If your body is distressed, I can hear you anyway and I'll come running."

"I know, thank you, but I'm sure I'll be fine."

"Yeah, but what about me?" he said and I could see his grin in the streetlight haze from the window.

"You'll be fine, too," I assured and smiled up at him.

He kissed the end of my nose. "I guess, but I'm always here for you. Even if I'm not here, I'm always tuned into you," he poked my chest gently, "in here."

"Yeah," I said and tried to keep the pout out of my voice at the thought of not seeing him until tomorrow night. "Night, Caleb."

"Night, Maggie."

Then he took my hand and placed it over his heart, his hand on top, rubbing circles over my knuckles, and I felt the beats of our hearts pounding together under my palm as I fell asleep.

Fourteen

That morning I woke rested. Completely rested and feeling great. I didn't feel the need to stretch or rub my eyes or lay there and adjust. When I woke, I was alert instantly. I thought I felt awesome after our nap yesterday but no, this morning was the epitome of a good night's rest.

Even Caleb seemed to be extra peppy.

I got up with him as he pulled his jeans on over his sleep pants and then changed his shirt. If I had a slow motion button I would've pressed it while Caleb pulled his shirt over his head. I bit my lip and watched intensely from my closet door. He smiled and shook his head reading my thoughts or feelings but kissed me chastely and told me I'd better watch it if I wanted him to ever leave. I just giggled while he lifted the window.

When he started to climb out he once again turned to me. I'm not sure who needed help being released this time, but we both just kinda erupted with it. He grabbed my face and I grabbed his shirt front and we both assured each other we'd see the other tonight that everything would be fine and they'd be missed. Then he kissed me again and practically shot himself out of the window and down the roof to the drainpipe. My body was already protesting a little at the distance, telling me I was going to need his touch sooner than I thought.

I watched and after one final wave as I lost sight of him after he left my yard. I went to unlock my door and got dressed. My uniform was a little dress with pockets and a half apron. My name tag read 'Sweet Pea'. The uniform was a little short but the owners wanted us all to wear white footless leggings underneath. It was kinda cute actually but without the leggings would have been borderline skanky dirty bar waitress.

So I got dressed. By this time it was almost 10:00. Caleb had left at nine. My dad never got out of bed before then with this job, his shift didn't start til 11:00, so it was perfect for him. My shifts used to be at night but they changed my schedule since I graduated.

So I went downstairs for breakfast which consisted of coffee and French vanilla creamer, which my dad had already placed in my travel mug for me. He hadn't done that since the 'event'.

Then Dad came back down and we talked for a few minutes about work and schedules and dinner plans. Then he actually picked up the paper to read it. He hadn't done that since the 'event'. Now that things were back to normal, that's what I planned on calling it; the 'event'.

I kind of felt proud that I brought him out of his funk, even if it was involuntary. He had reason to come back around to his old self, all because I was dating a new guy. Weird, but I liked it all the same.

After our completely normal morning, I kissed his cheek and thanked him for the coffee. He said 'bye, baby girl' which I've missed so much it clogged my throat with tears at knowing he was really back. Some girls might not like being called baby, especially by their father, but now, after everything that happened, I wanted it something fierce. It stood for something and the fact that he hasn't called me that since last summer and now just throws it around just like he always used to means that whatever had happened to him was serious. He really wasn't here and now he was back to normal, with all his old habits routine for him again.

So, there I was, heading into work. The five block walk in the mid morning was warm but not unbearably so. I passed a couple kids from school as they come bustling out of the coffee shop, giggling and holding each other's arms.

"Hey, Maggie," a girl, I thought her name was Leslie, called out.

"Hey," I returned, but didn't stop.

"What are you doing this summer?"

They fell into step beside me as I continued to walk on. They were both the grade below me, the grade I was in until I was stepped up from eighth grade to ninth.

"Um, right now I'm just working, college maybe in a couple months."

"Where are you headed? You following Chad to Florida?"

"Uh, no."

"Oh." She seemed perplexed by that. "Well, where are you going?"

"Tennessee maybe."

If only Caleb could hear me now. He would be grinning like a fool.

"Really. Why not Florida? I bet you could get Chad back if you went there."

"I don't want Chad back," I snapped, but sighed. "Sorry. Look, Leslie?" She nodded. "Chad and I haven't dated for almost a year now. I have no intentions of getting back with him."

"Aww, that's so sad," she crooned. "You guys were so cute together."

Thankfully, we came upon the diner, The 25 Hour Skillet. I turned to them and tried for a smile. "All right, I've got to go to work. Nice seeing you."

"You, too. See ya."

They waved and walked on and I turned into the revolving door and went inside. It felt like forever since I'd been there but the familiar warm air filled with the smell of homemade steak fries was as familiar as anything else in my life.

"Hey," Big John shouted over the sizzle of something on the grill, "cutting it close. You think just because you're so smart and you graduated you can be late anytime you want now? Is that it?" I put my hands on my hips and glared at him and he grinned. "Get over here, pretty girl, and give your ol' boss a hug."

I grinned, too, and ran behind the counter as he came from behind the grill and met me half way. He lifted my feet from the floor and squeezed me tight.

"Aww." I heard from behind me. When he put me down I turned to see Smarty, the boss' wife and head waitress, holding her order pad against her chest with her pen in her hair. "Our little girl is all grown up."

I hugged her, too. "Oh, come on. It's no big deal. People graduate all the time," I insisted.

"It *is* a big deal!" Big John said and grabbed something from under the register. He lifted it to my fingers. A small box. "Here, Sweet Pea. We got you a little something. We would have loved to have been there, but you know the grill never stops here."

"You didn't have to do this." I smiled at him and took it. I opened it slowly as Smarty and another waitress, Mena Bena, came closer to watch. I gasped. It was a little silver charm bracelet with a star charm already in place. The card underneath said 'We know we can't keep you forever, but we cherish you while we have you. Anywhere you go, whatever you do, you'll be a star. We love you, The 25 Hour Crew.'

The tears streamed down my face in record time. Smarty grabbed me into a warm hug. "Aww, sweetie," she crooned.

"Thank you guys," I squeaked out. "This means a lot to me. Really."

"No sweat. It's not much, but we wanted to do something for you," Big John said from behind me. He patted my back and went back to the grill. "So, how's your dad taking all this?"

I pulled myself from Smarty's grip and wiped my eyes as Mena put her arm around me. "He's actually...I don't know. He had some kind of breakthrough or something. He's almost back to his old self."

"Really," Mena said beside me, "well, that's great, honey."

"Yeah, it is."

I looked at them. Big John, I'm sure you can understand why he's called that. He's big and his name is...you guessed it. He's the owner and the best boss anyone could ever have, I might add. He's about forty five, bald, six seven and about two hundred seventy five pounds on him. So, big. His wife is Smarty, her real name is Alice but we all go by nicknames that Big John gives us so as to ward off stalkers. I think John just likes the feel it gives the place. She's about thirty five and a slim as a woman can be without being gross. Her blonde hair is always in a ponytail and she's the sweetest thing.

They both treated me like a daughter since I started working here right after both my parents abandoned ship, it was a perfect arrangement.

And then there are a few other waitresses that work here as well. Mena Bena, Rock Steady and Little Mama and another cook, Slim. I've never had any other job so I don't know what it's like anywhere else, but as much as I hear people complain it can't be like this place.

We all laugh and cut up. The cooks sling burgers, pancakes and eggs to each other. The crowd we get loves to see them doing their little show when we get busy. They yell orders loudly, along with our nicknames and we bustle about with the radio blaring country the whole time. The customers seem to eat up the atmosphere as much as the food.

The revolving door chimed to signal a customer so we all dispersed and I headed to the bathroom to clean up my smeared face.

When I returned, I grabbed my pad and got to work.

After the lunch rush and dinner rush my shift ended. It flew by today and I was surprised to find I wasn't as tired as I usually was. I blamed the good sleep I got from Caleb and secretly smiled. But I did feel the aches in my legs and back still. My head began to pound as I grabbed my purse and clocked out. I felt the ping of excitement as I realized I was about to see him.

I walked home briskly and put my bag on the foyer table as I came in the door. I went into the kitchen to see Dad trying to make dinner.

"Hey, Dad, what are you making?"

"Well," he sighed unhappily as he lifted a lid and wrinkled his nose, "I was trying to make risotto, but apparently, cooking rice isn't as easy as it sounds."

I stifled a giggle. "Well, I can make us some grilled cheese?"

"I guess if we want to eat you might have to. I can't cook. It's sad how much I depended on you and your mother to do everything for me."

"Dad." I hugged him from behind and he patted my hands. "It's ok. I'm not that great of a cook either. We'll work it out, but for now, grilled cheese sounds pretty good to me."

"You always take care of me," he said softly.

"It's no problem."

I went to the fridge to grab the stuff I needed and when I turned back he was gone. So I made the sandwiches and called upstairs for him. He came down and thanked me for the sandwich, but ate in easy silence. When he was done he washed his plate and then took mine from me to wash as well. Then he smiled and kissed my forehead.

"Night. Sleep tight."

"Goodnight, Dad."

I then made my way upstairs, feeling lots of aches in my legs and back. My head pulsed with a headache so I took a scalding shower, placing my new bracelet on the sink, and waited for Caleb to get here so he could take it all away.

He came up and climbed in the window I'd left open almost as soon as I sat down in my chair. I ran to the window to greet him. He dropped his bag to the floor and pulled me into a feet-off-the floor hug. I moaned out loud as my face rubbed his neck and it eased every pain away. He chuckled.

"Me, too," he whispered.

He cupped my chin and pulled my face up to kiss him. His lips were eager, but soft as he kissed my mouth and his arms enveloped me. The warm sensation spread from my lips to my face and neck. I finally pulled away and felt a ping of cold at the loss.

"Can we go to bed now? I'm just so ready to lie down with you," I pleaded.

"Yeah," he said firmly, like it was his idea.

This time he pulled off his jeans and stayed in his boxers leaving his t-shirt on. I silently compared him to Chad, mentally putting up a wall to block him first, of course…hopefully. Chad's legs were skinny and really hairy. Caleb's were thicker and tan with some hair, but not too much. The short view of his hips I had showed the same similarities. Where Caleb was more bulky and tan, Chad was skinnier and hairy. I have to say I was enjoying the change up.

We lay down after I put in Robin Hood, the one with Russell Crowe, on my little TV sitting on my dresser. I practically threw myself over him to lie on his chest as he wrapped his arm around me. He sighed several times as he ran his fingers through my hair and down my arm.

"You like Robin Hood?" he asked.

"I like all the Robin Hood movies, even men in tights."

"Really," he laughed. "That's an odd girl choice."

"I'm an odd girl," I sighed.

"You're not odd. You're just different, in a good way."

I smiled and nestled in closer. "So, how did it all go with your dad today?

"Good. We've got the family helping us try to figure something out. Try to see what it is that Marcus is doing." I nodded. "Today was almost unbearable," he admitted into my hair.

"Yeah, it wasn't fun," I said and wondered if he ached the way I had. "And I have to work tomorrow, too."

"Mmm," he groaned. "What time do you go in?"

"Same," I sighed.

"Well, we're definitely testing the limits of our separation, aren't we?" he said wryly. "Maybe we can see a movie or something after you get off. If you want to."

"Yeah," I said through a yawn, feeling utterly loose and at peace after spending the last few hours in complete knots.

"Great. Go to sleep, Maggie," he ordered softly.

"Thanks for staying with me so I can sleep. I felt better this morning than I ever have, I think."

He kissed my forehead. "There's nowhere else I want to be."

And I fell asleep before he even finished his sentence.

The next day was pretty similar. It was horrible saying goodbye to him that morning knowing I wouldn't see him until after work again, my veins protesting at the thought. He kissed me as we said goodbye and it was borderline painful. He tried to pull away and I reached around his neck to keep him there. He groaned a little against my lips so I didn't think he was complaining, but he had to go and I had to start getting ready for work so I pulled from him and licked my lips as if to keep the taste of him.

"Miss you already," he declared gruffly.

"I can't wait for tonight."

"Me either. Have a good day at work."

I nodded and that seemed to be enough to release me and he took off out the window as I ran to get ready.

I made sure to grab my bracelet before heading down and went slowly through my coffee and breakfast routine. Dad was MIA. Washing clothes in the basement I assumed as I heard the steady bang of the washer against the wood slats. I shook my head at him but smiled at the same time.

I got to work and it was pretty busy already so I got right to it. The hours flew by in unheard of fashion and soon I was clocking out with aching legs and a pounding behind my eyes. I longed for Caleb and knew I would see him in a few minutes had my fingers twitching with anticipation.

When I checked my phone in my purse, I had a text.

Sorry. So, so sorry. I can't make it tonight for movie. Helping my dad with some important stuff, but I'll come later tonight and climb through your window, Juliet, if you'll still have me?

My heart plummeted. As I waved to everyone and walked through the revolving door, I sat on the bench outside, not wanting to go home yet.

Though I was disappointed, I understood that I wasn't the only thing in his life, just like he wasn't mine - hello, I'd just spent all day at work - and texted back.

It's ok. And you can climb through my window anytime, Romeo. Can't wait.

I waited and leaned back on the bench feeling the effects of not being with Caleb all day starting to dominate my thoughts. I felt more tired and my back was starting to feel crampy. It was amazing how this worked. It sucked but it was amazing.

My phone dinged with a message.

You're an angel. I promise to make it up to you. Can't wait to see you. Be there after 10:00 with a snack :)

I stood, threw my phone into my bag and almost ran into someone.

Kyle.

"Hey," he said with a hand to steady me on my arm.

"Hey," I said and pulled away gently. "I'm just getting off."

"I know. I hoped I'd catch you before you got home."

I looked at him quizzically. "Caleb sent me to watch out for you." Now I knew that was a flat lie and gave him a look that said so. He recanted. "Ok. He didn't *send me,* but I knew he was gone so I figured I'd come keep you company."

"How do you know he's gone?"

"Because he's with my dad. All the men, including Caleb - if you want to call him that - are meeting tonight to discuss you."

"Me?" I said, my voice entirely too high.

"Yep, you. Apparently they are going to sneak onto the Watson compound and try to find out something about the echoling."

"Watson? Is that what Marcus is?"

"Yep."

Then I really heard what he said.

"Wait. They're going to sneak into the compound? You mean their house right?"

"Yeah."

"So, Caleb is off sneaking into a rival clan's house right now with who knows what kinds of abilities these guys have."

"Pretty much."

"You're not worried?" I asked in question to his easy tone.

"It's not my concern," he spat. "At least that's what I was told when I asked to go. But only those who have ascended are allowed at these meetings and since I'm most definitely not ascended, I was told to stay put."

"But Caleb isn't ascended either."

"No, but he's close enough," he said kicking the bench with the toe of his shoe.

I felt sick. Knowing Caleb didn't have his abilities yet but was breaking into a place where they had plenty of people who did and all because of me. All because some guy threatened me. I was sick thinking about what could happen to Caleb and his family. My hands trembled with wanting to call him but I didn't think that was a good idea.

An image of him sneaking behind someone and his phone ringing, alerting them to his presence, played over in my head.

"So anyway, since he abandoned you - because I knew he was supposed to take you to the movies tonight - I figured I'd come save you," he said and winked.

"Kyle," I said softly. "I'm not sure that's a good idea."

"Why? Because I'm in love with you?" he spouted bluntly and I almost choked.

"Yes." I started to step away. "I'm just gonna go home, ok?"

"Mags, I'm not gonna do anything about it, ok? It's useless. It's not like I could actually steal you from him. Please? You're still my friend aren't you?"

"Yes, but I…" I sighed. "I don't think Caleb would like it if we hung out."

"He can't tell you who to hang out with. Are you saying he doesn't trust you?" he said snidely.

"He doesn't trust you," I countered.

He grimaced.

"Come on, Mags. You have to know I'd never hurt you. Look." He stepped back another step. "If you don't want to that's fine, I'll just walk you home and head to mine, but I'd like to do something. I won't say anything remotely in the same ballpark as flirting and I'll keep at least three feet between us. Promise."

He smiled angelically and I couldn't help but chuckle.

"Kyle, It's not that I don't trust you. I just...I don't want you to be uncomfortable and I don't want me to be either. I miss hanging out with you and I want to still be your friend, I do, but we can't be anything more than that. I love-" I stopped and his eyes widened in horror but he quickly contained his expression to blankness. He knew I was about to say I loved Caleb. "I will never do anything to hurt Caleb," I rephrased.

"Ok. Ok. I understand and I agree. I mean, he was my best friend." He shook his head looking tired and sad. "We used to spend every weekend and summer together." He screwed up his lips. "I don't want to hurt him either."

"Ok." I smiled. "Then yes. We can do something but I'd like to change first."

I motioned to my outfit.

"It's ok. We don't have to see a movie. We can go to the park. You can push me on the swing."

I laughed. When Chad and I were together and we all used to hang out as a group, we used to go there and play around at night. There's a couple big playgrounds and a bridge over the lake, lots of huge oak trees. It was a good place to play Spotlight. Which is hide and seek with flashlights, if you didn't know.

I nodded to him.

"Ok."

He grinned and waved his hand, dramatically bowing for me to lead the way. We walked the few streets over to the park as he told me about the meetings Caleb was attending. They were called Rite gatherings. Every male that had ascended from the clan attended on a monthly basis. They scheduled the meetings on a different day every month so other clans wouldn't get any ideas about ambushing or attacking the ones left behind.

They discussed the company, the school, family issues or events, safety measures. It was the only time that everyone was together. And tonight, they were discussing me. I felt even sicker.

I couldn't stop the worrying for Caleb as I listened. If something happened to him-

I groaned involuntarily. Kyle sighed beside me.

"Don't think about him. I thought we went over this."

"I can't help it. You told me he's in danger, because of me, no less. What else am I supposed to do?"

"I didn't say he was in danger. I said he was sneaking." He looked at me and smiled. "He didn't tell you did he?"

"Tell me what?" I said confused at why he would be smiling at a time like this.

He chuckled.

"So modest, our Caleb. Our clan, the Jacobson clan, is famous. We are the most powerful clan in Virtuoso history. When we ascend, our abilities are way more useful and powerful than most clans. They fear us."

"Marcus didn't seem to fear you, or me," I muttered.

"That's because we haven't ascended yet. Think about it. They've had an echoling this whole time. Now granted, that's pretty powerful but it's usually unheard of in other clans. The last one I've ever known about was my great, great grandfather. So they've had this powerful weapon this whole time and were too scared to use it. They knew they didn't have the other resources for an attack so why bother? Once you ascend, they won't mess with you either. They are using it to their advantage right now. They have lame abilities like changing things from one color to another and talking to animals."

I felt some better at his words but still didn't understand everything.

"Caleb told me his parent's abilities, and I know about your parents and Gran but what about everyone else?"

"Well, I have an uncle who can see into the future, only fifty seconds, but still." I gaped at him but he went on. "His wife can see someone's past. My other aunt can recognize any herb, spice, plant, tree or weed and know exactly what to do with it. She can tell you what plant will cure a fever then turn around and make the most wicked quiche you've ever had. She's awesome. And then her husband can make anything grow. Like right then, he can make a tree bud grow to a full size tree right before your eyes. It's amazing. When we were kids, he would make vines chase us across the yard." He laughed. "And then I have this cousin..."

He smiled and laughed and I couldn't help but notice the affection and pride he had for his family as he continued to explain everyone's abilities. I could see what they meant by the abilities complimenting each other when you were significants. All the married members of his family's abilities went hand in hand with each other. I found myself being anxious and a little giddy at thinking about what Caleb and my abilities would be. Then I started thinking about Caleb again and the ache in my legs and arms got worse.

We made it to the park and sat on the swings. I laughed as he kept going higher than me in a silent challenge. We walked over the bridge and he told me that he was looking forward to getting to college and wondered if Caleb had talked me into going yet. I glanced at him curiously and he just smiled and shrugged saying he knew his cousin.

He was supposed to room with Caleb at his apartment, but that was apparently not going to work now. I felt bad for him and assured him that if the decision was made for me to go, and I hadn't decided yet, that he would be more than welcome to stay at the apartment with us. He smiled sadly and said, "We'll see".

Eventually it started to sprinkle and we made our way out of the park. Then it started to rain, then a torrential downpour. He took his jacket off and held it over us as we tried to swiftly walk to my house. By the time we got there I was drenched and dripping, freezing and my fingers were numb.

"Mags, I'm so sorry," he said fervently on my porch. "I had no idea it was supposed to rain. It was nice out earlier."

"It's ok," I said through chattering teeth.

My dad opened the door behind me and took in the scene.

"Good Lord, Maggie! Get in here. Kyle, you, too."

"No sir, thank you. I'm gonna head home."

"Let me drive you."

"No, no thank you. I'm already soaked."

"Kyle," he said firmly, "I will not let you walk home in this. You get your butt in here while I get my shoes on and then I'm driving you," he said leaving no room to argue.

"Yes, sir."

Kyle had been in my house many times over the years. Our group used to come here and watch movies sometimes together and we always handed out candy to kids on Halloween from my house. It was a tradition, but no more. This past year was the first year we hadn't done that since I was in third grade.

He came in behind me as my father pushed me towards the stairs.

"You go take a hot shower, right now. I'll check on you when I get back," Dad said.

"Ok. Bye, Kyle," I said as my dad went in search of his shoes. "And thanks."

"For drowning you?" he asked smiling.

"For thinking about me and taking the time to explain things. I really appreciate it."

He shrugged.

"Well, you're one of us now. It's only right you know what you're getting into," he chimed and smirked.

I just laughed softly as my father came back in.

"Let's go, Jacobson." He looked at me. "You. Shower. Now."

"Ok, ok."

As I trudged upstairs, heavy with rainwater, I hoped Dad checked on me sooner rather than later so I didn't have to worry about him coming in to find Caleb in his daughter's bed.

Fifteen

After my shower, I put on my pajamas and went downstairs to get something to eat, but my throat was already starting to hurt so I decided on a glass of juice instead and went back upstairs to sit in my chair and wait. It'd been almost an hour since I got home and I was already feeling sick.

I sighed in aggravation. One little rain and I was gonna have the flu and miss work. I heard a knock on my door and Dad peeked in.

"How are you feeling?"

"Fine," I lied so he wouldn't spend all night checking on me. "Thanks."

"How was work?" he asked as he came to stand over me.

"Good. They gave me this."

I showed him the bracelet still on my wrist. He examined it and smiled.

"Very pretty, what was it for?"

I was reluctant to say and now wished I hadn't said anything at all.

"Graduation present," I muttered softly.

Dad hadn't gotten me anything, barely said anything to me except a muttered congrats and I spent all graduation day doing laundry and dishes while he watched television.

"Oh," he said and looked about as shamed as I'd ever seen him. But then fit on a weak smile. "Well, that was very nice of them."

"Yeah, it was."

"I'll have to thank Big John for looking out for you." He squatted in front of my chair. "Maggie, I know I said it already but I feel like I need to say it again. I'm sorry."

"It's ok, Dad. I forgave you, that means it's done. Don't worry about it, you're more than making up for it now."

"And you're sweet to forgive me, but a father can't just pretend like he didn't abandon his daughter for months while he moped around. I promise you, I'm going to do everything I can to make it up to you. I love you, baby girl."

I accepted his hard hug and muffled a reply to him.

"I love you, too, Dad. I never stopped."

"I know." He pulled back to look at me. "That's what makes this all so surreal."

"Dad," I protested.

"I mean it. I expected you to be angry and you were, but... I never expected you to forgive me so easily. I don't deserve you."

"Come on, Dad. Jeez," I groaned.

"All right, all right." He kissed my forehead. "I'll check on you later."

"No need, Dad. I'm really tired from work. I'm fine, just gonna head to bed."

"Ok. Goodnight."

"Night, Dad."

I waited until I heard his footsteps on the stairs and then went to lock my door. I sprawled myself out on the bed and felt my throat with my hand. It was uncomfortably sore and I was very tired now. I knew I should get up. I glanced at the clock and saw it was still only 9:30. I needed to get up so I didn't fall asleep when Caleb wasn't here.

But that's not what happened.

I woke later. I must have just dozed off for a second and I sighed in relief as I looked around and realized everything was fine and the same. I silently chastised myself for being so stupid. I sat up and checked the clock. Yep, dozed. The clock read 9:36.

I ran my fingers through my hair and checked my phone. I decided I'd read again and wait for Caleb. I twirled a strand of my hair nervously and got about two sentences read when I heard a noise out my window.

I jumped up excited because Caleb was early. On my way to the window a spike of black hair entered my window instead of shaggy brown. I immediately backed away but he was in the window and closing it before I could think to do anything else.

Marcus turned to me and smiled sweetly.

"Maggie," he said softly.

"How did you get in here?" I said panicked.

"The window?" he said and cocked a brow.

"I'm not dreaming?" I muttered more to myself than him.

I tried to think, looked around at my room and the clock. Everything seemed normal when my other dreams had been strange and distorted.

"No, not a dream. I wanted to come see you myself." He took a deep breath and looked upset. "You see...your boyfriend and his family broke into my father's house tonight. They thought we didn't know. They thought we were planning something for you. It was just me. My uncle and I were messing with you. I'm sorry, I didn't mean anything by it. I was jealous. It wasn't fair that Caleb got to imprint and I didn't."

He shook his head and sat on the edge of the bed.

"My family was ready for them. I tried to tell them not to worry about it. That it wasn't a big deal, it didn't matter, but you don't tell my old man anything. He was determined that this was the chance we needed to end the Jacobson clan."

"What are you talking about?" I asked and heard the tears in my voice, understanding what he was getting at and not wanting to hear the words, but needing to.

"Maggie, I'm sorry," he choked.

"What? Tell me!" I yelled.

"He didn't make it. My father, he… I told him to stop! I told him we didn't need to go this far, but he felt threatened. He shot Caleb. Caleb is dead, along with his father and a couple others."

I fell to the floor to my knees, my legs refusing to hold me up.

"No," I breathed.

"I'm so sorry, Maggie. I never wanted this."

"No!"

My heart crumbled and my lungs heaved violently for air. My ears were ringing and the stars in front of my eyes made me think I might lose consciousness.

He crouched down beside me when I started to sob. But I focused on him to hear every word, I needed to hear it.

"Shh," he ordered softly. "You don't want to wake your dad do you? Look, Kyle brought me here. He's in his father's car outside. I just came from their house. Someone had to tell them what happened. He drove me here to tell you. He thought it'd be better coming from me."

"Kyle's here?" I sniffed and somehow got up on wobbly legs, walked to the window and saw the silver Audi on my curb. I could imagine Kyle fuming in agony in the car, feeling guilty because he had wanted to be there. "How is he?" I croaked and grabbed the window ledge for stability.

"Upset. It'd be better for both of you if you were together. I'm done, Maggie. I'm not going back home to live with that monster." He stood and turned full to face me again. "I'm sorry. I wish I could take it back."

I didn't know what to say. My heart was beating so fast I could barely see anymore. Everything was blurry and all I wanted to do was crawl under my covers and cry forever. I heard him say my name a few times and it sounded far away before I snapped back to reality.

"Maggie, come on. I'll take you downstairs to Kyle. Grab a jacket, its cold out there."

I followed his instructions numbly and went to my closet to grab my black hoodie. I didn't even change out of my cami and green sleep pants. I just slipped on my flip flops and let him open my door and lead me downstairs. I passed the clock in the hall and saw it was 9:51 now. My dad must have been asleep because the house was quiet and dark. I didn't turn on any lights just followed him outside.

The car was on and idling with its lights off. My porch light was on and it made the misting rain seem to sparkle in the dark. I wrapped my jacket tighter around me. The rain felt good on my hot swollen face, but I knew it didn't matter. The crying wasn't gonna stop anytime soon.

How do you go on without your soul mate? We'd barely even gotten to be together and now he was taken from me without warning and without cause and something inside me was missing. Not only was I upset and hurt and broken, I was angry.

A new desperate sob caught in my throat and Marcus looked back at me in sympathy. "Come on, Maggie. Let's get you out of the rain."

I nodded and stepped off the walkway and towards the car. I looked back at my dark house and knew nothing would ever be the same again. He opened the door for me and I hesitated.

I don't know why, but I did. I just felt like getting in that car made it official or...maybe that Marcus seemed to be hurrying me along. I wondered why. I once again examined the possibility of this being a dream but it couldn't be.

Everything was too real. I peeked inside the car at the driver, Kyle, but he was turned away from me with his head buried in his hands.

That's when I knew something was not right. I knew Kyle and even if his uncle and cousin were dead, he'd never just sit there. He would have gotten out and greeted me if nothing else. He would be worried about me, knowing how I'd feel about my soul mate being gone and most important of all, and the thing I should have noticed before, he would never have sent Marcus in my house to get me knowing how I felt about him. And that meant that the story about Caleb being dead was probably a lie, too. Hope soared in my chest.

I tried to stall without being obvious. The blood in my veins screamed for me to run. I decided to play it off easy.

"Oh, I left my phone. I need to grab it so I can reach my father later or he'll freak and call the cops or something," I muttered and rubbed my eyes, trying to seem like I was just upset and forgetful.

"Nah. You can use mine. It's ok. Come on, let's go."

"No, I'll just grab it really quick. I don't know any of the numbers because they're in my phone, so. It's right by the door."

I turned to go and he grabbed the hood of my jacket, yanking me back and slamming me into the side of the car. "Dang. We were so close, Maggie. So close to the easy way." He came right into my face, but didn't touch me. "What gave it away, huh? I was about to shed tears if that's what it took to get you in this car. What was it?" he asked mockingly.

The driver got out and came around the car as I stayed silent. He was a young guy like Marcus, one of them from the movie theater that day that I went with Kyle. He smiled at me when he took his place beside Marcus.

"Get in the car, Maggie," Marcus barked. I shook my head no. "I'm prepared to feel the burn of the offense mark to get your pretty little behind in this car. So. Easy way or hard way?"

I just stood there and looked at them. I had no way to get out of it, none at all. I glanced between them several times and when he sighed, I knew my stalling was over.

"It hurts you, too, doesn't it? Do you really want to do this?" he asked as he stepped forward another inch, almost touching me.

I stayed silent again but remembered something Caleb had said to me about calling to him. That if I was distressed, he could tell and would know something was wrong and come running. So I did. I yelled his name in my mind loud and long.

Caleb! Help! Caleb!

"All right."

He grabbed my arm and I felt the burn and jolt of revolt on my skin. He winced and gritted his teeth but held on as he tried to push me into the open car door. I attempted to pull free but he tightened a grip and pulled harder. So I kicked him in the shin and pushed off the door to run. He howled, grabbed my wrist and gave me a red hot glare that would scare any man.

Then he reached his free arm back and slapped me across my cheek.

I'd never been hit before, and didn't care for it, but I assumed it probably hurt worse than it normally would have because I got a zing through my cheek to warn him off as well as the pain from the slap. My vision spotted for a second with white hazy stars. It felt almost like I'd blacked out and then regained consciousness. He was still pushing me into the door and I just refused to take it. I started screaming, in my mind and out of my mouth.

"Shut up!" Marcus yelled.

"Shut her up and get her in the car, now!" the other guy yelled louder.

I was surprised no one had come outside to see what was going on yet.

"Help! Let me go! Help!"

No use. No one peeked or looked and I couldn't fight him any longer. Just as he placed me in the car door I remembered something. Something triggered, rather, in my mind. A flash of something crossed before my eyes and I found myself doing some strange roundabout kick thing and saw Marcus go down to the grass on his back.

"What the-" Marcus said as he looked up at me in disgust.

"Quit messing around! Get her in the car!" the guy yelled and came around to help. He grabbed my arm and jumped back, screaming as I felt the jolt ripple through my skin. "Ah! Crap! You weren't joking, man. That frigging hurts like hell."

Marcus jumped up at the same time that I sprung from the car. He came forward and my mind took over. The first flash vision I saw was a punch and then a block. Then another of a back hand punch then a side kick. I had no idea what they were called but I knew exactly what it was.

Karate.

Kyle's father had taught me karate that day and I was skeptical but no more. It was amazing. My brain was literally teaching me karate as I went along. And when Marcus reached for my arm, I used it on him. It was like watching a movie. I didn't control it, I just did it.

I heard screeching tires from behind us and peeked to see a black car and a SUV slam to a stop on the curb across the street, but I didn't stop fighting, couldn't.

When I looked back, Marcus was on the ground and his friend was coming for me again. He wrapped his arms around my middle from behind and yelped at the pain from my touch but held on as he tried to drag me to the open car door. I saw Marcus get up as I heard yelling and slamming doors behind me. I knew this was it.

I drop kicked the guy's shin with my heel and he threw me to the ground as he yelled. I scrambled up and threw my leg up into the air as my top half went lower. I kicked him square across the face and he went down hard with a grunt and curse onto the grass. Marcus cursed too and took off running, leaving his comrade behind and the Audi's tires squealed as he peeled out. The driver of the black car took off after him in the same flurry.

I turned to see Caleb, his father, Kyle's father and several others running towards me.

"Caleb," I said and saw everything go dark as I fell in sudden exhaustion. Warm arms caught me and hugged me tightly to a warm body, burying my face in his chest. "Caleb."

"I'm here."

"You're alive," I squeaked and muffled. I started to cry in relief. "You're ok."

"Of course I am." I felt the push of his mind peeking in mine, the fuzzy tingle. "Ah," he said with sudden realization and his tone changed from relief to anger, "that's how he got you out here. He told you I was killed by his father...and you believed him."

I opened my eyes to peek through my hair to see others standing over us as he held me in his lap on the ground. A couple of them were loading Marcus's friend into the SUV while a couple others searched my yard and the street.

When I turned my face up to look at him, Caleb pushed my hair back and kissed my forehead. When he leaned back he growled and several others made similar noises of anger, groans and grunts.

"He hit you," Caleb growled angrily.

I touched my cheek, forgetting. It burned when my fingers brushed it. I imagined I had several of those marks all over me from the way they both fought to get me into the car. And of course, they were going to see them sooner than later.

"Here." He took off my jacket and almost exploded with anger at seeing all the black hands, fingers and grab marks all over my arms and hands. His whole body shook and he stared at me with wide eyes and disgust written all over his face. At first I thought it was because they'd touched me. I was tainted or something, but he shook his head and held my cheek in his palm, covering the black mark from Marcus's swift hand. "No. I'm disgusted because they hurt you. I wasn't here, couldn't get here fast enough, and they hurt you."

Peter put his hand on Caleb's shoulder and he nodded and took a deep breath. His dad helped him remove his jacket and he wrapped it around me.

"We better get out of here before your dad comes. Someone had to have heard something."

He lifted me in his arms easily and I clung to his neck as his touch took the pain. I saw Kyle's father standing among the few around us.

"You saved me," I told him, remembering how he'd 'taught' me karate.

"I saw that," he said and smiled, placing a hand on my arm. "But you saved yourself, I just taught you how. Nice form by the way."

Despite it all I chuckled and winced at a slight pain in my stomach. Caleb's grimace got even tighter, if possible.

"Let's go."

We all piled into the SUV, with me on Caleb's lap still, and made our way to Kyle's house. Even with Caleb holding me, I still felt odd. Drained and foggy, like after the echo dream, but I couldn't get my mind to focus on that because my Caleb was right here.

I stared up at him and wanted to just burst with happiness at the knowledge that he was ok. More than ok, he came to save me, just like he said he would. Granted he came a little late, not his fault, but if he hadn't come, Marcus wouldn't have run off like that and I might still be out there fighting them or worse, in his car.

Caleb's mind was cluttered with anger and guilt and general madness. I wasn't touching his skin because of his heavy jacket so, even though the car was full of uncles, I reached up and touched his cheek. He startled at the contact and sighed loudly at the sudden release of anger. He looked at me and I looked back at him. He leaned over to rest his head against mine.

"You were amazing. Even I can't kick that high."

I wanted to laugh but it hurt so I smiled instead.

"Yeah. That teaching karate into my mind thing was pretty handy."

I saw Kyle's father smile in his profile beside us.

"Yeah. I'm so sorry, Maggie."

"It wasn't your fault."

"But we knew he was after you, we just didn't know why. I should have stayed or left someone with you."

The short ride to Kyle's house was over and Caleb lifted me into his arms as we exited the backseat and passed through the squeaky gate. I noticed they had the same filigree lined fence with half moons set in intervals as Caleb's house did.

Kyle ran outside and his eyes bulged when he saw me. Great, one more person to feel guilty.

"Gah! Maggie! What happened?"

"Marcus," Caleb answered and kept walking me inside.

"Oh, man. I was just with you not a couple hours ago. He must have been watching and waited for me to leave you."

"You were with her?" Caleb asked and looked at me.

"Yeah. He met me at the diner when I got off."

"We went for a walk in the park since you were *detained*," Kyle answered and grinned slightly. If I had the strength to glare at him, I would've. "It started to rain so we had to cut it short and I got her home."

"Is that why she's running a fever and her throat's sore? Because you took her for a walk in the freezing rain?" Caleb asked hotly as we crossed the threshold.

He must have felt that in me because I hadn't said anything.

"What? Are you sick, Maggie?"

I did feel sick and sore and in the general vicinity of hurting all over. Not only was I sick from being soaked in the freezing rain, but I had just gotten thrown around on top of it. But I didn't answer him.

We passed through the kitchen and I saw a few ladies in there around the table with coffee cups. Someone must have called them because they looked worried and when they saw me it wasn't surprise on their face, it was anger.

Rachel came up to me, forcing Caleb to stop. "Oh, no, Maggie." She brushed her fingers across one of the offense marks on my hand. "I'm so sorry. This isn't how things usually are."

"I'm taking her upstairs, Mom."

She nodded and everyone stood and watched as Caleb made his way up the stairs with me in his arms.

Sixteen

"You're burning up, Maggie."

Caleb had tucked me into his bed in the guestroom after changing my clothes from my soaking wet ones to a House of Heroes t-shirt and his boxers. I didn't complain and he didn't ask permission. He was my significant and he was going to take care of me. When my shirt went over my head and he saw the offense marks around my middle, he was thinking about anything but seeing me naked. His mind raced with curses and things he wanted to do to Marcus. Bad things.

"I'm fine," I croaked.

"You are not fine," he said as he pulled the covers up to my chin. "Are you still cold?"

I nodded. I was freezing.

He took off his shirt and jeans, leaving him only in boxers, and climbed in beside me. We laid on our sides facing each other as he twined our legs and arms, pressing our bodies close as they could get to warm me. He rubbed my arm with his palm and blew a frustrated breath.

"Caleb, I'm ok," I assured him.

"Only because you handled yourself. I wasn't there to keep you safe."

I wanted him to kiss me even though I didn't feel good, to take away his anger. I pressed my lips to his, hoping to ease some of his tension away, and I felt his arm relax a little, but his lips weren't into it. I pulled back, disappointed, and looked at him in the lamplight.

"But I'm ok," I protested.

"Yeah, no thanks to me. Or Kyle. What were you doing with him anyway?" he asked softly.

"He came to the diner when I got off. I'd just gotten your text and he said he knew you were gone and figured he'd come keep me company."

Caleb nodded and pursed his lips angrily. "Good old Kyle."

"I told him no funny stuff and he was completely normal with me, like he used to be. Then it started raining and we ran home but we were soaked and it was so cold. My dad took him home and I took a shower. Then a little bit later, Marcus climbed through my window telling me his father had shot you in the ambush of their house."

I shivered as I thought of it. He squeezed me tighter.

"I'm not going anywhere. I'm not leaving you here without me," he assured.

"At first I thought I was dreaming because I dozed off for a couple minutes but he was so convincing and..." I sniffed and could feel the tears burning as my body started to relive the pain of hearing those words. "And he said..."

"Shh. Don't, Maggie. I told you, I'm not leaving you. You and me, always together. From now on I'm probably going to be some form or version of a tyrant. This is your only warning."

I laughed and sniffed again. "That's ok. I don't care. I just want to be with you."

"And you will be, but first things first. We've got to figure out something to tell your father so he doesn't freak and you can keep him in your life but out of the loop. I don't want to ruin it with him."

"Me neither but what are we going to say? I sure can't think of anything."

"Well, I was thinking you could tell him - and my father can go and talk to him about it - that my family is going on vacation for a couple weeks somewhere and want to take you with us. My dad can be pretty persuasive."

"That might work. Are we going to stay at your house?"

"No. We're going away, just you and me. But your father won't know that. The farther away you are the harder it is for the echoling to reach you. My dad is going to stay here and try to work on figuring this out while I work on keeping you safe."

Though I found the idea of going off alone with Caleb extremely appealing, I was worried too.

"Where are we going?"

"Let me worry about that."

"You don't know or you won't tell me?"

"It's best if you don't know, just in case something happens until we can leave."

"Ah," I said understanding. He didn't want Marcus or his uncle to get our location out of my dreams and follow us there. "Well, I need to figure out my work stuff before we go."

I snuggled closer and he grunted. "You're still really hot, Maggie."

"Thanks."

He laughed and I smiled because that's what I had wanted. "Yeah, you're hot but you're also hot. Maybe I should get Gran or someone to get you something for it."

I grabbed him around his stomach. "Please, don't go."

He relented with a nod and nuzzled my nose. His fingers combed through my hair, tucked it behind my ear, traced down my cheek.

"I was so worried about you. All the way here I was yelling at Uncle Ben to drive faster. I heard you calling in my mind and it was like nails in my head. I had already felt your anxiety, but I thought you were just needing me there for the withdrawals. So I told them I was leaving, but then your heart just stopped for a few seconds." He laughed humorlessly. "I freaked and then you started breathing again, crazy fast. I knew something was wrong so I told them and they all jumped in the car with me. It felt like I was dying."

"That must've been when he told me you and your father were dead. They have a car just like Kyle's father's so when he told me Kyle waiting for me, I believed him. I'm sorry."

"Nuhuh," he crooned and kissed my lips sweetly. "Not your fault. I'm just so glad you're ok." He kissed my lips again and I started to feel warmer and more energized. "For the future, when your significant dies you know it. You can feel it. It's excruciating, like you're dying too."

"That sounds fun," I said dryly.

"You won't ever have to worry about it. I told you, I'm not leaving you."

I closed the distance to kiss him and he let me for a few seconds, but then pushed me back gently.

"You know I want to, but you need to rest, Maggie. You've been through a lot tonight and so have I, worrying like crazy about you. We have plenty of time for that later," he said completely concerned.

"Just give me what I want," I said as I took his mouth again more forcefully.

He chuckled against my lips and gave in. In no time his humor turned to passion and his hand found my side as he pulled me closer to him. Then he braced himself over me and though I felt the excitement lacing his mind, I could also feel his restraint, which he had claimed the other night to have none of. I mentally shook my head at him. He'd been so worried, so utterly devastated by what happened. He wanted to kiss me until I couldn't think straight, but knew I was hurt and planned to take it easy with me.

He didn't press me into the mattress as he had done before. He hovered above me and though his kisses were eager, they were gentle. When I moved my hand up into his hair to tug, I felt and heard his breath catch and exhale in a weird pattern.

I bit his lip gently causing him to groan and press me harder for just a second before pulling back and giving me a comically stern look. "Maggie. Sweetheart, are you trying to kill me?"

I just giggled and shrugged under him in innocence.

I loved it when he called me sweetheart. It zinged me in all the right ways to hear it.

He leaned down to my ear and whispered. "Sweetheart." I closed my eyes, savoring, and smiled. Then he kissed the side of my neck once, which he'd never done before and it did nothing to calm me down, and leaned back on his side before gathering me up in his arms again. "Go to sleep, Maggie. We'll have all day tomorrow for anything you want to do."

"But I have work," I protested.

"Do you remember when I said I was going to be a tyrant?" I wrinkled my nose and he chuckled. "We'll talk in the morning. Go to sleep. Sweetheart."

I smiled at his tactics and closed my eyes to block out everything but him. I fell into a peaceful, healing sleep.

I woke several times to a light. When I peeked over Caleb I saw Gran or Rachel or Peter, someone peeking in on us every hour or so. It was annoying and sweet all at the same time. Caleb's face was turned away so he never woke. Sometimes there would be two of them and I could hear them worrying over us. Two male voices but I couldn't make out who they were.

"I could kill them for this. How dare they go to this extreme, for someone who didn't even grow up in this."

"That isn't the way of our clan."

"Maybe it should be. Richard and his idiotic son are just going to get away with this. It's not as if we can go to the police."

"We'll keep her safe. We underestimated them, is all. We won't make that mistake again. We did all we could do. He heard her call and went after her. If we hadn't been so far away, it wouldn't have been a problem."

"Yes, but now we have a new problem. How do we keep her with us and safe and not disrupt her relationship with her father?"

"I don't know. Gran's family disowned her so, honestly, I've never thought about having to deal with the humans before this way but I won't force her to choose. It wouldn't be right. We'll just have to find a way somehow."

"No other way about it."

"Yes, but I don't see how. Her safety is paramount to anything else, and Caleb, he is adjusting remarkably well. He told me he has not only heard her heartbeat from the first second of the imprint but also has been able to read her feelings."

"So soon? Really? Fascinating."

"Yes. And apparently, she is advanced as well. She is already reading his thoughts and feelings at will and her withdrawals haven't been as severe as I feared."

I paled thinking about the withdrawals being worse than they already were.

"Well, that's great, but first things first. For her safety, Caleb has to convince her to stop working at that diner."

"She won't buy it. She'll think he's trying to control her."

"No, she won't I don't think. She's smart. She'll understand the need for such an act for safety. Besides, I think she'll probably be more prone to want Caleb's company from now on after what happened."

"Did you see her? She was fantastic. That idiot went down with little effort on her part."

"I know. She's pleasantly surprising us all, I think. I just hope she doesn't feel pressured by all the attention and concern."

"How could she not? But she's a remarkable young woman with a good head. Caleb is a lucky man. I'm very pleased by all this. It'll be good for our clan."

There was a pause.

"I'm sorry it wasn't Kyle."

"Don't be. Maybe it's coming back. Maybe in a few years when he's of age he'll imprint. Maybe they all will. Maybe this is the catalyst for the comeback we've been waiting for."

"I hope so. I don't know how long we can keep up the celibacy of our clan. It's not fair and soon we'll have to worry about carrying on our name and heritage. What'll we do when there's no one-"

"Don't even speak it. There's nothing we can do but wait. And I think watching your son and his new mate will be just what this clan needs, to give them hope."

And the little sliver of light from the door closed to darkness and the voices stopped for a while. All I could do was cling to Caleb's sleeping body and hope beyond hope that they were right about everything.

When light was full in the window, I opened my eyes. Though I'd slept fitfully and restlessly, I still felt refreshed and tons better. My throat still hurt and my head ached a little but nothing like what I had felt like the night before. And no withdrawal pains. That was the best part. The past couple nights, sleeping with Caleb, made me feel brand new in the morning and I wasn't sure I could go back to sleeping without him again, even if there wasn't an echoling trying to hurt me.

I turned my face from the window to see Caleb watching me, leaning on his elbow, with a little concerned frown furrowing into his forehead.

"Are you better today?" he asked as his hand coasted down my arm.

I ran my finger over the wire filigree tattoo on his arm. He shivered making me giggle. "Yeah, I'm better."

As he looked at my face full on for the first time he winced, closing his eyes for a few seconds.

"Oh, yeah." I palmed the black mark I knew was there. "Maybe we could see Gran now."

He nodded.

"She's already been in here, but I told her you needed to sleep. She's downstairs waiting. Everyone is."

"Why?" I said pulling the blanket up to my neck like that would help shield me somehow.

"Everyone was worried sick about you and apparently peeved at me for bringing you upstairs instead of letting them check you out last night. Quite a few have been in here this morning to chew me out already." He smiled crookedly.

"Really?" I smiled bashfully. "Wow. I've never had anyone so concerned for me before."

"Welcome to the family."

That thought made me smile wider. He leaned closer. "That's what I like to see," he whispered and then kissed me. He let his hand coast down my upper arm to my elbow. His next words were whispered against my lips. "Your skin is so soft. And you are really…beautiful in the morning. Did I ever tell you that?"

"No," I breathed and felt him tap over my heart with his forefinger, feeling it beating erratically, and smile in satisfaction against my cheek.

"Did I also mention how adorable you look in my shirt?" he said huskily as he fisted the large shirt I was wearing in his hand, pulling me closer to claim my lips.

As soon as I wrapped my arm around his neck and Caleb deepened the kiss we were interrupted by a loud banging knock and then an exasperated sigh as someone came in without waiting.

Kyle.

He had the worst timing ever, always.

"You can't even leave her alone when she's recovering, cuz?" he said and even I could hear the hurt and anger in his voice.

"What, Kyle?" Caleb asked harshly against my lips.

"I came up to see how Maggie was. I didn't know you'd be in here, too."

Caleb turned to frown at him. "You know I've been with Maggie at night because of the echoling. What are you doing?"

"What?" He shrugged innocently. "Nothing."

Caleb moved to lie on his back as he made noises of annoyance. I sat up and tried to tame my hair to some degree while Kyle came to flop himself down on the end of the bed.

"I'm fine, Kyle. Thanks."

He looked at me and I saw it in his eyes. The sympathy, the anger, the guilt because of this black handprint on my face. I sighed and covered my face with my hands.

"Kyle, can you tell Gran I'll be down in a few minutes if she'll help me with...these things, please." I peeked through my fingers. He continued to look at me with a soft grimace. "And go, so I can get dressed."

"Oh, yeah. Right." He got up and stopped at the door. "Uh, Caleb, she said she needs to get dressed."

"Yeah," Caleb sang dragging out the syllables.

"So, come on. Be a gentleman. Get out."

"Kyle," I said a little sharper than I meant to. I softened my voice and continued. "Kyle, we talked about this, remember? You promised me. Caleb and I are going to be together and we're all going to be family and you're gonna have to get over it. He doesn't need to leave, in fact, I don't want him to. Please, make sure Gran is still here."

"Fine."

He left in a huff and the door slammed a little harder than necessary.

"Whoa," Caleb muttered.

"What?"

"That was so..." he didn't finish out loud, but in his mind he thought it was 'hot' that I straightened Kyle out and was looking at me with those eyes that told me exactly what was about to happen.

He took my face in his hand and pulled me to him. His lips slid over mine. His hand found my leg and I assumed he was going to pull me into his lap when I heard a faint knock and then the door creak open. I pulled back from Caleb, licked my lips and peeked to see Peter at the door with a cocked brow with a concerned and amused expression as I settled back down to the bed and Caleb rubbed his face in his hands in frustration.

Peter cleared his throat before speaking.

"Good morning. I hope you both slept well. Maggie, Gran is here and more than willing to assist you with the offense marks whenever you're...finished up here."

"Dad," Caleb groaned.

Peter just chuckled and said for me to text an excuse to my father before he left, shutting the door behind him.

"There are too many people in this house," Caleb muttered and threw back the blanket.

I giggled as he helped me up and I texted a quick 'Left early. See you later on tonight. Love you' to dad.

Apparently, Kyle's mother had found some clothes somewhere for me to borrow and they were folded neatly on the end of the bed. I looked around and saw no other door in the room to escape to but tried not to be concerned with modesty. Caleb was my soul mate after all and he'd seen everything there was to be seen last night anyway when he changed my clothes for me.

So, I pulled his boxers off me, leaving his long shirt to cover me as I slipped on the jeans. Then I turned to look over my shoulder at Caleb and saw him watching me with a look that made me blush crimson as he fought to get his shirt on.

I smiled a little, bit my lip and pulled my shirt off over my head, keeping my back to him. When I did a quick peek back he looked about ready to keel over so I quickly put on my new shirt and turned around to find him right in front of me.

"That wasn't nice," he said softly.

"Oh?" I said with fake innocence.

"Ooooh," he groaned in mock anger. "No, not nice at all." His lips touched mine softly as he took my hand and pulled me out of the room. "I better get you out of my room while I still have some sanity."

I just shook my head at him as he stopped on the stairs.

"I want to warn you, I know how you are about crowds. There is definitely a crowd down there. And they are all going to fuss and bother over you all day, maybe more, and it's gonna aggravate the tar out of you." I wanted to giggle. Who says tar? "But if it's too much, say the word and I'll-"

"Caleb, I'm fine. Your family is so sweet."

"Our family," he corrected and I smiled.

"Don't worry about me...I think I'm falling in love with them." I held my fingers thumb and index finger up an inch apart. "Little bit," I said and smiled wider.

He stepped up to be one step under me, our heights matched.

"You're amazing," he said and lifted our entwined hands to kiss the back of my fingers. Then he led me down the last few steps to a kitchen full of watchful, weary and worried eyes all fixed on me.

Seventeen

"Well, come on, pretty girl. Let's get this over with," Gran insisted as soon as my foot hit the bottom step.

I looked around at the packed red brick kitchen. There were some faces I recognized and some I didn't, but there was a blast of titters and whispers at our arrival.

"Gran," Kyle's mother protested and I couldn't help, but think I needed to learn everyone's name. "Let her eat some breakfast first. I made coffee and honey buns. Caleb told me it was her favorite."

"I'm sure she's ready to not have that thing across her face anymore. Come on," she beckoned me again and took my hand to pull me into the next room. Her skin was cold and soft but I could feel her bones as she gripped me. "Caleb and Peter, you, too. This isn't going to be fun."

I felt my eyes bulge at her words and wondered what she meant by that. She pulled me to lay on the chaise lounge and propped a pillow under my head as I saw Peter and Caleb come into the den with us.

"Now, Caleb, come sit right here," she instructed and pointed to the spot on the floor by my head.

"Is this going to hurt?" I asked, unable to not ask. "It didn't really hurt the last time you removed one."

"Yes, I'm afraid it is."

Caleb looked at her sharply and I realized he hadn't known that either. "What do you mean?" he asked forcefully.

"Caleb, I'm sorry, sugar baby, but it was different last time. Yes, his intent wasn't pure then either, but this time it was pure malice and deceit. She's gonna have to feel that when I take them back and she'll relive every attack."

"No." He started to get up and grabbed my hand to take me with him. "No, she's not doing it then."

"It has to be done." She held him in place with a hand on his shoulder. "She won't get her energy back until we take them off. Plus she doesn't want to walk around with those things forever."

"No, I don't," I answered softly.

"I didn't know it was going to hurt you," Caleb said softly, squatting down in front of me, pushing my hair back. "We don't have to do this today. You've been through enough already."

"I want to. I want it over with. It's ok."

Caleb looked none too happy about that but nodded tersely to Gran and stroked my other cheek with his fingers before scooting over to my head as I lay back down.

She motioned Peter to sit by my feet so he pulled my legs up to sit under them, pulled them into his lap. He patted my leg and smiled weakly at me.

Then Kyle ran in. "What are you guys doing in here?"

"Healing Maggie. Now get over here and make yourself useful or hit the road," Gran said as she knelt beside me. For an older woman, she sure got around really great.

"Help how?"

"Hold her hand and the rest of you...hold her down." I heard Caleb sigh inwardly in aggravation. "All right." Kyle moved to kneel on the floor on the other side of the chaise and grabbed my hand. He even laced our fingers and his other hand held my arm by my elbow. He and Caleb glared at each other. "Let's get started. Maggie. You heard what I said. It'll be different than the last time I healed you because his intent was different. Before he was just trying to upset Kyle, this time, he was intentionally trying to hurt you. So it'll be worse but we'll get through it."

I swallowed and nodded. Caleb bent down to kiss my forehead and whispered that he was here and I knew his intention had nothing to do with Kyle being there. In his mind, he was extremely upset, pissed about the whole thing, and wanted to grab me and run upstairs. I wondered how he would react when he saw me in the pain from doing this. It was in his blood to protect me.

Gran didn't do my face first and I wondered why but didn't say anything. She did the one on my hand, placing her fingers and palm in exact alignment as the black handprint and as soon as she was in place the vision hit me and I felt his hatred for me as I watched and felt the scene as it ran its course backwards of how I received that mark. It showed Marcus grabbing me to push me in the open car door but it was in reverse and disorienting.

It choked me, burned in my skin and I yelped. Then it ended. When I opened my eyes everyone was watching, looking ill and angry. All I could hear was my erratic breathing.

Caleb grunted and breathed hard through his nose.

"Are you ok?" he asked gruffly.

"Yeah," I breathed.

He leaned his head on mine and I saw that he felt what I had felt, saw what I saw and was actually experiencing it for himself with me. It was killing him inside to see and feel what had happened to me before he got there to save me.

"Marcus better pray I don't ever see his sorry hide again," he growled.

"Go," I said to him as he lifted his head.

"No," he said firmly, knowing exactly why I was trying to send him away.

"You don't need to be here. The others won't relive it with me like you. Just go."

"Absolutely not."

"Caleb," I protested.

"Maggie."

"Did you know it was going to be like that for him?" I asked Gran, not unkindly.

"No." She looked at him curiously. "No, I most certainly did not. Caleb, maybe you should go wait in the kitchen."

"Not gonna happen, Gran. She stays, I stay."

"So noble," Kyle muttered sarcastically under his breath but everyone ignored him.

"Caleb, I've never seen it where one significant feels another's removal of offense marks or anything else I've ever done. I'm not sure it's a good idea-"

"Gran, I'm not leaving." He looked down at me. "You still want to do this now?" he asked and I nodded. "Then let's finish it but I'm not going anywhere."

"Peter," Gran implored.

He shook his head and twisted his lips. "Caleb knows what he can and can't handle, Gran. If this was Rachel, I wouldn't leave either."

"Well, you're of no help are you? All right, you two, brace yourselves."

She did all the ones on my arms next. There were four between the two of them and each one was excruciating, horrifying and I hated that Caleb had to go through it with me. And I hated that I had to go through it all twice.

Then she lifted my shirt and we all saw the long arm print with fingers wrapped around my side as Marcus's friend had grabbed me around the middle. She lined her arm up and began as I felt the pressure of Peter's grip on my legs and Kyle's on my arm. I tried not to scream, tried to ride it out with grit teeth. Sometimes it worked, sometimes it didn't. When she released me this time she told us all to take a minute because the last one, the one on my cheek would be the worst.

I barely contained my whimper at her words and dreaded it being worse than it already was.

They all took their place a minute later, holding me down tighter this time. Caleb gripped my shoulders and laid his forehead on mine. I heard a small girly gasp behind Gran and looked up to see Maria.

"What are you doing? I heard screaming. Uncle Caleb?" she squeaked and looked at him like he was a monster.

"Maria, we're helping Maggie."

"Why are you hurting her?"

"Maria," Gran stepped towards her, "listen, baby, sometimes you gotta do things you don't like in order to do something good."

"I'm fine, Maria," I told her as strong as I could, "Really. It's not pa-," I was gonna say painful, but knew that was a lie. "It just sucks that's all." I smiled weakly at her.

"Mama says I'm not allowed to say sucks," she whispered and gave me a look like I was in trouble.

We all burst out laughing, even me. "You know you're right. I shouldn't say that. It's not very ladylike is it?"

"It's ok. I won't say anything."

"Thanks."

"All right, child," Gran said. "Get gone. We're almost done and we're gonna be a hungry bunch when we are. Why don't you tell your momma to have some plates ready, hmm?"

"Ok," she said reluctantly and turned to go, but then looked back at Caleb. "Don't let her be hurt anymore, ok?"

He didn't nod or say anything as she walked out, just looked at me with regret and guilt and I felt it pouring out of him. I needed to tell him, but didn't want to in front of everyone so I focused in my mind and tried to send it to him. It worked surprisingly easy. And I felt the familiar beat of his heart as I always did when I focused on him or shared my mind with him.

Caleb.

His eyes jumped to mine and he leaned down to look at me upside down and stroke my cheek with his fingertips.

Yeah, gorgeous?

I smiled. And he smiled. But then I got serious.

You will not blame yourself for this. I was stupid. I was the one who let him tell me something that I should have known wasn't true. You didn't do anything wrong. You were out trying to help me.

I should have known they'd try something. I shouldn't have gone with my father.

That sounds a lot like blame. I'm serious. None of it.

He chuckled out loud and I glanced around and saw Peter watching in awe, Gran looking pleased and Kyle looking disgusted.

"I can't believe you're doing that. You know," Peter leaned forward on his elbows with my legs still in his lap, "your mother and I tried to do that for months after we imprinted and couldn't, until much later. It's amazing the things you two can do already."

"She started it," Caleb said and winked at me.

"Caleb, I mean it," I resumed my plea out loud since he'd been diverted. "Please."

He sighed. "I'll try. But I mean it, too. We've got to figure out a way for us to be together. I can't just let you go home and pretend everything's normal when I know that this isn't over. Marcus isn't going to just stop. We have to keep you safe and I can't do that sneaking in your window every night."

"Sneaking in her window!" Gran said scandalized.

"Gran, what else was I supposed to do? He was hurting her in her-" Caleb said while Peter said. "Now, Gran. You know with our kind there have to be exceptions."

"I know, but...Lord have mercy. Back in my day you'd have been shot for sneaking in some girl's bedroom."

"Well, her dad doesn't know, Gran. Otherwise it wouldn't work."

She threw her hands up.

"All right. Enough! My poor ears can't take much more." Peter and Caleb chuckled but then Gran knelt beside me and everyone sobered. "Ready, pretty girl? Last one, worst one. Let's be done with this."

"Ok."

Everyone grabbed on and Caleb resumed his previous spot, forehead to mine like he could take some of my pain away. She took a deep breath and laid her hands in line with the hand print and then pulled back.

"You've got a fever, Maggie."

"I'm ok." I glanced at Kyle and he rolled his eyes guiltily. "I'm ok, really. Go ahead."

She leaned over me, her gray eyes swirled green, making me dizzy to watch it. She realigned her hand and I saw her half moon tattoo on her inside wrist with 'Raymond' wrapped around the curved side right before the reverse vision came. In reverse and slow motion, I saw Marcus and his friend yelling something and Marcus grabbing my stinging wrist. Then a hand coming across my face and his hand dropped back to his side right after I pushed off the door. Marcus's mouth opened in a scream, then kicking him in the shin as he tried to push me into the open car door.

The whole time the vision was hitting me not only could I feel his hatred for me, I could taste it. Just like I knew Caleb's feelings, I could feel Marcus's. And taste. The taste was bitter and acidic, burning my tongue, pulsing the burn along with the flare of his emotions as the scene played out.

I also felt my fear, as ripe as it had been when it was really happening. I didn't realize I was crying. I didn't realize I was yelling. I was trying to kick and push them away. I felt their grips tighten on me and with the vision at the same time it frightened me even more.

When I opened my eyes, Peter was holding my legs with both arms, Kyle was fallen back on his butt looking at me with a 'what the' face and Caleb was still grasping my shoulders and hovering above my face with his own. Gran was standing over us with a tired expression.

Once I realized what I had done I immediately started to apologize.

"I'm so sorry. I didn't mean to."

"Don't you dare," Peter consoled gently. He patted my leg once more. "Are you feeling better now?"

I examined myself. There was no residual pain or weird feelings from the visions. My tongue tasted normal, my skin felt normal, and I felt normal again and completely energized. I hadn't realized how much those things were draining me until they were removed.

"Yes. I do. Thank you. I *am* sorry."

Peter shook his head at me, smiled, patted my leg again and got up. "I'll tell Rachel we're all done in here, and starving."

"You fought back from the very beginning," Caleb said proudly. "Good girl. I'm so proud of you."

"All right, let's go eat," Kyle blurted and stood up.

"Go ahead. I need a minute with Maggie," Caleb said.

"What? She's hungry, let's go eat."

"Kyle," Gran said sharply.

"Fine," he said as he stalked out.

As he waltzed out, I knew right then I'd have to have another talk with him about everything because he apparently wasn't getting it. I also felt horrible that I was the cause of their tension. They'd been best friends until literally ten minutes after I met Caleb. That one incident changed everything.

"Hey," I looked up to Caleb's voice and saw that Gran was gone as well, "he's being an idiot. If the situation were reversed, I wouldn't egg him on even if I did have a crush on the girl. It wouldn't be fair to either of them and with the imprint being so phenomenal anyway, like this is, they wouldn't need me being an ass."

"I know. I can't help but feel bad though and there's nothing I can do about it. I can't stand that you guys aren't friends anymore because of me."

"Not your fault." He slid his fingers over my cheek before coming to sit beside me on the chaise. "He'll get over it one day. He has to. And then, we'll be friends again."

I sat up and he automatically pulled me to sit sideways in his lap.

"Maggie," he sighed. "I don't think I can ever leave you alone again. How am I even going to finish college?"

I knew he was joking, but partly serious, too. He was so angry, so scared, so guilty. "I'll just have to go with you."

His gaze jumped to mine. "Really? You're going to go to Tennessee with me in the fall?"

"Well, I still hate the idea of your family paying for it so I'll look into student loans or whatever I have to, but...yeah. I'm coming with you."

His face split with a grin and he took my mouth forcefully and gratefully. I fisted his shirt front as his arms went around me. I begged that we'd have no interruptions this time as his skin worked like a sponge to extract all my worries and sorrows. It felt like the room took a spike in temperature, I felt too hot, but in a good way. My hand wandered to his hair, shaggy and soft. I let him devour me until I was sure I'd die of not breathing properly.

I pulled back a little, but he didn't release me, just let us sit so close, our lips almost touched and our foreheads did. His breath was hot and intoxicating.

"I'm so happy, Maggie. I hope you know that, even with everything that's going on, I'm so happy I found you."

"I'm happy, too."

He leaned back a little to look at me. "Are you really going with me or was that just a diversion to get my mind off Kyle and Marcus?"

"No," I laughed, "I'm really going. But that was a good idea, I should have thought of that."

He tickled me in retaliation and we laughed. His lips skimmed my temple before he stood up and steadied me.

"Are you good? We can wait a few more minutes if you need it. I'm sure we can find something to do," he said with inflection and clear enjoyment.

"I'm fine. I feel really good actually. Between you and Gran, I'm good as new," I crooned making him grin.

"Awesome, because," he let our lips graze, "as good as you taste, green eyes, I need some real food."

"Ditto," I said giggling at his lame line.

He took my hand and laced our fingers, pulling me along, but then stopped. "Oh, yeah, you better call work."

"Oh, crap. I forgot about that." I looked up to his face. I remembered last night talking about how he didn't think I should work today, or ever again, or at least that's where it seemed he was going with it. He looked at me like I might rebel and tell him to go screw himself. It was comical, actually. I giggled. "Caleb, I agree with you about not working today. I'm not gonna bite your head off."

He looked relieved. "Good. You understand that I have to keep you safe, right? It hurts to think about you in harm and I'm not sure I could sit here while you worked today after everything that happened last night."

"I understand."

"Besides, you don't have to work anymore. Not only is it not safe but I'm taking care of you now. And you'll be leaving in a few weeks for school so you'd quit anyway."

"Caleb, I told you I don't really feel...comfortable with you paying for my stuff. I don't need you to-" He cut me off with a kiss and then spoke his words against my mouth.

"In the words of some really beautiful smart girl I know, just give me what I want."

I laughed despite it all. "Ok, but...even though I'll call them and tell them I'm not coming in today, I can't just quit without any notice. They've been like family. I can't do that to them."

"Ok." He blew out a long breath. "We'll think of something." He smiled reassuringly.

We stepped into the kitchen and I looked around at my new family. Maria walked up to me with a plate piled high with homemade honey buns and strawberries.

"You're not allergic, are you?" she asked.

"Nope. I'm not allergic to anything," I said as I took the plate. "Thanks."

"You're welcome. I'm allergic to kiwi, but it's ok because I don't really like kiwi anyway."

"Really?" I pulled away from Caleb and gave him a smile over my shoulder. "I love kiwi," I told her and followed her out to the table where there was already about ten women seated.

"Hey, Maggie," Jen greeted and I was glad. I didn't want everyone to feel weird about me because they knew what had just happened to me. I prickled as I wondered if everyone had heard me screaming. "Feeling better?"

"Yeah, thanks. Gran is a lifesaver."

"And Caleb, I would think, too," a new woman said giggling.

Other giggles erupted and Rachel covered her mouth before going on.

"Now, now, leave them alone. It's been so long since we were that age, we've forgotten what it's like."

"Oh, I never forgot," the woman said. "That's exactly what I'm talking about!"

Everyone laughed, even me. Then, they told me some stories about Caleb when he was a kid.

"So, by the fifth go round, he finally realized that I was tricking him! He was so cute, all disgruntled," Caleb's aunt ended her story.

Everyone laughed as they remembered.

"Well, I remember the time he house sat for us and Ken charmed the house plants before we left. Every time Caleb came around a corner, my potato vine had moved something, a chair or the palm had flipped a picture frame. It was so hilarious the first phone call we got from him," she did her best Caleb impression, "Uh, Aunt Margo, I think something's up with your house." She laughed and cackled. "He finally figured it out at some point and when we got back he looked at us as sternly as a sixteen year old boy can and said, 'Very funny'."

I laughed so hard at their stories I was wiping my eyes.

"Well, Maggie, where are you going to school?" Jen asked after everyone settled down.

"Um, I think I'm going to go to Tennessee."

There were a lot of breaths of relief and I looked around curiously. Jen looked at me and smirked while Rachel explained.

"It's just that we're wading through uncharted waters, Maggie. Human girls are so...different. Demanding and independent and there's nothing wrong with that but it's just not the way of our kind. The Virtuoso have always been old fashioned and we were worried that you'd rebel against it all. Caleb is a good boy…uh, man." She sniffled and two ladies near hear patted her hands. She laughed through her tears. "I'm a mess. I never thought I'd see this day and now it's here and I can barely believe it." I bit my lip in uncomfortable respite. She smiled at me. "I'm sorry. I'm not trying to make you uncomfortable, I'm just so happy and very proud of Caleb. He's handling everything so well, as are you. He'll stop at nothing to make you happy, Maggie. Know that. You don't have to worry about mundane things anymore."

I nodded in understanding and smiled at her and her aunts, nodding and beaming with pride. I broke the silence by asking about their imprints.

I sat and finished my lunch with them, listening to their stories of when and how they imprinted and ascended. I was fascinated. I was sure they were sick of my questions, but they kept smiling and eagerly answered.

I so enjoyed them and no one treated me like I was a child or naïve. They sympathized, they laughed, some cackled more than once. I tried to keep my gaze off Jen, knowing she wouldn't have a story to tell, but when my eyes did drift to her she looked happy and content with Maria seated on her lap.

Eventually the guys came out and pulled some chairs to sit around us.

"You're alive?" Caleb jested. "I was scared of what I'd find out here."

"Yes, I'm alive. And I've learned a whole lot," I spouted with eyebrows raised.

"Oh, no, now I'm scared."

"You should be." I leaned forward to whisper loudly. "I know about the Scooby Doo underwear."

He groaned as I laughed and Kyle's dad, who I could never remember the name of, came over.

"Caleb, come play for us."

"No, no." He waved him off.

"Yes, yes. It's been ages since you played. Come on, play while we throw the shoes."

"Come on, Caleb!" someone else chanted.

"Fine." He grimaced at me and leaned forward to whisper in my ear, "Guitar. And Kyle's dad's name is Max by the way." Then he kissed my temple and smirked at me as he took the guitar from Uncle Max and sat back in his chair.

He started to play something and Max set up the horseshoes. I glanced at Caleb as I recognized the song he was playing, *Fake Plastic Trees* by Radiohead. He wasn't even looking at the strings while he played. He was looking at me.

Then I saw Kyle coming my way and I froze.

Crap. Crap!

I knew he was going to ask me to be his partner in horseshoes, I could see it on his face and I so didn't want to have any more conflict between Caleb and Kyle. That would do it for sure. So I jumped up from my chair quickly, acting like I hadn't seen Kyle coming, who had only been about seven feet away at the time, and made a beeline to Peter who was leaning on the next table over watching everyone.

"Hi."

"Hi there," he said easily.

"Do you want to be my horseshoe partner?"

He smiled. "An old man like me doesn't get asked that much anymore."

"Aw, come on, you're not old. And I've never played before so I'm not sure if you should play with me or run."

He laughed out loud just as Kyle reached us. Dang it. He followed me over there. "Mags, you wanna play with me?"

"Uh, I think I convinced Peter to partner with me, if he's brave enough."

"Oh," Peter said grinning as he stood and placed my hand in the crook of his arm. He walked us towards the others. "I'm brave enough, all right. But you better watch out because my wife taught me everything I know."

I laughed. "Aha. Well it's not like I could tell the difference between bad and good anyway. You're going to have to teach me."

He showed me how to line them up and how hard to toss. "So, feeling better now?"

"Much."

"Good. I'm worried about you and Caleb. I'm still trying to figure something out for you two."

"Thanks. You know, I'm not that worried though. Caleb's pretty crafty and it'll all work it out. I know it."

He nodded and smiled. I looked over to hear Maria squealing and saw an ivy vine racing across the yard towards her as she ran from it in zigzags. I looked around until I found the uncle concentrating on it. He winked and smiled at me.

"I'm glad one of you is level headed," Peter continued and I realized this was just a common thing with them, to use their abilities in everyday life.

We played a few turns and I actually won a few. He asked me about school and things. I told him about running track.

He threw a shoe and it stopped midair. I gawked at it, but he smirked and turned around to find Rachel. She smiled.

"Are you telling her that old lie about me teaching you everything I know?"

"Yes, ma'am, I am." He opened his arms and she went into them giggling in amusement. With their arms around each other they looked back to me. "Honestly, Maggie, my wife is terrible at shoes. Unless she cheats," he said grinning and guffawed when she playfully punched him in the stomach.

"I wish it weren't true, but it is," she admitted. "So, how is our Maggie faring?"

"Wonderfully. She's a natural at horseshoes." Then, he cleared his throat. "That was really thoughtful, what you did, Maggie."

"What?"

"I saw you before and I saw Kyle making his way to you. I could practically read your thoughts as you scampered over to me."

"Really?" I wrinkled my nose. "I wasn't trying to hurt Kyle's feelings, but he knows how to rub Caleb the wrong way and he does it on purpose. I'm just trying to avoid conflict."

"I know. And trust me, Kyle didn't see but I did. And so did Caleb."

He nodded his head to Caleb and I glanced over. He was looking at me with so much love in his eyes, it was terribly obvious but I didn't care. I smiled at him and then giggled when one of Caleb's uncles grabbed my arm to drag me away for another game.

I was handed off to several other uncles and cousins before it was over, one uncle, who was apparently the one to see almost a minute into the future, predicted with accuracy mine and all the other wins and losses.

He even gave me some pointers before shots and told me I was literally changing my future.

I really liked him.

Somehow, I kept away from Kyle. He looked like he maybe caught on before it was over with, but it couldn't be helped. He leaned back in a chair and sulked openly, leaning the chair back on its hind legs. I cared more about Caleb's feelings than Kyle's and Kyle was really pushing it lately.

They were all sweet and talkative as we listened to the tinks of metal hitting metal and the strums of guitar. They told jokes and Rachel passed out lemonade.

Caleb was so good, I couldn't stop my eyes from traveling to him every few seconds and even though he played a lot of modern stuff, his family seemed to really enjoy it. I guess they just enjoyed him. It still seemed so foreign to me to have so much family and be so close to them.

Then the music stopped and I turned to see Caleb standing behind me.

"I didn't get my turn," he said, cocky and grinning.

Eighteen

"Caleb, you were so good. I didn't know you could play like that."

He hugged me around the middle and grinned. "Believe it or not, there are still a few things you don't know about me."

"Oh, there's lots I don't know." I linked my arms around his neck. "Favorite color, favorite food, favorite band, favorite movie. Were you a band geek or a jock in high school?"

He smirked. "Would it matter if I was a band geek?"

"Absolutely not."

"Well, I was little of both, I guess. I played the drums and bass in the school jazz band and was also wide receiver on the football team."

"Wow," I sighed.

"What?" he laughed.

"You're just good at everything, aren't you?" He laughed again, but I kept going as I tugged him under the tree to get out of the sun. "We have guitar, piano, drums, bass, and I know I saw a trumpet on your wall, though I didn't see you actually play it, then football, swimming, geometry, motorcycles. I mean you are a serious overachiever," I joked as I leaned my back against the tree.

He shrugged and came closer, invading my space in a way that I wanted.

"What can I say? I've had a lot of spare time...waiting for you."

My heart skidded and now that I knew he felt every movement of it, I watched his face and saw him register it. His lips turned up slightly on the sides.

"Good answer. Add flattery to that list," I stammered as I stared at him, that dimple making me want to touch it.

He laughed again and shook his head. "You are the funniest person I've ever met."

"And you're the sweetest."

"I'm not that sweet," he insisted.

"You're honey bun sweet," I said with an accent as sweet as syrup.

"Oooh." He raised his eyebrows in mock seriousness. "That's like the ultimate compliment."

"Yeah, pretty much," I said grinning.

I glanced around and saw that we were once again under the microscope of his family as they sat, played horseshoes and talked, trying to look like they weren't watching us.

Then I heard Marvin Gaye blaring through the garden. Caleb scoffed and looked over with a raised brow at someone, I followed his line of sight to a guy I hadn't talked to yet. He saluted and winked at Caleb, grinning like a fool and I heard a lot of laughter floating around us. I realized he was using his ability somehow because the music seemed to be right in our ears, everywhere. He was trying to be funny.

It was pretty funny, though it made me blush. So, I started back on topic.

"So, what about tonight? I have to go home at some point."

"I know. I'll just come to your room again, though I wish I could keep you here. Maybe you can say you're spending the night with your friend or something."

My phone dinged with a message.

I can't believe you haven't called or texted me! I need details on you and college boy. Is he as dreamy as he looks? How was the kiss? You did kiss him didn't you? You better have! Come stay with me tonight. Pizza on me.

"Or." I had an idea and wanted to laugh at Beck's timing. "I could actually spend the night with my friend. I have barely seen Beck at all lately and she's leaving for Southern Cal U in a couple weeks. I know it sucks us not being together but it's not my house at least, Marcus wouldn't know to look for me there and I can leave first thing and come straight here to see you."

"But what about sleeping? He can still come to you in your dreams."

"Do you think he still would? After everything that's happened already?"

"I think he would now more than ever."

I sighed. I'm not a cursing person but I was silently cursing Marcus Watson. I had wasted so much time with my best friend being selfish and now, she was leaving soon and I was angry that I couldn't just be with my friend if I wanted to because of some jerk with a megalomania complex.

Caleb touched my cheek to bring me back to reality.

"I'm so sorry. I want you to just be able to do whatever you want; stay with your friend, work, sleep, whenever you want to. I want you to be happy and it kills me that you're not."

"I'm not *unhappy*," I insisted. "Everything is just happening so fast. Last week, I'd never even been in a fight let alone had enemies, now I have Marcus. Last week, my father didn't even speak to me and now he waits up to make sure I made it home safe. Last week, I hadn't spoken to Beck in weeks until the other night and now, I can't even see her. Last week, I wasn't going to college and now I am if I can get in. Last week, I didn't know you." I felt so strange. I wanted to cry. "And now I do. I just hate all the time that I wasted and now I feel like I don't have any. I feel like I can't make any-" I almost said decisions, but I knew what that word would do to Caleb, so I threw it out of my mind quickly. "I feel like I don't know what I'm doing. Like everything is happening around me and I'm just standing in the middle."

His face fell and I'd never seen someone look so guilty before. He grimaced and gripped my hips tightly.

"Ah, Maggie. I never wanted this. That day that Kyle said I didn't believe in all this, he wasn't lying. I did think imprinting wasn't real because I'd never seen it with my eyes. I thought it was over exaggerated. But then it happened to me and I was so happy. I felt complete for the first time, like I wasn't just following my parents and doing what everyone else wanted. It was finally what I wanted. And I hate - absolutely hate - that my happiness has to cause you all this trouble. I'm so sorry, Maggie. If I could take it back, I wouldn't want to, but I would if that's what you wanted. If that's what it took to give you your life back, I would go back and never have touched you."

"Caleb, no, that's not what I meant at all. I'm happy."

He smiled sadly and reached up to skim my cheek with his fingers. "Then why are you crying?" he asked softly.

I wiped the tears away and scoffed. I hadn't even felt them before that.

"I'm crying because it's a lot to handle, but that doesn't mean I want to change it. I don't want that, I want *you.*"

"Only because you think I'd be dead without you there to save me. Without that, I'm sure you wouldn't want it to be like this," he said, slightly harsh.

I pushed into his mind, as was becoming more common for me. It was almost second nature to me, like it had been implanted in me along with the imprint. Maybe it had.

I felt his heart beating erratically in his chest. It pulsed his sadness through my veins and choked me with it. He wanted me to be happy above all else, even at the cost of his happiness, his future, his life. I felt the tears coming fast as his remorse flooded me. It was painful to feel how upset he was, how much regret he felt for being so happy about something he thought made me so sad.

I mentally shook my head. I should never have said those things to him and I wouldn't have if I'd known he felt this way. Couldn't he see how I felt? That I loved him and wanted him and wouldn't go back for anything in the world, even if I knew he wouldn't die. I'd still do it all over again because I wanted him. He belonged to me and I belonged to him.

"I would want it. I do now. I don't want to change anything, that's just some of how I feel, not all."

Why was he not able to feel what I felt for him?

"Yes, I can," he said gruffly, reading my thoughts, "but it's hurting you. This thing between us is hurting you," he growled.

"Thing?" I whispered and felt a ping in my gut.

"Thing. I wish I'd never touched you sometimes because you would never have had to know this world even existed. You could have stayed in your pretty little bubble and never have known different."

"My bubble was not pretty, Caleb. You know that. And how dare you say you wished you'd never touched me!" I yelled and realized what I'd done. I lowered my voice and looked him straight in the eye. "Do you really wish that?"

"It would make things easier."

"No it wouldn't. For you maybe-"

"For you! Your world's been turned upside down, not mine. I was already stuck in the middle of all this and now I dragged you into it, too."

"If I had a choice, I would go back and do everything the same." I cut him off when I saw his protest. "And not because of saving you, because I want to..."

He read my mind. "Be with me? Really?" he spouted sarcastically. "I doubt that, Maggie. I've done nothing but cause you trouble from the moment I met you. You'd hate me if your body didn't force you to want me," he said bitterly.

"Just like yours does with me?" I countered.

"Exactly!"

What was he saying? Why was he all of a sudden so hell bent on putting it out there that we shouldn't have imprinted. He regretted meeting me. That's what he was saying. For some reason, I felt like I had when Chad broke up with me; left behind, unwanted, not special and naïve for feeling like I was different.

It was painful to fight with him, if that's even what this was, to feel his disappointment and hurt pound through my veins. It was physically painful. My heart squeezed and not in a good way as my blood was too hot. I leaned back against the tree to steady my legs. I heard myself whimper as my breaths pushed in and out painfully.

He pulled me close and framed my face with his big hands. I would've sighed at the contact, but I was too upset, though I could feel my body's want to accept his offering of calm.

It scared me because it was the very first time his touch didn't soothe me instantly.

"Ah, baby." He kissed me quickly. Keeping his face still touching mine he continued and I knew he'd been reading me from his tone. "I'm so sorry. I don't want to hurt you, that's not what I meant. I want you, I've never wanted anything more than you. You're everything to me and I just *need* you to be happy. I'm going to do everything I can to see that you are. I just feel responsible for you and it kills me that this has been forced on you, but...I'm so sorry. I take back everything I said. I'm an idiot, ok? Please don't think that I regret one second of waiting for you."

He moved his thumbs to wipe my tears away and I finally felt some of the calm seep into me. He watched me, his blue eyes looked so close to swimming and his expression was sorry and he wondered if he should just shut up or try to apologize again. He couldn't stand the thought that he had hurt me.

"I'm sorry. Baby, please say something," he pleaded anxiously.

"I think I like it when you call me *baby* just as much as I like *sweetheart*."

He gave a surprised laugh. "Maggie, you don't have to do that. You can be mad at me. You can yell at me if it would make you feel better."

"It wouldn't. Besides, it hurts to fight with you."

"It's because we aren't meant to. Like everything else it'll get easier. You'll be fighting with me like a pro in no time," he said joking, but his expression was somber.

"I don't want to fight. I don't want to doubt. Look, even though I can read your feelings for me, sometimes I just feel so...unworthy." He started to interrupt, but I pressed my fingers to his lips. "After everything that's happened to me in the past year, it's not easy to just know for certain that everything is as good as it seems. I'm sorry, too, ok? Will you please not doubt how I feel about you? I want this, I want you. I wouldn't change anything. You said I was everything, but you're everything to me. I promise not to doubt you again. Ok? Please, promise?"

He smiled against my fingers and pulled my hand down. "Promise. But you do know, right? How I feel about you is... You're so funny and amazing and sweet and beautiful. I was half a person before you. You make me feel like everything in my life has been for a reason. I'm just happy that I-"

I stopped him with a kiss because I *knew* and didn't need to hear it. I felt him chuckle as he pressed closer, pinning me against the tree, my hands on his chest in between us.

His lips took away everything. Every second of hurt or doubt in the past fifteen minutes was now a distant memory. I could hear his family around us again. It was strange that I'd completely forgotten where we were, and that we weren't alone, and now their voices seemed to float back to us.

I pulled back from Caleb a little and he pressed his forehead to mine to keep the contact. I could feel that he'd been hurting just as much as I had about our fight, about everything lately, and needed to touch me. So I let him.

"You're so amazing," he murmured. "I'm sorry. I can't say I'm sorry enough."

I nodded and we just stood, sharing breath and letting our touch soothe us as he kept murmuring things to me. I turned my head to look at his family. No one seemed overly worried about us, except Kyle who was glowering, but I almost expected that now from him. Then Caleb turned my face back to look at him.

"I have an idea. Why don't you go to your friend's house right now?"

"Uh, I don't know. Are you trying to get rid of me?" I joked.

"Absolutely not, but that way you'll see her now and then go home to sleep and I can be with you. This way, I won't go crazy worrying about you."

"Yeah, ok."

"Are you ok now? Really?" he asked sincerely.

"Of course," I insisted. "I think you could cure just about anything."

He chuckled bashfully which was so freaking cute.

"Are you sure you feel ok?" His hands coasted down my arms. "You still feel a little warm."

"Yeah." I did feel warm and my throat hurt slightly, but I felt good enough. "I'm fine."

"Man, I wish we were ascended already, then I could heal you." He sighed. "Ok, well, come on. Tell everyone goodbye and I'll give you a ride over there."

He held my hand tight even as I hugged his aunts and uncles, his parents. He wasn't looking forward to being without me at all today and was now willingly taking me to my friends to leave me there. For me, so I could see her. It was not something he wanted to do at all. He was worried about Marcus still, they'd try even harder to get to me.

Kyle hugged me and told me about four times how happy he was that I was ok and if I needed anything to call him. That he wished I'd stay there and not go home, that it wasn't safe for me. Caleb seethed beside me and I peeked back and couldn't help but want to giggle. In his mind he thought Kyle was trying to take his place. That Kyle had no right to worry over me and I agreed, but it was still slightly comical that they were silently fighting over me.

I never, ever in my life thought I'd be fought over before by anyone. And with Chad the other night too...I was just blown away. It wasn't as appealing as everyone made it sound.

Caleb took me to the garage and after the helmet was on and I was behind him he started it up and asked me which way to go. I explained the directions and he drove slowly through town to her house.

When we pulled up, Rebecca was just getting out of her little black Dodge Neon. She put a hand over her eyes to shield the sun and looked at us curiously. When Caleb helped me off the bike and took off my helmet she squealed and ran to me. Her bag slung over her shoulder banged me in the back as she grabbed me in a hug like she hadn't seen me in a year.

"Magpie! You came!" She pulled back to look at me, her face open wide with a smile and then she saw Caleb and her grin turned saucy. "And you brought dessert."

"Beck!" I chastised, but heard Caleb chuckle behind me.

"Since when do you ride a motorcycle?" she asked me.

I told her the same thing as Chad.

"Since Caleb drives one."

"Oooh. Good answer. Hi, Caleb," she said all sultry and I almost wanted to smack her.

"Hey," he answered as I pulled myself from her grasp to step back.

I grabbed his hand to try to fill myself with his touch before he left. He squeezed my hand and smiled at me knowingly.

"So, you came to stay with me? Where's your stuff?" she asked.

"I'm not staying the night. I figured we could just hang out for a while."

"Ok. I'll go call for pizza. Caleb, are you staying?"

"Nope. I'm gonna head out, but thanks," he answered and as soon as she was inside he smiled crookedly. His hand wrapped around the back of my neck.

He pulled my face to his and kissed me deeply and slowly. It was possibly the sexiest kiss I'd ever had. The few kisses we had already were desperate and needy. This was full of love and sweetness. He pulled me closer with his hand on my hip and continued to let his lips take me over.

He began to playfully nip and peck my lips. I laughed into our kiss before he eventually broke it gently.

"Are you trying to persuade me not to go?" I asked panting.

"Is it working?" he whispered against my lips.

I smiled. "So, I'll get Beck to drive me home later. You'll come, right?"

"Of course. Why don't you text me and let me know when you're home?"

"Ok." I kissed his dimple quickly. "Bye."

"Bye."

I turned, but couldn't step. I turned back to look at him and he knew.

"So...it's you again this time," he smirked.

"Shut up," I laughed.

"Go inside and have fun with your friend, Maggie. Then call me and I'll see you tonight."

"Ok."

"Oh, and uh...leave your mind open to me. I need to know what's going on with you, ok? I know," he held up his hands in acceptance, "tyrant. But after everything that's happened, I need it, Maggie."

"It's ok. I'd feel better like that anyway. Just don't listen to what I say about you," I jested.

"Never." He grabbed my face gently and I felt him pushing in my mind so I pushed into his. We'd only done this once before with totality. It was so intense how I could feel everything in him just like it was in me. It wasn't like normal, just picking up bits and pieces and his heartbeat never left me when we were like this. This was everything. "Ok. Now just keep the connection open and I'll see you tonight."

"Ok." I smiled up at him. "Bye, for real."

He waited until I was inside before leaving and as soon as I turned the corner Beck grabbed me by the shoulders.

"Holy cow, Mags! What was that?"

"What?"

"That! That wasn't just a kiss. That was a... something that is not just a kiss, kiss."

"What? I can't kiss the guy I'm dating?"

"You're dating him?" she exclaimed.

"Yeah. What did you think I was doing?"

"Trying to piss off Chad," she said matter-of-factly.

"No! Why would I do that?"

"Because he's still in love with you. He was livid at Pablo's. Li-vid. And I know you said nothing was going on with you and Kyle, but I just thought maybe, somewhere in your brain, you were trying to make Chad jealous. I saw him grab you up after graduation like nothing had happened. Like he hadn't dumped you. Jerk."

"No, absolutely not. I really like Caleb. This has nothing to do with Chad."

"Really?"

"Yes, really." I followed her into her kitchen and she began to pour some diet cream soda into glasses. "But Chad came over the other night."

She gasped and spilled some soda on the counter. "What? He did? Oh, my gosh. What did he say?" she spouted in a flurry.

"That he wanted us to get back together," I admitted softly.

"Ahhh, Mags. You have guys fighting over you. So sweet," she crooned.

I hopped up on the counter top.

"It's not sweet, it was sad. He waited on my front steps for me and when I pulled up on Caleb's motorcycle, he was so angry. He said he wanted to talk alone so Caleb left. Then he told me he made a mistake and wanted us back together."

"Wow."

"Yeah. I was pretty shocked. So, I told him I was with Caleb and he said Caleb didn't know me like him, that he knew every time I'd ever been sick, that he knew all my broken bones and Caleb knew nothing about me."

"Wow, Mags. If this wasn't Chad we were talking about I'd ask for his number. How romantic is he! Where was all that when you guys were dating?"

"I know! I told him that after he kissed me." She gasped again. "Yeah. He kissed me, like he's never kissed me before. It was all tongues and hands and...well, it would have been something if we were still dating. I told him that. I said, if you had kissed me like that when we were still dating, maybe we'd still be together."

"Holy cow. You're so lucky."

"What? Why?" I asked. Sometimes it was hard to keep up with her demented logic.

"Because having guys fight over you is hot!"

"No, it's not," I insisted, "it sucks. Why now? Because he was jealous? Because he finally decided he didn't want to go to college alone? Why? Why didn't he do this before I met Caleb? But then I wouldn't have met him, Beck. And I would take anything that happened to me all over again to meet Caleb like I did because..."

She gaped at me, her glass rolled with condensation in her hand. At first her expression was laced with unbelief and then worry and then realization.

"Ok, Maggie, listen. I really like Caleb, he's hot, but are you sure he's not just some college boy trying to get some booty before he goes back to school?"

"No, he's not."

"But how do you know? Boys can be very charming, Mags. Very believable."

"Caleb isn't like that. I know it's only been a few days, but you- you just don't understand. Trust me, that won't happen."

"So he hasn't tried to play shifty fingers with you yet? Or, 'oops my hand slipped onto your boob' or 'I have no idea why my hand is there, it just had a mind of its own but since it's there, let's have a go'?"

"No," I said bemused.

"Really? Hmmm. Every college guy I've ever met was like that."

"I told you, Caleb is different."

"He's never copped a feel," she said incredulously, "even a little."

"No!" I laughed. "Jeez, can we talk about something else?"

"Has he tried to take you to a party yet?"

"No."

"Hmm. Well, he will. And that's where he'll make his move."

"Ok, Beck. I'll be on my guard. Now, tell me what's going on with you."

"Oh, nothing but the normal."

The doorbell rang and she ran to answer it. She came back with two boxes. "Beck? Who else are you feeding?"

"No one, but I've got lots of questions and I want to keep you plastered with cheese to keep you talking."

I laughed as I followed her to the living room. She turned on her iPod and then sat with me on the couch. "Where are your parents?" I asked.

"Oh, they're at this charity thing for the school. They've decided to sponsor a student. You know, school supplies, new clothes, football dues."

"That's nice of them."

"Yeah, whatever. So." She bit into a huge piece and the cheese stringed from her mouth, but she kept talking. "What are you gonna do when lover boy goes back to school?"

"Well, I'm going, too."

"What? I thought you weren't going to college? I thought you couldn't get in?"

"I couldn't, but Caleb's family has ties to the school, Tennessee. So...I'm going."

"Oh, he definitely wants in your pants," she said with surety.

"Beck, he may want in my pants. In fact, I'm sure all boys want into the girls' pants that they're dating, but that's not why he's doing this."

I felt a little burst of laughter in my mind. It was warm and made me giddy. At first I was confused, but then I felt him. Felt him like he was standing right next to me. Caleb was here in my mind and he was enjoying the conversation. I tried to send him a thought to see if it'd work.

Are you enjoying this?

Immensely. But don't worry. I'm only checking in, not listening to everything.

I hid a laugh and tried to forget he was here so I'd be normal with Beck.

"Then why? You barely know him. It's creepy," she continued.

"I thought you would love this for some reason. It's so spontaneous and romantic."

"Yeah, for me! Not you! You're so responsible and a little naïve and sweet and...and responsible! You don't do things like this. It's scaring me a little."

"It's fine. Hey, why don't we all go out? And then you can grill him yourself. Double date?"

"Ok. Best idea so far. When?" she spouted all motherly.

"What about tomorrow night? I get off at seven so we can meet at eight? I'll ask Caleb if he's ok with that."

"But what about the farewell party at the school? That's tomorrow night at 8:00. Aren't you going?"

"I wasn't planning on it. I'd forgotten actually," I grumbled. "We'll see. So I guess we can all go out the next night then."

"I'll spy who I wrangle up to be my date."

"What about Ralph? He was really into you. You guys went out a few times."

"Yeah, I know...but his name is *Ralph*," she whined.

"Oh, come on, Beck, you are not that shallow."

"I could be! Ok, fine. I'll text Ralph. He is pretty cute. Maybe I'll see what his middle name is. I bet he'd let me call him that instead."

I rolled my eyes at her and then her iPod changed songs to '*Relator*' by Pete Yorn and Scarlett Johansson. She squealed, as this was our song. Well it was her song and I played along. She pulled me up and bounced and danced with me as she sang loudly. I laughed, missing her terribly.

We shook our fingers as we sang like we were scolding someone. Then lined our backs up and danced some more.

Then her parents walked in.

Nineteen

"Maggie. Rebecca," her father stated after Beck ran to turn down the music. He was clearly amused and trying to hide it. "I'm glad to see you two hanging out again."

"Hey, Mister T," I said as I went to hug him. They were the sweetest people. And their name was Thompson so I called them Mr. and Mrs. T. He loved it because of the joke. They always let me crash here, especially right after my mom left, and even though Beck was spoiled rotten, they were still really good to her and everyone else. "Long time, no see."

"Yeah." He hugged me tightly and then released me to snag a piece of pizza. "They feed us like birds at those things. So, Maggie, what've you been up to? Haven't seen you around much lately. We thought Rebecca had chased you off for good."

"Yeah," Mrs. T chimed as she too lifted a piece of pizza from the box. "We missed you."

"No, she couldn't chase me off. I haven't been doing much, just working mostly."

"And going out with a totally hot new guy," Beck blurted.

There was no point in trying to stop her. Her parents were as bad as she was.

"Really?" he asked in a fake girly accent. "Do tell."

Mrs. T and I laughed, but Beck did not.

"Daddy, eww." But she was over it quickly and threw her arm over my shoulder. "So, yes. Our little Maggie bagged herself a college boy."

"Really?" His brow furrowed in concern. As cool as they wanted to seem, they were still parents. "Now, Maggie, I'd be careful with this boy. Once guys leave high school, everything changes. I remember college, when I met the wife and I wasn't exactly noble-"

"Honey, no. Not appropriate," Mrs. T insisted.

"I'm careful. Don't worry," I assured them. "He's really nice and has already met my dad."

"And how is your father?" he asked sincerely.

"Much better."

"Ok, good. Well, we'll let you girls get back to it." He went to Beck to kiss her forehead and then they made their way out, but stopped at the door. "Make sure you come back, Maggie. We miss you around here, definitely not loud enough."

I smiled.

"Ok."

"Ok, so." Beck went right back to scheming. "Stay with me tonight. You can wear something of mine."

"Can't, have to work tomorrow."

"You don't go in until later. Stay."

"I can't." I thought hard for an excuse, but Caleb saved me.

Tell her your dad is really strict lately, which isn't a lie. I can also feel your fever, that you don't feel too good. You ok?

Yeah. Just tired. I'll take some Tylenol for the fever. I'm ok.

"Dad's kind of gotten over his funk. He's really been on my case lately."

"Really? Well, that's good, I guess. Ok, well it's ok. I'll see you tomorrow night anyway right?"

"Maybe."

"Come," she commanded.

I stayed for a couple more hours. We watched a 'wanna-be' scary movie in her mini-theater in her basement about a girl who is stalked because she answered a phone call or something. It was strange but Beck was appropriately girly and screamed and gasped at all the right moments. I just wanted to laugh but Beck loved these girly scary-but-not-scary movies. It was no Poltergeist.

After that it started to get dark, so Beck took me home. I told her I was excited about the next night, which was a lie. I was *so* not excited, but I knew that she would love Caleb once she got to know him and wouldn't think he was just some hot guy trying to steal my virtue and then skip back to college.

I'm home.

I sent him the message as I opened my front door. Dad was just then taking off his boots by the hall closet.

See you soon.

"Hey, Dad. How was work?"

"Good. Great actually. I got promoted."

"What? Awesome! What happened?"

I came to stand by him and tried to ignore the boot odor.

"Well, I saved a load of wood today from being destroyed by the new guy. He was an inch away from messing up the whole load and possibly cutting his arm off and I stopped him, right in front of the boss. So, I got promoted to general overseer because he said I had an eye for these things." I smiled at him as he beamed. I hadn't seen him so happy in a very long time. "So, I'm salary now and even get off an hour early every day."

"Dad, that's so great."

"Thanks, kiddo. Did you eat?"

"Yeah, Beck filled me with cheese pizza. You want me to fix you something?"

"No, I'll make a sandwich. I'm pretty beat so I'm gonna eat and go to bed, I think. You ok?"

"Yeah, I'm gonna go to bed, too."

"All right." He stood and stretched his back, then yawned. "Well, goodnight."

"Night, Dad."

I went straight to the shower. I didn't bring any clothes with me, thought I'd have enough time to change before Caleb got there. So I wrapped the towel around me and went to my room…and found Caleb sitting on my bed. I felt his instant desire and longing engulf me so I grabbed some clothes, wordlessly from my dresser, and went into the closet to get dressed quickly.

While at Kyle's I'd learned a few things. Like Caleb being so completely in tune with me and feeling everything I felt. He was hurting right along with me with the offense mark removal, and I never wanted to cause him pain again. Even if it was the uncomfortable kind from seeing me almost naked and his body responding, making him need me in ways that we weren't ready for yet. Well, I wasn't.

When I came out he was still sitting there. I didn't want to make things harder for him, seeing as how everything was so much more intense for him than me, which still didn't seem possible but there it was, right there in my head how conflicted he was and how much he wanted me. How much his body told him to have me.

I sat on the bed next to him and leaned my head on his shoulder. I laced our fingers, letting our touch cure my aches.

"Hey."

"Hey," he answered. "You're getting really good at reading me."

"Well, your mind was wide open."

"Yeah. If you had come over here with that towel on..." I laughed and snuggled closer. "You're still warm, Maggie." He placed a hand on my forehead, then my cheek. "Where's the medicine cabinet?"

"In my bathroom." I yawned. "My dad's room is downstairs so he shouldn't be up here."

He nodded and peeked out the door before disappearing and reappearing a minute later.

"Here, take these." He handed me a couple pills with a glass of water. I took them and lay down on top of the covers. Wow, I hadn't realized how bad I felt until right then. "Need anything else?"

"Just you," I said groggily and beckoned him to me. He lay down beside me to face me and played with my fingers on the pillow. I put my hand on his cheek, letting my fingers smooth over his dimple. "So, there's this thing at the school tomorrow, a party for the graduated seniors. I hadn't planned on going, but Beck begged me, so...but..."

"But?"

"I don't want to go."

"So don't go."

"But I promised."

"So, go," he said grinning.

"Will you come with me?"

"Of course I'm coming with you," he scoffed.

"We don't have to go," I reasoned.

"Yeah, sure we do." His smile was wry as he rubbed his chin. "You, uh, gonna be ok with introducing me to your friends?"

"Hmm." That was debatable. "We'll find out."

"Ashamed of me already?" he joked.

"No, of course not. I just don't want to try to explain...how I just met you a few days ago and can't stop looking at you with googly eyes."

He chuckled softly. "Googly eyes," he echoed and nodded. "Ok. Sure, we can go if you feel better." He cleared his throat. "You working tomorrow?"

"Yes."

"Well, the tyrant is going to sit in the back booth, ok?"

"For eight hours?" I asked incredulously.

"It doesn't matter." He sighed and sucked his lip in and out. "You're in my mind right now. Can't you see how it literally hurts me to even think about you in danger? Just letting you go to Beck's was hard but your work is..." He shook his head. "When we went to the Watson compound we found out who the echoling was and what they had planned. Marcus and his uncle plan to kidnap you and take you somewhere locked up where it would take me a very long time to find you. We'd both be in agony in just a day or two. They want to take you from me so neither of us will ascend. You see why I'm freaking? They know where you live. They know where you work. They knew I was going to be with my father that night. It's too risky and I'm sorry if you feel like I'm going overboard but I have to keep you safe. If you feel like you have to give notice before you quit, then that's fine, but I've got to be there with you. I'm sorry."

I sighed, knowing what he was saying was true. Marcus had told me that himself. "I know. Marcus told me once in a dream that's what he wanted to do."

"He did? You didn't tell me that."

"I forgot. It was always so stressful after I woke up. I understand, ok? I'll tell Big John something; that I'm in trouble or something, he won't care about you being there. But what are you gonna do sitting back there all day?"

"I have a couple papers due and a book list to read before school starts. I'll have plenty to do and I've been dreading it because none of it has to do with geometry," he said and smirked.

"Ok, if you're sure. Now I feel bad," I groaned. "I don't want you to sit there bored all day because of me."

"It's ok, really. The only way I'm going to get all this work done anyway is if you're busy. Otherwise, I'll just be distracted," he said gruffly, and leaned forward to kiss my chin.

"Oh, we wouldn't want that," I said with mock sincerity.

"No, definitely not."

I giggled as he kissed me and wrestled me under him. He tickled my sides and kissed under my chin at the same time. It was torture in every good sense. But when I reached my hand under his shirt to tickle his ribs I learned that boys can be more ticklish than girls. He jerked so quickly and laughed trying to squirm away, but I held on and he retaliated with gusto.

I'd forgotten about Dad.

I heard his footsteps up the stairs and thought quickly. Caleb looked at me with worry, his mind racing to whether he should bolt out the window or jump in the closet.

"Beck! Shut up! I can't believe you!" I yelled playfully, pretending to be on the phone.

Miraculously, I heard his footsteps stop and recede. We both sighed and chuckled softly in relief into each other's shoulders. I was glad because my eyelids were fighting with me anyway.

We called a truce and I reached down and pulled the blanket over us from the foot of the bed. He then rolled me over to put my back to him as he wrapped his arms around me. I sighed at the warmth and comfort, I nestled my back and bottom in closer. He pulled my hair behind me and to the side, then he placed a kiss on the back of my neck.

"Sleep. Feel better tomorrow."

"K," I muttered as I did what I was told.

"Wake up." Someone shook me. "You've got to get up, baby. You're going to be late."

"What?"

I opened up my eyes to see Caleb looking concerned. "It's after 10:00. You better get up. Or maybe you should stay home. Do you feel better?" He touched my forehead.

"After 10:00? Jeez, I thought I set my alarm," I groaned.

"You did. I've been trying to get you up for fifteen minutes. Are you feeling ok?"

"Yeah, I am." And I did. Sleeping with him was the best medicine. "Did you sleep well?"

"I always sleep best with you," he said sweetly, pulled me closer and kissed the top of my head.

"You're right, I've got to get up." I pulled from his grasp and was rewarded with a groan from him that made me turn to hide my smile. "I can't believe your parents condone you sneaking into some girls' window."

"You're not some girl," he corrected.

"I know," I smiled, "it's just strange."

"Well, my mom doesn't condone it at all. She's conflicted about the whole thing. She understands why we have to do it, but doesn't like it. She thinks it's all very scandalous."

I laughed and sat beside him on the bed. "Well, she's kind of right."

"You don't like me sneaking into your window all romantic like?" he asked and leaned close, his nose almost touching mine.

"I do like it, but it would be better if we didn't have to sneak, you know?"

"Yeah, I know." He leaned back a little and pushed my hair behind my ear. "But it's necessary. You're not upset about it, are you? I would never do something like this if it wasn't about your safety. I'm not one of those guys."

"I know that and I know it's only temporary. We'll figure it all out soon."

He nodded. "I'm sorry."

"It's fine, Caleb. I'm not upset, I promise." I leaned the few inches between us and rubbed his nose with mine. "It's very sweet, the things you do for me."

"Yeah, because sleeping with you is torture," he said sarcastically and kissed the end of my nose. "Ok. Well, I'm going to get out of here and then come pick you up at the door. I'll tell your dad I'm driving you to work today."

"Ok."

He got up and I saw he was in his clothes from yesterday still. He must have seen me looking at him because he looked down at himself, too.

"Oh, yeah. Let me run to my uncle's and I'll be back to take you to work." He picked up his book bag, slinging it over his shoulder and turned to look at me. "Don't leave until I get here, ok? I'll be right back."

"Ok. I'll wait. Hurry."

"Ok." He kissed me on the cheek and then looked at me imploringly.

I laughed. "I love it when it's you." I giggled at his expression. "Go to your uncle's and do what you need to do. Hurry back and I'll be waiting for you."

"Thank you, baby," he murmured sweetly.

He kissed my lips quickly before opening and sliding out the window.

I turned and got dressed as fast as I could. Running to the bathroom and fixing my hair and slicking on a little makeup, I thought about what to tell my boss when I gave him my notice today. They'd been so good to me and I hated having to leave them, but if I was going to college, it would happen soon anyway.

It took me about twenty minutes to get ready and I only had fifteen minutes left until I was late for work. I was about to run downstairs when I heard Dad yelling for me.

"Maggie! Caleb is here."

"Coming!"

I checked my hair once more in the mirror and then ran downstairs. I hadn't thought about Caleb not seeing me in my uniform. It was just a uniform after all, but by the way he was looking at me when I came down, he apparently thought differently.

Holy hell.

I gasped inwardly at his thoughts and looked down at my outfit. It was a little short, as I said, but I had footless tights on underneath. It was white, as were the tights and it buttoned all the way up with a little open collar and a little belt around the waist and a black half apron. I looked back at him curiously and quirked a brow.

You apparently don't see what I see. You work in that thing and you don't get asked out every five minutes? That's a bold faced lie!

I giggled out loud and Dad looked at me.

"Something...funny?" he asked all cocked browed.

"Nothing. Um, Caleb and I are going to the farewell party at the school tonight so I won't be here for dinner, ok?"

"Ok. You know the rules, before midnight."

"Yes, Dad, I know." I hugged him and he seemed surprised by it, leaning back to look at me with a half smile.

"Um," he cleared his throat, "ok, well have fun. And be careful. Caleb, you remember what I said about that bike?"

"Yes, sir; helmet, speed limit, careful. Promise."

"All right. See ya later."

"Bye, Dad." I grabbed Caleb's hand to pull him with me. "Good luck on your first day with your promotion."

"Thanks, Mags," Dad said softly and I looked over my shoulder to see him looking sad and conflicted.

I turned to Caleb and even though I knew I was going to be late, I had to see what put that look on my dad's face. But before I could ask Caleb he answered me.

"Go ahead. I'll wait at the bike."

"Thank you."

I walked slowly over to Dad as he sat on the bottom step of the stairs. I always loved these stairs when I was a kid. The carpet was plush and soft, almost baby blue in color, which is my favorite. I used to slide down on my belly all the way down from top to bottom until my stomach was red and sore but I just kept doing it.

I sat on the step beside him and sighed as I lay my head on his shoulder.

"What's up, Dad?"

"Nothing."

"Liar," I chimed sweetly and he laughed.

He sighed heavily, loaded with something he didn't want to talk about.

"I got a call from your mom."

Twenty

My heart jolted at his words. "What?"

"She called me late last night, crying. She wants to come home," he said somberly.

I was confused. I thought he'd be happy. All that stuff he'd spouted to me about us not loving her enough, taking advantage of her. I thought he'd be thrilled if she ever decided to crawl back.

"And what did you say?" I asked softly, my voice not even sounding like my own.

I saw Caleb come peek anxiously through the open door, no doubt feeling my crazy heartbeat and I smiled at him and waved him off.

"I told her... baby, I'm sorry. I told her no," he creaked and looked on the brink of tears.

I hugged him. My words muffled into his shoulder. "Why? Why did you say that, and why are you so upset about it?"

"Because, I know you need her. I should be able to just let her come home for you but I can't. She was furious. She thought I'd just let her come home and everything would be fine without even being sorry, pick up right where she left off. You were right, she was being selfish. She chose to leave, we didn't do anything wrong. We were a good family and she decided to just leave all that behind for God knows why. I forgive her for what she did, but she deserted you and needs to accept her consequences. I'm sorry."

"Dad, I don't want her to come back."

"What?" He turned to look full at me. "I thought you'd be angry at me. I thought you'd blame me for keeping her away."

"What for? She didn't just leave me, Dad, she left you, too. And I know she's my mom but she left and I agree with you. She needs to deal with the consequences. She made her bed and she can sleep in it. Nowhere does it say in the family handbook that when someone leaves and wants to come back without reason or sincere apology that you have to let them. It just says that you have to love them. And I do love her still and I'd be her neighbor any day, but it wouldn't be right for her to live with you just for me. She betrayed you more than me."

"But you forgave me."

"Yes, and I forgive her, too, but she shouldn't live here, Dad. She said you held her back. She's been living with other men. It wouldn't be-"

"She what?"

Crap. He hadn't known that. I bit my lip. "She told me she was dating. She talked about a few of them."

"A few of them?" He laughed a bark of a humorless laugh. "Well, I guess I made the right decision then. I told her she couldn't come back to stay with us and she shouldn't come see you without calling you first."

"Very smooth, Dad, way to handle things."

"How'd you get so smart?" he smirked, but sadly.

"I learned from my old man," I joked and bumped him with my shoulder. "You did the right thing. I don't know what happened to her but you are way too good for her to do this to you."

He laughed. "All right, kiddo. You're late now, I'm sorry. I'm fine. Get going."

"No worries, Dad." I kissed his cheek and he hugged me before standing.

"Have fun tonight."

"I will. Bye."

I went out to meet Caleb and he still looked a little worried but smiled sadly at me. "You ok?"

"You heard?" He nodded. "Yeah, I'm fine. I just can't believe she'd do this to him after being gone almost a year," I said vehemently. "She's so selfish!"

"I'm sorry, but I think your dad did the right thing."

"Me, too. I just hate that he has to go through this again. He's been through so much this year. He's just now starting to be normal."

"I know." He hugged me around my middle. "You want to stay here with him instead of going to work?"

"Nuhuh. He's fine. I just hope she doesn't try to come here or anything." I glanced at Caleb's watch. "Dang it, I'm so late. You might not have to worry about my quitting; I might get fired if I keep this up."

I put my helmet on and he buckled it for me. "Well, let's go then. I'd hate to not see you in action in that outfit."

"Hey!" I smacked his back playfully as I climbed on behind him. "I don't get it. Why do you like it?"

He shrugged and I could literally feel his attraction. "What's not to like? It's hot."

I just rolled my eyes and hugged him close from behind as he cranked it up and we drove to the diner.

When we pulled up, we got off the bike and he dragged his bag out of the back compartment. I took my helmet off and shook out my hair before twisting it into a messy up do. Caleb turned to see me and groaned.

"Ah, Maggie, you are making my fantasy so much worse."

"All right you," I laughed. "Get a hold of yourself," I said in as low a voice as I could muster, and pulled him down to kiss me.

It wasn't long before I had the urge to glance inside. I then had a slight moment of panic. Number one, Big John was walking out the door with a meat cleaver gleaming in his hand. Yes, a meat cleaver. Number two, he was glaring at Caleb like he was the devil himself.

"Maggie, get your butt in this diner, right now," he commanded.

"Big John, this is Caleb. I'm sorry I'm late."

"Get inside, Maggie. I'll handle this." He came to stand in front of us. "You. What do you think you're doing with my little girl, huh? She's only seventeen and I won't have you riding in here on your hog, all smooth and messing with my girl."

"Hog?" I asked and he pinned his glare on me.

"I thought I told you to go inside."

"B.J." I positioned myself in between him and Caleb. "I told you, this is Caleb. He's my..."

Dang it. I still didn't know what to call him.

"I'm her boyfriend, sir." Caleb extended his hand but Big John just continued to glare, ignoring the hand. "It's nice to meet you. I've heard a lot about you from Maggie."

"Oh, is that right? Boyfriend? You mean dead man! I know your type, ok? I used to be your type. You think you can trick a pretty little girl into giving you the goods and then skip town."

"Big John, eww. Enough. Look, Caleb is a nice guy. I'm sorry if you think he's a bad influence on me because I wasn't here yesterday and I'm late today, but there's a lot of stuff going on right now. Stuff you don't know. Can you lower the cleaver, please?"

He huffed and crossed his arms with it instead.

"What things?" His brow drew together and then it turned to rage. "Oh, my Lord, Maggie! Are you pregnant? I'll kill you!" He lunged for Caleb and I pushed him back with me.

Caleb was confused. He thought meeting my dad was going to be bad and it had been cake compared to this.

"Of course I'm not pregnant! I'm...being stalked," I blurted. Big John stopped and looked sharply at me. "There's this guy who's been after me. Caleb's been watching out for me. Making sure I'm safe."

"What? Who? Give me his address. I'll end this right now."

"It's not that simple. I don't know where he lives or anything about him really, just that he tried to kidnap me the other night and Caleb stopped him. He saved me."

Big John glanced at Caleb with new eyes and tucked the cleaver in his apron, like that helped.

"All right, thank you. Maggie is like a daughter to me. Get inside, you two. Come on."

We followed him in and Caleb whispered in my ear from behind. "What in the-"

"Honey!" Smarty yelled. "Oh, my goodness, I thought he was going to kill your biker friend."

"Me, too," Caleb muttered.

"It's ok, now. Smarty, this is Caleb. Caleb, Smarty and Mena Bena."

"Nice to meet you, ladies," Caleb said and it was hard to stifle the giggle at the look they got on their faces. I wasn't the only one affected by his charm. "Ok," he thumped my nametag and smiled, "Sweet Pea. I'll get out of your way and go park it in the back booth." He kissed my upturned lips softly and quickly. I heard a soft gasp and an angry grunt behind me. "Pretend I'm not here."

"That's not possible," I said breathlessly making him smirk as he walked away.

"Um, details. Now," Mena ordered.

"That's Caleb," I said aloofly as I started to stack napkins.

"Yes, we gathered that. And is he your man?"

"Yes," I said and heard the smile creep in.

"Oh! Yay. He's so cute, honey," Smarty chimed.

"I know. I'm sorry I'm late. I had a problem with my dad. But Caleb's going to sit in the back while I work. Because...someone's stalking me. Caleb saved my life."

"Ah! How romantic!" Mena said as she clutched her chest.

"Which one?" Smarty asked dryly. "The stalker or the saving her?"

"Both!"

Smarty and I both groaned at her as she bounced away. "I have more bad news," I confessed. "I'm officially giving my two week notice."

She sighed. "I knew this day would come. Big John!"

"Yeah," he said and came around the grill.

"Our girl is quitting."

"What for?" he asked and I could hear the hurt.

"I'm leaving for college soon. Caleb's father helped me and I can go to school in the fall. So, I'm going. Plus with this whole stalker thing...it'd be one less thing to worry about. I'm sorry. I'm gonna miss you guys so much." I hugged him around his middle. "You've been so good to me."

He hugged me back with gusto. "I'm gonna miss you something awful, girl."

"Me, too," Smarty said and wiped her eyes.

"You're sure it's not this boy. He's not gotten you mixed up into something has he? Not taking advantage of you?"

"No. I promise."

"Ok. Well, then you get your butt to work then if I only got you for two more weeks," he said gruffly and cleared his throat.

I laughed and pulled away from him, wiping my eyes, too. "Ok. Thanks."

I took my first table and kept glancing at Caleb. He wasn't getting much work done back there because he was watching my every move with eager eyes. One table was a group of guys there vacationing from Michigan to see the mountains. They flirted with me but I remained politely obtuse as I usually did.

I looked at Caleb on the way to place their order and saw him with his head propped up on his fist. His lips were twisted in irritation and his leg was bouncing under the table.

It's just boys. Don't get all worked up. You know, you're not getting much work done back there.

It's driving me insane how incredibly hot you look. Plus it's ingrained in me to want to pummel those guys for even looking at you. I can't help it.

Well, I'm sorry but I can't help how I look, I said and sent a laugh with it.

Very true. Ok, gorgeous, I'll get to work, but can you tone it down, just a little bit?

You are insane.

I looked to see him grinning at me. I grinned back and then got back to work. He stood by his statement and the next few times I glanced, he was going through his books and writing.

It went by slowly but steady. I told Smarty all about Caleb, how we met, how he was incredibly sweet and careful with me. She said she was happy for me and that he was extremely cute. We talked about college and my dad a little bit in between tables. I told her about my mom, too, and how she had called and wanted to come home and my dad had said no.

She listened and sympathized, but in the end did what she always did. She was an awesome listener but never told me what to do. She didn't make suggestions or criticize. She just listened and I loved her for it.

When it was time for my break, I sat with Caleb and brought him some sweet tea and a cheesy bacon burger with fries.

"Where did you get this bracelet?" he asked as he fingered the star charm.

"They gave it to me," I hooked my thumb over my shoulder towards the grill, "for graduation." He nodded. "What did Kyle get for a graduation present?"

"A car."

"I thought he already had a car?"

"He did, but his parents got him a new one, the first one was used. The silver Audi is his."

I balked.

"What? I thought that was his dad's car."

"Nope. Kyle just thought his car was messed up and in the shop. His dad actually pulled the battery cables off before school one morning so Kyle would think it was broken down." He chuckled.

"Wow. That Audi was pretty nice for a college kid."

"He's spoiled. Only child," he scoffed.

I smirked at him. "You're pretty spoiled, too, pal. A truck and a motorcycle?" I shook my head at him. "There are carless kids in Milwaukee and you have two! Disgraceful," I joked.

"Hey!" he laughed. "I'll have you know my truck is a hand me down from my dad and that bike was my graduation present."

"Oh, well that makes it better." I grinned at him.

"So, what did your dad get you?"

"Nothing." I smiled sadly. "He didn't even stand when they called my name."

"I'm sorry." I shook my head at him. "I wish I'd paid more attention at the ceremony now. I might have remembered you from when you crossed the stage."

"Yeah. That iPod is not good for you."

"You already know me so well." He smirked and rubbed my feet under the table with his, making me laugh.

"Ok, back to work, both of us."

Later that night after Caleb took me home and we both parted ways to get dressed, I was on the back of his bike. This time, headed back to the place I never thought I'd go again, the high school, the gym to be precise.

I wasn't even sure why I wanted to go. If it wasn't for Beck's begging... I wasn't sure why exactly but we were underway so there was no point in stopping now. Caleb seemed to be excited about the idea of seeing the people I went to school with, besides Kyle and Chad, excited to see pictures of me during school functions. I'd been so out of the loop this year, out of touch with friends, out of focus. I had no idea what they were going to do tonight, but I was pretty sure it wouldn't involve me since I'd barely been involved myself all year.

We pulled into the parking lot and he helped me take my helmet off, smoothing my hair back. I was nervous for some reason. I felt like everyone there would be able to tell that I was different somehow. We started walking towards the school and my heart beat faster and faster the closer we got.

"Hey," he stopped in front of me, "we don't have to go in there."

I swallowed and looked around the school parking lot. There weren't a whole lot of cars because this was only for the senior class but still...a gym full of my peers whom I abandoned for the past ten months.

He read my anxiety and started pulling me back to the bike. I halted my steps.

"No, it's ok. Let's go in."

"You're sure?"

"Yeah. It's stupid to be nervous anyway. It's not like anyone is going to care that I'm here."

I had visions of prom, streamers and flashing lights with glittery signs when we entered. But what I got was flashbacks that made me want to simultaneously smile and run.

The decorations were our school pictures, prom pics, candids at lunch. Big, blown up pictures lined the walls and the centerpieces on the tables were a school pom-pom and yearbook opened to the page of the people who were assigned to sit there alphabetically. I looked around at the photos as we made our way down the wall towards the tables and laughed at one of Beck and I sitting in art last year with paint on our faces, laughing.

Caleb smiled at it and let me tug and pull him as I got more enthusiastic about the photos and memories splayed out everywhere I looked. Then I heard my name across the room and turned to see Beck and Nicolette skipping across the gym, arm in arm towards us.

"Mags!" Nicolette cried and squeezed me. They both squealed and bounced around me, drawing attention to us and I cringed. "Oh. My. Goodness. You look so fab. Where have you been, girl?"

"Uhum," Beck said grinning and pointed to Caleb. "That's where she's been."

Nicolette perused him openly and gave a cocked little grin before coming up to him and holding her hand out.

"Nicolette."

"Caleb," he said politely and shook her hand quickly before releasing her and coming to put an arm around my waist. Her eyes bugged a little but she grinned all the same. "You girls ran track with Maggie?"

"And Cheerleading and Volleyball and just about everything else."

He looked down at me with a raised eyebrow, his lips parted.

Cheerleading? That totally just blew your little work outfit out of the water.

I pressed my lips together to keep from giggling.

It was only ninth and tenth grade. I did it because my mom wanted me to. I dropped out, it wasn't for me.

And yet my fantasy lives.

I smiled and tried not to laugh, to look normal and casual though an extremely hot guy was speaking into my mind about his fantasies.

Then an enraptured mass squeal erupted as Beck and Nicolette waved. The group of girls who I used to know all swarmed around us like they hadn't seen us in years, though it had been days. Technically, I guess it had been longer for me.

"Magsie! Where have you been?"

"Oh, we missed you at the meet last month. We could've used you when Brayers came up-"

"Dang, girl. You look so cute tonight!"

"Ok! Ok! I got it! Let's do a cheer! For old time sake!"

Meghan was the instigator, but everyone seemed to be on board and clapped and squealed as they made their way to the front of the room.

"Mags. You, too!"

I turned to the traitorous voice and was shocked to find it was Beck. "I haven't cheered in two years," I protested and clung to Caleb's arm.

"Oh, come on. We're doing the spirit cheer. It stays the same every year, it's tradition. Come on."

"No, no way." She had to know why I didn't want to do it. For the spirit cheer you paired with a football player. We danced and slid around them and at the end they lifted us in their arms. Chad was always my partner and there was no way in hell or high water she was getting me on that stage. "Go ahead, Beck. Really, I'm not going."

Beck pouted, but straightened up, glancing behind me warily. She bit her lip and bee lined for the stage. I didn't even need to turn to know Chad was behind me. Caleb also must have known and I felt his grip tighten on my hand. I remembered what he said about seeing Chad again, after I'd slipped and said that Chad had kinda sorta forced me to kiss him, and I felt really stupid for coming here now.

"Maggie, come on, we're an uneven number without you," he coaxed and smiled that smile that used to make me smile, too.

"No, thanks. You go ahead."

He had the gall to reach for my unoccupied hand.

"I don't think so," Caleb said softly with clear inflection and pulled me a little closer to him.

I felt protectiveness, even some possessiveness, and a flare of anger burst towards me from Caleb. He was angry at Chad for kissing me and even angrier that he had the gumption to reach for me and pull me from Caleb like he had the right to. I put my other hand on his arm, hoping to draw even more of his anger away. I visibly saw him take a deep breath and was proud that he kept himself in check at least, though his anger was practically crackling in the air between them.

Chad seemed to debate whether this was a fight he wanted or not. Apparently 'not' won out and he shrugged though I could see his eyes latched hurtfully to mine.

"Ok. Whatever. Just thought we'd have one last hoorah. You know."

"Yeah, but I don't want to, ok? It's been too long. I would just make a fool of myself. You go ahead. Have fun," I soothed, feeling torn and wanting to end the squabble.

He smiled sadly and nodded as he walked away.

I turned to look around and saw we had quite the audience, people almost begging, eyes glistening with excitement, for there to be a fight. I flushed and turned back to Caleb just as they started to do their cheer. I barely saw it as my own memories flooded me. In no time they were done and making their way back to us in a titter of cheers and giggles.

"It's starting. They sat us alphabetically so, we're over here," Beck said reluctantly and pulled Nicolette away. "See you tomorrow night, right?"

"Yeah. Absolutely."

"Tomorrow night?" Caleb asked and I felt him push into my mind for the answer. "Yeah, sounds fun."

I just shook my head at him as we made our way to the table. Luck would have it alphabetically, that Kyle was at the next table, in the chair right next to ours.

"Hey!" he said grinning and pulled me into a very intimate hug. "I didn't think you'd come."

"I came with Caleb."

"Oh." He put me down and regarded Caleb with a terse nod. "Caleb."

"Kyle," Caleb answered and pulled my chair out for me, turning his back on his cousin.

I felt guilty about that, but didn't feel it was my place to interfere, just yet anyway. Caleb pulled the yearbook on the center of our table closer to him and I realized it was tenth grade year. My hair was really curly that day and I'd pulled it to the side of my neck and smiled shyly.

He smiled at it and looked back at me. I rolled my eyes and took it from him. I glanced through it and laughed when Ben, sitting next to me, leaned over and pointed at a picture of him and me at a school assembly wearing face paint and chanting. I groaned and Caleb leaned closer to see. Ben began to tell him all about it. The way we used to paint our faces on school assembly day and wear wigs and all kinds of crazy things to make the school mad. It was a whole student body effort and we always pulled it off.

Caleb laughed and gave me a sidelong grin.

You were a bad girl. A rebel. I've been so misled.

I rolled my eyes laughing as the lights went down and the principal, Mr. Gurney, made his way across the stage.

"Welcome, seniors. Or should I say, adults, for you are no longer our pupils. You are the fresh new minds of our country. I am pleased to introduce this year's Farewell video. This video was put together by the yearbook staff and is quite lengthy, containing not just your senior year, but your entire school years collectively in a memoir that you can purchase at the end for a $10 donation. Now, let's begin."

The huge pull down projection screen flickered and there I was, first picture. I groaned out loud. It was me in the sandbox on the playground, Kindergarten. I was pouring a fistful of white sand onto Kyle's head. Kyle turned to grin at me in his seat and burst out laughing and clapping, as did lots of others. Each picture or video clip they showed had our names and the school year printed at the bottom. They played cheesy graduation music in the background, like Vitamin C or something.

The photos kept coming, so many years summed up. I found myself laughing sometimes quite loudly, but you couldn't hear me over everyone else. There were so many pictures and I was in lots of them. We saw third grade field day when I ran against the principal, and won. We saw fifth grade D.A.R.E program, us with our red t-shirts while we all stood beside the police officers, grinning. Steven holding Gretchen up to tack a Sadie Hawkins eighth grade dance banner to the ceiling, though if the school had paid attention to where he was looking - up her skirt - they wouldn't have put that one in there.

There was one of Beck and I in tenth grade, back to back, wearing wigs and making guns with our hands like Charlie's Angels making everyone laugh. I buried my face in Caleb's neck and groaned as he chuckled. I thought hard and could remember doing that, but not what it was for.

Then the school mascot, in full body paint, midair before he tripped face first over a pom-pom left on the basketball court. Then later, another one of Chad and I working in science lab together, grinning over a beaker of green something, his arm slung over my shoulders.

There was prom, dancing couples, homecoming, finals, last days, first days, Halloween, Spirit week, so much more.

Then they showed cheerleading and I felt Caleb snap more to alert, looking for me more intently among the faces. But there were plenty of pics of me there, too, among the skirted girls, some by myself, and to my chagrin, a lot with Chad and I. He was on the football team after all. The last cheerleading one, in slow motion only adding to my agony, was Chad on the football field after a winning game, ripping off his helmet and holding his arms open to something off camera. Then me, barreling towards him in my cheerleading outfit, jumping into his sweaty arms and kissing him, albeit closed mouthed, as he held me off the ground.

For some reason my eyes automatically snapped to Chad's and he was already looking at me, longingly and sadly.

I felt horribly guilty about it all and glanced at Caleb. He glanced at me, too, and smiled knowingly, shrugging like 'what are ya gonna do'?

I'm sorry.

It's in the past, Maggie.

Yeah, but you shouldn't have to watch it.

It's ok. I got the girl, right?

He grinned at me and squeezed my hand in between us making me smile.

You definitely got the girl.

He put his arm around my shoulder and kissed my temple.

They showed Football games, Basketball, Volleyball and Track, plus all the sports and clubs and activities, dances, lunches. There was some of me running on the track and some warming up. Some of me playing Volleyball in the gym. I felt Caleb's interest in these pics was just as noticeable as the cheerleading ones had been.

It was long, but felt oddly satisfying to watch. Like maybe I had accomplished something after all. I felt like tearing up, but dammed them back.

As the music started to die down they showed our procession as we marched to graduation. Some were cutting up in line and some seemed nervous. The camera passed me but I wasn't looking at it. Then the last frame, the money shot, the tear jerker, was a large group walking out to the parking lot afterwards, half were still wearing their robes, some still had on their caps, some had their diplomas in hands. A couple had their arms around the other's shoulder as they walked into the sun, making them appear nothing but a dark silhouette against the backdrop of parking lot and football field. The caption read 'And then we walked boldly out of the sunset of our pasts and into our futures. The End'

The lights came up and I saw several people wiping their eyes and laughing. Mr. Gurney made a small speech about that concluding the presentation and wishing us luck in our future, then left the stage.

I was quite ready to leave and Caleb seemed ready as well. I waved to Beck across the room, but of course she was standing with my old group. Kyle and Chad included. They both watched us go with wistful looks. I hated to have put those looks on their faces so I held on tight to Caleb as we made our way out.

A few people and teachers said goodbye to me on the way out but for the most part, I didn't stop. I felt good about graduating and was ready to be gone.

That night at my house, I fell asleep quickly. The next day was all a fast blur as Caleb sat in the back again and tried to study. We didn't talk about the party except him making jokes about pictures he remembered and several funny comments about cheerleading. He didn't mention Chad or the fact that Chad seemed to be everywhere I was back in school. We were pretty much attached and that was the truth, but no more.

I was grateful and hoped he understood that that part of my life was behind me and I was right where I wanted to be.

In no time at all, the work day was over and I found myself climbing on the back of his bike again and heading home. He dropped me off and released me with his words. I ran in to get ready for our double date while he went to his uncle's to do the same.

After my shower I chose my clothes, a pair of jeans and a yellow tank with my brown cardigan and light brown wedge sandals. My charm bracelet hung just under the hem of my sleeve. I left my hair down and pulled my bangs back to help tame it after the bike ride but then I wondered what we'd drive tonight. Beck's little two door Neon was small and uncomfortable but we could take it if we have to.

I heard the knock on the door and made my way to answer it. For once I beat Dad. Caleb was wearing something similar to me, jeans and a brown leather jacket. His brown shaggy hair was curling very cutely around his ears.

And he had a single flower in his hand. A yellow rose.

I gaped at him.

"Are you trying to score points?" He just grinned as I took it and smelled the petals. "How did you know these are my favorite?"

He leaned close and kissed my cheek, speaking his words against my skin.

"When you left your mind open to me, I did some digging around."

I leaned back to look at him and he was serious.

"Really? I wish I'd thought to do that," I muttered.

"There will be plenty of time for that. Once we ascend we can pretty much go all in the other's mind anytime we want."

"Hmm," I hummed nervously, smelling my flower again.

"Don't worry." He wrapped his arms around my lower back. "I won't go poking in your head unless you want me to. And you will want me to," he said low and foreboding.

Before I could ask him what that meant, he took my lips gently, kissing the top then the bottom and sucking as he did so. I felt the temperature in the room go to uncomfortable levels. He pulled back a little to murmur against my lips.

"You look amazing." Then he moved to skim his nose over my chin and under my ear. "And you smell so good. What is that?"

"Ch-cherry blossom," I stuttered breathlessly, my breaths were practically nonexistent.

He came back to my lips and continued what he had started. His hands moved lower to my hips right as I heard my dad clear his throat obviously behind us.

I pulled back and looked over at Dad with a guilty smile. I didn't look at Caleb at all.

"Sorry, Dad." I bit my lip. "All right, I'm gonna go put this in water. We're just waiting on Beck and then we'll be out of here."

I went to the kitchen and Dad followed me. "Maggie, you better be careful with him."

"I am, Dad. It was just kissing. Wouldn't you rather that we did that here, at the house?" I asked as I pulled the vase from under the sink.

"Yes, I would actually, but I think you guys are a little serious after only a week of dating."

I blew a steadying breath to stall, to give me thinking time. "Dad, he's different. He's not going to take advantage of me."

"I hope not, because I'd hate to go to prison for murder."

I laughed and went to hug him but he wasn't amused. "Dad, I'll be ok. Caleb is a nice guy and very responsible. I promise you I won't do anything stupid and neither will he. I'm sure he wants to stay alive and keep all his limbs intact. Ok?"

"Ok," he conceded with a sigh.

"Ok," I agreed. "Well, let me go call Beck. She's late."

When I came back to the door I heard yelling outside. Caleb was standing in the doorway with his head cocked to the side.

"What's going on?"

"Well," he said slowly. "It looks like Beck and her date are here." He looked back at me and grinned. "And it looks like love to me."

Twenty One

I peeked over his shoulder and saw that they were fighting and yelling by the curb, right by the trash cans. I groaned.

"Leave it to Beck to start trouble before we've even started the date. Bye, Dad!"

"Bye. Be safe," he said as he came around the corner.

"We will, Mr. Masters, thanks," Caleb assured him politely.

"Call me Jim, please, Caleb," Dad said and extended his hand to Caleb. "Mr. Masters makes me feel old."

Caleb laughed and took his hand. "Jim. Thanks. And don't worry about Maggie. I won't let anything happen to her."

Dad nodded and waved to me as we left. I slowly made my way to the curb and could hear some of what they were saying instead of just the noise of it.

"Well! What do you expect! She texted you with me in the car!" Beck yelled and tapped her pointy booted foot.

"Rebecca, come on. You called me just this morning to go out with you. We've been on like four dates. Am I supposed to delete every girl's number I have even though I haven't heard from you in weeks?"

"Maybe! Just turn your phone off at least. You didn't have to text her back."

"I was telling her I was out with you!"

"Oh, sure," she said sarcastically and rolled her eyes just as she saw us coming. "Hey, guys." She jumped and grabbed Ralph's arm affectionately. "We were waiting for you. Ready to go?"

I looked up at Caleb and he looked torn between laughing out loud and smirking.

"Ok," I started. "What are we driving?"

"I brought my uncle's car," Caleb volunteered and jingled the keys in his hand.

I looked behind Beck at the black Lexus.

"See," Beck said smartly and smirked. "Told ya, Lexus."

"Great. Let's go," Ralph said hotly and stalked to the car door.

Beck looked at me and nodded her head to the side. I followed her behind the car while Caleb waited by the front passenger side door. "Can you believe him! He-" she started but I'd already heard enough.

"Beck, I know. We heard everything. You weren't exactly being quiet. Look, please be nice and don't fight the whole time. I want to have fun."

"But he texted her, right in front of me!"

"He said it was about you. He told some other girl - a girl he might have been possibly about to go out with, but instead chose you - that he was out with you. You should be happy that he'd do that. Ralph really likes you. What are you doing?" I asked softly.

"I don't know. You're right. But if he texts anyone else, so help me..."

I rolled my eyes and pulled her to her door. Caleb opened it for her since Ralph was already in.

"At least someone has manners," she muttered.

"Be nice," I commanded. He shut her door and I turned to look at him. "I have a feeling we aren't going to have very much fun."

"Yes, we will." He kissed my forehead fast and soft. "You'll see."

I climbed in after he opened my door and waited in the stiff silence of the car for him to get in himself. Once in, I introduced them all and I asked where to go.

"Take us somewhere we've never been," Beck said sweetly. "Somewhere from your town maybe."

Caleb looked at me and I nodded, knowing what he was thinking.

"Ok. Buckle up."

"Where are we? I feel like we're in Deliverance," Beck said as she clutched the back of my seat.

We had just pulled into the lot at Mugly's and though she was my best friend, I wanted to smack her. We had barely spoken a word on the drive over. She spent her time filing her nails and answering questions with Hmm's and Uhuh's.

Caleb eventually turned on a CD, Cold War Kids, and clasped my hand. We talked a little, some in our minds too, but mostly, we let them both just cool off before we got to the restaurant.

And now, we parked and I got out before Caleb could come and open my door. Ralph tried to open Beck's for her and she just scoffed and walked to catch up with me. She laced her arm through mine as we made our way through the lot to the door.

I looked back at the guys and they were walking a few feet behind us, talking about something. I looked back at Beck and she was seething but with a nasty little smile on her face. I was so confused why she even wanted to come out. I didn't remember her being so petty before.

"Oh, my goodness, look at this place! It's right out of the boonies!" she exclaimed loudly when we entered. I turned and pinned her with a stare. "What?" she said just as loudly.

I pulled her arm to make her come closer.

"Jeez, Beck. What is wrong with you? Just because you're mad at Ralph doesn't mean you have to be rude to everyone else. Caleb knows the owner here, don't insult them, please. I brought you here because I thought you'd like it."

"Ok, ok. Fine. Whatever."

Caleb came forward and greeted the hostess, a new girl I hadn't met before, and she said to follow her. He reached back to grab my hand and tugged me along to a back booth. I sat beside him and Beck and Ralph sat on the other side.

Our peppy little waitress came and explained the different barbeque sauces to us, to which my rude best friend laughed at like it was a joke, and then took our drink order. We all ordered sweet tea except Beck, who ordered bottled water.

I'm so sorry about her. I have no idea what's wrong with her tonight.

It's ok.

He smiled reassuringly and put an arm around me to pull me closer. He kissed my temple and Beck rolled her eyes.

"So, Ralph. Where are you going to school?" I asked because his date wouldn't.

"Columbia."

"Really?" Caleb said interested. "That's a really good school."

"Yeah. Is that where Bish went?" Ralph asked me.

"NYU. But he's actually interning now," I said and he nodded.

"I wanted to go here, to Tennessee, but my mom is so set for me to go to New York and since they're paying, it's not like I have much say."

"I hear you there, man."

I heard something in Caleb's voice then; longing. I peeked into his mind without looking at him, though he could tell, you always can by the little fuzziness. I knew he wanted to go to Arizona, but I didn't know if it was just a flashing fancy or if he really truly wanted to go. Maybe he didn't even want to be an architect. His mind told me I was right. He had looked extensively into Arizona. He was good at it but had no real desire to do architecture except to please his family. He had no idea of what he wanted to be except maybe be a geometry teacher. It wasn't that

Arizona was a particularly fantastic school, it was away from here, on his own and no one to stop him if he wanted to take an art or astronomy class or something else useless, but it was *his* time right? He just wanted to do what he wanted to do.

I smiled up at him and he shook his head at me, the corner of his lips turning up in his profile.

"Uh, hello? Can you come out of La-La Land and answer me?" Beck spouted in irritation.

"What?"

"I asked what we're doing after we eat."

"I don't know but let's look at the menu. We haven't even ordered our food yet."

"Fine." She snatched the menu up and grimaced when she opened it. "Ugh. Meat, meat and more meat."

"You're not a vegetarian," I countered.

She didn't say anything else and I told Caleb to get me what he was having again.

"So, we have a theater in town if you want to catch a movie," Caleb suggested.

"Ugh. No," Beck groaned. "Do you have any clubs in town?"

"Not anything underage, but a friend sent me a text earlier. He's throwing a party tonight at the beach."

"Yay! Sounds good. Let's do that."

"Beck," Ralph said and looked at her funny. "Maybe they don't want to go to the party. You didn't even ask."

"He wouldn't have brought it up if he didn't want to go!"

The waitress brought our drinks and we all ordered our food. Then Beck went to the bathroom so I decided to find out what the heck was going on.

"What is wrong with her? She can't be this upset over a text message," I asked Ralph and he rubbed his neck, looking uncomfortable and guilty.

"The girl who texted me was my ex-girlfriend. Beck was really weird about it when we went out before and when she wouldn't return my phone calls, me and Christina went out again a few times. She freaked in the car on the way over. What am I supposed to do? She doesn't act like she wants to be with me, but calls me out of the blue. Am I supposed to not ever go out with any other girls and wait for Beck to realize that I'm freaking in love with her?"

We heard a gasp behind us and turned to see Beck with a struck expression. She'd heard him. I bit my lip as I watched him stand and move towards her. She smiled and threw her arms around his neck and kissed him. He laughed after a few seconds and pulled away.

"We'll be right back," he said quickly and pulled her away, giggling.

I felt extremely giddy and leaned on Caleb's shoulder. I was glad when the waitress brought our food right as they came back, about eight minutes later. Beck's lips were red and her hair was a bit disheveled. She beamed at me and when Ralph was getting a refill she looked at me and mouthed 'Holy Cow!'

"Try these, Beck." I pointed to the corn nuggets. "They're really good."

Ralph stabbed one with a toothpick and nodded in appreciation.

"So. Caleb," Beck started and laced her fingers into a fist under her chin. "What's your major?"

She gave me a concerned look and then turned her gaze to Caleb with a little frown. I realized this was the grilling she'd been waiting for.

"Architecture."

"Really? And what exactly are your intentions with my best friend?"

He choked on his sweet tea, laughing, and I looked at her in disbelief.

"Beck. What the heck?" I asked.

"What? It's my job as best friend to make sure he's not a serial killer. Or an English major, not sure which one's worse," she spouted indignantly and Caleb and Ralph both laughed.

"Well, uh, I adore Maggie." He looked at me and smirked at my stunned expression. "And I am most definitely not a serial killer. But I do know a little English," Caleb said grinning.

"Well, that's a relief. So are your parents loaded?"

"Beck, oh, my gosh! Are you serious!" I yelled, but she ignored me and looked at him imploringly.

"Well, I'd say we're well off enough," Caleb answered carefully.

"Oh, yeah. Loaded," Beck said and tossed her hair. "So what about siblings?"

"One sister."

"Parents still together?"

"Yep."

"When's the last time you talked to your best friend?"

"Yesterday. Text," he answered.

"And your mother?"

"This morning."

She raised her eyebrows at that. "Really. When was the last time you went to the dentist?"

"Um. Three months ago," he said grinning.

"Have you ever been engaged?"

"Nope," he said laughing.

"What do you think about the current economical state of Iran?" Ralph and Caleb were laughing so hard, they looked about to cry. I just shook my head at her while she bantered. "Hey! That's a legitimate selling point!"

"Don't answer that, Caleb," I cut in. "Ok, Beck, enough. Are you done?"

"Yes. You have my stamp of approval."

He raised his glass in toast to her in gratitude and smirked. "So, are we going to the party or a movie or what?" Caleb asked after everyone settled down.

"I vote party," Beck said and then recanted. "If that's what everyone else wants to do."

"I don't care what we do," Ralph said sweetly, looking at Beck.

"What about you?" Caleb asked me.

"Whatever you want."

"Well. We can go to the party. He's a pretty nice guy so I wouldn't think it'd be too crazy."

"Ok. Party."

We finished up just as Mrs. Amy came by and said hello.

Caleb drove us to a dark parking lot in the woods. I took my sweater off in the car and we piled out. As you came over the dunes you could see the red and orange bonfire lighting the sand and trees behind it. There were probably fifty people out there on the beach.

Beck jumped out of the car quickly, towing Ralph behind her. Caleb and I walked slowly hand in hand. I took my shoes off and put them in the pile along with a lot of other girls who hadn't worn appropriate sand shoes.

Quite a few people called out to Caleb and he waved or said hello or bumped fists. A guy came and offered us drinks.

"I don't drink," I said as he forced the sloshing warm beverage into my hand.

"It's just soda, cutie," he said and winked before stumbling away.

I didn't know if he was joking or not, but Caleb took the drink from me and threw it in a passing trash can.

"I'll get us something *we can drink* in a minute," he whispered as we walked over to the fire.

I wondered for just a second what his telling tone meant, but forgot all about it once I saw the crowd. They all turned to look at us when a guy yelled loudly to Caleb.

I felt my cheeks burn and was glad the red glow of the fire would hide it. And I swear there were a couple girls glaring at me, openly giving me dirty looks. I looked at them curiously as Caleb hugged a guy and bumped backs with their fists.

"Hey, man. Glad you could make it."

"Yeah. Thanks for the invite. Tristan, this is Maggie."

"Hi," I said softly.

"Hey, there." He smiled widely. "Caleb, dude, you've been holding out. It's nice to meet you, Maggie. Any friend of Caleb is a friend of mine." I smiled and he looked back to Caleb. "Where you been, man? I haven't seen you in a while."

Caleb nodded his head towards me. "Maggie doesn't live here so I've been traveling back and forth."

"I didn't think you were dating anyone. I told Ashley to come because you might be here."

I silently groaned.

"Man, come on. I've told you before, I am not interested in Ashley, at all. Never was."

"Caleb!" The Ashley in question crooned sweetly from behind us. She even came up to him and grabbed his arm. "I'm so glad you're finally here. I've been waiting. It's so boring without you," she whined.

She glanced at me and smiled unkindly. Caleb pulled from her grasp making her pout more pronounced.

"We're going to get something to drink," Caleb announced and pulled me by my hand.

Ashley called out behind us. "I'll take a martini, dirty."

He cast a rolling eyed look over his shoulder at her. "Give it a rest."

"Come see me once you take preschool home to meet curfew."

He turned back to glare at her. "Enough, Ashley. You really have to wonder why I never wanted to date you?"

She looked genuinely hurt and I wanted to feel sorry for her. Her look of hurt turned to snideness as she flipped us off before turning and almost tripping over a log. I laughed into Caleb's shoulder.

"Oh, no. Did she really just flip us off?"

"Yeah." He didn't laugh though. "I'm so sorry. I wish we hadn't come here, now. This isn't my scene, even though I come to them a lot because there's nothing else to do, but I thought Beck might have fun."

"It's ok. I'm not worried about Ashley. I'm not worried about anything." I hugged him around his middle, pressing my face to his chest. "I'm going to be with these people in a few weeks anyway, right? I better get used to it."

"I guess. It's really making me look bad with my choice of friends."

"I've only met two of them. Let's get a drink and then you can introduce me to anyone you want."

"Really?" he asked curiously and looked down at me. "I thought you'd hate this."

"I kind of do," I admitted laughing, "but I want to like it."

"I know I've probably said this twenty times already, but...you are amazing." He cupped my face and kissed me with gentle pressure. I stuck my hands into his open jacket, grasping around his back for warmth and closeness. My lips tingled and it spread to my cheeks, then my neck. I pulled back before we got too carried away and licked my lips. I felt him sigh, his breath blowing across my face.

"Drink?"

"Yeah," I answered in a squeak and looked up to see his smug smirk.

"Caleb!" I turned to see a very nice looking and very tall black guy strolling towards us with a wide easy grin. "My brother from another mother! Man, where you been?"

They hugged and verbally jabbed back and forth laughing, then Caleb took my hand.

"Maggie, this is Vic. Vic, this is Maggie, the girl I was telling you about."

My gaze shot to him in surprise. I didn't know he'd told anyone about us, especially someone from school.

"Maggie, Maggie, Maggie," Vic crooned and hugged me. "I can't tell you how happy I am to meet you, girl. You know, my boy hasn't stopped talking about you."

Twenty Two

"Vic, come on. We only talked like three times," Caleb said and I could feel his embarrassment and also his glee about this guy liking me.

This was his best friend, the friend he mentioned that day. He had an over pronounced southern accent that was very cute. His hair was short and he had an earring in one ear. His sunglasses were hanging from his polo shirt collar and he wasn't wearing shoes.

"Yeah, and it was all about this girl, right here." He shook his head, pointing at me above my head and laughed. "I've been Caleb's friend for ten years and I've never seen him with a girl, not once. Not even prom, he just skipped it. The guy's a monk."

I laughed as Caleb rolled his eyes and rubbed his chin. "I know. He kinda told me all about it."

"Well, come on, Maggie. Let's get you a very non-alcoholic beverage."

He put an arm around my shoulder and pulled me with him, Caleb trailing behind us. We came to a big flat rock where it seemed all the food and drinks were set up. He handed me an unopened can of soda.

"Want something to eat? We've got shrimp, oysters, ribs, chips-"

"Nah, I'm ok. We just ate, but thanks."

Vic looked me over in a very objective manner with his chin between his thumb and forefinger.

"Caleb. I have to say you did good, brother. She's sweet, she's polite, she's southern, cute. I approve. You two can continue to date."

"Thanks, man," Caleb said with fake sincerity.

"So where did ya'll eat?"

"Mugly's."

"Oh!" he shouted and laughed. "Caleb's pulling out the big guns!"

We all laughed and went to sit around the fire. There wasn't much room because that's where most of the people were. I kept looking for Beck, but hadn't seen her or Ralph since we got there. I imagined her pulling him behind a tree and doing who knows what, that thought made me want to gag and giggle at the same time.

So we sat down and Caleb put me in between them on the log. He kept looking around protectively which made me wonder what he was looking for.

"So, where's Molly?" Caleb asked.

"She's here somewhere. Probably with Ashley which means she probably won't come over here."

"We've already run into Ashley actually," Caleb explained and his voice got harder. "She's in rare form tonight."

"You know how she is, man. She ain't gonna change, unless maybe you asked her to. Then, I bet she'd wear purple hats with green shorts and call herself Sally."

"Dude," Caleb laughed, "you need help."

"Yeah. So, Maggie, what's the plan for school? Caleb talked you into Tennessee yet?" Vic asked me while he loaded up a marshmallow on a palmetto stick to roast.

"He has," I said. "I'm really looking forward to it."

"He must have some serious skills to get you to come to our school after only a week," he mused and stuffed the mallow in his mouth. His next words were muffled, making it even funnier. "Must be the hair. Girls go nuts over that hair."

"It *is* good hair," I agreed and Caleb covered his face beside me making Vic laugh.

"Great. Now you've joined his side," Caleb groaned. "He'll talk you into anything."

"Have you met his parents yet? I haven't even met his parents," Vic grumbled. "Even though the guy has been to my swimming pool in my back yard a million times, I've never set foot in this guy's house. His parents are like super secretive or something."

"I have actually met them...and been to his house."

"Oh, sure!" He yelled and threw his hands up. "Of course she gets to. I hear the guy is loaded. Is it true? He's always so modest, but I know his parents have to be loaded."

"Don't answer that, Maggie," Caleb said and leaned towards me to whisper loudly and conspiratorially. "He's trying to get you to feel sorry for him. His parents live in a three story complex with an inside pool and a *real* butler."

I gasped in mock surprise. "You tried to trick me!" I pawned good naturedly.

"No! Don't listen to him!" Vic yelled playfully and waved his hands back at Caleb.

I laughed as they went back and forth.

"All right, guys," Vic said. "I better go see my girl or I'll be in the doghouse. I'll catch up with you later. Text me, brother."

"It was nice to meet you," I said and Vic turned and smiled gorgeously at me.

"It was good to meet you. Please don't go anywhere. You've done that kid good."

I laughed as Caleb continued to groan and moan beside me.

"He's really nice."

"Yeah. He's a good guy." He stood and held his hand out to me. "Come on."

I took his hand as he helped me up.

"Where are we going?"

"Well, it is a party," he said and smiled.

He took me to the spot on the sand designated as the dance floor. The music was so loud there was no point in trying to speak. Luckily, we didn't need to use our mouths.

Caleb, I can't dance.

Sure you can. Everyone can dance. Plus, I'm an excellent teacher. They don't call my kind Charmed for nothing.

He took my hands and put them on his shoulders. His hands gripped my hips just as the music changed to something slower. I was swept over with relief and he laughed and shook his head.

You got lucky on that one, but you're still dancing with me. That's all I care about.

I wrapped my arms tighter around his neck and he pulled me closer, our bodies touching all the way down as he used his hands to sway my hips. His slightly stubbly cheek rubbed against mine as he moved us with our heads together and I was consumed with calm and warmth.

It felt so right to be there in his arms. Wherever he was is where I needed and wanted to be.

I had never danced before, ever. Not even Prom. Chad had been very focused on goofing off with our group of friends that went together and we never made it to the dance floor. I was relieved back then because I couldn't dance and still can't. Beck tried several times to get me to shake it with her on the dance floor, pulling me ungracefully in her sinfully low cut purple gown, but I refused. She even tried to get me to sneak out to clubs with her sometimes when I stayed at her house but once again, I refused.

Now, I didn't know if I'd go to a club or not, it sounded appealing with Caleb there with me, but right now, all I could think about was him, pressing me to him with his big warm hands through the thin fabric of my shirt. I liked his hands there.

I like my hands here, too.

I smiled and thought back to the very beginning, when we first saw each other. We'd both had a reaction to the other before the imprint even took place. I remembered that I'd never told him how I'd felt before that. That I had been feeling similar feelings for him that he had felt for me from just our short little walk to Kyle's house. I'd never shown him how I loved his curly hair and how affected I'd been by his eyes when he had leaned close to check my head. How endearing it was for him to be so worried about me. How I dreaded leaving him when Kyle was trying to pull me away. How I had no idea why I was so enraptured with him but seemed to be drawn to him somehow as I offered him my hand and told him my name, hoping he'd remember it.

You're showing me now.

I kept forgetting that he was so in tune to me.

Well, it's all true. You were very cute, all concerned for me.

He pulled back to smile crookedly at me.

I can't wait for you to come up here with me for school. I've been meaning to ask you...

His hands flexed on my hips. His nervousness for the question he was about to ask was apparent as it pulsed through me. He was worried that I'd think it was too soon or inappropriate. Or I'd just flat say no.

Just tell me, Caleb. It can't be that bad.

I was just wondering if you were planning to...live with me at the apartment. I'm asking you to, I guess.

Oh.

I hadn't seriously thought about it. Kyle had mentioned to me the fact that he was supposed to room with Caleb and I'd said he still could. I doubted that was still ok, but I hadn't really thought beyond that. So I answered truthfully.

I hadn't really thought about it.

Ok. No pressure.

He so, so wanted me to live with him. Wanted for us to not have an obstacle in the mornings when we needed each other most anymore, to not have to worry about me at night with the echoling or sneaking in and out.

But I wasn't so sure. I mean I did want to live with him but I didn't want to lie to my dad anymore. I didn't want to continue to have to come up with stories for him and other people about where and who I lived with.

Would I tell everyone else that I lived with my boyfriend off campus if they asked? Would I tell my dad that I lived in the dorms? What if he tried to visit me, which I'm sure he would? Would I - Could I - tell him that I was eighteen and living with my boyfriend and he couldn't stop me? He would be furious. Plus, I had always had a subconscious plan. To get married first before I moved in with my guy but things weren't even in the same ballpark as normal anymore so exceptions had to be made.

Caleb was reading me.

It's ok. You don't have to worry about it right now. We'll figure it out later.

It's not that I don't want to. I do. I'm just worried about my dad. It would be so much easier and safer if I stay with you. And more fun.

I sent him a little smile, but he was still hung up on the worry; the worry for me if I wasn't with him and how this was going to work out. It was not only his desire to protect, it was ingrained in his veins.

I decided to distract him because his feelings of worry and upset and need to protect were choking me.

I pulled his face to mine with my arm around his neck. He sighed in relief against my lips at the contact and release of coiled emotions. His arms tightened and his gratefulness was all around me. He knew I was saving him with this kiss as I tried to forget the things that would have to be dealt with very soon...but not tonight.

We continued to sway with the slow music as we kissed slowly and sweetly. The song was something I wasn't familiar with, but it didn't matter.

Someone bumped us, breaking our kiss.

"Oopsy. Shouldn't you be heading home, preschool?" Ashley said as she swayed with a guy who was somehow even drunker than her. They both stumbled and grasped each other to keep from falling. She laughed. "Ahh! Did I interrupt something?"

Caleb quickly pulled us further away from them when someone else bumped against us. We both looked up to Beck and Ralph, writhing in rhythm to the music beside us on the sand, practically dry humping and I felt like I needed to avert my eyes but then I saw hers and realized she'd been drinking. They both had. I sighed at her stupidity at taking alcoholic drinks from a bunch of college kids she didn't know.

"Hey, girl. Having fun?" she yelled over the music.

"Where have you been?" I asked feeling very motherly at the moment.

"Oh...somewhere," she yelled and they both laughed maniacally, falling into each other, giggling and groping.

I rolled my eyes and wanted to go away. It's not like we could talk anyway. There were entirely too many people around and it was so loud. And Beck, although I was happy for her and Ralph, had been driving me crazy all night. We were growing apart, in different directions. I still wanted to be her friend but it felt like we were just in different places. Right now, I wanted to spend my time with Caleb more than anything else.

Say no more.

He took my hand and tugged me away from everyone to a little trail in the wooded area off the beach. The music died down as we kept going, hand in hand, and I leaned my head against his shoulder.

"What's your biggest pet peeve?" I asked him finally after some minutes of comfortable silence.

"Hmmm." He scratched his chin in that familiar way I was beginning to adore. "Probably lying, but since I'm forcing you to do it because of our imprint, I guess that's pretty hypocritical, huh?"

"Caleb," I protested but he kept going.

"But if you want an easier, less in depth answer, I'd say...a whiner. Someone who complains about everything gets on my nerves. I know there's nothing wrong with letting loose sometimes but there are some kids, especially since I got to college, who just whine and cry about every little thing. They are so spoiled, it kills me." He looked over at me to see my smirk. "And you? What's yours?"

"I'd have to say, in depth would be cheating on someone. I can't stand it, hate it. That's one reason I'm so mad at my mom. But the easier, less in depth answer, would be meanness. What about...what you like to do when you go home from school?"

"The same thing I like to do at school. Play music, write music, listen to music, attend concerts and friend's gigs at clubs. I should really change my major, I think." I giggled and shook my head. "You? Favorite thing to do?"

"Um...read, I guess. I'm a nerd."

"I like to read too, that doesn't make you a nerd. Unless you're calling me one." He cocked a comical brow at me and I smiled then bit my lip, thinking.

"Favorite person?" I asked.

"You, that's an easy one."

"That's not what I meant," I laughed.

"I know, but we're here." He pulled back one last tree branch, like a curtain, it opened up to a postcard pretty picture in front of me. The moon was casting a mirror reflection on the water. The sand was white and clear. The waves were small and there was probably fifty yards of beach, right in between two rocks that seemed to be deserted and un-messed with. It was gorgeous.

"Wow."

"Yeah. I found this place at another one of these parties. It gets to be a little much for me too, so I took a walk and here it was."

"And did Ashley follow you here?" I joked and fluttered my eyelashes.

"She would have if she'd seen me."

He took my hand again to pull me to the water's edge. He took off his jacket and spread it out on the white dry sand. He lay his head down on the jacket and beckoned me down to him. I smiled as I snuggled up against him, using his arm and shoulder as a pillow.

You liked the stars last time...

I turned my face to look up and saw that it was possible to be even more beautiful than before. There were a million of them up there and, as cheesy at it sounds, it took my breath away.

We just lay there for about twenty minutes, just like that, watching, listening, being together. It wasn't hot or cold, it wasn't loud or quiet, the sand wasn't hard or soft. Everything was perfect and add his calming touch to that, his hand coasting up and down my arm, and it couldn't have gotten better.

He started to think about things. What was he going to do when I was in class without him? What if our schedules conflicted so much that we never got to see each other during the day at school? He'd never get any work done worrying about me.

You're in my head, remember? You'll always know if I need you. Everything should be fine.

I know you think that and I'd like to, but what if the echoling never stops? What if Marcus never stops? I don't know what I'd do.

Caleb. I pulled his face close to mine with a hand on his cheek. *I like it that you worry about me and I'd never tell you to go against that. But why worry about something that hasn't even come near to time yet? Who knows what'll happen by then? This whole thing may be sorted out.*

He chuckled and tucked my head under his chin.

You're so cute when you're all optimistic and take-charge.

Ha ha.

You're right. No point in worrying about it yet. But eventually, all of this will have to be discussed. Especially...the living arrangements once you start school.

Your parents are fine with my living with you? Because I know my dad would be livid.

No, they're not ok with it, not really. I told you, they don't really see another choice. It's not like I can sneak into the campus dorms every morning to see you.

I know. I just don't know what to do. Why does everything about this have to be so complicated?

Well, it's usually not. Usually...we're older when we imprint. No one else has ever had to worry about all this stuff before. We are a new thing and no one really knows what to make of our situation. See, before when they imprinted, they just got married and that was it.

I realized what he was saying; we were the first Ace couple to imprint and not get married right away.

How long did people wait to get married?

They didn't wait. It was more like, how soon can they get married. My parents only waited three weeks.

I balked. My heart slammed. My head spun. What!! Three weeks!

Maggie, breathe. It's ok.

I'm sorry. I just... Three weeks? That just seems...

Crazy, I know, but they're meant for each other. It's not like they were going to decide to date someone else, you know? They were it for each other, forever. Why not get married and get started on your life?

You've thought about this already, haven't you?

Of course I have. He leaned to hover over me on his elbows and looked seriously at me. "I've thought about it ever since you first touched me and I knew you were mine."

What did you say to something like that? I didn't know whether to run, or cry in joy. I wanted to marry him right this second. I knew he was it for me and there was no point in waiting, but I was only seventeen. My dad wouldn't forgive me or understand and I'd have to tell everyone I met that I was a teenager and married. That shouldn't matter, what other people thought, but for some reason, it kind of did a little.

I also wondered why we were chosen so young when everyone else imprinted in their early twenties; appropriate marriage age. There had to be a reason, but right now, I was just scared.

We heard a ruckus behind us. We both looked up to see a couple drunk guys barreling through the brush at the edge of the woods in a clumsy and uncoordinated fight. Caleb groaned and got up. They were yelling loudly and taking swings at each other.

"Stay here for a second. Let me pull these idiots off of each other."

He left and I sat up to look at the water. I continued to think as I heard Caleb trying to settle them behind me. I felt the stick in my arm before it registered that something was wrong. I felt one second of panic before my heart slowed to a sleepy rhythm. The last thing I saw was the beautiful scene of where Caleb had taken me before my eyes closed and I fell back into the sand.

Twenty Three

I woke up in the dark. I smelled Caleb all around me and moved my arms to feel that his jacket had been draped over my head. I pulled the jacket down to my shoulders and felt the chill hit my face. I was somewhere cold, musty and dark. I felt groggy and unhinged.

There was someone there, that's why I'd woken up. They were laying my arms and legs out and strapping them down, my arms over my head. In my mind my heart spiked in panic, but my body didn't respond. My heart stayed at its slow lazy rhythm and I didn't understand why. I didn't even fight whoever it was.

I tried to focus my brain. Tried to tell myself to look around and see what was going on. Caleb. Where was Caleb? I popped my eyes open as wide as they'd go and looked up to see two faces over me. One I didn't recognize but looked slightly familiar, a woman, and the other had my insides screaming.

Marcus.

I tried to move my hands and feet but they wouldn't budge. My arm hurt. My eyes drifted to see wires and tape around my hand, an I.V. What were they doing to me?

I tried to speak. "What-" My throat felt like sandpaper. "What are you doing?"

"Maggie, finally. It's been hours," Marcus said happily.

"Don't talk to her, Marcus. This isn't a game," the person I could only guess was his uncle barked at him. "Get out of here."

He smiled cruelly at me and left the room. I looked over to see a very heavy looking door slamming shut behind him as he left. The room I was in was small and metal, a box really.

"Now listen to me," the man said and I jerked my face to look at him instead. "You have medicine in you to keep your heart rate low so Caleb won't be able to follow you here. You might hear him, he might get through enough to talk to you a little bit, but you'll just be torturing yourself if you think that he will come and rescue you. He won't. I'm sorry to have to do this to you, but we can't allow the Jacobsons to have the power over us anymore. They've always had a hand over us and now this? I saw an opportunity and I took it." He shook his head. "No more."

He started to leave. "Wait. How long am I going to be here?"

"Until Caleb stops looking for you and forgets about ascending."

"That'll never happen."

He looked at me poignantly and smiled sadly. "I know."

The slamming door was like a nail in my coffin. I understood him exactly. They had no intentions of letting me go, ever, and they fully expected Caleb to spend the rest of his life looking for me in agony. Which from what I'd heard, when two imprinted Aces are not with each other, may not be long. I could already feel the ache in my back and legs for him which made me wonder how long I'd been here already. In just a couple days time we'd be in so much pain we could barely think from what I'd been told. And the medicine they were pumping into me with apparently didn't have pain medication in it because I could feel everything.

How had they pulled me away and Caleb not seen or heard them? What had happened to Caleb, had they hurt him? What happened to Beck at the party? My dad would be freaking if I hadn't made it home by midnight. I couldn't think anymore. My eyes started to drift closed and I could no longer command them to remain open.

I woke with a startled gasp as something warm and wet was on my face. I looked up to see a girl, about my age, wiping my face and hands with a cloth. She dipped her rag and wrung it out moving to my neck and belly under my...wait a minute. Where was my tank top? I was naked under a sheet.

"What are you doing?" I creaked through the pain in my back.

My head pounded behind my eyes, blood rushing in my ears so loud I could barely hear myself speak. The withdrawals. I needed Caleb.

"Washing you," she said with a 'duh' face. "You don't want to stink, do you?"

I saw she was being extremely careful with the extra large sponge to not touch my skin with hers. "Who are you?"

"Marla, Marcus' sister. You're Maggie, right? Marcus was a little shifty on the details."

"What are you talking about?" I muttered and tried to sit up, realizing then that I was no longer strapped down. But I may as well have been. My head swam and my arms felt like Jell-O as I tried to use them. "Where am I? What are you doing to me?"

"Well, where you are is the million dollar question isn't it? If you knew, then your knight could come and rescue you couldn't he?"

I looked at her, hearing the disdain in her voice. She looked an awful lot like Marcus; dark, wavy hair that hung past her shoulder blades and down her front shoulders. Her face was pale and heart shaped with dark brown eyes. Very thin and looking at me with...envy?

"Are you in love with Caleb or something?" I blurted.

She laughed a genuine laugh. "Uh, no. Granted, that boy is hot, but I would never date a rival clan. That's like not only forbidden, but disgusting. Why do you think that?"

I tried to shrug, but it came off jerky and very 'seizurish'. "I don't know. Your brother kidnapped me and you're helping him?"

"I'm helping him because I have to and he kidnapped you because of exactly why they told you. The Jacobsons have always had better abilities than us, always. So I'm told. I guess back in the day, like sixty years or something, they used to be friends, but then there was this girl. Almost sounds romantic doesn't it? This girl was beautiful and of course everyone prayed they'd be the one to imprint with her. She apparently wasn't waiting for that though. She secretly dated two guys from different clans without the other knowing it. They were of imprint age already and knew what they were doing but for whatever reason, kept seeing her. So, one of them finds out about the other. Guess who they were? A Jacobson and a Watson. So, they're furious, right? They somehow all wind up together out on the cliff with the old well behind our complex. The guys fight and as she's pushing them apart in between them...she imprints, with the Jacobson. Well, you can imagine how pissed the Watson was and was so enraged at what she had done, using him until she found her significant. Word is they even had sex which is just dirty without it being your significant." She visibly shivered like it was gross to think about. "So, he pushed them both over the cliff while they were too wrapped up in each other to notice."

I waited. Was there some punch line I had missed? She stayed silent and looked at me expectantly. "That's a terrible story."

My headache was only getting worse by the minute.

"I'm just giving you a history lesson."

"So, because your ancestor pushed Caleb's ancestor over a cliff, I'm supposed to feel sorry for you and Marcus?"

"No, you're supposed to see why we hate the Jacobson clan."

"I still don't get it. That was so long ago. Three stupid people, that has nothing to do with any of us."

"Oh, but it does. She imprinted with the Jacobson. Though she had used them both, the Jacobsons always won when we battled for something. He won the girl then, and the Watson never imprinted. He was the first in our clan to never imprint with anyone and therefore never to ascend."

"It was probably punishment." I couldn't help but spout the first thing that came to my mouth and I wondered if they'd slipped me something to make me speak the truth into my medicine.

"Probably. I'm not saying I condone what he did. I'm saying it wasn't fair that the Jacobson won twice. Not only did he imprint with the girl they were both in love with but then the Watson didn't imprint at all. A double whammy. It was bad enough that the Jacobsons always have better abilities."

"What are your parent's abilities?"

"My mom is an empath. She can feel what other people feel, totally useless in a clan of vicious bitter people and my dad is a weather man. He can tell you what weather is coming our way which is also totally useless."

"That's harsh."

"Their words, not mine. They hate it. The Jacobson's can move metal and do things in each other's minds. Our gifts are lame and have been for a long time. They think you are gonna solve that somehow."

"How?"

"Not sure. First, they are going to see how long we can keep you from Caleb. And if you live through that, I'm not sure, but I guess my uncle has some experiments planned."

"Experiments?" I squeaked.

"Yeah, like blood work and other stuff. My uncle said you have to have come along for a reason. He wants to see if we can find out what that is. You're a celebrity, you know. Every clan from here to London is talking about you and Caleb."

"Why?"

"Because you're the youngest to imprint and no clans have imprinted in a really long time. I'm sure they explained this to you."

"They did. I just wanted to see if you'd lie."

She laughed again. "We could so be friends if you weren't the enemy. Sorry, I gotta go. Here are some clothes. They aren't going to tie you up anymore, but you will be pumped with meds often so don't try anything. Someone will be down to check on you and feed you. I put a couple magazines on the nightstand and the bathroom is in the corner. But soon, you'll be in so much pain, I'm sure you won't care about any of that."

I looked over to see a solitary toilet, with no walls sitting in the corner. No sink, nothing else. Great.

She stood to leave and I panicked but once again my body didn't respond, just my brain. I decided to plead.

"Please help me. I didn't mean to imprint with Caleb, we can't control it. I have nothing to do with your fight. I love him. It hurts so bad. Please, please help me. I can't stay here."

"Sorry," she said, but didn't look a bit sorry to me.

I slumped against the bed. The room looked like a cell - an old, musty, nasty cell. There was nothing to do but wait and feel the wretched pains and kinks in my muscles from withdrawals. Would it be like drugs? Would I be in withdrawal and sweat in pain for a few days, then be all right and not need him anymore? I knew that wasn't true, but I had to think that the Watson clan had a purpose. Not just to kill Caleb and I with our own bodies turning against us just to see what happens. But that could be exactly what they were doing.

Caleb. Caleb, can you hear me? Please hear me.

I waited. I waited so long. I kept saying his name, trying to send him my feelings of longing, even letting him feel my pain, anything if I thought it would help.

Nothing.

But then something, faint, hazy and broken. Like a CB radio that was way out in the boonies.

Maggie? Can you...me?

Caleb! Are you ok?

I'm...you better be ok or I'll...Oh, G...Maggie. Please be ok. Tell me...you are?

I don't know where I am. A cell or basement maybe? The Watsons have me.

I know. I'm...sorry. Baby, p...forgive me. I'll get you...there, I promise. I'll find you. What happened? Your heartb...

They're keeping me drugged so you won't find me. They want to keep us apart so we won't ascend and then find out why we imprinted. Caleb...

I choked. I didn't want to tell him how scared I was. He was scared plenty for us both and it would just make him feel worse.

I know. I know. I...I'm coming for you. Just...

My dad? Beck?

He hesitated.

It's been a day and a half already. I had to...Dad. He freaked. Call...cops. They are looking...find you. But they won't. They are...things worse. I'm keeping...on your dad. He's fine. Are you ok?

I'm ok. I hurt, so bad.

Me, too. Baby...sorry.

It wasn't your fault.

It was...trick. They followed...to get to you.

I know.

No, no! You're fading out. Stay with me.

I *felt* like I was fading out, too. My head swam worse and I felt drained and even more tired and out of control.

I'm sorry. They did something to me. Can't stay awake.

I will find you...promise. I love...Magg...you're scared. Don't be. I love you.

I love you, too. I'm sorry I didn't say it before.

Me, too.

And then he was gone and I was in so much agony I couldn't even enjoy the fact that he said he loved me. It seemed for the short time we'd talked, I felt a sliver better. But as soon as our connection broke, I felt like cold water had been thrown on me. Too cold, freezing, stinging water and it hurt all over to be separated from him. I believed his words. That he'd keep my father safe and would never stop looking for me. But if he never found me and spent his whole life looking in pain and agony, somehow, that sounded worse than even death.

I woke up again some time later with the worse headache of my life. I felt nauseous as my back was locked in spasms. My legs cramped, curling my toes painfully. I heaved over the side of the bed but they hadn't given me anything to eat or drink so nothing came up. My stomach cramped violently as I leaned back on the pillows and tried to catch my breath.

I now had an even bigger respect for Gran.

And this was only day two. As my body jerked on its own accord, I heard the creak of the door opening. I looked over as much as I could and saw Marcus there. Smirking.

"Dead yet?"

"Get out, Marcus."

Someone else was already in my room. I looked further over to the corner to see his uncle sitting in a chair, watching me.

Marcus slammed the door, leaving me alone with his uncle.

"The next time you're alone I'd put those clothes on Marla gave you if I were you."

I looked down and saw my bare legs tangled up in the sheets. I quickly pulled them under with me and tried to glare at him but I felt terrible and I'm sure I didn't pull it off. He was handsome, which irked me. His hair and eyes were dark and he couldn't be more than forty five. If this was Harry Potter, he'd definitely be in Slytherin.

"What are you doing in here?"

"Watching you sleep. Watching you withdraw. Studying you."

I continued to feel like death was kicking in the door, but I kept my eyes on him. I did not feel safe with him in my room, especially with a lack of clothing.

"So, you're the one who hacked my dreams."

"Yes. You are very special, Maggie."

"I wish everyone would stop saying that," I muttered. "I definitely don't feel special."

He laughed and leaned back to cross one leg over his knee.

"Well, we could argue about it all day, but you are. And Caleb, too," he grumbled, "though I hate to admit that. This has happened to you for a reason. I can only imagine the abilities you would have possessed. I bet they'd have been exquisite. But that's behind us." He sighed and leaned forward on his knees. "I am not happy to do this to you, by any stretch, but I feel, as the champion of my clan, that I have to stop this. *For* my clan."

"Even though I have nothing to do with your stupid feud? Even though Caleb wasn't even born yet? We met at a stoplight. It wasn't something we could control. We didn't choose it, it chose us."

He stood abruptly startling me.

"Yes! Exactly. That's why! Why you? Why him? Of all the clans to pick from, why the Jacobson's again? They are always favored with whatever it is in the universe that controls us and our imprints, our lives. Why them again when the rest of us have plenty of willing and waiting people to claim their mates and abilities?"

I just shook my head and closed my eyes. There'd be no reasoning with him. He was a mad man.

"Just go. I want to get dressed and I don't really want you to watch me while I sit and cry in pain…that you caused me."

"I told you, I don't want to do this to you."

"But you are! You have no intentions of stopping even though I haven't done anything to you. You actually have to wonder why God would pick other clans for special treatment when this is how you treat people! Just get out!"

"I know what you're going through-"

"No you don't! Have you ever been away from your significant before?"

He paused and had the good graces to look a little guilty. "No."

"Then you have no idea what this feels like. Get. Out!"

I started to cry big fat, hurtful tears. It wasn't just physical pain, though there was plenty of that. It was anger and frustration and feeling useless and hurting for Caleb, knowing he was feeling every pain I was and more.

I heard him shuffle out and shut the door gently so I tried to get up, wrapping the sheet around myself just in case but my legs cramped and hurt so bad that I collapsed to the floor.

I lay there in a heap and I screamed. I cried. I yelled. I cursed. I did anything and everything that came to mind. I called Caleb's name over and over, screamed it. I could feel it when I yelled his name in my bones. Like it wasn't just my mouth but my entire being was calling to him.

It hurt so bad, I didn't know how it could be worse. No one came in again and I didn't get dressed; just continued to lay there. Eventually someone slid a tray of something into the door slot and left it there but I didn't look.

The day dragged on or so I thought. I had no concept of time except that every excruciating minute seemed to pile on top of each other. I tried to call Caleb again and again, but couldn't reach him. I imagined him, laying there on his bed, his dad and mom standing over him as he groaned and rolled in pain, just like I was doing. Maybe he wasn't lying on his bed. Maybe he was stronger than me. Maybe he was up pacing with his family and trying to come up with a plan.

It hurt so much to think about him, but I had to. I *needed* to. It could be that last thing I did.

I fell asleep again. I dreamed I was on the beach with Caleb, the same small beach between the rocks he brought me to. My clothes were the same as that day, the wind felt the same, smelled the same. I saw him standing on the sand in front of me a few feet away. I knew instantly it was a dream, but I still wanted it so badly that I ran to him. He smiled and held his arms out for me. But when I touched his arm with my hand it burned and jolted me. Like an offense mark does. I leapt back to see him and saw that it was still Caleb's face, but his eyes were dark and brooding. His t-shirt had changed from green to black, like Marcus's.

"What are you doing? I'm already your prisoner, why do you have to torture me in my dreams, too?"

"Because it's fun," Caleb\Marcus said snidely. "Uncle Sikes says you're having a real hard time. That it's real painful to be without this face." He rubbed a hand down his cheek and then smacked it hard with his palm.

I winced and he seemed to like that response. He took a step forward.

"Isn't he the one helping you do this echo dream?" I stepped back.

"He doesn't have to be awake to help me anymore. He'll remember it in the morning, but he doesn't know I'm here until then."

"Why? I didn't do anything to you," I creaked.

"Ahh, cutie," he crooned and tried to touch my cheek, but I jerked back. "You made me look bad in front of my clan. I couldn't kidnap one little human girl. You know how incompetent that made me look to them? Plus, Caleb doesn't deserve you. He doesn't deserve to have this handed to him like he was more important than the rest of us when-"

"Maggie!"

I gasped and turned to see Caleb, the real Caleb, my significant, my imprint, my soul mate, running over the dune and down the beach toward me.

Twenty Four

"Caleb?" I whispered in awe.

"You don't belong here," Caleb\Marcus roared behind me. "How did you get in here?"

Caleb reached us quickly and swallowed me in an embrace of warm arms. I sighed, but not in relief because I got none. His touch didn't soothe and calm me of the withdrawals because it wasn't real.

But he was really there, in my dream, right then.

"Caleb," I cried. "How did you get here?"

He pulled back to cup my face and kissed me forcefully. His mouth opened mine, his lips were filled with all the longing we'd felt in the past two days without each other. It didn't last long and he whispered his next words against my lips.

"He can't keep you from me. No one can. I told you I'll always find you."

"Answer me," Marcus growled again. "How did you get in here without an echoling?"

Caleb startled like he just noticed we weren't alone and pulled me behind him.

"Because you underestimated us, like always."

"Whatever. I'll just go wake her up, right now, and I won't do the echo dream anymore. You'll never see her again so you better enjoy it while you can."

"At least she can sleep in peace and not have you crawling through her dreams anymore," Caleb growled back.

"You better get to it," Marcus said and disappeared.

Caleb immediately turned and pulled me back to him, speaking into my hair.

"Where are you, Maggie? Tell me what it looks like."

"Like a jail cell or a basement storage room maybe. It's all metal walls and concrete floors. It stinks."

"What does it smell like?"

"Musty mold. And it's cold. How did you get in here?"

"No idea. I just was thinking about you, trying to get a read or fix on you. I was lying on my bed, must've fallen asleep, then landed on the dune. Who have you seen?"

"Marcus, his uncle and his sister, Marla."

"Did he hurt you? Did any one of them hurt you?"

"Not yet," I squeaked.

He sighed and squeezed me.

"I'll find you. I will."

"Is my dad freaking out?"

"Absolutely. My parents have actually been at your house a couple times with him already. They've been working together with the police. He called your mom, brother and your boss, too. My whole family has been going nuts." He ran a hand through his hair harshly. "Maggie," he sighed and put his head against mine. "I need you to be here. I miss you."

"I know. Me, too," I cried. "I'm so sorry."

"This is not your fault."

"Your's either. I just want to come home. Caleb, I-"

"I know, baby, I know," he said gruffly.

He kissed me again, but it was so desperate, so painful because I knew he was about to be ripped from me and I'd be back in my hole with the pain of our separation gripping me violently. I wrapped my arms around his neck and he lifted my feet from the sand as he squeezed me to him. His mouth was gentle and slow like he knew there was no point in trying to rush. It didn't matter. I just wanted to keep him there as long as possible.

But it didn't last long enough.

Something happened.

I felt a jolt go through me and my blood turned cold in my veins. Caleb's skin felt too hot to touch but then mine matched it and I was burning and freezing but in a good way. His heart was beating through my chest along with my own, making me startle. I opened my eyes to look at Caleb and saw he was experiencing the same thing as me. His eyes were wide and then he laughed which seemed odd at the time but I knew this wasn't something awful. It felt like...like imprinting. Wait…he had said we'd be together when it happened and it would feel like imprinting when we ascended. Could it be?

"It's ok, Maggie. It's for real. It's happening."

"How? This is a dream."

"I don't know, but I'm not complaining. This is going to help me save you somehow. I know it." He pulled me close to him again and held me tight. "Just wait, don't fight it. Once it's all done, we'll figure out a way to get you out of there."

As we held on, our bodies continued to pulse with warm and cold and seemed to breathe for themselves. It's like our souls took a back seat and let our bodies transform and configure into something else. My limbs burned and tingled, my head tingled, too, and I closed my eyes against the pressure.

When I finally felt like I'd settled back into myself, I felt different; more lithe and womanly than I had in my previous, awkward body. I felt more right and stronger, like I finally belonged and had purpose.

It didn't really make sense, but I went with it.

"Maggie."

I opened my eyes and looked at Caleb as he, too, looked a little different. His muscles under my hands on his upper arms were slightly more defined and harder. His facial features looked more rugged and grown up, as if he had aged, but not in a bad way.

"Caleb. You look..." I had no way to describe it to him.

"I know. You're gorgeous. I didn't think it was possible for you to be more gorgeous than you were before, but man, was I wrong." He looked as if in awe as he cupped my cheek and caressed it gently like I was something precious. "You are so insanely beautiful."

He smiled and I felt it all the way to my toes. I reached up and traced my finger over his brow, down his nose, over his lips as he closed his eyes, his lips parted. Everything about him seemed to be different. He *felt* different. I pressed my ear to his chest, hearing and feeling our heartbeats under his skin, beating in sync. Reminding me that nothing could literally ever separate me from Caleb, or him from me. We were one.

Oh, my… He was mine and he was perfect. Not just his looks, his everything. I could see and feel his soul and goodness all around me like it was a tangible thing. He glowed with love for me. And he was mine.

"Yes. And you're mine," he murmured into my hair, reading my thoughts. "Forever."

But then something yanked at me, something that felt like a tether or leash I was connected to. I could feel myself being pulled towards consciousness and gasped as I pulled back from him a little.

"Caleb, he's taking me. He's waking me up."

"No, not yet," he begged and ran his fingers through my hair, pressing his nose to mine.

"Caleb, please stay with me," I said my voice breaking as the tears rolled down my face. "I love you."

"Not goodbye, Maggie." He wiped my tears away with a thumb and kissed my forehead. "I love you so much. I'll find you. We're ascended now. I promi-"

I was awake, gasping and aching like never before by Marcus throwing a bucket of water on me and my bed and the sheets.

"Finally. The pillow didn't work. Fighting it weren't you?" He chuckled and turned to leave. "Stupid human."

I lay there cold, shivering and writhing on the bed in utter devastation but utter revelation as well. I was not a human anymore. Even though that was abundantly clear and the pain was wretched and volatile, the loss of Caleb was incomparable.

Once again I had no sense of days or time. The pain just took me over and I screamed and cried, yelling for Caleb and feeling my body jerk and jar with a slow steady heartbeat. During it all, no one came to see me. No one opened the slot to see if I was ok. No one gave me water or tried to calm me. They just let me scream myself back to sleep.

I woke fuzzy, like I was drugged. But I had refused to eat their food or drink so I didn't understand how they were still getting their drugs in me to keep my heart rate low. I wiped my face of drool but stopped. It smelled funny. I smelled my hand and tasted it, spitting it out once I realized it was the medicine. Someone had been coming in, knowing I'd pass out from exhaustion from withdrawals, and slipping me the medicine then. Their cleverness was beginning to make my hope fail. I tried to not scream from the pain this time. My throat was raw and scratchy from it and the lack of water. I guessed there was no point in holding out any longer because they were already giving me the medicine.

I rolled out of bed, the sheet still damp around me but I crumpled to the floor with a whimper and dry heaved over and over. How? How could it still be getting worse? There was no way I'd survive. If I didn't get out to Caleb, I'd die. No other way about it. And Caleb...He would die, too. I had to get to him.

I crawled and pulled myself to the door where today's food tray was and found a big bottle of Gatorade and a turkey and cheese sandwich. I woofed it down and was amazed to still feel my stomach growl after it was all gone.

"I'll have Marla bring you another one shortly."

I turned to see Marcus's uncle sitting in the same corner that he had before.

I wondered if he would be able to tell I was different, that I had ascended and was no longer human, but I guessed not since I was so disheveled. I looked down at my see through white wet sheet and then glared at him.

"I told you to put those clothes on, didn't I?" he said clearly amused.

"Great. I can add pervert to your list."

"I'd cooperate if I were you. You see, the bad part is about to begin. My wife is coming in to take your blood. You put one scratch on her and I'll kill you myself. Got it?"

I sat and looked at him like he was a total idiot.

He nodded like my silence had been an answer and banged once on the wall with his fist. The door opened and a short, pretty little woman came through. She refused to look at me but came right to me and helped me off the floor. She placed me on the bed and motioned for me to lie down.

She then placed a hand on my forehead, like she was checking for a fever. That's when I realized something was different. I wasn't shocked or jolted by her touch. There was no offense mark.

"Why aren't you burning my skin like they do?"

"Well, I'm not here to hurt you, dear. But also, I was human, like you. So I don't produce those kinds of marks on others."

Human? But Caleb has said there were only three humans. Could it be that they didn't know about her?

She pulled out a needle and a couple tubes with labels and I felt sick. I turned, groaning and pressed the side of my face into the pillow.

"She needs more liquids," the woman called out to her husband. "I won't get much blood from these dry veins."

He banged on the wall again and a young guy I'd seen somewhere before opened the door.

"Bring me two bottles of orange juice, unopened."

He nodded and left quickly. She continued to poke the inside of my elbow with her fingers until he came back with the bottles.

"Drink one now, one after," Sikes said as he tossed them to me. The guy who brought them stared at me with a little smile. His eyes roamed over me and I realized with chagrin I was still wearing the damp sheet. I pulled my legs up and placed my arms on top of my knees. He chuckled at my reaction but Sikes barked at him. "Get out."

Then I recognized him, the guy who tried to help Marcus kidnap me. He had put a majority of the offense marks on me that night. I glared at his back as he left.

"Drink up, dear. I need to get this blood so we can let you rest."

I wanted to laugh at her attempt at humanity. It was a little late for that now. I drank the orange juice eagerly, as I needed it. While she waited for the juice to hit my system I decided to small talk.

"What's your ability?"

I fully expected her to not answer, but she did.

"I can see through things. Skin, for instance. It's why I'm so good at taking blood and things like this."

That gave me pause and I was surprised I could follow and focus so well after everything that had happened to me. My body felt disoriented but my mind was sharp. I wondered if the ascension had anything to do with that.

"Wait. I thought the abilities were supposed to complement each other? But if he," I pointed to the jerk still sitting, leaning on the wall, "can go into dreams, that doesn't go together with seeing through things."

"That's only a Jacobson rule," Sikes muttered. "The rest of us just have to make do."

"Oh."

"It's time," she chimed and began to get my arm ready again. I felt bile rise in anticipation of the stick. I hated needles. "Just relax. I'm very good at this. It won't hurt. Lean back and close your eyes."

I did what she said though I didn't trust her, I had no other choice.

"I can't believe I have to do this to this poor girl." She took a deep breath. "It's for the good of the clan, the good of the clan."

"What?" I asked, wondering what she meant by what she said.

"I didn't say anything, dear. Lie back."

I looked at her curiously because I knew I heard her say something. Then her lips didn't move but...I heard her.

"This better work. I'm not spending the rest of my life experimenting on teenagers, Sikes."

I coughed a shocked laugh.

"What?" she asked out loud and began to look worried. She looked at her tubes in her hand. Then in her head she said, "Did I take too much? She's acting funny."

I watched her and listened to her inner monologue, sometimes to Sikes and sometimes with herself, until she was done.

"All done," she chimed happily and took the rubber band from my arm. "There. You didn't even know I was doing it, did you?"

"No," I breathed because it was all I could do.

Holy crap, I could read minds. That was my ability? Somehow the way everyone had made such a fuss over me, I thought it'd be cooler than that. How the heck was that going to get me out of here?

"Ok, Maggie, drink your juice and put those clothes on. The next time I visit, we're taking a little field trip," Sikes said and left behind his wife.

I tried to process and think, reach out to Caleb but got nothing. I washed up in a bowl of water left beside my bed. The water was cold and it didn't feel good but I did it anyway. I hurriedly put on the clothes left for me, a pair of old jeans and a black baby doll t-shirt that said 'Bite Me' with two red blood dripping vampire holes in the collar. Ugh and Eew.

I tried to pull my hair back in a twisted bun but my arms ached so bad, I couldn't make it work. I hurt all over, like I'd been hit over and over, my muscles refusing to cooperate. I needed Caleb.

By then Sikes had returned to find me sitting on the bed's edge.

"Ah, you look like a new girl."

"I'm sure I do," I muttered sarcastically.

"Come on. We have work to do."

He didn't touch me but beckoned for me to follow him. When I came out of my cell, I saw that there were other cells, too, but no one was in them as we passed. We did pass a few people out of cells though and they gawked openly as we passed them every so often. Some looked like they wanted to spit on me, others wanted to put me in their bag and run with me like I was the Holy Grail. I didn't like either of those options.

"Where are we going?"

"Somewhere."

"Hilarious," I muttered and tried to stretch out the ache in my back.

"Keep your questions to yourself for now."

I rolled my eyes at him but he didn't see. I kept shuffling along through the pain. I considered the karate I'd learned from Kyle's dad, but I was so weak from withdrawals, I was barely dragging myself down the hall. And the meds they were giving me probably had something in them to keep me from something like that. I'm sure Marcus told them what happened the first time he tried to kidnap me.

Speak of the devil. I heard someone behind me and turned to see Marcus smiling cruelly behind me. Then Sikes started spouting something ahead of me.

"Maybe we should try to test the blood first. Maybe we could pair her with one of ours and see if we can break the imprint or trick it."

"What?" I asked him, confused and terrified.

"I didn't say anything. Be quiet."

I realized I'd heard his thoughts. I decided to test it since we were apparently headed down the longest hall in history. I tried to open my mind, my ears, my senses and listen to a group of three people as I passed them in the hall.

Plan backfire.

I heard all kinds of voices at once and it was too much as my head stung and buzzed. I collapsed with a scream to the floor, cupping the sides of my head as I felt like I'd black out. A couple of them tried to run to help me but Sikes held up a hand to stop them.

"Wait. Don't touch her! No offense marks!" Then I heard his thought.

Other than the one Marcus already put on her hand.

"What's wrong, Maggie?"

"I, uh..." It was all right if I didn't push it, so I eased myself off the floor on shaking, achy legs. "I'm ok, just a sharp pain in my head, headache, I guess."

"Well, come on. Fresh air will do you good."

"Outside?"

"No tricks, Miss Masters. You are still pumped with meds. Your Caleb will not save you."

"Not like he could even if your heartbeat was blaring like a foghorn," Marcus remarked snidely.

I ignored them and tried again to focus on hearing someone's thoughts. If I focused on one person it worked. It was strange how my body just seemed to know what to do. Just like Caleb had described. There was no denying it. We were meant for this.

There was a man by a door with a gun. I opened my mind and focused on only him, thought of his face only and it worked. He thought this was ridiculous and they should just kill me. Then the imprint would break and Caleb would never ascend. Problem solved. I inched against the wall around him, eying him warily. He smiled sweetly and reassuringly at me which completely contradicted his thoughts and I wondered if my whole life had been led this way; with people saying or acting one way and then thinking and believing a complete other way.

I kept at it. I discovered that if I was hearing a thought, my head felt a little fuzzy, like I was talking on the telephone with a metallic connection. I had to focus to notice it, but it was there. I'd have to master that skill so as not to answer something that wasn't asked out loud.

We came to a ladder at the end of the hall, or tunnel. It went straight up so Sikes went up and unscrewed the bolt on the lid and lifted it straight up and over. He went out and I assumed I was supposed to follow. I climbed the steep ladder slowly and with labored breaths and bare feet because they'd taken my shoes. I knew I couldn't make it. I was going to fall the short distance I'd made but then felt a hand on mine. I looked up to see Sikes' wife smiling.

"Come on, dear. I know it's hard, but you can do it. Let me help."

She pulled me up the rest of the way and I collapsed on the ground. When the sun hit my cold face it was painful and good. I'd missed it.

"Get up," Sikes barked. "Almost there, then you can rest."

"It hurts. It's been...I don't know how many days since I've seen Caleb. I can't. It hurts too much."

I didn't want to cry anymore but after the exertion, it was ferociously painful and pronounced. My head pounded so hard that my vision bounced when I tried to focus on something.

"I can't help you. I don't want to taint you with an offense mark until we've tried every other avenue in our experiment first. Come on, just a little further."

His wife looked displeased as she helped me from the ground.

If we hadn't been married for as many years as we have, I swear...

I wanted to look over and laugh at her but my body would absolutely not have cooperated with that. Sikes' wife was practically dragging me behind him as we made our way through a wooded area that was really grassy and overgrown. The grass was so tall it was up to my thighs, which made sludging along that much harder and the blades were scratching and itching my feet.

I felt like I'd collapse again but we came upon a well. I could see the cliff just beyond it and knew exactly where I was. Did they know that Marla had told me that story? That she told me about the well behind their house? I knew where I was! If I only could tell Caleb.

I looked at Sikes. I tried to push into his mind just like Caleb had pushed into mine that first day. Focusing and honing in on him, picturing his mind. It didn't take much of a push and I was in. It was the strangest thing I'd ever experienced. It wasn't like Caleb's mind at all.

Sikes' mind was murky and I could feel his anger and bitterness like slime on my skin. It consumed him. I realized I wasn't just reading his thoughts, I was looking into his mind; all of it, every corner. I could sort through and look at things he had planned or thought and done before this. I saw what he was planning for me and this well.

And I wanted no part of it.

We stopped and I looked around to see Marcus and about five other guys had joined us there, big burly dark guys. Their thoughts were all different and I discovered, just like Sikes' wife, not everybody was thrilled to be here.

"Oh, man, I'm so ready to be done with this."

"We can't even call ourselves human beings after this. Sikes is crazy."

"I wonder what mom's cooking for dinner. Hurry up, Sikes'. I'm ready for some fried chicken."

"Why are other clans always so much hotter than ours? I'd pay a lot for ten minutes with this one."

"So stupid. It's not even gonna work. All this wasted time, torturing some teenage girl. Ridiculous."

I felt the onslaught crushing over me but staved off the collapse of my control with focus. I could control this but I hated hearing what people said. Well, these people anyway, so I shut them out.

"All right, Maggie," Sikes stated suddenly, "let's get you in."

"Please, no. Please don't put me down there," I begged and tried to pull from Sikes' wife, but she held me tight.

"Don't start. If you don't cooperate, I'll send Marcus to Caleb's house right now and we can see first hand what happens when an imprinted Ace dies."

"No!" I yelled and collapsed to my knees. The pain in my stomach at just thinking about it was insufferable. "Please, don't."

"You see," he said conversationally, "this well is supposedly what started it all. Over three hundred years ago, my ancestor fell down this well. The legend says he was betrothed to a beautiful girl and was in the well for four days. He thought she'd be worried sick about him and prayed to God, made every promise he could think of, to help him. He became so enraged when no one came to his aid, that on the fourth day he started to scream and beat his fists on the walls. His blood from his hands and arms mixed with the water in the well and it started to glow. He was scared but then he saw a face over the well. Someone had come to rescue him. He was pulled out and was eager to see his beloved, but when he came up, she was not among the ones waiting for him. You see, she thought he had cold feet and had left, decided not to marry her, so she married another. He was heartbroken and went to the church where they were to be married to pray. There in the cemetery in the church yard, he met a girl, placing flowers on her father's grave. When he helped her stand and they touched, that was the first imprint. He was relieved of the pain from the woman he loved and immediately loved another. Within a few days he and his significant both ascended. By then others had started to imprint in the village as well. A village occupied by mostly Watsons. Then they ascended just as my ancestor had and it started it all. No one in the village was married again without an imprint and their abilities helped them to conquer and fend off their enemies. You see, when he bled into the well, in his rage, legend had said that's what started it all. He eventually told everyone that the water had started to glow and it must have meant something. And it was the village well, so everyone consumed this water. Now, you see why I want to test the theory of the well water. Now. Get on the platform," he said evenly and I heard Marcus chuckling behind me.

Sikes' wife helped me to stand and moved me towards the board attached to rope on all corners over the well opening. I couldn't fight, I just moved where she moved me. She placed me on it and I curled up in a ball and tried to hide my fear from them. I didn't look at them or speak to them as they lowered me down. I heard Sikes' wife muttering in her mind but she kept right on doing what he wanted.

And Sikes, he wanted to see if the water would reverse the imprint or break it since it had given it to someone who had none. As for Marcus's mind, I couldn't even look into it without being sick. All the vile and horrible things he thought about me, about the Jacobsons, about Caleb. It physically hurt me to look in his mind with its gray fog and thick barrier of pure hatred.

So I let them lower me until I felt water come over the edge of the board and I sat up. I didn't know if I'd have the strength to swim and I started to panic, but felt no increased heart rate to go along with it.

When the water reached my stomach the pulley stopped and I looked up to see Sikes leaning over the edge.

"We'll be back to get you in a couple days, Maggie."

I felt my breath rush in and out in panic.

"Please don't leave me down here. I'm scared," I called up.

"That's the idea," he yelled back and moved away.

Twenty Five

I felt my stomach bunch and cramp. So this must be the third or fourth day away from Caleb and they were going to let me sit in a well for days, testing a theory. And what would they do with me if it did break the imprint? Should I fake a broken imprint? Could they tell?

I sat for a long time, trying not to shake and jerk my muscles in pain because the sloshing of the water was driving me insane.

I listened to see if someone was up there waiting for me. I listened for their thoughts but got none. I tried to call Caleb but got nothing from him. After a few hours my teeth chattered so much that my jaw ached and I bit my tongue several times. I had an idea.

I spit my blood into the water around me and waited and waited. No glowing apparitions, nothing. I scolded myself for buying into his lame story and wanted to lay down so bad I could barely think. I couldn't lean back on the wall because the platform started to buckle.

Eventually, I gave in and began to cry again. All day, I sat there. I watched and felt the sun making its way across the sky, but the water was so cold that I couldn't feel any warmth from it. Then the darkness came. I heard awful noises out there, animals yelling and howling, birds hooting and chirping, breaking twigs, crickets. It was excruciating. I couldn't sleep because I couldn't lie down. My eyes kept closing against my control and I rested my head on my knees, but I fell over several times into the water, splashing it everywhere and wetting me more, making me colder so I eventually stopped trying.

Then morning came. The sun starting making it's was across the sky. In the light I could see the bricks were out of alignment in the well wall. I stood wobbly, holding the pulley rope for leverage and tried to set my foot on them and climb. I got a little footing but it was all so slimy and lined with algae that I never made it more than a step before I slid back down and scrambled to not fall further in the well. The last time I was reaching for a brick with one foot and slipped, slicing my arm on the hard, dirty rocks.

My blood, once again dripped into the water beside me and I watched it in anticipation, grimaced at it. It was stupid to believe maniacs.

I tried yelling again. I tried reaching Caleb. I was so exhausted, I could barely think. When it was almost so dark and I could barely see, I heard voices.

I hoped and prayed they were the voices I wanted, the Jacobson's, Caleb, but they weren't. I saw Marcus's face above me as he smiled.

"Dead yet?"

I slumped in defeat and wanted to scream as they began to pull me up. Two days. Two days they'd left me down here. All the water left me and I thought the warm air would help but it didn't, it made it worse. My skin burned and shivered at the same time. Whoever was pulling was jerking and pulling so forcefully that the board was banging on the walls, jabbing my muscles with the force. It felt like my bones were hitting against each other. I heard myself scream and whimper. My chest hurt with it. I screamed Caleb's name and thought it, begged for him to hear me.

When I reached the top, I rolled off the board and side of the well to land forcefully in the grass. I gasped and shook. I opened my eyes and saw that Sikes' wife wasn't there, but Marcus, his uncle and three other guys were. I wondered how they were going to help me without putting offense marks on me, but by the looks on their faces, they had no intentions of that anymore.

Marcus smiled cruelly at me and grabbed my arm, yanking me up before jerking his hand back hissing.

"That still stings as bad as it did the first time."

"All right. We can't do this outside she'll make too much noise. Inside, now," Sikes barked.

Oh, no. What- Then his thoughts were blaring to me. He was so, so mad. He didn't want to do this and, in fact, had no intentions of watching. He was going to let Marcus loose on me and see how many offense marks they could put on me at one time. See if it affected or drained me so much that it changed something. I couldn't have that. I shook my head.

"No. No, please stop," I begged Sikes, looked right at him to implore his humanity. "Please don't hurt me anymore. I'm only seventeen. I can't handle this anymore. It hurts so badly, please."

He looked away and repeated his order.

"Take her inside."

I screamed as Marcus came to grab me once more, wrapping a fist in my hair. Something silver and gleaming glinted in the light in his hand. I felt the sting and pressure across my shoulder and the edge of my throat before it registered what he'd done. He'd cut me, with a knife.

I flung my hand to my shoulder and felt the warm sticky mess in between my fingers. I also felt warm soaking up the front of my shirt.

"Marcus! No!" Sikes yelled and pushed him aside. "I did not give you permission to harm her with worldly goods, only supernatural! Finn, take her inside, now!"

I pushed at the one who came, and then they all came for me. I felt stings and slaps in several places all over me as they all tried to contain me, but were jerking their hands back in pain themselves. I slung my arms out and my brain kicked in with karate maneuvers but my body had no strength behind it as I lamely fought back with feeble kicks and blocks.

I thought, if I could just hold them off, maybe something would happen. And then it did. One of the men, Finn I presumed, yelled and screamed, grabbed my arms and pulled me up to stand. He pulled me against his chest from behind and wrapped a hand around my mouth, still screaming in his own agony, but determined to end this now. I bit his hand as hard as I could muster and he pushed me away in instinct, over the cliff's edge.

I heard yells and screams as I soared through the air. Sikes roared above me as I fell, out loud and in his mind, "No!"

I looked down and saw only dark greens and blues moving rapidly towards me.

I landed in freezing ice water. Raging around me and swallowing me. I fought it but just like up on the cliff, I had no strength to actually make progress. So I just took a deep breath and let the current of the river take me. I floated roughly until I felt scratching and jarring on my legs. I looked up to see I was slamming into a downed tree, leaning over the river's bank.

I reached and pulled, slowly I managed to get myself half out of the water. I knew it wasn't smart to sit there in plain sight. I was sure that Sikes and his bunch would be looking for me. But my body wouldn't go any further. I passed out with my top half on the dirty freezing bank and my bottom half submerged in tree branches and dirty freezing water.

I had no idea how much time had passed, but it was dark when I woke up again. The pain that shot through me was like nothing ever before it. It coursed through me, on a mission to end me. I couldn't scream. I knew they were looking for me and it would lead them to me. Plus, I knew this was the Watson compound. Who knew how many of them lived out here, but I wanted to scream so badly. I fought it. My mouth opened in a silent scream as my body spasmed and bowed in reflex to the cramps, my fingers digging into the dirt. I contorted in on myself as I spat and coughed up river water when I tried to move up the bank and out of the freezing water.

I eventually pulled myself up completely out of the water and army crawled to the dry grass up past the beach. I rolled to rest on my back and tried to catch my breath.

I could see every star, just like that night at Mugly's with Caleb. Just like the beach the night I was taken. I imagined Caleb beside me, holding my hand and us just looking up at them so casually as we'd done before. My chest clinched as I thought of him. The stars bounced in my vision as my head pounded against the ground under it. I had to get to Caleb. I was free. I had to get moving.

I rolled back over and it took all my strength to stand. I started to walk as I continued to shiver. I felt twigs and rocks under me cut my feet and my arms scratched by passing branches and I rammed through like a lump. I felt the gash on my collar break open when I fell to the ground once. I wrapped my fingers around it and kept going, ignoring the pain in my shoulder. The longer I walked the more I couldn't feel my toes or fingers. I had no way to warm myself and, after what seemed like several hours, felt my resolve slipping. I was going to die out here. If it wasn't by the Watsons hand it would be by the woods.

I didn't walk on the trails or the beach instead walking through the bushes and trees to hopefully keep anyone from seeing me. I was so exhausted, so in pain, but I kept going. I saw a shed or cabin ahead of me. I felt hope soar then plummet. I debated whether to go in or not. Who knew whose shed it was? It could be one of theirs and they'd find me there. I couldn't help it. I was freezing and had to get dry.

I pulled myself up the short hill to the top by some roots and vines. I crept up to the cabin, wincing when the stairs creaked under my feet. I peeked into the dark window and seeing no light decided to try the door.

Unlocked.

I eased it open and heard the lock rattling from my shaking fingers. I took a deep breath and swung the door open. The moon illuminated the room to show a small bed and kitchen. I searched for a light switch and found one by the door. The lights were bright and I quickly turned it off in case of alerting someone. I spotted a flashlight on the floor by the door and tried it instead.

As I looked around the cabin it was clear that no one had been there in forever. It was undecorated, unclean, and efficient. Across the room, the closet was full of clothes, jeans and coats. I immediately pulled off my soaking wet t-shirt and threw on a long ugly men's warm sweater. I took my jeans and laid them across the bedrail to dry. There was nothing to do for my cut and bleeding feet.

I walked over to the kitchen and found a stack of emergency candles all ready and lined up by the sink with matches. I lit a couple of them and then looked into the cupboard for something to eat. I found two cans of Vienna sausage - yuck - but I ate them quicker than I had any tasty burger I'd ever had. There were a couple jugs of water by the sink, too. They were unopened and smelled all right so I took a couple big swigs from one.

I felt ready to pass out again. My stomach was full but hurt for other reasons. I had no idea how to reach Caleb or where I was exactly, geographically, but I knew I had to find a way. In the morning, I'd be able to see and could find my way out.

But when I looked at the bed I was skeptical about being able to sleep in it. It was old and dirty, dust and cobwebs everywhere, but I wasn't in a position to be picky. I decided to just sleep on the top cover and used a blanket thrown over the end to cover up with.

When I lay down, I sighed. Who cared whose bed it was, it was like heaven. I balled myself up, pulling my knees to my chest and felt the shivers slowing just as I drifted to sleep.

Something startled me awake. I opened my eyes and was too terrified and anxious to think about the blinding pain hitting me. Someone was there.

I hobbled to the closet, grabbing my shirt and pants on the way. Once I sat down, I felt the full force of the withdrawal and it was all I could do not to scream. My stomach started to heave and cramp but somehow I managed to keep it together as I heard the front door creak open.

I held my breath and prayed I could keep myself calm as I waited for them to find me or not. My heart was beating against my ribs so hard, it hurt. Wait…

My heartbeat.

The medicine was out of my system. Caleb could find me now! If I could only make it until he could get here. My joy sang in me even as I feared the worst of my intruder. The long cut on my throat and arm were pulsing and pounding painfully with my rapid heart but I was thankful for it. I peeked through the coats that hung in front of my face. I couldn't see who it was but they were looking around the room, like they were looking for something. I silently cursed myself for running to the closet instead of out the back door.

But I heard the voices calling to each other outside and was thankful for the closet. The man inside yelled something back and I held back my gasp. It was the guy who'd brought me orange juice and ogled me in my see through sheet.

Crap. They were here looking for me.

"Not here," he yelled and walked swiftly through the door.

I focused to see if I could hear Sikes thoughts, if he was near and got nothing but when I thought of Marcus, I got a lot more than I wanted.

Stupid human. I'll kill her. And Sikes thinks he's just running things now. I have had it with this. When I find her I'm gonna teach her something about what a real Ace is. She'll wish she'd never met me. Maybe I'll show Caleb in an echo dream. Ha! That'd be freaking hilarious! Oh, no! Maggie I love you! Ha! Idiots. I'm so glad I'll never imprint and have to deal with that crap. Just wait til I find you, little Maggie. You'll wish you'd died in the fall.

Oh, God help me. His mind was pure evil coated with malice. I shook myself and peeked out the closet. I fell out of it really because I was hurting so much. I breathed through it and managed to wiggle my jeans back on but threw the vampire shirt under the bed, just in case. I looked around for shoes but once again, found nothing.

I took a few more big gulps of water from the jug and then tried to reach Caleb. I called out to him in my mind. I didn't get him but I got flashes and glimpses, like before. That's when I realized I was doing it wrong. I shouldn't be trying to tune myself into Caleb like I had before, connecting us. I should try to read his mind, one way, like I had everyone else. That's what I could do now. So I did and I immediately heard him. He was talking to his father.

"I don't know, Dad. Only about ten minutes ago, but it's real. Let's go. Now," Caleb said vehemently.

"I know, son, and we will, but we have to get everyone together. We can't just run half-cocked into the Watson complex. We need numbers."

"I know," Caleb sighed and banged his fist on the wall, leaving a mark in the plaster. "I can feel her, Dad, and she's terrified of something. What if someone is hurting her right now?"

"You'd feel that. As soon as her heartbeat returned to you, so did your ability to tune into her body. If she's in pain, you'll feel it now. We'll get her back. I promise you that."

I saw Peter walk toward Caleb, though it looked like he was walking towards me and hugged him. Caleb sighed harshly and patted his father's back roughly.

"We'll find her," Peter promised.

"Ok. Let's get things rolling. I'm dying here, Dad. I'm not gonna be cool much longer if we don't go soon."

"They're already on the way here. Go sit and wait-"

"I can't!" he growled. "I can't just sit here and wait! I've got to do something. It hurts so bad...and I can feel her in me. She's hurting and... It's too much. It's-" He gasped and growled and kicked a chair that slammed into the desk across the room. "If they hurt Maggie, I'll kill them. I swear to-"

"I know." Peter grabbed Caleb around his shoulders. "I know, but you aren't going to help Maggie by losing it. We will get her back."

I pulled away from Caleb's mind. It was too painful to see him losing it like that. I had no idea how long it would take them to get here to the Watson compound and I knew they were already out looking for me. Should I stay here in the cabin or try to get to a road? I could open my mind, like I did before and then I could hear the thoughts of those near me and hide. It would work.

I peeked out the door slowly and cleared my mind, opened it wide and listened. I didn't hear anything so I inched my way down the porch, trying to not trip on my aching legs, and winced when my feet hit the gravel. I held the porch rail in one hand and lifted one foot to see a bloody mess on the sole. Great.

I started towards the woods again. The opposite way I had come before. It was so different during the day. I could see how thick and full the woods were which made me feel some better about being able to elude the Watsons.

I walked for a couple hours, hobbling, holding my stomach as it ached and burned. I had to stop a couple times to breath and try to talk myself into going forward. I just wanted to find the nearest rock and crawl under it. I had no idea how long it had been but I was thirsty, hungry and my vision was starting to blur and bounce again. It wouldn't be long and I'd pass out from the withdrawals, just like before.

I tried to find a large low tree to hide under so no one would find me when I did pass out. I saw a cave-like thing under the cliff and knew that would be too obvious of a hiding place so I went around it. There were cliffs all around so I hoped and prayed this wasn't the same one I'd fallen from. On the other side of the cave was a large group of Christmas tree evergreens. I sighed in relief and went to go crawl under the low branches to wait out my sleep, but as I pushed a large branch away I heard his thoughts, just a second before I saw a man.

His eyes went wide as he saw me and in his mind he'd been looking for me. He was holding up his hands as if to say he meant me no harm. I knew better. I took off running. I could hear him behind me, gaining ground. I was a runner for crying out loud, but my body couldn't keep up with my spirit. I held in my scream when I felt his arms go around me. He didn't tackle me like I thought he would.

"Maggie, wait. Don't scream."

I realized then that his arms were still around me and he wasn't burning me with an offense mark. I slowly turned and looked at him, brown curly hair and kind eyes.

"Caleb's here?" I squeaked.

He nodded. "I'm Rodney, Caleb's cousin. I'm sorry I scared you."

I didn't care if he was the pope. He wasn't a Watson and that was gold to me. I collapsed in relief against him and felt him lift me in his arms. I went in and out of consciousness as he carried me swaying. He swiftly made his way, to where I didn't know. It wasn't too long before I heard yelling. I looked up thinking this man had somehow tricked me and taken me back to the Watsons but it was Peter and...Caleb.

I gasped and wiggled out of Rodney's grasp. He put me down easily and steadied me. I tried to run but couldn't. Caleb grabbed me before I hit the ground and the aches and pains left my body with a harsh sigh from us both as we collided and wrapped our arms around each other. Then there was a burst of energy all around us as our skin made contact for the first time in days.

I saw Peter and a few others behind him fall to the ground behind Caleb, like they'd been knocked back by some force or invisible trip wire. A few were pushed back mid air as they ran our way. The energy was visible, in streams of iridescent blues and it seemed to flow through my skin. I lifted my arm to see the ribbons making their way through one side of my hand and out of the other.

I gripped Caleb's neck tightly in my fingers and felt his grip on my back tighten. "What's happening?" I whispered.

"I don't know," he spoke into my hair, "but I don't care."

He kissed me softly all over my face, my lips the most. I could barely stand and he held me up as he let me feel everything in him, all his worries and anger and longing. Or maybe I was just able to feel it now because of the ascension.

"Yes," Caleb answered me. "I told you you'd be able to feel everything from me after the ascension without even trying." He pushed my hair back from my face and made a pained face from seeing offense marks around my mouth. I grimaced wondering what the rest of me looked like and smelled like. He chuckled and shook his head. "I don't care. I have you back and that's all that matters. I'm sorry I didn't get to you first. A few of the family who were closer got here before us. I told them where you were."

"That doesn't matter. I'm just glad you're here."

"I'm here," he agreed and pulled me closer by my shirt front. He saw the angry red slash across my neck and shoulder and at first he blared hot fury as he ran his fingers across it scowling and growling low in his throat. Then he perked up and the sides of his mouth turned up, making me wonder what in the world had just happened. Then he looked back to me and smiled happily. "And now, I can do this."

He closed his eyes and concentrated. One by one I felt the offense marks on my body and face, the slice down my arm from the well wall and the bruises and cuts on my feet tingle and burn away. The long cut across my shoulder burned for a second before searing away to nothing. Then the cold left my body as well. I was filled with warmth and a glow of rightness. This was exactly where I was supposed to be.

"Caleb," I said and he sighed and pulled my face to his, our noses touching.

"I have missed hearing you say my name."

"Me, too."

"Ok, I'm sorry. What were you saying?"

"What about the Watsons? They were out here looking for me this morning."

He pulled back and looked at my face seriously.

"You saw them?"

I nodded.

"I hid in a cabin in the woods last night."

"Wait…What? We thought they let you go because they knew we were coming for you."

I bit my lip and tried to block that part instantly from my mind so he wouldn't see. Should I show him everything they did to me?

He growled at my thoughts. "What they did to you? What do you mean? Show me, right now, Maggie," he ordered gruffly.

"Please, don't leave me again. Even to go and hunt them down. Please?"

He shook his head and looked in as much agony as I felt.

"I'm not leaving you for anything. You are staying right here." His arms tightened around me. "I'm sorry. I wasn't angry at you."

"I know that, but I just didn't want you to run off in a rush to crack someone's head."

"What did they do to you, Maggie?" he asked softly. "I *need* to see it."

I bit my lip again and closed my eyes, leaning my forehead against his. I showed him from the first second I awoke with his jacket, then woke naked and being washed by Marla, then Sikes, Marcus. Once the vision got started, I couldn't turn off certain parts so he had to live through my withdrawals as well. Even living it again was almost unbearable.

He grit his teeth so hard I could hear it. Then I showed them taking my blood, and when he saw me able to read Sikes' wife's mind he gasped and pulled back to look at me, awestruck. I smiled and leaned my head back to his. Then I showed him going down the hall and up to the well, waiting all day and night and another day down there, freezing and trying to climb out. Then the Watsons attacking me and my being pushed, accidentally, off the cliff. He growled and cursed and huffed through it. Then we saw the water, the cabin, them looking for me and my hiding, my opening my mind to hear all thoughts and reaching out to read his mind, hearing him and his father speaking to each other about my heartbeat returning to him, then his cousin Rodney finding me, then here, now.

I pulled back to look at him and he was red and shaking.

"They're still human. How could they do this to someone?" he muttered more to himself than me.

"Caleb," Peter said behind us. "I'm sorry but they'll know we're here by now. They'll run and we'll miss them if we don't go."

"I'm gonna kill-"

"I saw. We all saw," Peter said shakily and Caleb and I both looked sharply at him.

"What?"

He pointed above us and our thoughts mingled and bounced into view on the ribbons and streams of energy around and above us still. Right then, I could see a fuzzy blue broken picture of Caleb and me looking up at the ribbons, because that's what I was thinking about and him, too, apparently. It was a strange revelation. That reminded me of when I'd first heard Sikes' wife's mind and the picture shimmered and changed to that vision of her taking my blood on the bed. I could even hear our voices.

"Can you hear that, too?" I asked and Peter nodded. "Am I doing that?"

He nodded and smiled proudly, coming to lay a warm hand on my cheek.

"Maggie, your ability is a most rare and precious one. We haven't had a Seer in our family in over a hundred years."

"A Seer?"

He took the hand from my cheek and placed it on Caleb's shoulder with the same look of proud respect for his son as for me.

"Someone who can read minds, see into minds and read their feelings and desires, see the past thoughts and actions of someone. You can read anyone's thoughts or plans. There have been no known ways to block a Seer, either. Just like you did Caleb, they don't even have to be near you, you just have to focus on them and you can read them like an open book in front of your face. You also can receive visions, usually of the past but I've heard of Seers getting glimpses of the future as well."

"And that's good?" I asked, remembering when I'd thought reading minds was a lame gift.

"Yes," he laughed. "That's very good."

"What's your ability, Caleb?" I asked, turning to face him.

"Don't know yet. Don't care yet." He smiled widely. "I've said it a lot but...you're amazing." He kissed me with a hand cupping my cheek, right in front of his dad. "Come on. Let's get you taken care of and then we're going to go find the Watsons and kick some a-"

"Caleb," his dad barked, both amused and parental.

Caleb just grinned at me, lifted me in his arms and carried me to the SUV.

Twenty Six

"Where's my dad?" I asked as I sat in the backseat with Caleb and woofed down a to-go bowl of corn chowder his mom had made for me.

"He's at his house. We didn't tell him we'd found you yet. He'd want to come with us and we couldn't let him...you know."

"Yeah, I know."

I felt so much better it was like night and day. I was still tired but felt like I could at least function properly. Caleb hadn't left me at all. He sat right next to me and had a hand on my thigh the entire time I ate.

When he'd walked with me to the car, the energy ribbons and streams followed us, but as soon as he'd placed me in the backseat, losing skin contact, all the energy ribbons fell away and sizzled into the sky as his family looked on in awe. When he climbed in on his side and touched me again, I almost thought the energy burst would return. I worried that every time we touched each other now we'd light up like a Christmas tree, but they didn't come.

"What about Beck? What happened to her and Ralph after the party?"

"I found them and told them that you'd been kidnapped. I didn't know what else to say, so I just told the truth. Beck was freaking out. I called my dad, dropped them off and then had to go tell your dad." He shook his head and swallowed. I saw pieces and glimpses of their conversation in his mind, my dad red faced and yelling. "Man that was not fun."

"I bet," I muttered. "Was he mad at you?"

"Oh, yeah." He chuckled humorlessly. "I haven't been called names that bad since...ever."

"I'm so sorry. He-"

He wrapped an arm around me, pressing my face into his neck.

"He's your dad. I'd think something was off if he hadn't freaked. I had just told him when we left for our date that I'd keep you safe and then had to come and explain that someone had taken you right out from under me."

I looked up to see his face and decided to see for myself what had gone on while I was away.

I didn't have to try hard because we were already in each other's mind, the ascension like Caleb had said, but his memories of his losing me and the withdrawals zoomed to me in a hazy rush. Some parts were normal and others were like they were on fast forward.

I saw him out of his mind with worry and grief on the beach looking for me. He called my name over and over. He knelt in the sand and beat his fist over his heart to make it work, anything to pick up my heartbeat again, to find me. He knew what had happened; the Watsons had taken me somehow. He knew it and he was puzzled as to how they had kept my heart steady to hide me from him.

He ran back to the bonfire, snagged Beck and Ralph and sped the entire way back to Beck's as he talked frantically with his father on the phone. Then he went in to talk to my father without waiting for his, like his dad had told him to. He knew I'd want my father to know as soon as possible and he felt responsible; wanted to meet his punishment head on.

Then I saw glimpses of my dad in Caleb's face yelling. Then all that flew past and I saw Caleb on the couch at Kyle's, sitting, pulling at his hair with his fist as his dad tried to get him to try to sleep.

"You'll be no good to Maggie this way, son," he said but Caleb just pushed off his hand and continued to rock and moan in agony.

"I have to find her. I have to find her," was all he would say.

Then more flashes and glimpses of him sick and in pain, him rolling and groaning on the floor in the guestroom at Kyle's where someone had taken him to rest. Him yelling my name over and over as his father and mother watched, Rachel burying her face in Peter's shoulder to cry loudly for her son.

It was too much to watch. I tried to yank away from it and soon, I was caught anyway.

"Maggie, no!" Caleb said harshly. "You don't need to see that."

"Caleb," I squeaked and took a deep steadying breath. "It wasn't your fault."

"Well... It'll never happen again, I can tell you that much," he muttered angrily. He took a deep breath and smoothed my hair back. "Anyway, your dad called the cops and calmed down a little once they got there. He even apologized to me later for yelling at me but said he still didn't forgive me." He rubbed his chin and I saw in his mind he was upset by that. "My parents rushed right over and they have been at your dad's every day since then."

"How many days have I been gone?"

"Four. Long. Days,"

I swallowed. Four days.

"Dad's going to make things so much harder for us now."

"I think you might be surprised." He smiled sadly. "Just wait. You feeling better now? Dad looks like they're ready to go."

"Yeah, but I don't like this. I don't want your family going after them because of me. They're dangerous. Someone could get hurt."

"My family is very powerful. I'm not bragging, I'm just telling the truth. Our family has the most powerful abilities, always has. We'll be fine. Don't worry about them, they know what they're doing. The Watson can't get away with this. If we had taken care of them after the first time they tried to kidnap you, this wouldn't have happened."

"Okay. All right," I conceded and tucked my brushed hair behind my ears.

Caleb's mom kept a brush in the SUV and I was so grateful.

He took my face in his hands.

"My family loves you. They'd do anything to keep you safe and I promise you they can handle themselves, they'll be fine. Don't feel guilty about us protecting you. That's what family does."

"Okay."

I smiled weakly at him and he smirked at his victory, shaking his head. He leaned closer and kissed my forehead.

"I love you, Maggie," he whispered, his lips moved against my cheek.

I smiled at hearing it, real and out loud, for the first time without being pulled and yanked away from it.

"I love you, too," I said, my voice breathy with emotion.

He grinned big and proud and happy. "Let's go."

I climbed out, then Caleb and I saw about fifteen men and women waiting for us on ATV's. Some had weapons. Some had smiles. I saw the guy who had found me there, too. He was smiling bashfully. I smiled at him and that seemed to encourage him. He came forward to greet us.

"Thank you," I said sincerely.

He was young, a lot younger than I had noticed before, couldn't have been more than twenty two or so. He had light brown hair and a square chin that fit him. He had a large frame, as all the Jacobsons seemed to have, and he had his hands in his pockets.

"No problem."

"Yeah, thanks, man," Caleb said and hugged him a bit awkwardly as he still held my hand tight. "I owe you."

"No, you don't. You'd have done the same for me. I'm just glad I found her. I think I scared her pretty good," he said and winked at me, making me smile and nod.

"Yeah, I saw in her vision," Caleb said and laughed. "This wasn't a very well thought out plan was it?"

"It all worked out. I'm happy for you guys."

"Thanks. Oh, I'm sorry. Maggie this is my cousin, Rodney. They live near the Watsons so they were closer to you when I could finally reach you again, because we'd been with your dad all day."

I nodded in understanding.

"It's ok." I turned back to Rodney and took a step forward to hug him. "Thank you. Really."

"No sweat," he said softly and patted my back. "Now, let's go find these bastards and show them who they messed with."

"Let's," Caleb and I both said at the same time and we all laughed.

"Come on," Caleb said and tugged me to a four wheeler.

He climbed on and I climbed on behind him.

"Won't this be loud? They'll hear us coming a mile away."

He turned to grin at me. "You haven't met all my family yet." He kissed my bottom lip quickly and softly. "Hang on, gorgeous."

I grabbed him around the middle. "Not gorgeous right now," I muttered into his back.

Hush.

He cranked the ATV, or so I thought. I could feel it rumble under us but couldn't hear anything. I read in Caleb's mind that one of his uncles had an ability to control technology. Basically anything with a motor or computer brain, he could control it. He had charmed the ATVs so the motors would be quiet for our surprise attack. He was called an Automator.

"That's awesome," I said aloud in awe and Caleb chuckled.

"Yeah, it is. Here we go."

I hung on as Caleb and his family roared on through the woods on silent four wheeled vehicles to go and hunt down the family who had kidnapped and planned to torture me. I could have laughed. Never in a million years would I have ever dreamed this would be happening to me. I have abilities! I have a new family full of people with abilities, too, who care about me. Never in a million years would I have believed I'd have found the love of my life at a stop light after I saved his life.

Caleb squeezed my knee.

"Believe it." I smiled and leaned my head to rest on his back. Within a minute I felt my eyelids begging to close. I could feel his next words vibrate through his back. "Sleep. We're still about twenty minutes out. I've got you."

And the lulling of the ride along with the quiet calm of the woods, Caleb's warm back under me put me right to sleep.

I woke up to the sound of yelling. I gripped Caleb tightly in reflex and saw ahead of us that we'd found the Watsons. We were on top of the same hill, the one with the well and the cliff and everyone was scattering, running.

Running away I realized. They had been back in the bunker or basement or whatever it was and were now trying to flee but we'd caught up to them. A couple of ours and theirs started throwing punches. I saw one man holding his hand out towards one while the other man grabbed and clawed at his neck like he was choking.

Then Caleb stopped the ATV abruptly and leaned forward to jump off, but stopped and looked back at me. I could see in his mind that he had seen Marcus and wanted to go after him, but couldn't leave me alone. It physically hurt him to think about it right when he just got me back. He cursed in his head at the dilemma, but as I looked up I saw Marcus coming to us. I pointed behind Caleb and screamed for him in my mind in just enough time for him to turn and evade being grabbed as he jumped off to shield me, slamming his fist to Marcus' cheek.

Marcus turned a 180 and punched Caleb's chin. Caleb recovered quickly and pulled him back, slamming him over the front of the ATV bending him backwards before punching him in the jaw.

I whimpered and bit my lip to stop from screaming. As much as I didn't like Marcus and what he'd done to me, that didn't mean I wanted to see this.

Marcus laughed and spit blood off to the side.

"You think you've won? This has just begun," he sang and laughed again.

"If I catch you near her ever again, I won't hesitate to end you," Caleb enunciated every word and banged Marcus's head several times as he spoke. "The rules of the council won't matter."

"You're so weak. She makes you weak."

"Shut. Up," Caleb growled.

Then we saw Peter jump off his still moving four wheeler and tackle Sikes. They were the champions of both families so, naturally, everyone stopped and watched as Peter punched Sikes in the jaw and gripped his shirt collar in his fist.

I saw the fear on Sikes' face, on all their faces. He didn't even try to fight back. They were terrified of the Jacobsons and I wondered why, if that were true, had they kidnapped me and risked getting the Jacobsons even angrier at them? There had to be something I was missing. Some reason other than just jealousy and petty family squabbles that Sikes didn't want Caleb and I to ascend.

"I have never been more ashamed of being an Ace until I saw the things you did to my daughter-in-law," Peter growled and it was so intense I couldn't even be excited about the daughter-in-law part. "You are not a man, you're a monster. And you know what? It was all for nothing. Even with all your meddling and torture, they ascended anyway."

Every Watson eye turned on us and Sikes looked devastated.

"No," he muttered and closed his eyes. "No."

"Yes," Peter spat. "Now you take your family and go with your tail stuck between your legs somewhere where I can't find you. Our family has never attacked yours and I resent this juvenile and idiotic behavior over something that happened between our families years ago that has absolutely nothing to do with us. I am not a murderer but I will *not* stand by and watch you try to destroy my family again. The next time, and you better be smart enough for there not to be one, I. Will. Kill. You. Now, go."

I was floored. I never knew that amount of venom could come out of the sweet man who'd done nothing but comfort and help me. I was floored because all this upset was over me. I didn't know whether to be flattered or frightened.

He leapt off Sikes and we all watched as he turned his back on him and got on his ATV again. Sikes sat up and looked directly at me. His face was so distraught and forlorn I almost felt sorry for him.

"Don't you dare," Caleb hissed under his breath to me and then threw Marcus towards his uncle.

He tripped backwards and fell in the grass. Sikes was helped up by his wife, who wouldn't look at me at all. Marcus got up and went to stand by them, looking murderous.

Everyone let go of whoever they were holding mentally or physically and made their way back to their own ATVs. I held on tight as this time, our ATVs cranked to life loudly and rumbling. I looked back to see Marcus smiling at us as we left. I shivered.

"He's just grandstanding for his ego. He better know not to mess with you again," Caleb assured me and I sighed as I leaned on him. "Just hold on, baby. We'll have you back home in no time."

Home. Dad.

I couldn't remember a time I'd ever seen my dad move so fast.

I had ridden the whole long ride there with my head in Caleb's lap in the backseat while Peter drove way above the speed limit. I had been so anxious, so worried about Dad and though I very much wanted to see him, I was worried that he'd forbid me to see Caleb or never let me leave the house again because of what happened.

And now, with my dad rushing to meet me at the SUV side, I couldn't think about anything but the red eyes and dark circles on my father's pale and sleep deprived face.

"Oh, baby girl." He grabbed me up from the ground and held me too tightly, but I didn't complain. Caleb looked like he wanted to, feeling what I was feeling but I smiled at him to show I was ok. Dad needed this. "I'm so glad you're ok." He placed my feet to the ground and looked angrily over at Peter. I was just about to jump in and defend him, but Dad spoke first. "Who was it? Who took my daughter and why? If I ever get my hands on him-"

"We took care of it," Peter said coolly. "You don't have to worry about anything."

"Thank you, Peter. I'm in your debt," he said and looked back at me.

"No, I'm afraid you're in Caleb's debt, Jim," Peter said, slapped my dad on the back and smiled. "He found her, not me."

My dad's gaze shifted over to Caleb and Caleb shrugged his shoulders, his side of his mouth curling up in a little sad smile.

"Caleb," my dad started, but stopped. He looked on the verge of tears. He released me and went to Caleb, grabbing him in a rough hug. "Thank you son." I could read all the thoughts my dad had about Caleb and Caleb could read them through me. My dad was grateful and regretful for the things he'd said to Caleb. He was also worried that this was going to increase the intensity of Caleb and my relationship even further and he thought I wasn't ready for that. If only he knew. "I don't know how I can repay you for this."

"You don't have to." My dad pulled back from Caleb but didn't move away. "I love her, sir." Caleb's voice was rough with emotion. "I will always do whatever it takes to keep her safe."

"I know that, now. I mean it. You are always welcome in my house." Then Dad cocked his head a little. "Will he try this again? Taking her? Who is this guy? What does he want with her?"

"No. We'll keep an eye out, she'll be safe," Peter assured. "We took care of it, but Maggie is the one who got away from them. We found her in the woods after she escaped from them the day before. She survived over night out there. She's quite a capable young lady."

That was it. The dam broke. My dad burst with silent sobs, shaking, and pulled me to him again. Once I calmed him down with small murmurs and pats to his back he spoke gruffly as he pulled back, holding my upper arms to look at me.

"You slept in the woods? How- How did you get away? What did they do to you? What did you- Did they hurt you?"

He looked me over and saw no bruises, but that's only because Caleb had already healed me of them.

"Dad. I'm-" I hadn't really thought of a way to explain yet. "I'm really tired. I don't want to relive it yet."

"But, we've got to call the police and tell them to stop looking for you."

"We will. Tomorrow ok? I can't talk to them tonight."

"Ok. Yeah. Yeah, of course."

His mind was still raging with unanswered questions about what had happened. He was wondering if they had done something to me and I just was down-playing it all.

"I'm ok, Dad."

"I'm so glad you're home and safe, kiddo."

"Me, too."

He turned to Caleb and his dad. "Thank you again. I don't know what I can do, but if there's ever anything-"

"No need," Peter insisted. "Maggie is like family to us. We take care of our family."

Dad nodded. "Ok. Well, I'll take her to bed then. Good night."

My heart gave me the most violent clinching it ever had at his words and the thought behind them. Putting me to bed alone, he'd be checking on me every five minutes because he was scared to death now that something would happen to me again. He might even sleep in the chair in my room for who knows how long.

Caleb grunted and grabbed my arm as if to halt my dad's progress.

"Mr. Masters, please."

"I told you, it's Jim." He looked at Caleb's hand on my arm and gave him a sympathetic look. "I know you missed Maggie, too, but after everything she's been through, I think it's best if she goes on to bed for tonight. You can come over, first thing in the morning."

I started to panic. I didn't think Sikes would attack in an echoling dream again but we'd learned that Marcus could channel his uncle because they'd done it so many times. I wasn't so sure about him. Plus the thought of being without Caleb after four days was excruciating.

I heard Peter's thoughts and looked at him. He knew I heard and was waiting for the ok from me. Tell him? Tell Dad everything about us, about the Aces. About my abilities and Caleb being my soul mate. Caleb read his father's thoughts through me.

Up to you. And just so you know, your dad will be the first human to know about us. My dad is making a huge leap of faith with this. We never, ever tell humans. What do you want to do? Can he handle it?

I don't know.

My dad was a lot of things but gullible wasn't one of them. As badly as I didn't want to lie to him anymore and it would be so much easier for him to know, I hoped he would be able to believe me but I wasn't sure. What if he didn't give us a chance to explain and tried to drag me inside? That wouldn't go over well on either side.

Baby. I looked up at Caleb. *Whatever you want, I'll do it. But you read his thoughts. He's gonna be a little nuts about you if we don't tell him. I'll go home if you think it's best...well, I won't go home but I won't come to your room if you don't want me to. Whatever you want. Just tell me.*

"Maggie?" Dad said and looked at me curiously.

I looked at him as he stood on the curb, the uncut grass long and curling up around his ankles as he stood in his bare feet, in his wrinkled striped short sleeve button up shirt and jeans. His hair needed to be cut something awful. The signs on his face showed just how much he'd aged this past year. This wasn't fair to do this to him. But the alternative - just running away or fighting with him constantly - wasn't an option either. My dad deserved the truth, even if he resented me for it in the end.

"Dad, can we go inside and talk for a minute? With Peter and Caleb? We need to explain something to you."

He looked between us all and then grabbed his head.

"Oh, no. You're pregnant!"

"No, of course not." I rolled my eyes as he sighed long and loud. "We just need to talk to you."

"Are you getting married?" he said and cut his eyes at Caleb.

I blushed at the idea and hurriedly shut my mind, focusing on Dad, so I didn't hear Caleb nor Peter's thoughts on that one.

"No, Dad."

"Maggie, we can do this tomorrow. It's late and you've been through a lot. You need rest and whatever you have to tell me can wait."

"No, Dad. This needs to be done now. Please?"

He lifted a brow at me and I read his thoughts before he said them and it was so very strange.

"All right," he conceded unwittingly to the cause. "Come on. Let's go to the den."

He looked perturbed when I reached for Caleb's hand instead of his but led the way inside and got everyone a glass of sweet tea as we sat, me on the loveseat beside Caleb, his hand in my lap holding mine.

"Ok. What's so important that this couldn't wait?"

I looked up at Peter who sat on the opposite sofa beside my father. He smiled encouragingly at me. I nodded to him and he began to tell my father all about them and us, Caleb and I, everything. He started with one loaded sentence.

"Jim, my family is a supernatural one that obtains abilities through imprinting with a mate, a soul mate, which my son is to your daughter."

I waited for him to bolt, but my dad just stared at him. So Peter continued…and continued…and continued. He told him everything there was to tell, some things I'd never even heard before. I had to give my dad credit for being attentive and seemingly open minded as he was told a load of things that I wouldn't have listened to if I hadn't imprinted with Caleb and felt it first hand.

Caleb squeezed my hand soothingly as his father explained how we needed to be together, touching, reading each other, everything. How we were it for each other and would always be together. Then he told him about my newfound abilities. Through it all my father remained stoic.

Then after almost an hour, Peter ended.

"I know it's a lot to take in, but we're family now and I want you to know that though we love Maggie, we have no intentions of taking her from you. You are the only human that we've ever told, the only one who knows about us. This is an unusual situation but a remarkable one. We want this to work easily and not have discord between you and Maggie over it. I'm sure, as a father myself, that you feel an array of things right now but above all else know that we'll never lie to you from this day forward and that Maggie is important to us and we'll protect her with our lives."

Dad looked at me. His eyes were guarded but his mind was filled and overflowing with thoughts. Scrambled. Some were angry, some were skeptical, some were down right hurt. I winced at the onslaught and he leaned forward a little towards me.

"Maggie." He swallowed hard, spoke softly. "Are you really going to sit there and tell me that you can read my thoughts?"

Twenty Seven

I'd known it was coming. I'd known he wouldn't just believe us but it still hurt to see his disappointment. He thought I was gullible and naïve. That I'd let them dupe me into believing this crazy scheme. He was scared for me. He was thinking that he needed to call the police again - for a restraining order this time. He was worried that they'd take me or I'd run away with them if he threw a fit so he tried to remain calm, for my sake.

"Think of something," I told him and winced again as he bombarded me. "Think one thing," I clarified quickly.

He sighed and pursed his lips, clearly not wanting to continue but humoring me, thinking he'd prove me wrong. He thought of the time he was teaching me to ride my bike and I crashed into the back of mom's car, scratching the bumper in the process, but I also scratched my forehead. I still had a scar on my hairline.

She had been worried about the car. He had been worried about me.

"You always worried about me," I said softly remembering everything. "We should have seen the signs about mom back then. We should have realized something was wrong with her, that she wasn't happy. What kind of mom cares more about her bumper than her kid?"

Dad's jaw fell open and he looked at me with bordering fright.

"It's ok, Dad."

He reigned in and his features were replaced with a flat expression. He never took his eyes from me. He lifted an eyebrow in contest and thought again some things to test me. He wasn't giving in that easy. His first thought...

What's my birthday?

"Dec 24th."

His eyes went wide, but he kept going.

What's the capital of Georgia?

"Atlanta."

His face got even more determined.

What's two plus two?"

"Six." His brow lifted higher. "I'm kidding dad. It's four."

Who's the thirty second president?

"Come on, Dad. I wouldn't know that answer even if you asked me out loud."

He covered his mouth and chin with his hand and continued to look at me. His eyes softened a little. I saw it happen before his thoughts hit me. He believed me. How could he not after that demonstration? But that didn't mean he was thrilled about it. He blamed Caleb for doing this to me.

"So, this is your fault?" His eyes left me for the first time in five minutes and he turned his gaze to Caleb. He scowled furiously. "You knew this would happen, that she'd be a freak and you did it anyway?"

"Dad," I said sharply and he looked back at me. "This isn't his fault, he had no control-"

"But he knew what he was. He shouldn't have ever touched you if that was the case. You don't belong to this life. You're not like them and now, you'll never be the same." He shook his head and in his mind he decided he wouldn't go quietly into the night about this. He was gonna let me have it. "And now, look at you. Following his lead and listening to every little sweet nothing he says just because you think you're stuck with him for life? Well, I'll figure something out, to break or stop this...this imprint thing. You don't have to be a freak against your will-"

"I'm going to stop you right there," I shouted. "Caleb and I imprinted. I know you were listening to Peter, I can see your thoughts, Dad, so don't act like now you didn't hear him. You know that we didn't choose this, it happened *to* us. It's not something you can control. My abilities didn't come until a couple days ago; they've had nothing to do with Caleb and I up until now. And I'm not a freak and neither are they."

"Maggie." He leaned forward and grabbed my free hand. "They knew this would happen to you and they let it. You're a sweet, young, pretty girl and they just-"

"No. Stop."

"You don't even know him that well. You're not ready for-"

"Dad-" I cut in and jerked my hand away but he didn't stop.

"-something like this yet. You've barely graduated high school and now you're supposed to be someone's soul mate? I don't fully understand all of what you're telling me, and I know that there's still things I haven't heard yet but-"

"Dad."

"I understand enough about relationships to know that you can't just base it on feelings and pressure-"

"You're not listening to me," I blurted loudly and he finally stopped his plight. "It's not about whether you think I'm a freak or gullible or naïve or even if I'm ready. I love him, Daddy."

He slumped in defeat and slid to kneel on the floor in front of the couch.

"I always knew you were serious when you called me Daddy," he admitted and I went to the floor, too, on my knees. He looked at me. "So, this is it? You're leaving me," he phrased it as a statement, not a question, like he knew my answer already.

"No, that's why I wanted to tell you. It's really rare for humans to imprint with Aces. They don't have to deal with this very often but they were willing to risk telling you, for my sake, so that I could keep you. Do you understand? I can't be without Caleb without it hurting me, and even if I could I wouldn't want to. But I want to be with you too."

He took a deep breath.

"It's not fair. It's not fair that I have to just take a backseat and watch someone else have you."

I laughed softly.

"That's what happens, Dad. Did you think I'd never leave home? Never move out? Never go to college? Never get married?"

He cracked the first small smile.

"Yes. Yes, I did think that."

Peter chuckled behind Dad and it was like my dad realized then that we weren't alone. He looked over at Caleb for a long time. Then he smiled again and so did I reading his mind.

"It's mostly my fault, but my daughter hasn't been happy in a very long time, until now. I saw it but..." he shook his head, "I didn't want to believe it was over a boy. I can't deny that as much as I might not like how young she is, that she's happy with you."

Caleb nodded and looked down at our still intertwined hands.

"I'm sorry. I never wanted to take her away from you. I just want her to be happy."

"I know." Dad sighed and pinched the bridge of his nose. Then he turned a forced smile on Peter. "So, your whole family has these...abilities? You all get married for life? Everyone?"

"Yes," Peter answered, "but, like I said, Caleb and Maggie are the first to imprint in a very long time and Maggie's gift is rare and coveted. I'm not sure what it all means, I won't lie, but it's something good."

Dad looked back to me and blew a long breath. "College now?"

"Well," Peter interrupted, "first things first. We need to make sure that the echoling is actually going to stop. That Marcus will stop."

"But I thought you said you took care of it?" Dad asked.

"We did but we can't just call the police like humans can when we have a problem. The only way to truly take care of it is to kill him. I...will if I have to, but I'd rather not resort to that unless it comes to it."

Dad looked scandalized but kept his composure. In his mind he was wondering if he could ask someone to do that; kill someone - take a life, for me.

"Ok, what do we have to do?" Dad asked with a new resolve.

"Well...I think if Caleb and Maggie get out of town for a while it would be best while I monitor the Watsons. The further away from the echoling she is, the less chance he has of reaching her."

"But I thought you said if they slept-" Dad choked on the word and cleared his throat. "Slept together - were together at night - that he couldn't harm her."

"He can't, but he's already tried a kidnap attempt here at your house once before."

"What!"

"It's all right. Maggie handled it, but I think it's just best if we send them away for a while."

"Maggie handled it? What does that mean?" my dad said and looked between us all.

"My family has many gifts, Jim. Maggie will attain many herself, self defense being one of them. She fought the two of them off until Caleb was able to get to her."

"What? Get to her?"

"Yes."

"You saved her...twice?" Dad said and looked at Caleb with an awe I only hoped I would see and I felt my eyes water.

"It was only fair," Caleb said and winked at me, "she saved me first."

"I can't believe this." Dad scrubbed his face with his hands and then fiddled with the top button of his shirt. "All this time I resented you two spending so much time together and you were saving her... I really wish you had told me then, Maggie, at the beginning."

"I didn't have my ability then, Dad. You never would have believed me."

"You're right," he laughed sadly, "I wouldn't have. Where are we sending these two?" my father conceded gruffly.

"Somewhere out west," Peter suggested.

"Arizona," I blurted out.

I peeked back at Caleb and saw a grateful little smile. He knew I wanted to go there because he wanted to go to school there. He'd never been and I wanted him to see it. He spoke to me and I could feel the love attached to the words in warmth and tingles.

I love you.

I know. I love you, too.

"Arizona, huh?" Dad tried to process everything. Me in Arizona, anywhere really, with my soul mate and not him and every scenario brought bad outcomes and pregnancies and shotguns and Vegas weddings. I couldn't help but laugh. He looked up at me and twisted his lips. "I forgot about your *ability* already," he muttered.

"Dad." I pulled from Caleb and went to hug my father around his neck. "I'm not going to do anything stupid." I pulled back to sit on my heels and look at him. "I know this isn't ideal but it wouldn't matter if I'd met Caleb now or at thirty. It would be the same for me, but, even with that, I know what I'm ready for and not ready for."

"You were always so smart." He chuckled then took a shuddering breath. "Look at me. If you run off and get married in some justice of the peace's office or make me a grandpa before I'm gray, I will not forgive you."

Everyone laughed again and I felt like bursting with happy tears.

"Deal, Dad."

"Deal."

He hugged me tightly and then stood, pulling me with him and although in his mind he believed everything we'd said, he was still wrapping his thoughts around it all. He was ready for bed, to be alone and think.

"Ok," he looked between Caleb and me, "you knew, from the very beginning, from the first time you brought him here, that you were...were…" he sighed and gripped his neck, "imprinted?" He finally got it out and I nodded. He nodded back. "Ok. No more sneaking. No more lying. No more secrets."

"Yeah, Dad," I said as Caleb said, "Yes, sir."

"Now, uh... How about you two sleep on the sofa tonight. I may be coming to terms with all this, but I'm still your father."

"Ok, Dad, that's fine," I said amused. I turned to Peter and reached up to hug him. "Thank you for coming for me." He hugged me tightly, just like my own father had.

You're family now and we love you. Wouldn't have it any other way.

I smiled through tears but held them back from falling to my cheeks. Caleb said goodbye to his father and then while Dad and Peter were saying theirs, Caleb laced his fingers through mine. I looked at him and he was watching me with a smile.

Are you happy?

Yes. Thank you for this. He took it better than I thought. I know my dad's a little nuts , but he'll keep your secret- Our secret, I corrected.

He put his forehead to mine and rubbed my arm from elbow to wrist.

I know he will. I just want to you to be happy, whatever that is.

You. Me. Alone. Arizona.

He laughed out loud and started to frame my face with his hands but looked over to see our fathers watching, not hearing our internal interlude. He smiled bashfully at me and turned to wave at his father as he left.

"Ok, kids," Dad said and rubbed his hands together, "I'm going to bed." He hesitated. "I'll come check on you guys later," he said hurriedly and I heard his thoughts.

"Dad, I promise you we will be fine. We'll sleep on the couch, nothing else, and won't runaway into the sunset before you can get up."

He laughed ruggedly.

"Ok, ok." He hugged me. "Night, baby girl." And he said it like he always had. Not like I was a freak or different but like I was his daughter and always would be, no matter what. Then he shook Caleb's hand. "Night, son. Thanks again and uh...I'm sorry, for what I said to you before-"

"No need, sir, it's forgotten. Good night."

Dad left and I could have collapsed right there. It was like it all hit me at once and I sat down swiftly on the couch.

"I need a shower," I muttered and yawned.

"Not tonight. Sleep first."

"Wait." I stopped him and held his cheek in my hand. "Your face. Marcus punched you."

"Barely," he scoffed. "It'll be fine," he assured.

"Let me heal you."

"You've been through enough tonight-" But I just closed my eyes, put my hand on his jaw and focused, hearing him sigh in defeat.

I wasn't sure what I was doing or how to but somehow my body knew just what to do. My body felt suddenly heavy as if I was weighed down and then my hand...I could feel me drawing it out of him, like a magnet; the pain, the blood, the bruises. It all went in me and then through me. Then it was over. I opened my eyes to see his jaw was no longer pink.

I smiled in triumph.

"Happy now, doctor?" he smirked.

"Yes."

He pulled the afghan off the recliner and I didn't have the strength to argue as he gently urged me to lay down, then slid beside me and pulled the blanket over us, wrapping his arms around me and tucking my head under his chin. My body practically sighed.

Sleep, Maggie. No worries tonight.

No worries. Ok. Thanks for coming for me.

I'll always come for you. I'll always find you, I told you, you're everything now, Maggie. I love you so much.

He squeezed me as he spoke to me in my mind and I felt that he hadn't really gotten to relax and just feel his relief of my being found yet. He was shaking with the release of it all now, finally taking his turn to relax.

I leaned back and reached up to press my lips to his. His happiness and relief coursed through me. When I closed my eyes I saw the energy ribbons bouncing around us but when I opened them, nothing was there. He kissed me back gently and caressed my cheek with his fingers, pushing my hair behind my ear, raking his fingers through it.

I missed this, I told him as he continued to kiss away all my troubles.

Me, too. Me more, I think.

I laughed against his lips. He gave me one last kiss on my lips, then on my forehead.

Sleep, sweetheart. There'll be plenty of time for that later.

I love you.

I love you.

So it turned out, Arizona was not where we were headed. Apparently there was an uncle I still hadn't met who had a vacation beach house in California. Ugh. Just the thought of being in the same state that my mom had fled to made me want to hurl.

We were woke up the next morning by Peter as he came over early. He and my dad had all the details worked out before we even got up. I apparently needed the sleep because we slept on that couch soundly until 11:00 in the morning.

I remember feeling warm and absolutely content. My body zinged with energy and happiness as I slowly came out of sleep. I opened my eyes to see Peter over me with a smile as he shook Caleb gently. I could see Caleb and I hadn't moved an inch during the night, awaking in exactly the same position as we'd fallen asleep in.

Caleb opened his eyes then and looked at me first. The smile that crept to his cheeks was illuminating. Then he saw his dad and his expression went back to neutral.

"Oh. Hey, Dad," Caleb muttered.

Peter looked amused.

"Oh. It's good to see you, too, son." He leaned up and nodded his head to the kitchen. "Come on you two. We've got a lot to talk about."

He made his way that direction, I heard his thoughts about the beach house and our flight leaving that night as he left. I looked back at Caleb.

"Did you sleep ok?" I asked.

"You know I did. It's impossible to sleep without you now."

I nodded and pushed the thoughts of the fitful and painful sleep I'd had at the Watsons away. He pulled my face back up with a finger under my chin.

"Don't think about that anymore. That's all behind us." He kissed my forehead. "Now, go take a shower and I'll see what these two clowns want," he joked. "I'll grab a shower down here if your dad doesn't mind."

"Ok."

I didn't need any more convincing. He helped me up and I ran upstairs. I was shocked at the amount of energy I had. I felt like a completely different person.

As much as I wanted to just sit in the shower for hours, I knew they were waiting for me so I hurried through a hot one and went to get dressed in my room. As I took my towel off in front of my mirror I did a double take.

That was not me. I looked like a woman. I remembered after the ascension how Caleb had subtle changes to him that I'd noticed but I hadn't seen myself then at all nor since then. I had no idea what I had looked like yesterday, all matted and dirty but today, clean and brushed, I barely recognized myself.

My cheek bones were slightly more defined. My hair was shiny and a little longer. My upper arms were still soft but I could see the muscles more clearly. I *felt* stronger. My stomach and legs were a little slimmer and the, uh, womanly parts of me were - well - more womanly.

I leaned closer to the mirror and examined my face. My eyelashes were longer and fuller. My face was completely clear. My complexion tan and glowing, making my freckles stand out more, but for some reason it looked good on me. My green eyes looked like sea weed swirls with dark and light.

I wondered why my dad hadn't noticed the changes last night. Maybe the changes weren't as noticeable as I thought. I did see myself everyday; I would notice them more than someone else. I shrugged, knowing it was all caused by the ascension, I just didn't know why, so I didn't worry about it right then.

I put on a jean skirt and my coral tank. I had no idea what we were doing today, so I just put on something comfortable. I slid on my silver hoop earrings. My charm bracelet had been taken from me at the Watsons along with my phone. I missed it already. I put on a long necklace Dad had given me a couple years ago for Christmas. It was a jumble of charms on the end: a heart, a cross, a circle swirl, a quarter moon, a dangle of gems. I'd always loved it, but had stopped wearing it this past year because I was so angry with him.

I padded my way barefoot down the stairs and stopped by the kitchen door. I could hear them talking about me. Caleb must have taken a quick shower.

"So, sleeping with you not only keeps her safe from someone hurting her in her dreams, you anchor her or whatever, but also makes her physically feel good in the morning?"

"Yeah, we both do. We energize each other, with...skin contact, we heal each other." I could tell Caleb was uncomfortable by his tone, but didn't know if Dad could sense it or not.

"Huh." My dad got a thought and I almost burst in to stop him, but waited. "Wait. Did you heal Maggie already? Did they hurt her and you healed her before you brought her home?"

"Um. Well," Caleb started but Peter stepped in to elaborate.

"When someone touches her - any of our women - who means them harm, it leaves an offense mark, an almost burned looking handprint wherever they touch them. Maggie's skin also shocks them, kind of, to warn them that they don't have the right to harm her. It hurts them to touch her, even through clothes. The significant can remove the mark when they touch once they are ascended. The marks, they don't harm her just to make her very tired, they drain her energy. When we found Maggie, she had quite a few of these handprints on her and Caleb did heal her. That's one reason we're so worried about the echoling. See, he can hurt her in her dreams. She can receive an echo, an offense mark or other injury that occurs in a dream. My grandmother healed her of some of these injuries before."

"Gah, I can't believe all this was going on the whole time right behind my back and I never thought to be suspicious. So this guy is after Maggie because of you?" Dad asked but his tone was easy, he wasn't accusing, just asking.

"Well, in a sense, yes, and I'm sorry about that. See, they would have gone after anyone in our clan who imprinted in this day because it hasn't happened in so long. It just happened that Maggie was it."

"So, Maggie has met your grandmother?"

"Maggie's met the whole family," Caleb explained softly. "I brought her over the day after our imprint to explain everything to her. To let her see my family so she wouldn't be afraid and ask any questions she had."

"Huh."

I heard a tongue clicking.

"Well," my dad continued, "I'd love to meet them, too."

"I was hoping you'd say that," Peter said. "I explained to them last night that we told you everything and they are anxious to meet you."

"Really? Ready to string me up by my ankles?"

Peter guffawed, the one he did when he was truly enjoying himself. His thoughts confirmed it.

"Ah, no. My family is very...affectionate. They love Maggie and can't wait to meet you. I told them I'd try to talk you into coming over for lunch before we send these two off tonight."

"Sounds good," Dad said but he was freaking out.

His thoughts were scared.

A house full of people with abilities. Hmmm. And Maggie has met them all. All these things she was keeping from me. But it's not like I deserved to know. I was barely a father two weeks ago. Now she's growing up too fast. Way, way too fast. She's leaving me, starting tonight.

I decided to make my entrance. I came slowly around the door frame and saw three sets of eyes widen and three mouths drop.

Twenty Eight

At first I thought I'd left my tank top upstairs, but with a quick look I saw that I was dressed.

Their thoughts all hit me at once. Peter had seen the ascension changes before on others but none as drastic as this. He smiled, knowing why I looked different and looked proudly on me.

Caleb was in awe. In his mind I saw that he always thought I was gorgeous, but now I just seemed confident and a finished masterpiece. He hadn't been able to really see the extent of the changes because I'd been disheveled when he rescued me and the dream was rushed and crazy. I looked at him, too, and saw his differences as well, though his were more subtle. He had never been more handsome. He'd showered and changed clothes and I could see his tan arms flex as he shoved his hands into his jean pockets. I bit my lip at how good he looked.

Then he looked me over, head to toe, and started thinking about my legs and arms and plenty else. I blushed from my neck to my cheeks at the things he wanted to do and turned from him before it was obvious what Caleb was thinking to everyone else.

My dad was devastated and I'd been so wrapped up in the other thoughts to see it. To him, my life had been sped forward, years taken from, and he was looking at someone who was no longer a teenage girl, unsure and fragile and needy. I was someone who was grown up and called home to Dad on holidays and birthdays. Someone who didn't ask permission because she didn't need to anymore. She was sure of her future and taking the reins away from him completely, someone who didn't need nor want a father anymore.

I stepped to stand in front of him.

"Dad, never. That'll never be me." I looked down at myself and shrugged. "This is just the ascension, just my looks. I'm still me, I haven't changed."

"But you have," he said softly and cupped my face with his hard callused hands. "You grew up while I was being an idiot." He smiled. "You're beautiful, inside and out. I'm so sorry if I ever made you doubt that."

I nodded, taking a deep breath. I was about to ruin the mascara I'd just put on if he didn't quit it. He released me and put an arm around my shoulder. He kissed my temple and started to explain what was in store for me.

They told me about the beach house and the flight. I didn't bother to tell them I knew all about it because I could read their thoughts. Caleb smirked at me from over the counter, reading me. He knew I was just letting our fathers seem like they were controlling and handling everything for us. They needed it so I didn't stop them.

"Now, I'll get you another cell phone this afternoon and you better keep it on you at all times," Dad explained again and I nodded. He looked at Peter. "Now, who did you get to go and watch out for them?"

"I have a few to ask at lunch today."

"We don't need a chaperone, Dad," I insisted.

"I'll be the judge of that."

My comeback was interrupted by the doorbell. Everyone looked around. We weren't expecting anyone but I heard thoughts of an anxious person who was worried. Then the door opened and I heard shouting.

"Dad! Dad, are you home?"

"Bish!" I yelled and took off toward the voice.

I turned the corner and my brother looked exactly as I remembered; big, beefy, tan, dark haired and smiling in confusion. "Bish! Oh, my goodness!"

"Maggie? I thought-" He grabbed me as I jumped to him and held me off the floor against him. "Dad called and said you'd been kidnapped." He put me down but didn't release his bear grip on me. "Was this some sick joke just to get me to come home?"

"I wish," Dad said from behind me and grabbed Bish in a hug. "It's good to see you, son. Wow. I didn't think you could get any bigger," he mused and Bish smiled bashfully.

"Well, you know." Bish rubbed his upper arm. He was always naïve about how nice looking he was. He was a very muscley guy, always had been. "I do a lot of lifting at work, boxes of supplies and stuff." Then he remembered why he was here. "What the hell, Dad? I thought you said-"

"She *was* kidnapped." Dad pulled me to him. "We just got her back last night. Haven't even had time to tell the police yet."

"What happened?" Bish asked and looked at me. He turned his head and squinted. He pulled me from Dad and looked closely at me with his hand on my shoulders. "Have I been gone that long? You're so..."

He was thinking how stunning I looked. How grown up and different I was.

Holy crap, what happened? How could I have missed so much? She looks more like mom than ever. Man, she was always pretty but she's just so... beautiful.

He had also noticed the two men standing behind us but hadn't acknowledged them yet, on purpose. He suspected they had something to do with all this and he'd have to hurt someone. He suddenly felt very extra protective of me and wondered if I had run away with that boy and was discovered or something and that's why Dad thought I'd been kidnapped. He mentally took a deep breath to calm himself for what I was about to tell him.

Then, since his thoughts seemed to be streaming to me, everything else did, too. All his errant thoughts, his loaded memories, his past thoughts came flooding to me like a landslide. His mind was clean and sincere with a barrier of guarded reluctance, but his memories were anything but.

I saw a flash of him as a kid, hiding in a blackened closet, a yellow light peeking under the doorway while yelling and banging on the door was all around him as he held the knob tightly pulled to with all his ten year old might.

Another glimpse of a man who seemed to tower over him, literally. He looked like a giant with shadows across his face and his eyes seemed to almost glow red as the man drew his hand back swiftly to slap him.

Then, a kid being pulled away from a raggedy house while a woman covered her face and cried. The kid, a teenager, was dirty and his lip was bloody. When he looked back, there was a man beside the lady, if you could call him a man. He was broader than any normal man with arms like a cartoon wrestler and he looked strangely satisfied, his grin too wide like a clown, as the officers placed the kid, Bish, none too gently into the back of the squad car with lights blaring for all to see the criminal. Bish's thoughts were only for the woman with the monster's arms around her and how he hadn't gotten there fast enough to stop the last beating. And now, his foster mom didn't have him there to save her anymore.

I realized then that this was Bish's perception. His memories were distorted but as real as anything I'd ever felt. This is what his child mind was filled with; pictures and flashes of monsters of every kind and variety, human monsters. This was what his childhood was like.

I pulled desperately out of his mind and threw my focus to Caleb instead to block Bish altogether, with my hand covering my mouth to hold in the scream. Caleb was fighting to hold himself in check as well, so as not to run to me.

"Oh, Bish," I sighed as goose bumps ran down my arms.

"What's the matter?" Bish asked and bent to see my face as I held tight to his arms for support. "You look a little green, Mags."

What is going on with you?

I heard Bish in my mind but forced it shut. Caleb was watching me with wary eyes, seeing what I had seen through me and his legs twitched, seconds from making their way across the room to rescue me with his calming touch.

I'm ok. It just surprised me, that's all. I'm all right.

He didn't look convinced but nodded slightly where only I could see.

"I'm fine. And I grew up is all." I punched Bish playfully in the stomach and tried to keep my own self in check with a plastered on little smiled. "If you hadn't run off to New York, you'd have noticed how different I look isn't so drastic."

He ignored my dig and pressed on. "What happened, Mags?" His glance flickered to Caleb and Peter. He did not look happy. "Someone better tell me what's going on."

"Oh, sorry, Bish," Dad said and stepped forward, "I forgot. This is Peter and Caleb Jacobson. This is my son, Bish. He's been interning in New York."

"Nice to meet you, Bish," Peter said and shook his hand.

"Likewise," Bish muttered snidely.

"Bish," I protested.

"They apparently have something to do with this. That's why you're just now introducing them when they've been standing back there the whole time." He went to stand ominously in front of Caleb. "So what is it? What do you have to do with Maggie disappearing?"

Caleb was tall but Bish still had about two inches on him and though Caleb was plenty big in the chest and arms, bigger than most guys I knew, Bish was the biggest guy I personally knew. And he was pissed.

I'm gonna have to kill this guy. I can see that right now.

"Bish, no," I protested again and went to stand in front of Caleb. "What are you doing?"

Caleb wasn't scared of Bish, he just didn't want there to be a problem with him and upset me. I felt him grab my arm from behind and squeeze affectionately. I turned to look at him and he smiled, pulling me to his side

"It's ok." He held his hand out to Bish. "I'm Caleb. I'm dating Maggie." Bish still didn't take his hand so Caleb lowered it.

"Bish," Dad said and put a hand on his shoulder. "Caleb found Maggie. She was kidnapped by some...men. She escaped from them. Caleb and Peter found her in the woods yesterday and brought her home."

"What? Why didn't you just say that?" Bish asked me.

"Well, you were all...on offense," I answered.

Bish chuckled and looked back to Caleb.

"Sorry. She's my baby sister," he explained and extended his hand out to Caleb, "you know."

"I get it," Caleb laughed and shook his hand, "I have a sister, too."

"So...you said you're dating? Did you know each other before yesterday?"

"Yeah. We were already dating before that, I was out looking for her."

Bish looked back at me and all humor went away. His mind was confused as to how he should react to this. He didn't know whether to just be happy I was safe or go berserk and ask who needed to die.

"I'm fine," I told him and grabbed his hand, "really."

"Stop, Mags. It's not like you had a bad experience at the dentist, ok, you were kidnapped."

"But I'm fine now. I just want to forget it."

He pulled me to him roughly, my head under his chin. I squeezed him, still feeling the slime of his memories of the men and women who had abused him all around me. My chest was tight and I fought to keep tears in check.

"I missed you, kid." He sighed. "I shoulda been here. After mom left... I should have come home to make sure you both were ok." He pulled back. "Has she called you?"

"No."

"Yes, actually," Dad answered. "She's called everyday since you were gone."

"You shouldn't have called and told her, Dad."

"She's your mother, Maggie."

I leaned my head back and looked at the ceiling.

"Well. I don't want to talk to her. I'm not being disrespectful but she has a lot of things to make up for, with you," I pointed to Dad, "before she does with me. She may have abandoned me but she left you, Dad."

"Maggie, she's your mother," he repeated with more inflection.

"She's your wife! It's not the same thing."

"You're right, it's not the same thing." Dad came up to me. "You can't hold what your mother did to me against her. She and I will work out our problems or we won't, but that doesn't have anything to do with you and her."

I did not want to talk to her or be talking about her anymore. You just don't do that to people. They were married for a long time, they promised to love each other forever and she just left. How can you do that to someone who had devoted their life to you? What kind of chance did people who loved each other have if they had to worry about the other person flipping out and leaving you one day for no apparent reason. I didn't think that Caleb would ever do that to me but it was only because of the imprint. He *couldn't* leave me. His body wouldn't let him.

"Don't," Caleb said across the room and looked at me sternly. "Don't you do that."

I looked at him and bit my lip, suddenly wanting to cry. One minute everything seemed so sure and certain and the next I was in limbo. The truth was...that I missed my mom. I missed her the way she used to be and yet I was so angry at her for the way she was now. She did leave me and as much as I wanted to never see her again, if she walked through that door, I had no idea what I'd do.

I'm sorry, baby.

Caleb walked over and pulled me to him. I breathed him in and put my arms around his middle, letting him calm me.

I'm sorry I'm such a girl.

He laughed and pulled back to look at me.

"That's the way I like you."

"What am I missing?" Bish muttered under his breath.

"Nothing," I said and scolded myself for forgetting that he didn't understand everything. "Um, we better get going if we're going to make lunch at the Jacobson's." Crap, Bish. "Oh, uh, Bish is here."

"It's fine," Peter assured, "we made plenty I'm sure. Bish you're welcome to join us."

"Ok, great," he said and looked at me with a raised brow. "Maggie, why don't you ride with me?"

I halted my steps, my body protesting, but it was only a ride down the street, right? I'd see Caleb in like five minutes. Normally, it wouldn't matter so much but I didn't want to be away from him at all for a while. I sighed and got a grip on myself. I'd have to learn to function like a normal person.

"Yeah," I agreed, my fingers scratching at the side of my thigh and glanced at Caleb. He smiled.

I know it's hard. It's just really bad right now because of everything that happened the past few days. Go with him and I'll see you at Kyle's.

I smiled and nodded, then told Bish I had to go grab my shoes. Caleb, Peter and Dad went on and were gone by the time I came back down.

"Ok, before we leave," Bish said and cornered me on the stairs, "what the heck is going on with you and this kid?"

"Everything," I answered softly and truthfully. "Everything is going on with us."

"What do you mean *everything*?" he boomed.

"Not *that*. Everything as in…I'm in love with him."

"Crap." He sat down roughly on the bottom stair. "What happened to Chad?"

"What do you mean what happened?" I sat down beside him. "You know exactly what happened. He dumped me."

"Yeah, but I thought you...I don't know."

"And what's up with you? Why were you being such a jerk to Caleb?"

"Why haven't you told me about him?" he countered.

"I don't know." I put my head on his shoulder. "It's different with him."

"Chad was a tool."

I laughed.

"Yeah, but I thought you liked Chad."

"I did, but that's only because I knew he was a tool and nothing bad would come out of you two dating."

"Why does everyone say that?" I muttered.

"And I'm protective with you and all your boyfriends. Chad got his fair share, it's Caleb's turn."

"He's nice, Bish. He's really good to me. He loves me."

"How long have you known him?"

"It doesn't matter. Just be nice to him, he's gonna be around for a while."

"All right. He did save your life. I can be nice I guess."

He pulled me from the step and opened the door for me.

"How long are you here for?" I asked and as much as I missed him, I hoped he'd be leaving soon.

I was supposed to be leaving with Caleb tonight and Bish knows Dad wouldn't let me go on a vaca with a guy. He'd think something was off if I made up something about staying at a friends the night after I was kidnapped.

"No idea." He opened my car door and then quickly went to his before slumping roughly into the drivers' seat of his rented Ford Taurus from the airport. This was so not a Bish car. He leaned his head back on the seat. "I hadn't thought about it. I just couldn't sit up there and wait for news from Dad anymore. So I spent my savings on a plane ticket."

"Ah, Bish. I wish you hadn't. I miss you and I love you but I hate that you have to struggle so much. Your boss is such a jerk."

"It's ok. It was worth it. I just don't know what I'm gonna do now. New York is like a different universe, Mags. Everything is so expensive I barely have any money left over after my bills. I've been working for this guy for almost three years thinking he'd promote me but I'm still his intern."

He looked over at me. I was trying to keep my face neutral so he wouldn't know but his thoughts were desperate.

He hadn't been telling Dad and I what a hard time he was having. Apparently, it was really bad. His apartment was crap and he was behind on rent. His job was tedious and his boss always had him doing extra errands and things for no extra pay and on his time, threatening to fire him if he didn't do them without complaint. He had to do odd jobs, give blood and walk dogs on weekends just to have money for food. He was thinking about quitting but there was nothing else to do. He'd looked. He wanted to come home but didn't want to ask. He felt like a failure.

"I'm sorry. Maybe you should just come home? Dad would let you move back for a while until you get settled into another job."

He brightened a little.

"I've actually been thinking about that. I even looked at the classifieds in the city so I could commute from Dad's. I don't know," he shook his head, "I'm not sure what I want."

I leaned over and kissed his cheek and he smiled in surprise at me.

"You should do what makes you happy," I chimed sweetly. "So, how about girls?" I said conspiratorially.

"Girls?" he scoffed. "I've got no time for girls," he laughed and cranked the car, "unless she worked at my boss' coffee shop, I'd never see her."

I laughed and he did, too. It was a sad truth and I didn't blame him but it still sucked. I wanted him to be happy. He wasn't. I hated it.

"I can't believe you're dating that guy. He's strange."

"What?" I asked, puzzled by why he was bringing it up again.

"I didn't say anything." Crap. I'd read his thoughts. I'd have to watch it around him more carefully. "Where are we headed?"

I spouted the directions and he pulled out.

"So, how's Beck?" he asked.

"Crap!" I yelled. "I completely forgot about Beck. Can I borrow your cell?"

"Sure."

He tossed it to me and I dialed her number. She picked up and I could hear her thoughts. Ralph was there and she was irritated about being interrupted.

"Beck?"

"Maggie! Maggie, where are you?"

"I'm fine. I was brought home last night."

"OMGosh. I can't believe this. You're like a celebrity around here!"

"I am?"

Oh, man I hoped not.

"Yes! Of course! Everyone knew about it. Are you ok? Where were you? What happened?"

"Beck, I'm sorry, I can't talk right now what with the police and family and all. I just wanted to call and tell you I was home safe."

"Ok," she said and I could tell she was perturbed but she let it go. "Call me later, Mags, I've been so worried about you."

"I know," I muttered. "I'm sorry. I'll call you, k?"

"K. Love you, Mags. I'm glad you're ok."

"Love you, too."

I hung up just as we pulled onto Kyle's street and...oh, boy. The street looked like a parking lot. There were cars everywhere.

"What's going on? Is the fair in town?" he grumbled as he pulled into a spot way away from Kyle's.

"It's kind of for me," I admitted softly.

"What? What do you mean? Oh, because you were rescued and all, but...this is his parent's right? They're making a big deal over you, huh? They must like you."

"You have no idea."

We made our way down the sidewalk and I was grabbed sideways and lifted as we passed the hedges on the edge of Kyle's yard.

"Holy crap, Mags! I've been worried sick about you."

"Kyle, hey."

He put me down and kissed my cheek, especially close to my lips and beamed at me. His hand still held mine and I glanced over to see a confused Bish.

Now who is this Joker?

I pulled away quickly and was hit with Kyle's thoughts and…wow. I had no idea before how he really felt about me. This was not some crush. He was in love with me, seriously in love with me. And I felt nauseous.

"Wow, Mags. You look awesome."

I wanted to take it all back. To block him from the start and not have listened to his thoughts about me, but it was too late.

He had been so worried he'd barely slept while I was away. He was angry at his family for not thinking it was important to keep him updated, because he was my friend. He hadn't even been told that I'd been found until this morning, by his mom. He was mad at me and Caleb for not telling him ourselves. He thought I looked hotter than I ever had and wanted nothing more right that second than to kiss me, like he's wanted to kiss me for two years straight.

I wanted to hurl.

I felt terrible and horrible inside. I hated hurting people and I was hurting Kyle, though I never meant to. "Bish, you remember Kyle?"

"Oh, yeah, man. How are you?"

"Good, man. How's New York treating you?"

"Awesome," Bish muttered sarcastically and was thinking about finding Dad and what the heck I was doing with this boy if I was with Caleb.

"All right, well everyone's waiting for you, may as well get it over with. Come on," Kyle said and tried to take my hand again.

"I need a second with Bish," I stalled.

"All right." He smiled. "I'm so glad you're all right, Maggie."

"Thanks, Kyle." He left and I turned to Bish to see his what-the face.

"I know, ok. I know. He's Caleb's cousin. I went to school with him. He was friends with Chad and me before all this. It's all very complex."

He grinned. “Look at my little sister. A player,” he laughed.

“Shut up!” I smacked his arm and he laughed louder. “I can’t help it if someone has a crush on me.”

“Well, you are pretty great.”

“Oh, please,” I rolled my eyes. “Can we go in now?”

“I’m ready if you are.”

It was my turn to grin. “You have no idea what you’re getting into.”

I pulled him through the yard to the porch and as the door opened it exploded with light and laughter, blaring thoughts, my name called on lips in minds. Add their concern and relief to that and I was overloaded.

I fainted, right there on the porch in front of everyone.

Twenty Nine

Well, fainted was a strong word. Pre-faint was better. I could hear them. It was like I wasn't completely conscious but not completely asleep either. Bish steadied me as I swayed and sat in the rocker on the porch with me in his lap. My head pounded as I rubbed my temple.

"Maggie!"

"Someone get Caleb!" I heard Gran yell. "Back up everyone. She's fine, just got a little overwhelmed."

"Overwhelmed?" Bish said angrily. "Why are you calling Caleb? Call 911!"

"She'll be ok, son. I'm Caleb's grandmother. You must be Bish."

"This is not the time for introductions. Why are you all just standing there? Call an ambulance."

"I'm fine, just dizzy," I insisted.

"Maggie," Bish breathed and then I felt Caleb pushing through the throng of people gathered around me as I heard his thoughts blaring to me before I even saw him.

He was angry.

"Guys, I told you before she got here to turn it off," he growled and went to take me from Bish, but Bish held tight.

"What are you talking about, turn it off? What?"

"Nothing," Caleb muttered and knelt down beside me to brush my cheek with his fingers and my headache instantly went away. "You ok?"

"Yeah. Just, uh…" I looked up at Bish and back to Caleb with Gran and the others watching me. "I'm sorry. I just can't seem to…"

Crap. I couldn't even explain myself with Bish here.

It's ok. They know what's going on. My dad and I told them to keep their thoughts quiet when you got here, but they were so excited... It's too easy to get overloaded in the beginning. It takes a while to control it, but Dad said that it's easy once you get the hang of it.

Ok. Will you please take me inside so everyone will stop staring at me.

He smiled and held out his hand to me. I took it, but Bish grabbed my other one.

"You need to go to the hospital, Maggie. You don't just pass out for no reason."

"I'm fine, just haven't eaten anything today. Really, let's go find Dad."

"Whatever," he said and threw his hands up like he was giving up.

I turned to see Gran still waiting.

"Hey, Gran."

"Hey, pretty girl. You make a good entrance," she said with a twinkle of amusement in her eyes. She hugged me tightly and rubbed my hair. "It's so good to have you back, safe and sound."

"Thanks. It's good to be back."

"I didn't think you could get much prettier," she observed and lifted my arms out to my sides. "But my, my..."

I smiled shyly and I was sure I was blushing.

"Yeah. My, my," Caleb repeated and smiled down at me.

"Yeah. It's...something," I muttered.

"You doing all right?" Gran asked me.

"Yeah, just thinking about the…about everything." I remembered thinking about Gran in my cell. About how she'd been through the withdrawals like I had. She and Caleb were the only ones who had been through anything like that. "I, uh, well, I...wanted to say that what you told me before, I..."

"I know." She shook her head. "You can never understand until you go through it, can you? And I'm so sorry that you had to. Both of you." She looked at Caleb and back at me. She swallowed and I winced as I watched her memory of her withdrawal. "But never again. You keep each other safe from now on and all will be well."

I nodded and turned to Bish.

"This is my brother, Bish. Bish, this is Gran."

"It's nice to meet you, Bish." She grabbed his arm, lacing hers through it. "So, New York? I went to New York once."

She pulled him away and I was grateful. I squeezed Caleb's hand as we passed through the doorway. After we explained to Dad that I was fine we continued on. I was hugged and patted by everyone.

Kyle's parents said they barely recognized me. I wasn't sure if that was a good thing or not. His parents, Dad, Peter, Caleb, Kyle and I stood and talked for a long while about it all; getting my ability, the ascension and how the energy ribbons were all around us and how I'd projected my thoughts into them. They all crooned about how wonderful it all was. Dad listened intently with a look of amazement the whole time.

Kyle's mom told me about her ascension and how she thought she had man arms afterwards and hated it. I laughed with her and Kyle's dad went on to tell her he loved her arms.

Dad and Peter followed along with us as we made the rounds. Dad had been introduced to just about everyone before I got there and everyone told me how much they loved him already. He was a hit.

Jen and Maria I hadn't seen yet, but Rachel hugged me long and hard.

"Oh, Maggie. I'm so sorry about all this. I'm glad you're safe."

I pulled away to see her crying as she wiped her eyes and in her mind, she felt like they'd dragged me into a crazy life of turmoil and she didn't know how to fix it.

"Me, too."

"You look so beautiful. You always did, but...you look complete now," she said with a hand on my cheek.

"Thanks," I said because I didn't know what else to say to that. "Rachel, have you met my dad yet?"

"No, I was in the kitchen." She held her hand out to him. "It's so nice to meet you. I'm Rachel, Caleb's mother."

"Nice to meet you, too."

"Maggie is such a darling."

"That she is. This is a great house you have here."

"Oh, we don't live here." She wrung her apron in her hands. "This is my cousin's house. We live about thirty minutes from here. Just about everyone here does. We only come here to...well, for Maggie."

I blushed, embarrassed and saw Dad's eyes take in the room full of people, all here for Caleb and me. He was thinking that he'd see even less of me than he originally thought because he thought Caleb lived right here near him and now learned he doesn't. And he couldn't believe all these people drove all this way just for me.

He was also in awe of all the couples, all different ages, who had been married for years and were still so happily married. He felt a twinge of longing for my mom, but pushed it away.

"Well. I'm famished," Peter said and then clapped his hands loudly, drawing everyone's attention. "Everyone, we all know why we're here. Our Maggie has come back to us." There were claps and cheers and Caleb put his arm around my shoulder to shield me, knowing I hated the attention. "Let us not forget the struggles of the past few days for Caleb and Maggie and give them our respect and space. Also there are new developments that need to be handled... delicately. We are very glad to have Maggie's father and brother here with us as well and I smell something heavenly from the kitchen. I'm sure Rachel has outdone herself once again." He looked over at her affectionately and she beamed under his praise. "Let's eat folks."

We all went through the line of chicken pot pie dishes and casseroles and then made our way to the patio. Caleb and I sat and I just looked at everyone. I got smiles and glances. They were happy. They were proud to have me in their family. It was surreal.

I saw Bish coming out the sliding glass door with a plate piled high, along with Dad and Peter. I waved to him to come sit with us.

"Maggie!" I heard and saw Maria bounding passed him towards us. I stood and received a very enthusiastic hug from her. "Maggie. My goodness, you sure know how to scare people."

I laughed and so did Caleb.

"Did your mom teach you to say that?" he asked.

"Yep. She's been worried like a crazy person."

Then I saw her coming. Bish, Peter and Dad had taken a seat around our table and I saw Bish do a subtle double take of Jen as she came to hug me and Caleb.

Who is that creature?

I had to press my lips together at his thought and also give her props for looking pretty great. Her dress was flowy and blue, her hair was down and she looked awesome.

"Maggie," she said sweetly, "oh, it's so good to see you."

"You, too. Jen, this is my brother, Bish and my dad, Jim. This is Jen, Caleb's sister."

She smiled at Dad and shook his hand and then turned to Bish. He stood and they just kind of stared at each other for a few seconds.

"Hi," she finally said and cleared her throat and sat down beside Caleb without shaking Bish's hand. "Nice to meet you," she said softly and was thinking that he had the kindest, most focused eyes she'd ever seen.

I thought it was comical that she didn't even think once how hot he looked or about how muscley he was.

"It's nice to meet you, too," he said, not having taken his eyes off her yet.

I looked at Caleb to see if he saw. And oh yeah, he saw. He scowled at his sister and glanced down at his dad. Peter frowned, but shrugged at him.

I understood, the no-dating rule, it had a purpose but my brother didn't date. Ever. Even in high school, he'd been very focused on his work and withdrawn. He'd even been shy and had no idea the reactions girls had to him. He thought he was a burden to our family though grateful we'd taken him in. He wanted to work hard and earn his keep and get a good job. He'd never been on a date since I'd known him.

The way he was looking at Jen was something I'd never seen on him before. He thought she was sweet looking and pretty. He had to physically keep his eyes from drifting down to her bare shoulders, which he liked, a lot.

I was blushing just listening to his thoughts. She eventually smiled shyly and pulled her hair to one side of her neck, looking over at Caleb.

"So, you're leaving tonight?"

"Yep. Our flight's in three hours," Caleb answered as he leaned back in his chair. "In fact, we need to get going pretty soon and pack."

His hand found my leg under the table and he squeezed my knee.

"Where are you going?" Bish asked and glanced between me and Caleb. "You're going somewhere the day after you were kidnapped? Alone with him?" he said and I didn't have to be a mind reader to see that he disapproved.

"Not alone," I threw in.

"Bish," Peter explained, "the ones who took Maggie aren't in police custody. We want to send them away for a while, for their safety, to make sure that these men don't try again. Someone will go with them."

It took about ten minutes of back and forth with Peter and Dad to get Bish to settle down about the 'men' who took me not being under arrest and still out there after what they did. He was furious. Finally he calmed down enough but kept looking over at me and biting his thumb nail. In his mind he wanted to snatch me and run with me. He thought something fishy was going on. Everybody was a little too calm and collected about it all.

First, no one cared when I almost fainted, now this? He couldn't figure it out but he didn't like it. He went to put his arm around me and his hand ran into Caleb's arm, already around my shoulder. He glared at him. Saved me or not, he was liking Caleb less by the minute.

Then I could hear Peter's thoughts. He was thinking about Jen, worrying really. He hoped he wouldn't have a problem with her and Bish but wanted her to be happy at the same time. He was conflicted.

I could also hear Rachel somewhere upset because she had broken a glass in the kitchen and Maria was looking at a butterfly and Dad was worrying about me leaving and Jen was back to thinking about Bish, how sweet he was to be so worried about me.

Then an uncle was wanting seconds but his wife was reminding him of his cholesterol. A cousin was shooing an annoying fly and flitting thoughts of dinner through her mind. Another uncle was looking at Caleb and hoping his son would be just as lucky.

Caleb was worried about me, feeling the wave of overwhelm coming, but couldn't fully stop the onslaught in my head even when he touched my hand with his. It lessened but the voices all around me seemed to compile and compress in my head in an annoying haze of fog and thickness that was almost painful in its uncomfortable-ness.

I covered my face with my hands and took a deep breath as Caleb rubbed my back.

"Are you ok?" Bish asked. "You feel faint again?"

"No," I muttered.

"No, you're not ok, or no you don't feel faint?

"Either one."

"Maggie," Peter called from across the table. I peeked up at him. "Calm down, ok? Don't let it upset you. It's worse when you're upset. Just block it all out. It'll get easier, I promise."

"What? What's going on?" Bish said angrily.

"Stop being so paranoid, Bish," I muttered tersely. I felt someone raking their hand through my hair and looked up to Caleb. I blew a breath and tried to clear my head. It was hazy and full but when I stopped and breathed through it, it helped. Caleb's fingers grazed my cheek and the rim of my ear, pulling the too-tight feeling from me with his touch. "Thanks."

"I'm sorry," he whispered to me, "I know it sucks."

"It's ok," I whispered back and smiled at him. "I'll be fine."

"All right, kids, you need to get going. You've gotta pack and all before you go," Dad said, thinking he could divert Bish. "We've got to get to the cell phone store, too, Maggie, so let's go."

"Ok," I answered and turned back to Caleb.

"We'll come pick you up in an hour," he stated, "that'll give us plenty of time to get to the airport. Just bring one bag and we'll buy anything else we need when we're there, ok? I have no idea how long we'll be in California."

"I don't need you to buy-"

"Maggie," he scolded. "It's fine. Let me do this. I'm not worried about the money, I'm worried about you."

He kissed me softly and I ignored the grunt behind us. Then he stood and pulled me up from my seat.

"You guys get going and we'll pick you up in an hour or so. Jim, you're coming with us to the airport right?"

Dad nodded. "Ok, let's go," Dad said and stood, along with Bish.

Our movement was noticed and everyone wanted to say goodbye. Maria ran to Caleb and I, hugging us both.

"Who are you?" she asked Bish sweetly.

"This is my brother, Bish. Bish, this is Maria, Jen's daughter."

"She has a daughter?" he asked softly and looked at Maria in awe as she took his hand and shook it. He laughed and smiled. "Nice to meet you, Maria."

"Thanks," Maria said and skipped off.

Jen was behind us and laughed, rolling her eyes. "She's something else," she said and hugged me. "Maria will miss you for sure. I'm glad you're all right. Be careful, ok?" She pulled back to look at me sternly and I read in her mind what she meant. "Careful," she reiterated.

"I understand," I said and gave her a wry smile that said what my mouth couldn't in front of everyone else - no sex. "We'll be careful."

"I've got to go, too," she turned to Caleb, "so I won't see you before you leave. You be careful, too." She grabbed Caleb in a big hug around his neck and whispered in his ear but I could hear in her mind. "I'm glad you finally got everything right again. I've been so worried about you two."

He looked sadly down at his big sister, knowing she would never have this.

"Thanks, Jen. Keep Mom from going nuts, huh?"

"Yep. Love ya."

"Love ya."

She turned to Bish.

"Maybe we'll see you around again."

Translation in her mind: *I really wish things were different.*

She glanced at me knowing I'd heard her thoughts and smiled a little bashfully.

"Maybe. I'm supposed to head back to New York, so..." Translation in his mind: *Wow, I wish I could stay here and figure out what's going on around here. Especially with this one.*

His eyes were locked on hers and I knew I needed to help him, by removing him. He finally gets all gooey eyed over a girl and it's the one he can't have.

"Come on, Bish, we gotta go," I hurried and felt like a peeping tom for eavesdropping on our families all night.

"Ok. Nice to meet you, Jen," he said as we turned, him shoving his hands in his pockets.

"You, too, Bish." She gave a little wave.

I pulled his arm and we said goodbye to everyone else. When Gran came I swore I saw a smile on Bish's face.

"Bish, you come and see me anytime. You're family now," she crooned and hugged him.

He raised an eyebrow at me over her shoulder.

"Family?"

"Course!" She pulled back and hugged me next. "Bye, pretty girl. Keep my boy out of trouble, hear?"

"Yes, ma'am. Bye."

"Don't you worry about your father now. You two get everything settled with you, I've got my eye on Jim."

"Thank you," I said and meant it. We made our way out to Bish's car and he climbed in none to gently, slamming his door. I looked up at Caleb. "This ride will be fun. I've never seen him so paranoid before."

"He's just worried about you."

"I know, but we can't afford for him to be worried can we? I'm not so sure he'd accept the idea of my being an Ace like my dad did, even if we could tell him."

He smiled and pulled me to him.

"Everything will be fine. We'll wind up telling him or we won't. He's going back to New York anyway. Being away from it all will help, I'm sure."

"You're probably right. So you don't know who's coming with us?"

"Not yet. All the older ones they want here, my dad and my uncles, because of their abilities. They either need to use it or want them here in case Dad finds something and they have to attack the Watsons."

"Attack," I whispered under my breath.

"One more good reason we won't be here. Don't worry about it." He pulled my face up. "Are you gonna be ok with Bish and all?"

I nodded just as Dad came across the lawn.

"Let's get going, baby girl," he said and climbed in the back of Bish's car.

"Your dad will be a good buffer," Caleb said and smiled. "See you in a bit." He stopped. "Are you excited? I mean, I know it's not good circumstances but...I'm pretty happy to be going away with you."

I smiled, too, thinking about it.

"Me, too. I've never even been out of Tennessee."

"What? How's that possible?" he mused.

"It's possible. We never took vacations. I've never ridden a plane either."

"Well, you'll like it. It'll be late, so we'll sleep most of the way, anyway. I promise we'll have a good time in California."

I nodded and went up on my tip toes to kiss him. We hadn't been kissing two point two seconds when Bish honked the horn. He actually honked.

I glared at him, but Caleb laughed. "He's not liking me too much, I don't think."

"That's not funny. He's being so rude. I've never seen him like this."

"You're his sister. It's ok, he just needs time to figure me out. He'll get it while we're gone. Get going, I'll see you in an hour."

"Ok."

"Oh, and don't worry about the cell phone, I've got it covered."

"Caleb," I protested in my most whiny voice.

"See you later, gorgeous," he said grinning as he walked backwards away from me.

As he turned away I stopped in a revelation. I realized that I never felt the stuck feeling of needing to be released from him just now, even a little. It was the first time we'd both walked away of our own free will.

Bish honked again. I rolled my eyes as I got in. "Rude much," I spouted and glared daggers at him.

"You're going to see each other in like five minutes. I thought we were in a hurry to get home?"

"He was explaining the details to me about our flight. What's wrong with you?"

"What's wrong with *me*?" he said incredulously and turned onto the street.

"Now, Bish-" Dad tried, but no good.

"Gee, I don't know," Bish kept going in his deep voice but the sarcasm was making him boom even more, "you almost faint on the porch in front of everyone and no one seems to care. You are so incredibly serious about this boy and everyone acts like you're about to get hitched or something, even Dad, and it's weird. You're acting funny, like you're sick or something, but once again, everyone acts like it's just normal and nothing's wrong."

"Bish, you've been gone a while. Things aren't the same as when you left," I tried to explain.

"That is very clear but that doesn't explain anything. Something weird is going on here." Then he jerked the wheel, righted himself and turned to look at me with wide eyes. "Oh no, are you pregnant?"

"No! I'm not pregnant," I grumbled and wondered why everyone thought that.

He sighed long and heavy, just like Dad had done, and it irked me as much as it had when Dad did it.

"Well, that's good, but something is going on."

"When do you leave?"

"Not sure, I told you. I don't know what I'm doing. I was hoping I'd get to spend some time with you, but you're running away with your boyfriend."

I stayed silent. There was no point. He was thinking about punching Caleb's jaw when he came to pick me up. I wanted to punch Bish's jaw right then.

We pulled into the driveway and we got out. Dad went inside and I pulled Bish to a stop by his arm.

"Wait. Look," I tucked my hair behind my ear, trying to look vulnerable and small, "everyone thought you'd be just like this. I love Caleb, he's different and his family is different. They are really close and everyone...likes me. Dad has come to terms with Caleb and I, you're going to have to, too."

"Mags." I felt him soften in his mind and his face visibly softened, too. He placed his hands on the tops of my arms. "I'm sorry, ok? I came home expecting one thing and found something completely different. You're so...different. You look different, talk different, act different. You're different with Caleb, too. I don't remember you being like that with Chad." I mentally rolled my eyes. I wish everyone would stop being so perceptive. "I'm just worried about you. It seems no one else is."

"Believe me, I have enough people worrying about me. I want my brother back. I missed you." I hugged him and heard his thoughts cave. He didn't want to fight with me either. "I want you to come back and see me soon, ok? I have no idea how long I'll be gone, but," I shrugged, "don't stay gone for so long."

"I'll try, Mags. I want to like Caleb, I do."

"Well, you better get started because he's it for me."

"What? You're so young, you can't know that. I bet you thought Chad was it for you, too. Now Caleb, he may not feel the same way."

"I know it. Please. You don't have to like him, though if you'd give him a chance you would, but you do have to be civil. He's here to stay."

"Ok. I'll try," he repeated. "I love ya, kid."

"I love you, too."

"All right, go pack."

We walked inside and I heard his question before he asked it and I still didn't know what to say.

"So, Caleb's sister, Jen, seems nice. Is she married?"

"No."

"Divorced?"

"Caleb's family doesn't get divorced."

"What does that mean?"

"They don't believe in it. No one has ever gotten divorced in his family."

"Wow. That's pretty amazing but isn't that one more reason to be cautious? What if things don't work out with you and Caleb? You'd be the first ones to fail in the family."

"Gee, thanks for the vote of confidence."

"No pressure, huh?" He elbowed me playfully.

I chuckled with him because it was better than anything I could think of.

"So, Jen's not married and not divorced but she had a kid," he mused.

"Date rape," I blurted and he looked at me sharply. "She doesn't date, Bish."

"Wow. Ok. Well, I'm gonna go, uh...catch up with Dad while you get packed."

He walked away and I regretted laying it out there like that but I had to nip it in the bud. I felt terrible, flashing back to his memories of a horrible life before he met us, but I stopped them and took a deep breath.

It was for the best to stop it now. He wouldn't see her that much, for a while anyway.

Thirty

I ran upstairs and pulled out my school track duffel bag. I didn't own a suitcase because we never went anywhere. I stuffed as many dresses and skirts I could in it then a couple pairs of jeans and shirts then the essentials and I was done. By then it was almost time for Caleb to be here and it amazed me how I still got butterflies thinking about him. I wondered if it'd ever go away. I hoped not.

I pulled and dragged my bag down the hall and stairs because it was too heavy and bulky, shouldering my purse at the same time, and heard laughter behind me. I looked down the stairs to see Caleb, Peter, Dad and Bish all chuckling, watching me struggle. I placed my hands on my hips and gave my best glare but it didn't stop the laughter. If anything it made it worse.

"I'll get that," Caleb said, swiftly scaling the steps and lifting the bag easily, smirking at me.

I thought with my new man arms I would be able to lift a duffel bag.

Caleb laughed in my mind.

You're stronger than you were but you're still not Wonder Woman.

Ha, ha.

"Ready?" he asked still smirking.

"Yeah."

"Let's go then."

We all piled in the cars and they went straight to the police station. I gave my brief statement as Peter explained that we were needing to catch a flight. They were perplexed as to how Caleb had found me but Peter could be very persuasive and smooth talking. We were out of there in ten minutes.

As I sat in the back with Caleb, I rubbed my wrist, mourning the loss of my bracelet, the only real thing I had to remember the only people who were there for me this year. Caleb reached over and wrapped his fingers around my wrist. When I looked up at him, he smiled sadly, feeling my pain. I just shrugged. What else could I do?

We had about forty minutes until our flight left by the time we made it to the airport drop-off, cutting it close. Peter spoke to me in my mind, advising me about the explosion of voices and information I'd get when we got to the airport.

Ok, Maggie, he started, but didn't look at me, just faced forward so Bish wouldn't see him staring at me. *Now, whenever you're in a crowd, just focus on Caleb. When you focus, you won't let anything in but what you want to. It's only when your mind is open or caught off guard that you're overwhelmed. It'll take a little practice but you'll get the hang of it in no time. You'll be ready for it before it happens. So, when we get there, just focus on someone before you step out of the car and you'll be fine, ok?*

I couldn't nod or anything, because he wouldn't see so I just took it that he knew I'd heard him.

We pulled up and I knew the person who was going to grab me first would be Dad, so I focused on only reading him. When he opened the door, I winced waiting for the overload of voices, but heard nothing but Dad's wary inner monologue as he hugged me to him. He looked at me closely and tested his theory.

Can you hear me?

I nodded slightly.

I want you to be careful. Be watchful, don't let your guard down and I want you to know that I'm...proud of you. You're a beautiful woman now with a sweet heart, trying to keep your old man from worrying about you, but I'll always be your dad and I'll always worry. Comes with the territory, but I like Caleb and his family is...something else. I like them, too. You did good, kiddo. Now, listen. I know what you have to do but I want you two to sleep on the couch, ok? I don't think it's a good idea for you to share a bedroom, though I understand the need to sleep with him. Got it? I nodded again. *I love you more than life and I want you to have a good time but not too good. Why don't you think about college while you're there...and be careful...and don't do anything crazy...and call me everyday.*

I had to suppress a laugh and nodded again and squeezed him.

"I love you, Dad."

"Love you, too, baby girl."

Then I hugged Peter, turning my focus to him, and he gave me a similar internal pep talk but with less gush. I thanked him for the advice and told him it was working well and he smiled. Then it was Bish's turn.

"Be careful and don't worry. They'll find these guys," he said and hugged me tightly. "Text me, ok?"

"Of course."

"Don't do anything stupid and give me a reason to have to kill your boyfriend." I rolled my eyes and looked drolly at him. "Love ya, kid."

"Love you, too. Bye."

Bish just smiled and cocked his head at Caleb in contest. Caleb laughed, nodded good naturedly, took his luggage and my bag as we made our way through the revolving doors of the airport entrance way. I looked back over my shoulder and saw them still watching us go. I waved and followed Caleb to the ticket counter. He handled everything for us.

We went to sit at our gate after going through security and he asked me if I was ok.

"Yeah, I just hope Bish goes back to New York and doesn't cause trouble. I mean, I love him and miss him, but he's being way *overprotective brother* right now."

"I can handle Bish if you're worried about me."

"Well, it's not just you, though he seriously needs to stop that, I just don't want him digging around finding something he shouldn't. Your family has already taken a huge risk by telling my dad."

"Was he like this with Chad?" he asked and put his arm along the back of my seat, not worrying about his family in the least.

I guess that should've given me comfort that he wasn't worried about it.

"Um, not really. He jokingly bashed him in the beginning, you know, 'I'll kick your butt if you hurt my sis', but he was never hostile like he is now. Maybe it's because I'm older. It can't be because of you, you're so... charming."

"Charming," he mused and chuckled. "Ok. From a brother's point of view we have this. You're dating a guy you never told him about, you mysteriously are kidnapped and returned and then take off to a picnic with that guy's family like nothing happened. Then, you jump on a plane, alone, with before mentioned guy while your dad acts like this is totally normal right after a semi-breakdown. If you were my sister and everyone was acting this way, I'd think everyone was nuts and go berserk on someone. Personally, I think he's taking it pretty well."

I just looked at him. He was so funny and cute.

"Ok, so you don't think we should worry about it. If he finds out, he finds out?"

"Yep, it's gonna be pretty hard to hide this kind of thing from him for the rest of our lives. It's probably best if he finds out sooner than later."

"But I thought it was so secret."

"It is," he looked over and down at me, "but your happiness is more important than a secret. I learned that when we told your dad. You were so happy to be able to tell him, to not have to lie anymore."

"Yeah, but I understand your side, too. I don't think Bish would run to USA Today or anything, but he may not be so accepting."

"We'll deal with that later. Right now," he pulled me to him to kiss my temple, "your safety is more important than anything else."

I nodded and leaned my head on his shoulder. “And yours. And our family's.” I took a deep breath. “Everything will work out.”

“Right.”

I ran my finger over his wrist, over his tattoo. “So, how come we don’t have to release each other anymore?”

“I’m not sure. That part doesn’t last forever, so maybe it was just our time to know that we’d always come back to each other.”

I smiled up at him. “That was a very good answer,” I whispered.

He smirked at me and kissed the end of my nose. “I’ll get us some drinks. You’re thirsty,” he announced.

“A diet-”

“Diet cream soda if they have it.” He laughed and tapped my forehead. “I know, remember?”

“Kinda takes the fun out of it,” I grumbled and he laughed as he walked across to the food court.

He kept looking back to me, watching me as he stood in line. I heard people all around me as I looked at an older man, a grandpa I assumed, as he played tic-tac-toe on a cocktail napkin with a little girl. He saw me watching and smiled, shrugging.

“A three hour layover with a four year old. What are ya gonna do?” he said and shrugged again.

I laughed and nodded. Then I felt a hand on my shoulder and gasped as I jerked up from my chair to spin expecting Sikes, or worse, Marcus. It was Chad. Of all the luck.

“Whoa, Mags. Chill,” he said in surrender. Then his eyes widened and his mouth fell open. “Wow. You look...” he licked his lips, “great. Wow.”

“What are you doing here?” I asked tersely.

“I’m leaving today for Florida. I thought you were kidnapped or something.” He crossed his arms. “I’ve been going out of my mind. What are you doing here?”

I glanced over and saw that Caleb was watching us with a frown but stayed in line.

You ok?

Yeah. He just scared me. I’m fine. Hurry back, please.

He grinned.

I can’t refuse a request like that.

“Maggie?” Chad said and waved in front of me. “I said, what are you doing here?”

“I’m leaving, too.”

“What happened? Everyone thought you’d been kidnapped?”

"I was," I answered and his eyes went wide, "I'm fine now. It was a...it's over now."

"Where are you going?"

"California, for a while."

"Huh. You going to see your mom, after what happened?"

"No, just going away for a while. Caleb's uncle has a vacation house there."

"Caleb." He adjusted the backpack on his shoulder roughly and sighed. "I should've known. Does your dad know you're leaving? I wouldn't think he'd be ok with you taking off with some guy."

"He drove us here, actually," I said casually.

"When are you coming back?"

"You're leaving, why does it matter?"

"I'm coming back in a couple weeks to finish packing and all." He stepped closer to me, like it would keep our conversation more private. "I figured we could get together when I come back. Talk."

"About what? Chad-"

"Just hear me out, ok? I know I messed up at your house the other night. I was being stupid but I'm in new territory with you. It's important to me that we try to work it out. I miss you, so much, Maggie." He reached out for my hand and I pulled it back to rub my neck before he could reach it.

His mind was clean and airy, not mucked up with deceit or meanness like other minds I'd been in. His thoughts said he was being truthful. He wasn't just jealous, he really did miss me. In fact, the only reason he broke up with me last summer was because his father pressured him to. He told him it would be easier on me that way and he'd never be able to focus or make it in college if he dragged me along. Chad was torn between making his parents happy and me. He thought we'd just be friends and I'd wait for him until he was settled into college and then he'd come and make things right with me. He thought that would make everyone happy. He had no idea I'd take the breakup so hard and stop talking to him all together and regretted it immediately. He wanted to take it back but couldn't tell me what he'd done and why. He was ashamed and now was scared for me, he thought I was making a mistake with this guy because I was angry. He missed me, he still loved me and wanted me. I was his biggest regret and he was miserable.

I felt like I'd been kicked in the gut.

"Maggie," he rubbed his face, "I don't know what to do, here. I love you and I don't want to see you hurt. I wish I could just get you to see how sorry I am and how much I want to make it up to you."

"Chad, I'm sorry that things happened the way they did. I'm sure you got pressure about college and all. You had no idea what was going on in my life. I should have told you about my mom. We weren't as close as we should have been, like real couples are. I'd always known you. You were always there and I was comfortable. I didn't want to take it any further with you but for some reason, I thought we'd always be together. I'm sorry, but it's too late. It's not just about Caleb, I was just never who I am now, with you. Now, I'm who I was always supposed to be." I shrugged and heard them call his gate number over the loud speaker. "You're gonna be so great in Florida. I know your dad is proud of you."

"Yeah," he mumbled, "he is, but I don't think it was worth it."

"It was. You'll see."

"I hope so." He nodded his head over my shoulder. "Caleb."

"Chad," Caleb said not unkindly and handed me my drink. "Small world."

"Yeah. Well I'm off. See you around, Maggie."

He was yelling in his mind. He so didn't want to leave and it hurt me to see him like that. He just wanted one more shot, so bad.

"Bye."

He started to turn, but stopped. "Call me...or something. Let me know how you're doing, that you're all right, ok?"

"Sure." I smiled and relented. I went to hug him briefly. He squeezed me so tight, I could feel his breath in my hair and his hands pressed against my back. I noticed Caleb had blocked his thoughts from me. I couldn't even feel his emotions. I thought that couldn't be good. Chad held on for a long time before I finally said something to end it. "Have a good flight, ok?"

"Yeah," Chad pulled back and glanced between Caleb and I. "You, too. See ya."

"Bye."

Once he was gone I turned and expected to see an upset face on Caleb but he surprised me. He looked amused.

"You're so sweet." He kissed my cheek and then sat down. "How's your drink? They didn't have cream soda so I got you-"

"Wait." I sat next to him and looked at him, perplexed. "You're not mad?"

"No. Why would I be?"

Well, I just hugged my ex-boyfriend right in front of you for one.

"You forget." He put his drink down on the floor, turned back to my guilty face and placed his hand on my knee. "I can see straight into your mind. You can't hide anything from me anymore. Neither can I, unless we're trying to. I saw that you were upset by how he still feels about you. That you hate how it all happened but you don't regret it. You didn't have lingering feelings for him, you just felt sorry for him and didn't want to hurt him. There's nothing wrong with that. Now," he screwed his lips up, "I admit, it's not fun to watch my girl with her arms around another guy, but I saw in your mind that this was goodbye with him. You never got the goodbye, the 'closure' I told you that you needed. Well, now you do."

"You're pretty amazing," I said softly.

"Hey, that's my line," he said grinning.

"I'm serious. Any other guy would be upset."

"Any other guy," he leaned close, "wouldn't be in their girlfriend's head." He kissed me. "I have an advantage other guys don't. Plus, the whole soul mate thing," he said flippantly and waved his hand like it didn't matter.

"Yeah, just that." I grinned at him. "So, you never told me what your ability was."

"Well," he dragged out and looked at me a bit oddly.

I felt his amusement drain away, replaced with humiliation and an unease that threaded through me, and I felt like an idiot for not getting it sooner. He had been hiding it from me. He hadn't received his ability yet, which was unheard of.

"Ah, Caleb." I put my hand on his knee. "I'm sorry. I was so involved in my own drama I didn't even care about yours. What does it mean? Maybe you just haven't figured out what it is yet?"

"We always can sense our ability," he explained. "Like you knew you could reach out to people to go into their minds even when they weren't thinking something specific. You just know and I just...don't."

"What does it mean?" I asked again softly.

"It's one more thing Dad's looking into. No one else knows but him. It's never happened before. He's freaking out a little bit."

"I'm so sorry."

"Don't be," he commanded and put his hand on mine on his knee. "I'm not happy about it, but I'm happier that you have an awesome ability. Maybe you've got enough power for us both. I can practically read minds myself since I can read everything that comes through yours. Like with Chad just now, I saw everything you saw in his mind, through you. I saw it all just like it was my own thoughts."

I nodded, but didn't like it. He was the Ace, I was some imposter. He'd waited his whole life for this, to ascend and get his ability, and now I took it and he got nothing. I felt wretched.

"Don't." He pulled me under his arm. "I'm fine, really. I mean...I'm not *fine* but I'll worry about that later. One thing at a time, remember? Oh, and here's your new cell." He pulled a black square object with a touch screen out of his pocket. "It's the same number as before, I just added you to my plan and I went ahead and programmed the numbers I knew you needed to be in there. You can do the rest later."

"This is the new iPhone. I had a cheap Motorola."

"I know, but you can check your email and use the internet on this, too, while we're gone, keep in touch with your father better. See." He showed me how to go to the web and smirked in smugness as I looked on in awe.

"You didn't have to do this," I protested softly. "I don't want you spending so much money-."

"Flight #197 to San Diego Airport, first class only is now boarding at gate #3B," the loud speaker announced.

"That's us," Caleb said and jumped up.

"She said first class, Caleb."

"Yep."

"We're riding first class?" I asked incredulously.

"Yeah. It's a long flight. We're going to sleep most of the way. I wanted you to be comfortable."

I stood and looked at the men in business suits with their rolling luggage heading to the too peppy attendant who checked their tickets and wished them a happy flight and wondered if I was ever going to get used to the idea that Caleb had loose pockets when it came to spending. He was the kind of guy that didn't worry about money at all and I always had been responsible and cautious with mine. He was going to try to spoil me, I could see it now.

He laughed and kissed my forehead as he shouldered our bags. "You bet your pretty tush I am."

"Caleb, I am perfectly fine with riding coach. If that's what it's even called," I muttered. "You don't have to impress me, really."

"This is not about impressing you. It's about you being happy and comfortable. I have the money, you were right, money doesn't matter to me. I'm not taking it for granted I just think that's the point of having money to begin with, to live and to do things for the ones you love. Let me. It makes *me* happy."

I groaned and knew I was going to get nowhere. "Your dad doesn't care that you're spending all his money?" I said and knew I was reaching.

"No," he handed our tickets to the attendant who smiled angelically at him and waved us on, "he doesn't, especially if I'm spending it on you but I'm not spending his money right now. I'm spending mine."

I balked. "What? How do you have money for first class last minute tickets to California?"

We smiled at the stewardess as she directed us to our seats and he pushed me gently to the window seat with his hands on my hips. He sat down beside me and smirked at me.

"Believe it or not, my love, I am not the spoiled brat you have me pictured as in your mind."

"I don't think that-"

"I know," he said laughing. "I started a tutoring service for middle school age kids. I always had the hardest time then and as you know, I love geometry, so that's what I started teaching. At first it was the community service thing, you know, for college kids to put on apps for scholarships and stuff but it really took off and soon I had a company want to partner with me to offer an affordable statewide service that works out of community buildings to keep cost down. So the parents can spend practically lunch money on a tutor for their kid, college students who tutor make book money and application credit and I have a little spending money for my girl." He kissed my cheek and smiled. "I just don't ever tell anyone about that. It makes me look all geeked out."

Holy crap. How did I not know about this? He was a saint, an angel. I did that girly little sighing thing you do when you can't handle all the sweetness anymore and bit my lip. The corners of his mouth lifted slightly and he rubbed his chin bashfully.

"It's nothing," he assured me.

"It's not nothing. Here I was, running you down the river because of you spending your dad's money and you're like the sweetest guy ever."

"Geek," he said and raised his hand like he was claiming the title.

"Not geek. Sweet. And very hot," I whispered and bit my lip again.

"Really?" he said hopefully and leaned closer. "Well, I also give them apples to snack on."

I laughed and received an amused knowing look from the stewardess as she asked if we wanted a drink. Caleb ordered us something and then turned back to me.

"How did I not know this?" I said once she was gone. "I have got to stop worrying so much and start digging around in your brain like you do mine."

"Maybe we should wait until we get to the house," he said quickly.

"Why?" I asked, perplexed.

"Well..." His mind was filled with possibilities. He was excited about it but cautious. "I told you before how you'd like it, to be in each other's minds, right?"

"Uhuh."

"Well, you will like it, a lot. That's why I haven't really showed you how to do it yet. Once you get started looking into someone's mind and you're completely into it, it's very...intense."

"But we've done that before haven't we? And you've been digging in mine apparently."

"Yes, I have but it's one sided. Before, that was peanuts compared to what we can do now. See, when we do it together, on purpose, with intention, you kind of consume the other person." He looked amusedly entertained and his cheeks seemed to pink a little. I tried to look into his mind to see why but he was holding back. He wanted to explain without me seeing first and not rush me. "It's like nothing you've ever felt or done, even with me, even imprinting. It's amazing, from what I hear."

"What you hear?"

"My dad. He explained it to me. We got this talk along with the birds and bees talk."

"What do you mean?" I said in complete misunderstanding.

"You see," he started and then switched to speaking in my mind. *It can be kind of like...sex.*

Thirty One

I felt my eyebrows rise and I stared at him. He stared back with a little smile.

I don't understand. We're just reading each other's thoughts, right?

No, I told you it's different. It's like we can feel each other, though we're not touching. You can feel every emotion, every feeling of the other person all over you. It's all consuming and intense and can be very...sexual. It's Ace non-sex. They call it mutuality.

But Gran said that Ace's get pregnant the human way, so you have regular sex, right?

We do, after the wedding, but mutuality is different, we don't need to wait.

After the wedding?

Yeah. We wait until our wedding to...consummate. He had a little grin. *Just like you want to*. My mouth opened for a second before I remembered that I didn't have to tell him things anymore. *But remember that most people only wait a couple weeks to get married so it's not that big of a stretch.*

But you do both...sex and mutuality once you're married?

Yes, and when you do them together...it's supposed to be insane. Like uncontrollable, really powerful...pleasure.

I was blushing just talking about it, let alone doing it.

I'm not pressuring you. He smiled and ran a finger over the length of my jaw and chin. *I'm just letting you know that if we get all entangled in each other's minds, our bodies will go that direction. It's instinct. It's not sex, it's all in the mind but it's definitely sexual. And I was just joking about waiting until we get to the house. We'll wait as long as you need to, no rushing.*

He smiled reassuringly but I'd already seen in his mind how excited he was about it. It's one of those things you have to wait until you're ascended to do, like a lot of other things. He asked his dad about it since we had imprinted. He knew real sex was out of the question for a long while and I was grateful for that but he was very intrigued and interested in the other, the mutuality.

You don't want to wait...to do that? I asked.

He smiled and rubbed the back of his neck. I could feel his embarrassment and caution. No. He didn't need nor want to wait but he did and would if I wanted to.

Baby, listen. Even though the fasten seat belt sign came on he leaned over in his seat towards me and put his head to mine. *I did used to think that all this was a sham, that everything my parents used to talk about was over exaggerated and more about personal perception than facts. Then it happened to me - you happened to me - and even though I used to act all aloof about it, I had waited for that day my entire life. When it happens to other Aces, they jump right in to being together and starting their lives. It's instinct, I know you feel it, too. But...with us being so young, especially you* - He continued quick when I mentally rolled my eyes - *we need to keep it toned down and not just jump in all at once, like our bodies want us to. But. I have wanted all of you, all of us, since that first second. It's drilled in my bones from the imprint to... I don't want to scare you.*

He shook his head and started to move back, but I stopped him by grabbing his shirt sleeve.

"You'd never hurt me, I know that. I'm not scared of you or anything you have to say. Tell me," I pleaded and he sighed, then continued.

It's rooted in my blood to consume you and be consumed by you. To protect you. To please you, in every way. His fingers raked through my hair. *To make you shiver when I touch you.* And to his enjoyment, I shook with goose bumps. He smiled and skimmed his fingers down my arm. *To cause your heart to beat faster.* He tapped his finger over my heart as he'd done once before and it didn't make me calm down any more than it had before. *To make you happy, to do anything and everything with you, to date you, spoil you, love you...marry you. So yes, I want to make love to you. I want to mutualize with you. I want to live with you. I want to marry you and have kids with you. But not today. Not right this second. We have all the time in the world, Maggie. I told you in the very beginning that I'll let you set the pace and that still stands. I'm ready for anything, whenever you are but I'm not pushing you, ok? I've waited this long for you and I'm happy.* He kissed my stunned lips softly as I fought to keep my composure and breaths even. *I'm happy, just like this, for now.*

I had no idea what to say to him after that. My chest was too shallow and my eyes were brimmed with tears, but I wasn't sure what they were for, happiness, gratefulness or fright. My vision was spotty and blurry and Caleb's breath blowing in my face wasn't helping anything. He smiled cockily and brushed my bottom lip with his thumb.

"Breathe, Maggie."

I took a deep breath and felt more clear just as the captain came over the intercom and instructed us we were about to take off. I felt the floor and seat vibrate and shake beneath me. I gripped his hand on the armrest between us and gasped at the jolt as the engines fired.

"It's ok, it's normal," he said as he turned his hand over under mine to lock our fingers.

I took deep breaths and scoffed at myself. I was not scared of a plane. I leaned back and tightened my seatbelt as tight as it would go. I felt Caleb's eyes on me in concern.

"I'm fine."

"Let me distract you," he said and pulled my face to his. Our noses touched and he sighed his words. "I can't wait for us to get there."

He showed me a vision of us on the beach, walking and holding hands, him chasing me down the shore as we passed a campfire at nighttime. Him kissing me on a big porch swing as he pressed me down further into it's big cushions and pillows. A huge white breakfast nook window sill where we're sitting, reading a book together and eating orange slices. My legs wrapped around him as we float in the pool and he kisses me witless.

When he pulled his face away I was breathless, but the plane was long forgotten.

"Is that your plans for me?" I joked.

"Absolutely." He smiled, his dimple driving me insane and tweaked my nose. "We're ten thousand feet. How do you feel?"

"Perfect. Thank you."

"Well, we can sleep. We've got a long flight but we'll get there really late and it takes about an hour to drive to the house, so."

"Ok. Hey," I grabbed his arm, "thank you."

"For what?"

"Everything. Dealing with my ex, my brother, my dad. My insecurities about all of this, coming to find me, taking me away from everything, explaining things to me a hundred times, keeping me calm on the plane, being patient with me. For always telling me the truth even if it embarrasses you or you think I won't like it."

"You never have to thank me for those things," he said sweetly, but forcefully, and wrapped a hand around the back of my neck, his fingers curling and flexing as he spoke. "You're mine now, Maggie. You'll always come first and I'll do anything for you. Anything."

"I know. And I love you for it."

"I love you, too, baby. I don't see how I can love you anymore than I do right now."

I smiled at his words, feeling the warmth and caress behind them. I leaned forward and kissed him. I opened my mouth and let my tongue touch his bottom lip, then pulled it gently between my teeth. His breath left in a rush. I smiled inside and pulled him closer with his shirt in my fist. I let my fingers trace his jaw and neck and move to his hair. I ran my fingers through it, tugging gently. I heard and felt his small groan so I decided to pull back from him. His eyes were bright and glimmering with something I didn't want to think about on a plane. He licked his bottom lip and continued to breathe erratically.

Just so you know, it makes me insane when you call me baby.

"I'll remember that," he said breathlessly.

I giggled. "It's good to know I'm still not the only one affected."

"I told you, it's so much worse for me." He leaned forward, so close our faces were almost touching. "That wasn't nice. I can't exactly do anything about it on a plane, now can I?" He nipped my chin and then kissed the same spot. I gulped and he smiled. "Now we're even."

I laughed breathlessly and bit my lip. His smile was smug as he brought his hand to cup my cheek. Then his fingers coasted down my arm to my hip and I sucked in a breath as he found my thigh then my leg...as he pulled a pillow out from under my seat. Oh, boy. Caleb was going to play dirty. The plane's air didn't seem to be working properly.

He chuckled at my thoughts as he fixed the pillow for me under my head, leaning my seat back.

"Touché," I muttered and he laughed harder.

"There will be plenty of time for that later," he assured amusedly.

"So, what's this tattoo on your wrist?" I rubbed it with my fingers. "I've seen them on your family, too."

"It's our Virtuoso crest for the Jacobson clan. Every family has their own crest. Ours is half moon, simple and classy. We're born with them and only other Aces can see them. It's one more way to show others who we are, what Clan we belong to."

"But I've seen names on the other ones. Their significant's names."

"Yeah," he murmured and sucked his lip in and out which I'd learned was a thinking tactic. "Well...it happens to us. See, we're not sure on the exact details but supposedly, the first significant couple started it. The first time they practiced Mutuality on each other, the tattoos came along with the names of their significant appearing on the inside of their wrists. From then on, we were all born with their family tattoo. See, when two significants line up their wrists, their half of the tattoo added to the other one becomes a whole and the names create an outline or border. It's really cool, actually."

"So what about us? I don't have one," I said, rubbing my wrist and felt extremely sad for some reason about that.

"You can get one, if you want to."

"How did Gran get hers?"

"She got it done for Papa's birthday one year." He chuckled. "Ever seen a grown man cry?" He chuckled again.

I thought how incredibly sweet that was and I guess I could go get it done but for some reason, it didn't seem the same. I felt left out. Caleb would never have a match for his tattoo unless I went and got the thing myself, which I just might do.

First Class was nice, though I had no idea what Coach was like. We ate our dinner they brought us and they started a movie but I took Caleb's advice and curled up beside him as best I could with my blanket and pillow.

"Sleep, Maggie. I'll be right here."

His hand snaked under my blanket and found mine. He curled his fingers around mine and tugged it, hugged it to his chest, pressing it to his heart so I could feel the two heartbeats. Mine and his, always right there together. We both fell asleep in blissful peace.

I woke up some time later in the dark quiet cabin. I had no idea what time it was but I needed to think when Caleb wasn't in my mind so I lay there, looking at him facing me on his side in his seat. His hair had fallen over on his forehead and around his ears. I brushed it back and then ran my thumb over his dimple and heard his little noise of contentment.

It was still so surreal. He was mine. It seemed impossible that the past nine days had been real. Only nine days since I'd met Caleb. It was crazy.

I thought about the things he had told me about earlier; the mutuality. I had no idea if I was ready for that. I knew I was if I was honest but it was a step for me, a step I'd never taken before, never gotten close to before and even though it wasn't real sex, it still sounded intimate enough that it may as well be.

It wasn't that I was afraid it would change things between us, though it would in a good way, or that I wasn't ready to commit or whatever. I was just scared in general. Scared I wasn't good at whatever it was he wanted me to do. My mind and my insides wouldn't be as good and sweet like he thought I was. I thought bad things all the time. I was no saint, like he apparently was. Tutoring service. Ugh! How could I compete with that?

What if once we got into our minds and true feelings that couldn't be hidden away and he saw the raw me, real and open…he no longer liked it? He was just stuck with me? Everything else about this imprint is different from what I've heard. What happens if he wants out or is unhappy with the results?

Even if that never happened, what if he never gets his ability? He'd resent it, resent me, eventually. I took what was rightfully his and it wasn't fair. I'd fork over my ability to him in a heartbeat if I could. It bothered him, it had to. But, wait! He was asleep. I can go in his mind, he wasn't in mine right now. He said we could poke and prod whenever we wanted and he'd been in mine and I never felt the hazy feeling I had before when he did it.

I pushed a little and slipped into the mind that I couldn't believe I had doubted. I swore to him I wouldn't doubt again and I'd just spent the last ten minutes doing it. His mind was gorgeous. And he loved me, adored me. His mind was lined with my face and a protective barrier so thick. He was worried about my safety above all else, just like he said. My happiness and contentment was right above that.

I pushed further to see our memories lined up and on loop; our greatest hits. I loved how a lot of them were from that short few minutes before the imprint and it made me warm all over. The one that played the most was the first time he saw me. So not even paying attention and absorbed in my own stuff and him completely and utterly taken by me.

I could feel his heart pounding like it had that day. His want to get to know me and his wish that things could be different just like he'd showed me that day at Mugly's.

I pushed further. I saw his desire to please his family but also to do his own thing. He did not want to be an architect, which I already knew, but I didn't know that he had absolutely no intentions of even trying to do anything different. Family was so important and after me, they came next. He was selfless and would be happy if we were. That thought didn't sit well with me. I filed that away to work on another day. I wanted him to be happy, too, really happy, and I'd find a way to make that happen.

The further into his mind I got, the warmer and more out of body I felt. He was all around me, all in me. I could smell him and feel him everywhere and finally understood what Caleb had meant by consuming each other. It was like he was made to be everywhere and everything to me and in me. I got the sensation of euphoria, being drugged, that feeling you feel right at the end of a roller coaster.

It took my breath away how good it felt to be consumed with him. But...there was a little part that held back, that I wasn't allowed to experience. I immediately knew that that part wouldn't be unlocked unless we were together, consuming each other.

When I got to the inner most parts everything was all jumbled, floating around like pieces of a hazy puzzle. His favorite pizza topping was sausage. He loved seeing brand new bands at concerts. His all time favorite movie was The Matrix. He hated to be in the mosh pit. He was upset about not getting his ability but was genuinely happy for me and loved that his family loved me so well. He loved school cafeteria pudding. Was scared of what he'd do if he ever met the guy who hurt his sister. He couldn't stand it when people smacked while they ate. He thought it was so hot when I looked over my shoulder at him with a smile. He loved the beach. His favorite thing to do was take walks at night, wherever he was, because the city and country and beach or whatever looked so different at night.

It was all jumbled and a mess and came at me in no rhyme or fashion. I couldn't pick or choose and couldn't even stop it from coming at me in droves. It felt too hot and unorganized and started to be uncomfortable so I pulled out all the way and felt the chill of the plane air on my face. It felt odd to be me again. I looked at his face and he was still sound asleep. I smiled, strange knowing so many things about him I would have never thought to ask in so little time.

I wanted to know everything. I could see why Caleb seemed to enjoy it. I did, too, and couldn't wait for him to show me how to do it for real and look for specific things.

Being in his mind gave me a taste for it. I wanted all of him. It was like a need, not just a want anymore, to do anything and everything for him and to him. His happiness was paramount and I wanted his happiness to be mine.

My smile grew wider as I had a thought. I pushed it aside, tucking it in the back so he wouldn't see it. Sex was still *way out there*, but whenever the time was right, soon, I'd try the other. Mutuality.

I still felt tense and apprehensive, I had no idea what it was really or what it entailed or what it would feel like but this was Caleb. I had to stop thinking of him as just a boy. He was mine, for life, my soul mate, my significant. There was nothing to fear with him. He was always careful and loving with me and he would be with this, too.

I pressed my hand a little harder into his chest and felt my heart beat speed up under my fingers as I thought about what mutuality would be like. I giggled silently and took a deep breath to calm my fast heart rate so I didn't alert Caleb and wake him.

Suddenly, I couldn't wait to get to this beach house.

Thirty Two

"Wake up. Maggie, wake up. We're in Cali, baby," Caleb teased and did a surfer dude hand signal making me giggle as I stretched and rose from my seat back. "No dreams, right?"

"Nope. All good."

"I was a little worried last night. I figured as long as we were touching it didn't matter but..."

"I slept great," I announced and it was true.

I'd finally fallen back asleep after poking around in his head and could now see the lights from the airport through the window. I peeked out and everything looked the same as it had in Tennessee. I couldn't help, but be disappointed. This was California for crying out loud. My mom left us and came here. Movie stars and famous people lived here. Arnold Schwarzenegger! I expected something more than sleepy flight attendants and a dank airport runway with no glitz or glam.

"It gets better," Caleb assured me and we listened to the Captain welcome us to the Eureka state.

We sat through all their instructions, then Caleb grabbed both our carry-on bags from the overhead and we were off. I followed behind him all the way through to the car rental pick-up desk. He had rented a black Jeep Wrangler for us to use while we were there.

He threw our stuff in the back and headed out. Once we were on the highway he asked me if I was hungry. I wasn't, so he told me to shut my eyes and rest until we got to the house. He didn't want me to know where we were exactly so as not to disclose info in a dream by accident to the Watsons, just in case. He said we'd go shopping in the morning for the things he knew I forgot or wouldn't fit. A bathing suit was number one on the list.

I argued but it didn't help. I'd have to get used to him buying stuff for me. The measly amount I had saved in my bank account from waiting tables wouldn't have even paid for one of those plane tickets, I was sure. He smirked at my pout and gripped my hand in my lap, rubbing the back of my fingers with his thumb. It didn't take long for me to soften when his touch sent warmth and tingles through me. When I laced our fingers he sighed in satisfaction and pulled my hand up to kiss it.

I closed my eyes and it didn't seem like an hour had passed, but as he told me to look, we were pulling into the driveway of a very pretty white house that looked anything but a vacation place in the Jeep's headlights. It was as big as my regular house. It had blue shutters and a wrap around porch. There were vines and flowers blooming everywhere and a sign made of driftwood that said 'Jacobson' by the front door.

"Wow."

"Yeah," he agreed and put the Jeep in park. "The fam comes up here at least twice a year. I love it here. Come on, it's even better on the inside."

We grabbed our stuff and went in. It was all white and crisp and clean. It even smelled clean and airy. It wasn't done in some tacky beach-shells-and-nets-with-starfish theme. It was nice and classy. I loved it right off.

Caleb threw our bags down at the bottom of the cherry wooden stairs and pulled me with him by my hand.

"Come back here with me. The best part is right..." he pushed open the French doors and came behind me to push me to the banister with his hands on my hips, "here."

I blew a surprised breath and brought my hands to my face. It was gorgeous. They had a huge garden in full bloom in the back with strung white lights everywhere around the pool. All the trees and shrubs had white Christmas lights on them, too. Little bricked paths were laid out between the flowers and there was a huge table with umbrellas behind that. If you looked beyond that, the ocean was loud, the waves beating on the beach just past the backyard.

I laughed in joy. This was my temporary home and I was in love.

"I knew you'd like this."

"I love it," I told him. I turned to look at him. "Oh, my gosh, Caleb. This is so great."

"Good, I'm glad you like it. Now maybe I can get you to relax." He smiled and pulled me close with his hands on my hips. "Take it easy for a while and not be so wound tight."

"I've had good reason to be so wound," I countered.

"I know. Now you have good reason not to be," he said smirking. "This," he waved his arm around us, "is a no-stress zone. No worrying, no over-thinking, no pressure. No stress." He tapped my nose with his finger.

"Easier said than done," I muttered.

"Look at this." He turned me back to face the yard and ocean, his tan arms went around me and he placed his head on mine. "This is our bubble."

Then he leaned down and kissed the side of my neck. I gasped inwardly as I realized this was my vision. The very first vision I'd had while we were imprinting of us on a porch - this porch. We had been seeing the future and it was now.

"Yes," he agreed and spoke the words into the sensitive skin under my ear. "When you imprint you see what will happen to us in the future. Pretty neat, huh? I can't wait for my visions to come true."

"What did you see?" I whispered.

"Lots of things that are way down the road, gorgeous. I'll show you one day."

I let him end it with that. I assumed it had something to do with weddings or babies and it was too soon for that.

But one thing made me wonder. "So, all this was planned or...destined from the beginning. Everything that happened. Marcus kidnapping me, Sikes, us coming here, all of it. This was supposed to happen."

I didn't phrase it as a question because it wasn't one. I knew with certainty now. It was clear to me. I still had two more visions to see, so I'd at least make it that far, long enough to see them come true.

"Yeah. Everything is driven forward to destiny. We have a long way to go to the end, Maggie. Nothing is going to happen to you."

"Or you?"

"Or me. My visions were...far down the road." He kissed the side of my neck again. "We were happy and together and all in one piece."

"Why won't you tell me what you saw?"

"Your visions are yours and mine are mine. Yours are probably not very long off. Mine are very involved. There's a reason for that. I wouldn't want to scare you with it and our imprint understood what we both could handle. It gave us those particular visions for a reason."

I thought about that and it made sense. "So, one day I'll know what they are? I'll see them?"

"Yes. One day, when they come true, you'll see them and understand it for what it is."

That was good enough for me. I nodded. "Thank you for bringing me here. It's perfect."

"You're welcome. Ready for bed? Or, uh...couch?"

I laughed and nodded. "Yeah, I'm ready for couch."

We walked inside and he locked all the doors as I pulled the cushions and pillows off the couch. I changed quickly in the bathroom and when I came out, he was already in sleep clothes, a white t-shirt and Vols fleece pants. He pulled the couch bed out and we curled up under a blanket I retrieved out of the hall closet.

He pulled his arm up for me to lay on and tugged me to lie against him. I fell asleep almost immediately.

The next morning we got up and went to grab some breakfast. There wasn't any food in the house so Caleb took me to a little coffee shop he knew of and got me a Cappuccino and a homemade honey bun. Then he took me to the mini mall and practically dragged me into the Old Navy by my arm.

"Caleb, no. Please. All they have are little string bikini things in there."

He grinned. "I know."

"Caleb," I protested.

"What did you wear to the beach before? A smock?"

"No," I groaned. "All right, fine, but if I can't find something to cover at least three percent of my skin, we're out of here."

He laughed behind me as he directed me to the back with his hands on my hips. "Deal. You go this way," he pushed me left, "and I'll go this way." He went right and called over his shoulder. "We'll meet at the cash register in fifteen minutes," he turned back to point at me, "with a suit."

"Ok!" I yelled playfully and shook my head at him.

As I turned I felt his mind skid to a stop. He realized he'd just left me alone.

Are you gonna be ok? I can come with you?

Nope. I'm good. I'll be quick.

I'll be right over here. I can feel you, don't worry about anything.

Not worried. Remember? This is a stress-free bubble.

I felt his laughter in my mind and giggled into my hand so no one thought I was nutso.

That's right. How stupid of me to forget.

I grabbed five suits to try on and went into the dressing room. I tried on the first one and knew I didn't need to go any further. It was a baby blue top - I knew Caleb loved me in blue - and it had brown dots and a brown little somewhat skimpy wrap for a bottom, but not as skimpy as others were. It had straps at least. I smiled at my reflection and tried not to cover myself. I was alone in the dressing room after all. I chewed the inside of my cheek. I looked different than the last time I'd been in a suit. Not terribly so but enough.

I wondered what Caleb would think of it.

I took the suit off and put my clothes on quickly. I found Caleb at the register line with a pair of swim trunks and black flip flops.

"Found something, did we?" he chanted and twirled his dark blue Hawaiian swim trunks around his finger.

"Yes."

I quickly threw my wadded up suit on the counter. The checkout guy held up the suit and Caleb's eyes went wide.

Ah hell, Maggie.

He sighed my name ruggedly in my mind and I saw in his that he almost regretted coming here. He didn't know how he'd keep his sanity around me with that on and kicked himself, wondering what he'd been thinking. Everyone would see me with that on and he wanted to growl at the thought. I just bit my lip.

The check out guy smirked at me. That turned into a wide smile when I blushed when he continued to stare and hold the suit up.

The guy was thinking about me wearing that suit and the picture in his head was hilariously disproportioned; the top way too big and the bottom way too narrow. I wanted to laugh at him, but Caleb cocked his head when the sun bleached blonde guy just kept staring.

"Buddy," Caleb said and made a motion with his hands to get going. "Let's get on with it."

"Oh, right."

He rang up our stuff, throwing it all in the bag and told Caleb the total. When Caleb was digging into his wallet the guy winked at me. I looked at him with squinted eyes and wanted to ask what he thought he was doing. My boyfriend was right beside me.

Caleb ran his credit card and took the receipt. He glared at the guy as he waved to me as we walked out the big window doors to the sidewalk. I laughed at him.

"Not funny. That dude was way out of line," he grumbled.

"He's a jackass, but he's harmless."

"Harmless? I saw what he was thinking in your mind. Jerk off," he muttered and jingled his keys with excessive force.

I stifled my giggle and followed him to the Jeep. "It's your fault. You wanted me to buy a suit."

"Yes, I did," he conceded. "What was I thinking? I think the tyrant needs to make a comeback."

I shook my head at him. "You're hilarious," I replied sweetly as he opened my door for me. "So what now?"

"What? You want me to go teach surfer boy a lesson?"

"No," I laughed. "I meant what now for us? Isn't someone supposed to be meeting us at the house?"

"Yeah. I haven't heard from my dad yet about it. Let's just go back to the house and change into our suits. We can go out to the beach and then if he hasn't called by this afternoon, I'll call him."

"K. Who is it do you think?"

"Don't know. Dad wants to keep the big guns there in case of an attack or something."

I stiffened. "Would the Watsons do that?"

"I don't know. They've never out right attacked us before like this. Dad's scared of what they'll do now. He should of just…" He sighed harshly as he cranked the Jeep and drove out of our spot.

In his mind he was thinking 'killed Sikes', but he stopped himself because he couldn't have done it either.

"It's ok," I assured to soothe him. "It'll all work out. I'm not worried."

"Well that's something new," he mused with a smile. "And about time."

"I know between Peter and you, I'll be safe, and you're here with me so you'll be safe, too. I've got nothing to worry about," I sighed easily and leaned my head back.

He grabbed my hand as we drove back to the house and squeezed it. He was practically oozing with adoration and it warmed me all over.

"I love you, Maggie."

"I love you, too." I smiled at him, but then got a thought. "How come you don't call me Mags, Magpie or Maggsie or whatever like everyone else does?"

"Do you want me to?"

"Not really. I've just never met someone who didn't eventually make up some little nickname for me. Dad, Bish, everyone called me Mags in school, the teachers, even Chad."

"Ding ding, we have winner," he sang.

Light bulb. "Aha. You don't want to because that's what he called me."

"Yeah."

"And Kyle, too," I realized.

"Bingo."

"I see."

"Besides, you don't look like a Mags to me. I'll stick with baby if you don't mind."

"You know I don't mind," I said grinning.

"Freeze, just like that." We happened to be stopping at the red light and he leaned toward me. "Keep that smile pasted on that pretty face until I say stop, ok? I miss seeing that face."

He took my chin between his thumb and finger and kissed my lips sweetly. It only took a second and I was nodding, breathing funny and blinking my eyes to shed the cross-eyedness. I know he could feel my heart speed up.

He smirked smugly at me as he pressed the gas to go and we made our way through one of the prominent shopping streets.

He was right. Everything looked very 'Californy' today, in the sunlight. Just like TV. Palm trees and shopping signs everywhere, bikini clad girls on every street. Blonde, blonde and more blonde, even the store mannequins were blonde.

We ran into a little mom and pop shop for some groceries near the house and I secretly laughed as he grabbed my favorite foods and grinned at me.

I helped him bring everything in from the Jeep and put it all away. The house was still empty of anyone else and it didn't look like anyone had been there either.

"Wanna go out to the beach? I can't get Dad on the phone, but I'm sure whoever they're sending will be here soon. I for one am not worried about it."

"Me neither. I'll go put on my suit."

I went to the bathroom and put it on. Once again I couldn't believe that was me I was looking at. I'd forgotten my cover-up dress so I peeked out and heard him banging around in the kitchen, putting up groceries. I made a break for it. Just as I reached my bag he came around the corner and his mind slammed into mine with his desire and effort; the effort to keep himself in check and not rush me even though his insides were screaming for me.

I found my dress and went to pull it over my head but he was there in front of me, stopping me with his hands covering mine. He was wearing his suit, too, only his suit, and I felt my skin burn hot.

"Nice suit," he said huskily.

"It wasn't the skimpiest I could've bought," I defended.

"Thank God for that," he muttered and pulled me to him.

He gripped me tightly around my waist and his mouth took mine with hungry abandon. His lips moved against mine with intent and purpose. His tongue and teeth played with my lips and I gasped at the pleasure of it. When he pushed my hair back from my shoulder and kissed my neck, I shivered. Then his hands slid down to glide from my hip to the back of my thigh and then back up, all the while, his lips nibbled my collar bone and throat. He'd never been this focused on exploring me before.

I swore stars bounced behind my eyes at the intensity of his wanting, his love, his need to consume me and be consumed.

I finally understood what he meant by that. Our bodies were made to be enthralled and taken over by our significant. I wanted him to and I knew without a doubt he wanted me to. It was instinct.

So I pushed him backwards as he continued to ravish me, his chin and lips rubbing against the soft skin of my throat and jaw. When we reached the chair I pushed him down to sit in it and sat on his lap, one leg on either side of him.

"Maggie," he groaned, "you're killing me-"

I stopped his feeble protest with a kiss and felt his hands tighten and grasp at the spot where my hips and thighs connect. I opened my mind wide and willing and pushed into his. I saw his protective barrier for me and pushed beyond that, past everything and straight to the core. I no longer cared if it was too much and took me over; I wanted it to.

When I finally felt him all around me, everywhere, in my veins, my mind, my blood, on my skin, I focused on him. I felt his shock at what I was doing, him realizing, his needing wonder and want to do it, then his restraint as he pushed me out.

"Maggie, wait," he said against my lips as he barely pulled back enough to speak. "I think we should just hold on a minute."

"For what?" I whispered and pulled his bottom lip between mine.

He moaned and growled, his harsh breaths coasted across my face and neck. "Maggie. I don't..."

He didn't want to hurt me. He thought he might get carried away. His father told him mutuality was just as good as and better in some ways than real sex because it was so intimate and something that only the two of us can do with each other. There was no way to be any closer physically or mentally, but he also told him it was very easy to lose ourselves in it and Caleb was worried that I'd get too wrapped up in it to stop at just mutuality and then regret it later.

He wanted to so bad but needed me to be absolutely sure that it's what I wanted and not just be going on his feelings in my mind; me feeling his longing for me.

I placed my hands on either side of his face.

"You would never hurt me. I know that more than anything else, especially after being in your mind. You'd never do anything that I didn't want to do and I'm not worried about losing ourselves either. Haven't I always kept you a gentleman?" I joked and kissed his dimple.

"Baby, you know I want to, but why do you? Is it because of me? I can't help it, I know you've seen in my mind that I want to, but I can wait. I'm not pushing."

"I know. I want to because I love you." He looked at me, my face close to his. His mind was a tangle of emotions and as his eyes roamed my face I smiled in happiness, seeing his surrender. I pushed back into his mind, wrapped my arms around his neck and kissed his lips before laying my forehead against his. He pulled me closer against him on his lap with his hands on my hips and I felt him enter my mind, like the click of a lock.

I heard my swift intake of breath at the completion of our melding but didn't feel my breaths. I felt nothing but him. His feelings of want, his chest rising under *his* breaths, his hands on my hips as his fingers that flexed felt like my own. It was so very strange to feel his cold blood running through his hot veins. Then I was me again but he was still there, in me and consuming me.

His mind was always the same, adoration and concern flooding my mind for me and his longing to please his family, to make us all happy. It made me love him even more for it.

More thoughts flew to me in an awkward lineup as we pressed further into each other's head. I knew he was feeling and seeing the same things but different, because it was all me. I saw a vision of him in kindergarten as he read his first word, bat. Then I saw his dad teaching him to ride his motorcycle at his graduation party. A flash of him mowing the grass at his house, the smell of summer and green surrounding me. How much he loved BBQ pizza. He missed his friends from school but would leave them all for a chance at Arizona. He admired his professors.

Then, I felt the hand on my hip move higher, gliding up my spine to my neck and back down again in a slow torturous caress. It felt mind-blowing. I held a gasp in check when I looked down to see his hands hadn't moved from my hips. My gaze jerked to his and behind him I saw the blue energy ribbons were bouncing in the air around us again, going through our bodies, and filling the room.

He looked around in awe and then looked back to me, holding my gaze. He smiled sweetly. Not smugly, not cockily, just Caleb. He moved his hand on my back again with his mind and I shivered.

This is what it's like. We see it all. Past, present, wants, memories, things we want to do. We can do anything in mutuality with each other without actually doing it and it's all magnified and extreme.

His caution and bashfulness coated his words. It was strange to feel his every feeling, hear his every word in my head and yet not be able to tell what was his and what was mine anymore.

I focused on my hand in my mind, it coming down from his neck, sliding along to splay my fingers against the hard skin of his chest and ribs, then his stomach. His breaths came out fast and he laughed nervously.

"That feels amazing," he whispered against my mouth and then kissed it. "Do it again," he ordered gruffly.

I laughed, too, and as I formed the thought to do what he asked, I heard the knock to the tune of Shave and a Haircut on the front door.

The energy ribbons crackled away as if they were fireworks as we yanked out of each other's minds. I felt irritated and cold from the separation. I thought Caleb would throw me off his lap in anticipation of whoever it was, but he lifted his head from mine and glanced that way, his hands tightened on my back.

I heard Bish's thoughts before I saw his head poke in the door. He was worried about what he'd find us doing, then Kyle walked in right behind him and the worry in his mind was the same. Both looked equally unhappy to find us in our bathing suits with me in Caleb's lap.

"What are you doing here, Bish?" I asked as Caleb asked Kyle the same question, but with much more edge in his tone.

"I'm your chaperone," Kyle said grinning in clear enjoyment of the situation and Caleb's reaction.

"And I'm his," Bish muttered and glared at us. "They couldn't spare anyone else so I volunteered to come. Kyle insisted on coming, too. So here we are. What are you doing?"

"We were about to go to the beach," I answered.

"Great, I'll go put on my suit," Kyle said chipperly and flung his duffel bag on the club chair before running upstairs.

"So, you're going to be here with us the whole time? What about work?" I asked.

"I quit."

"What?"

"It wasn't for me anymore. Besides, like I said before, no one seems to have your best interest in mind so I'm here to stay."

I rolled my eyes at him and secretly growled inside. Well, there went our fun getaway.

Hey, it's ok. He can't keep you from me and this'll be a good chance for him to get to know me, maybe even like me.

Yeah. Me on your lap is a good way to start.

I could kiss you if you think that'd help.

Ha, ha.

He grinned. *I'm totally serious. I'm feeling a little unfulfilled right now. We were interrupted during the encounter that* you *started.*

I smiled, biting my bottom lip and felt my cheeks pink. He grinned wider, running his hands up and down my arms.

Later. We'll finish this later, I promised.

You bet we will.

He gripped my chin between his thumb and finger and kissed me. I shivered in anticipation. I wrapped my arms around his neck, forgetting our guests and remembered when I heard an angry grunt and exasperated sigh.

"All right, all right, you two. You said something about the beach, right?" Bish said.

I sighed, pouting, and Caleb smirked at me. "Later," he assured quietly, where only I could hear.

Caleb lifted me gently to my feet and went to grab us some towels from the hall closet.

"Could you put something on?" Bish asked me, but not looking right at me.

"This is something, my bathing suit. We're going to the beach. Generally, people wear these at the beach, unless times have changed," I said sarcastically.

"You're such a smart a-"

"Hey! Are you going to be like this the whole time?" I asked.

"Probably. Are you going to be strutting around in practically nothing and hanging all over your boyfriend the whole time?"

"Probably," I replied cheerfully and heard Caleb snicker behind me which earned him a glower from Bish.

"Whatever. I'm going to put on my suit," Bish grumbled.

"You don't have to come," I volunteered.

"Oh, I think I do."

Once he was gone I turned into Caleb, feeling the strain and irritation leave me with the touch of his skin. I couldn't help but sigh. "Crap, Caleb. I was really looking forward to this."

"I still am. It'll be ok."

Ah, jeez. You have got to be frigging kidding me. She can't be this sexy all the time. No flaws! None? Really? She's so hot...

It wasn't Caleb's thoughts blaring through my mind. It was Kyle's. We both turned to see him looking hotly at me, unabashedly, and Caleb having heard all Kyle's thoughts through me was beyond peeved.

"Let me grab a shirt," he said loudly, glaring at Kyle, "and you one, too, apparently, Maggie."

Kyle smiled in contest as Caleb went to our luggage. Kyle walked over to me and licked his lips as I tried to shrink myself, crossing my arms over my chest. He wasn't even trying to hide his thoughts from me.

Man, look at those legs. Jeez, Chad's an idiot.

"Kyle, stop." I looked at him with a look of amazement at his boldness. "You know if I can hear you that Caleb can, too, through me. Stop it."

"I don't care if he hears."

"I care."

"Why? Afraid he'll get jealous?"

"Kyle," I protested.

"I figure you probably like Caleb's tattoos," he mused. "I have one, too, you know. Two in fact but the other one's in a much more interesting spot. Wanna see?"

"No, I'm good. Are we ready? Bish!"

"I'm coming!" he yelled from the bathroom door.

"Why so skittish, Mags?" Kyle said with a mysterious grin.

"I'm not skittish, I'm irritated."

"Why? We interrupt your little interlude earlier?" he said snidely.

"Yes! You did, actually," I said and put my hands on my hips to emphasize.

He grimaced and turned away, heading for the door. He put his hand on the knob and looked back at us.

"Ready? Let's go."

Bish came back and I had to smile at him. He bashfully had a towel thrown over his shoulders and was thinking about how he didn't want to get burned so he stopped mid stride and turned towards his bag for the sun block. Then he went to stand by Kyle. He made an impatient motion with his hand, like he was waiting for us and not the other way around.

I rolled my eyes and looked up to see Caleb standing beside me, towels in between his knees as he pulled one of his t-shirts over my head. I looked down and saw it was his 'Spill Canvas' tour shirt. Then he took the towels in one hand and the other grasped mine.

This is not going to be as fun as we thought.

He smiled sadly at my comment.

Ah, yeah it will.

I gave him a questioning quirked brow and he relented.

Ok, yeah. This isn't going to be as fun. But. He smiled wider and pulled me close. *We're together and you're safe. The prison won't last forever and then you'll be all mine.*

Mmmm. Yeah. Can we fast forward to that part?

He laughed out loud and kissed my forehead.

"What's so funny?" Bish asked tersely.

Kyle coughed uncomfortably, glancing at us and rolling his eyes. His thoughts said we were being reckless with our significant abilities and had better watch it. He opened the door, walking out swiftly.

"Nothing. Inside joke. Let's go," I said.

"Whatever," Bish grumbled and held the door open for me.

Caleb pushed me through it with a hand on my lower hip and I heard Bish cussing up a storm in his mind.

"Can we keep the PDA to a minimum? I just ate," he said snidely.

Caleb and I looked at each other, a disgruntled Bish behind us and a begrudged Kyle in front, leading the way. Our chaperones. No. This was definitely *not* going to be fun.

The End...For Now.

Be sure to pick up the sequels to Significance, Accordance, Defiance and Independence as the story of Caleb and Maggie continues…

Thank you to my God first of all and my family for supporting me through my endeavors of writing. It was a whim one day that has turned into this thing that I love. Thank you all who have helped me and to the ones who purchase my books, I hope you enjoy reading it as much as I enjoyed writing it.

Thank you.

You can contact Shelly at the following avenues.

www.facebook.com/shellycranefanpage

www.twitter.com/authshellycrane

www.shellycrane.blogspot.com

Enjoy Shelly's other series

Collide

Devour

Stealing Grace

Wide Awake

Smash Into You

Letters To Henry

Shelly is a bestselling YA author from a small town in Georgia and loves everything about the south. She is wife to a fantastical husband and stay at home mom to two boisterous and mischievous boys who keep her on her toes. They currently reside in everywhere USA as they happily travel all over with her husband's job. She loves to spend time with her family, binge on candy corn, go out to eat at new restaurants, buy paperbacks at little bookstores, site see in the new areas they travel to, listen to music everywhere and also LOVES to read.

Her own books happen by accident and she revels in the writing and imagination process. She doesn't go anywhere without her notepad for fear of an idea creeping up and not being able to write it down immediately, even in the middle of the night, where her best ideas are born.

Shelly's website:

www.shellycrane.blogspot.com